Oscar Fingal O'Flahertie Wills Wilde (16 October 1854 – 30 November 1900) was an Irish poet and playwright. After writing in different forms throughout the 1880s, he became one of London's most popular playwrights in the early 1890s. He is best remembered for his epigrams and plays, his novel The Picture of Dorian Gray, and the circumstances of his criminal conviction for homosexuality, imprisonment, and early death at age 46. Wilde's parents were successful Anglo-Irish intellectuals in Dublin. Their son became fluent in French and German early in life. At university, Wilde read Greats; he proved himself to be an outstanding classicist, first at Trinity College Dublin, then at Oxford. He became known for his involvement in the rising philosophy of aestheticism, led by two of his tutors, Walter Pater and John Ruskin. After university, Wilde moved to London into fashionable cultural and social circles. (Source: Wikipedia)

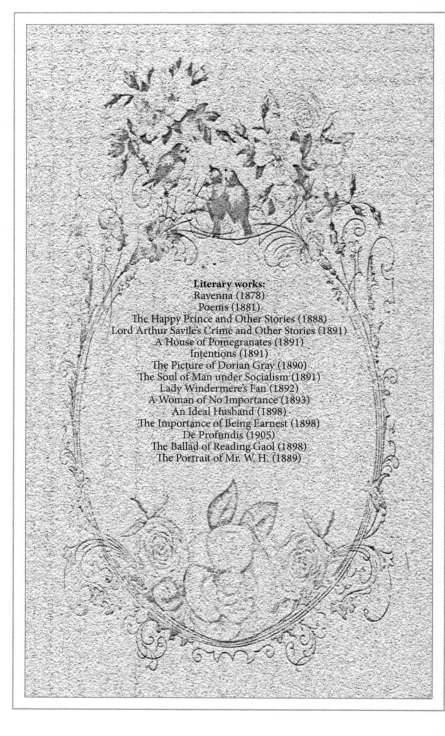

Literary works:
Ravenna (1878)
Poems (1881)
The Happy Prince and Other Stories (1888)
Lord Arthur Savile's Crime and Other Stories (1891)
A House of Pomegranates (1891)
Intentions (1891)
The Picture of Dorian Gray (1890)
The Soul of Man under Socialism (1891)
Lady Windermere's Fan (1892)
A Woman of No Importance (1893)
An Ideal Husband (1898)
The Importance of Being Earnest (1898)
De Profundis (1905)
The Ballad of Reading Gaol (1898)
The Portrait of Mr. W. H. (1889)

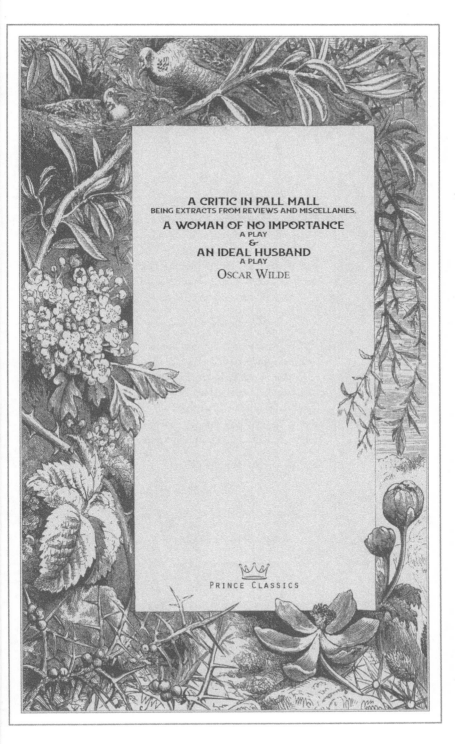

A CRITIC IN PALL MALL
BEING EXTRACTS FROM REVIEWS AND MISCELLANIES,

A WOMAN OF NO IMPORTANCE
A PLAY
&
AN IDEAL HUSBAND
A PLAY

OSCAR WILDE

PRINCE CLASSICS

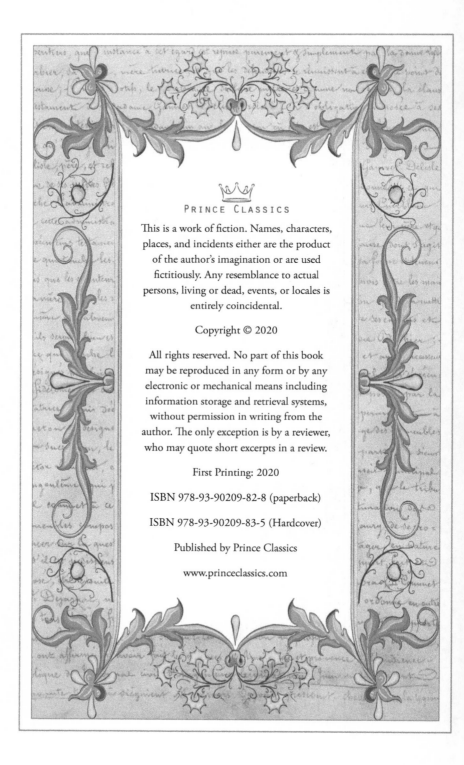

PRINCE CLASSICS

This is a work of fiction. Names, characters, places, and incidents either are the product of the author's imagination or are used fictitiously. Any resemblance to actual persons, living or dead, events, or locales is entirely coincidental.

Copyright © 2020

First Printing: 2020

ISBN 978-93-90209-82-8 (paperback)

ISBN 978-93-90209-83-5 (Hardcover)

Published by Prince Classics

www.princeclassics.com

Contents

A CRITIC IN PALL MALL
BEING EXTRACTS FROM REVIEWS AND MISCELLANIES.

A WOMAN OF NO IMPORTANCE
A PLAY
&
AN IDEAL HUSBAND
A PLAY

A CRITIC IN PALL MALL:
BEING EXTRACTS
FROM REVIEWS AND
MISCELLANIES

THE TOMB OF KEATS

(Irish Monthly, July 1877.)

As one enters Rome from the Via Ostiensis by the Porta San Paolo, the first object that meets the eye is a marble pyramid which stands close at hand on the left.

There are many Egyptian obelisks in Rome—tall, snakelike spires of red sandstone, mottled with strange writings, which remind us of the pillars of flame which led the children of Israel through the desert away from the land of the Pharaohs; but more wonderful than these to look upon is this gaunt, wedge-shaped pyramid standing here in this Italian city, unshattered amid the ruins and wrecks of time, looking older than the Eternal City itself, like terrible impassiveness turned to stone. And so in the Middle Ages men supposed this to be the sepulchre of Remus, who was slain by his own brother at the founding of the city, so ancient and mysterious it appears; but we have now, perhaps unfortunately, more accurate information about it, and know that it is the tomb of one Caius Cestius, a Roman gentleman of small note, who died about 30 b.c.

Yet though we cannot care much for the dead man who lies in lonely state beneath it, and who is only known to the world through his sepulchre, still this pyramid will be ever dear to the eyes of all English-speaking people, because at evening its shadows fall on the tomb of one who walks with Spenser, and Shakespeare, and Byron, and Shelley, and Elizabeth Barrett Browning in the great procession of the sweet singers of England.

For at its foot there is a green sunny slope, known as the Old Protestant Cemetery, and on this a common-looking grave, which bears the following inscription:

This grave contains all that was mortal of a young English poet, who on his deathbed, in the bitterness of his heart, desired these words to be engraven on his tombstone: HERE LIES ONE WHOSE NAME WAS WRIT IN WATER. February 24, 1821.

And the name of the young English poet is John Keats.

Lord Houghton calls this cemetery 'one of the most beautiful spots on which the eye and heart of man can rest,' and Shelley speaks of it as making one 'in love with death, to think that one should be buried in so sweet a place'; and indeed when I saw the violets and the daisies and the poppies that overgrow the tomb, I remembered how the dead poet had once told his friend that he thought the 'intensest pleasure he had received in life was in watching the growth of flowers,' and how another time, after lying a while quite still, he murmured in some strange prescience of early death, 'I feel the flowers growing over me.'

But this time-worn stone and these wildflowers are but poor memorials [2] of one so great as Keats; most of all, too, in this city of Rome, which pays such honour to her dead; where popes, and emperors, and saints, and cardinals lie hidden in 'porphyry wombs,' or couched in baths of jasper and chalcedony and malachite, ablaze with precious stones and metals, and tended with continual service. For very noble is the site, and worthy of a noble monument; behind looms the grey pyramid, symbol of the world's age, and filled with memories of the sphinx, and the lotus leaf, and the glories of old Nile; in front is the Monte Testaccio, built, it is said, with the broken fragments of the vessels in which all the nations of the East and the West brought their tribute to Rome; and a little distance off, along the slope of the hill under the Aurelian wall, some tall gaunt cypresses rise, like burnt-out funeral torches, to mark the spot where Shelley's heart (that 'heart of hearts'!) lies in the earth; and, above all, the soil on which we tread is very Rome!

As I stood beside the mean grave of this divine boy, I thought of him as of a Priest of Beauty slain before his time; and the vision of Guido's St. Sebastian came before my eyes as I saw him at Genoa, a lovely brown boy, with crisp, clustering hair and red lips, bound by his evil enemies to a tree, and though pierced by arrows, raising his eyes with divine, impassioned gaze towards the Eternal Beauty of the opening heavens. And thus my thoughts shaped themselves to rhyme:

HEU MISERANDE PUER

Rid of the world's injustice and its pain,

He rests at last beneath God's veil of blue;

Taken from life while life and love were new

The youngest of the martyrs here is lain,

Fair as Sebastian and as foully slain.

No cypress shades his grave, nor funeral yew,

But red-lipped daisies, violets drenched with dew,

And sleepy poppies, catch the evening rain.

O proudest heart that broke for misery!

O saddest poet that the world hath seen!

O sweetest singer of the English land!

Thy name was writ in water on the sand,

But our tears shall keep thy memory green,

And make it flourish like a Basil-tree.

Rome, 1877.

Note.—A later version of this sonnet, under the title of 'The Grave of Keats,' is given in the *Poems*, page 157.

KEATS'S SONNET ON BLUE

(Century Guild Hobby Horse, July 1886.)

During my tour in America I happened one evening to find myself in Louisville, Kentucky. The subject I had selected to speak on was the Mission of Art in the Nineteenth Century, and in the course of my lecture I had occasion to quote Keats's Sonnet on Blue as an example of the poet's delicate sense of colour-harmonies. When my lecture was concluded there came round to see me a lady of middle age, with a sweet gentle manner and a most musical voice. She introduced herself to me as Mrs. Speed, the daughter of George Keats, and invited me to come and examine the Keats manuscripts in her possession. I spent most of the next day with her, reading the letters of Keats to her father, some of which were at that time unpublished, poring over torn yellow leaves and faded scraps of paper, and wondering at the little Dante in which Keats had written those marvellous notes on Milton. Some months afterwards, when I was in California, I received a letter from Mrs. Speed asking my acceptance of the original manuscript of the sonnet which I had quoted in my lecture. This manuscript I have had reproduced here, as it seems to me to possess much psychological interest. It shows us the conditions that preceded the perfected form, the gradual growth, not of the conception but of the expression, and the workings of that spirit of selection which is the secret of style. In the case of poetry, as in the case of the other arts, what may appear to be simply technicalities of method are in their essence spiritual not mechanical, and although, in all lovely work, what concerns us is the ultimate form, not the conditions that necessitate that form, yet the preference that precedes perfection, the evolution of the beauty, and the mere making of the music, have, if not their artistic value, at least their value to the artist.

It will be remembered that this sonnet was first published in 1848 by Lord Houghton in his *Life, Letters, and Literary Remains of John Keats.* Lord Houghton does not definitely state where he found it, but it was probably among the Keats manuscripts belonging to Mr. Charles Brown. It is evidently taken from a version later than that in my possession, as it accepts all the corrections, and makes three variations. As in my manuscript the first line is torn away, I give the sonnet here as it appears in Lord Houghton's edition.

ANSWER TO A SONNET ENDING THUS:

Dark eyes are dearer far

Than those that make the hyacinthine bell. [5]

By J. H. REYNOLDS.

Blue! 'Tis the life of heaven,—the domain

Of Cynthia,—the wide palace of the sun,—

The tent of Hesperus and all his train,—

The bosomer of clouds, gold, grey and dun.

Blue! 'Tis the life of waters—ocean

And all its vassal streams: pools numberless

May rage, and foam, and fret, but never can

Subside if not to dark-blue nativeness.

Blue! gentle cousin of the forest green,

Married to green in all the sweetest flowers,

Forget-me-not,—the blue-bell,—and, that queen

Of secrecy, the violet: what strange powers

Hast thou, as a mere shadow! But how great,

When in an Eye thou art alive with fate!

Feb. 1818.

In the Athenæum of the 3rd of June 1876 appeared a letter from Mr. A. J. Horwood, stating that he had in his possession a copy of The Garden of Florence in which this sonnet was transcribed. Mr. Horwood, who was unaware that the sonnet had been already published by Lord Houghton, gives the transcript at length. His version reads hue for life in the first line, and bright for wide in the second, and gives the sixth line thus:

With all his tributary streams, pools numberless,

a foot too long: it also reads to for of in the ninth line. Mr. Buxton Forman is of opinion that these variations are decidedly genuine, but indicative of an earlier state of the poem than that adopted in Lord Houghton's edition. However, now that we have before us Keats's first draft of his sonnet, it is difficult to believe that the sixth line in Mr. Horwood's version is really a genuine variation. Keats may have written,

Ocean

> His tributary streams, pools numberless,

and the transcript may have been carelessly made, but having got his line right in his first draft, Keats probably did not spoil it in his second. The Athenæum version inserts a comma after art in the last line, which seems to me a decided improvement, and eminently characteristic of Keats's method. I am glad to see that Mr. Buxton Forman has adopted it.

As for the corrections that Lord Houghton's version shows Keats to have made in the eighth and ninth lines of this sonnet, it is evident that they sprang from Keats's reluctance to repeat the same word in consecutive lines, except in cases where a word's music or meaning was to be emphasized. The substitution of 'its' for 'his' in the sixth line is more difficult of explanation. It was due probably to a desire on Keats's part not to mar by any echo the fine personification of Hesperus.

It may be noticed that Keats's own eyes were brown, and not blue, as stated by Mrs. Proctor to Lord Houghton. Mrs. Speed showed me a note to that effect written by Mrs. George Keats on the margin of the page in Lord Houghton's Life (p. 100, vol. i.), where Mrs. Proctor's description is given. Cowden Clarke made a similar correction in his Recollections, and in some of the later editions of Lord Houghton's book the word 'blue' is struck out. In Severn's portraits of Keats also the eyes are given as brown.

The exquisite sense of colour expressed in the ninth and tenth lines may be paralleled by

> The Ocean with its vastness, its blue green,

of the sonnet to George Keats.

DINNERS AND DISHES

(Pall Mall Gazette, March 7, 1885.)

A man can live for three days without bread, but no man can live for one day without poetry, was an aphorism of Baudelaire. You can live without pictures and music but you cannot live without eating, says the author of

Dinners and Dishes; and this latter view is, no doubt, the more popular. Who, indeed, in these degenerate days would hesitate between an ode and an omelette, a sonnet and a salmis? Yet the position is not entirely Philistine; cookery is an art; are not its principles the subject of South Kensington lectures, and does not the Royal Academy give a banquet once a year? Besides, as the coming democracy will, no doubt, insist on feeding us all on penny dinners, it is well that the laws of cookery should be explained: for were the national meal burned, or badly seasoned, or served up with the wrong sauce a dreadful revolution might follow.

Under these circumstances we strongly recommend Dinners and Dishes to every one: it is brief and concise and makes no attempt at eloquence, which is extremely fortunate. For even on ortolans who could endure oratory? It also has the advantage of not being illustrated. The subject of a work of art has, of course, nothing to do with its beauty, but still there is always something depressing about the coloured lithograph of a leg of mutton.

As regards the author's particular views, we entirely agree with him on the important question of macaroni. 'Never,' he says, 'ask me to back a bill for a man who has given me a macaroni pudding.' Macaroni is essentially a savoury dish and may be served with cheese or tomatoes but never with sugar and milk. There is also a useful description of how to cook risotto—a delightful dish too rarely seen in England; an excellent chapter on the different kinds of salads, which should be carefully studied by those many hostesses whose imaginations never pass beyond lettuce and beetroot; and actually a recipe for making Brussels sprouts eatable. The last is, of course, a masterpiece.

The real difficulty that we all have to face in life is not so much the science of cookery as the stupidity of cooks. And in this little handbook to practical Epicureanism the tyrant of the English kitchen is shown in her proper light. Her entire ignorance of herbs, her passion for extracts and essences, her total inability to make a soup which is anything more than a combination of pepper and gravy, her inveterate habit of sending up bread poultices with pheasants,—all these sins and many others are ruthlessly unmasked by the author. Ruthlessly and rightly. For the British cook is a

19

foolish woman who should be turned for her iniquities into a pillar of salt which she never knows how to use.

But our author is not local merely. He has been in many lands; he has eaten back-hendl at Vienna and kulibatsch at St. Petersburg; he has had the courage to face the buffalo veal of Roumania and to dine with a German family at one o'clock; he has serious views on the right method of cooking those famous white truffles of Turin of which Alexandre Dumas was so fond; and, in the face of the Oriental Club, declares that Bombay curry is better than the curry of Bengal. In fact he seems to have had experience of almost every kind of meal except the 'square meal' of the Americans. This he should study at once; there is a great field for the philosophic epicure in the United States. Boston beans may be dismissed at once as delusions, but soft-shell crabs, terrapin, canvas-back ducks, blue fish and the pompono of New Orleans are all wonderful delicacies, particularly when one gets them at Delmonico's. Indeed, the two most remarkable bits of scenery in the States are undoubtedly Delmonico's and the Yosemité Valley; and the former place has done more to promote a good feeling between England and America than anything else has in this century.

We hope the 'Wanderer' will go there soon and add a chapter to Dinners and Dishes, and that his book will have in England the influence it deserves. There are twenty ways of cooking a potato and three hundred and sixty-five ways of cooking an egg, yet the British cook, up to the present moment, knows only three methods of sending up either one or the other.

Dinners and Dishes. By 'Wanderer.' (Simpkin and Marshall.)

SHAKESPEARE ON SCENERY

(Dramatic Review, March 14, 1885.)

I have often heard people wonder what Shakespeare would say, could he see Mr. Irving's production of his Much Ado About Nothing, or Mr. Wilson Barrett's setting of his Hamlet. Would he take pleasure in the glory of the scenery and the marvel of the colour? Would he be interested in the Cathedral of Messina, and the battlements of Elsinore? Or would he be indifferent, and say the play, and the play only, is the thing?

Speculations like these are always pleasurable, and in the present case happen to be profitable also. For it is not difficult to see what Shakespeare's attitude would be; not difficult, that is to say, if one reads Shakespeare himself, instead of reading merely what is written about him.

Speaking, for instance, directly, as the manager of a London theatre, through the lips of the chorus in Henry V., he complains of the smallness of the stage on which he has to produce the pageant of a big historical play, and of the want of scenery which obliges him to cut out many of its most picturesque incidents, apologises for the scanty number of supers who had to play the soldiers, and for the shabbiness of the properties, and, finally, expresses his regret at being unable to bring on real horses.

In the Midsummer Night's Dream, again, he gives us a most amusing picture of the straits to which theatrical managers of his day were reduced by the want of proper scenery. In fact, it is impossible to read him without seeing that he is constantly protesting against the two special limitations of the Elizabethan stage—the lack of suitable scenery, and the fashion of men playing women's parts, just as he protests against other difficulties with which managers of theatres have still to contend, such as actors who do not understand their words; actors who miss their cues; actors who overact their parts; actors who mouth; actors who gag; actors who play to the gallery, and amateur actors.

And, indeed, a great dramatist, as he was, could not but have felt very much hampered at being obliged continually to interrupt the progress of a play in order to send on some one to explain to the audience that the scene was to be changed to a particular place on the entrance of a particular character, and after his exit to somewhere else; that the stage was to represent the deck of a ship in a storm, or the interior of a Greek temple, or the streets of a certain town, to all of which inartistic devices Shakespeare is reduced, and for which he always amply apologizes. Besides this clumsy method, Shakespeare had two other substitutes for scenery—the hanging out of a placard, and his descriptions. The first of these could hardly have satisfied his passion for picturesqueness and his feeling for beauty, and certainly did not satisfy the dramatic critic of his day. But as regards the description, to those of us who look on Shakespeare not merely as a playwright but as a poet, and who enjoy reading him at home just as much as we enjoy seeing him acted, it may be a matter of congratulation that he had not at his command such skilled machinists as are in use now at the Princess's and at the Lyceum. For had Cleopatra's barge, for instance, been a structure of canvas and Dutch metal, it would probably have been painted over or broken up after the withdrawal of the piece, and, even had it survived to our own day, would, I am afraid, have become extremely shabby by this time. Whereas now the beaten gold of its poop is still bright, and the purple of its sails still beautiful; its silver oars are not tired of keeping time to the music of the flutes they follow, nor the Nereid's flower-soft hands of touching its silken tackle; the mermaid still lies at its helm, and still on its deck stand the boys with their coloured fans. Yet lovely as all Shakespeare's descriptive passages are, a description is in its essence undramatic. Theatrical audiences are far more impressed by what they look at than by what they listen to; and the modern dramatist, in having the surroundings of his play visibly presented to the audience when the curtain rises, enjoys an advantage for which Shakespeare often expresses his desire. It is true that Shakespeare's descriptions are not what descriptions are in modern plays—accounts of what the audience can observe for themselves; they are the imaginative method by which he creates in the mind of the spectators the image of that which he desires them to see. Still, the quality of the drama is action. It is always dangerous to pause for picturesqueness. And the introduction of self-explanatory scenery enables the modern method to be far more direct, while the loveliness of form and colour which it gives us, seems to me often to create an artistic temperament in the audience, and to produce that joy in beauty for beauty's sake, without which the great masterpieces of art can never be understood, to which, and to which only, are they ever revealed.

To talk of the passion of a play being hidden by the paint, and of sentiment being killed by scenery, is mere emptiness and folly of words. A noble play, nobly mounted, gives us double artistic pleasure. The eye as well as the ear is gratified, and the whole nature is made exquisitely receptive of the influence of imaginative work. And as regards a bad play, have we not all seen large audiences lured by the loveliness of scenic effect into listening to rhetoric posing as poetry, and to vulgarity doing duty for realism? Whether this be good or evil for the public I will not here discuss, but it is evident that the playwright, at any rate, never suffers.

Indeed, the artist who really has suffered through the modern mounting of plays is not the dramatist at all, but the scene-painter proper. He is rapidly being displaced by the stage-carpenter. Now and then, at Drury Lane, I have seen beautiful old front cloths let down, as perfect as pictures some of them, and pure painter's work, and there are many which we all remember at other theatres, in front of which some dialogue was reduced to graceful dumb-show through the hammer and tin-tacks behind. But as a rule the stage is overcrowded with enormous properties, which are not merely far more expensive and cumbersome than scene-paintings, but far less beautiful, and far less true. Properties kill perspective. A painted door is more like a real door than a real door is itself, for the proper conditions of light and shade can be given to it; and the excessive use of built-up structures always makes the stage too glaring, for as they have to be lit from behind, as well as from the front, the gas-jets become the absolute light of the scene instead of the means merely by which we perceive the conditions of light and shadow which the painter has desired to show us.

So, instead of bemoaning the position of the playwright, it were better for the critics to exert whatever influence they may possess towards restoring the scene-painter to his proper position as an artist, and not allowing him to be built over by the property man, or hammered to death by the carpenter. I have never seen any reason myself why such artists as Mr. Beverley, Mr. Walter Hann, and Mr. Telbin should not be entitled to become Academicians. They have certainly as good a claim as have many of those R.A.'s whose total inability to paint we can see every May for a shilling.

And lastly, let those critics who hold up for our admiration the simplicity of the Elizabethan stage remember that they are lauding a condition of things against which Shakespeare himself, in the spirit of a true artist, always strongly protested.

HENRY THE FOURTH AT OXFORD

(Dramatic Review, May 23, 1885.)

I have been told that the ambition of every Dramatic Club is to act Henry IV. I am not surprised. The spirit of comedy is as fervent in this play as is the spirit of chivalry; it is an heroic pageant as well as an heroic poem, and like most of Shakespeare's historical dramas it contains an extraordinary number of thoroughly good acting parts, each of which is absolutely individual in character, and each of which contributes to the evolution of the plot.

To Oxford belongs the honour of having been the first to present on the stage this noble play, and the production which I saw last week was in every way worthy of that lovely town, that mother of sweetness and of light. For, in spite of the roaring of the young lions at the Union, and the screaming of the rabbits in the home of the vivisector, in spite of Keble College, and the tramways, and the sporting prints, Oxford still remains the most beautiful thing in England, and nowhere else are life and art so exquisitely blended, so perfectly made one. Indeed, in most other towns art has often to present herself in the form of a reaction against the sordid ugliness of ignoble lives, but at Oxford she comes to us as an exquisite flower born of the beauty of life and expressive of life's joy. She finds her home by the Isis as once she did by the Ilissus; the Magdalen walks and the Magdalen cloisters are as dear to her as were ever the silver olives of Colonus and the golden gateway of the house of Pallas: she covers with fanlike tracery the vaulted entrance to Christ Church Hall, and looks out from the windows of Merton; her feet have stirred the Cumnor cowslips, and she gathers fritillaries in the river-fields. To her the clamour of the schools and the dullness of the lecture-room are a weariness and a vexation of spirit; she seeks not to define virtue, and cares little for the categories; she smiles on the swift athlete whose plastic grace has pleased her, and rejoices in the young Barbarians at their games; she watches the rowers from the reedy bank and gives myrtle to her lovers, and laurels to her poets, and rue to those who talk wisely in the street; she makes the earth lovely to all who dream with Keats; she opens high heaven to all who soar with Shelley; and turning away her head from pedant, proctor and Philistine, she has welcomed to her shrine a band of youthful actors, knowing that they have sought with much ardour for the stern secret of Melpomene, and caught with much gladness the sweet laughter of Thalia. And to me this ardour and this gladness were the two most fascinating qualities of the Oxford performance, as indeed they are qualities which are necessary to any fine dramatic production. For without quick and imaginative observation of life the most beautiful play becomes dull in presentation, and what is not conceived in delight by the actor can give no delight at all to others.

I know that there are many who consider that Shakespeare is more for the study than for the stage. With this view I do not for a moment agree. Shakespeare wrote the plays to be acted, and we have no right to alter the form which he himself selected for the full expression of his work. Indeed, many of the beauties of that work can be adequately conveyed to us only through the actor's art. As I sat in the Town Hall of Oxford the other night, the majesty of the mighty lines of the play seemed to me to gain new music from the clear young voices that uttered them, and the ideal grandeur of the heroism to be made more real to the spectators by the chivalrous bearing, the noble gesture and the fine passion of its exponents. Even the dresses had their dramatic value. Their archæological accuracy gave us, immediately on the rise of the curtain, a perfect picture of the time. As the knights and nobles moved across the stage in the flowing robes of peace and in the burnished steel of battle, we needed no dreary chorus to tell us in what age or land the play's action was passing, for the fifteenth century in all the dignity and grace of its apparel was living actually before us, and the delicate harmonies of colour struck from the first a dominant note of beauty which added to the intellectual realism of archæology the sensuous charm of art.

I have rarely seen a production better stage-managed. Indeed, I hope that the University will take some official notice of this delightful work of art. Why should not degrees be granted for good acting? Are they not given to those who misunderstand Plato and who mistranslate Aristotle? And should the artist be passed over? No. To Prince Hal, Hotspur and Falstaff, D.C.L.'s should be gracefully offered. I feel sure they would be gracefully

25

accepted. To the rest of the company the crimson or the sheepskin hood might be assigned honoris causâ to the eternal confusion of the Philistine, and the rage of the industrious and the dull. Thus would Oxford confer honour on herself, and the artist be placed in his proper position. However, whether or not Convocation recognizes the claims of culture, I hope that the Oxford Dramatic Society will produce every summer for us some noble play like Henry IV. For, in plays of this kind, plays which deal with bygone times, there is always this peculiar charm, that they combine in one exquisite presentation the passions that are living with the picturesqueness that is dead. And when we have the modern spirit given to us in an antique form, the very remoteness of that form can be made a method of increased realism. This was Shakespeare's own attitude towards the ancient world, this is the attitude we in this century should adopt towards his plays, and with a feeling akin to this it seemed to me that these brilliant young Oxonians were working. If it was so, their aim is the right one. For while we look to the dramatist to give romance to realism, we ask of the actor to give realism to romance.

A HANDBOOK TO MARRIAGE

(Pall Mall Gazette, November 18, 1885.)

In spite of its somewhat alarming title this book may be highly recommended to every one. As for the authorities the author quotes, they are almost numberless, and range from Socrates down to Artemus Ward. He tells us of the wicked bachelor who spoke of marriage as 'a very harmless amusement' and advised a young friend of his to 'marry early and marry often'; of Dr. Johnson who proposed that marriage should be arranged by the Lord Chancellor, without the parties concerned having any choice in the matter; of the Sussex labourer who asked, 'Why should I give a woman half my victuals for cooking the other half?' and of Lord Verulam who thought that unmarried men did the best public work. And, indeed, marriage is the one subject on which all women agree and all men disagree. Our author, however, is clearly of the same opinion as the Scotch lassie who, on her father warning her what a solemn thing it was to get married, answered, 'I ken that, father, but it's a great deal solemner to be single.' He may be regarded as the champion of the married life. Indeed, he has a most interesting chapter on marriage-made men, and though he dissents, and we think rightly, from the view recently put forward by a lady or two on the Women's Rights platform that Solomon owed all his wisdom to the number of his wives, still he appeals to Bismarck, John Stuart Mill, Mahommed, and Lord Beaconsfield, as instances of men whose success can be traced to the influence of the women they married. Archbishop Whately once defined woman as 'a creature that does not reason and pokes the fire from the top,' but since his day the higher education of women has considerably altered their position. Women have always had an emotional sympathy with those they love; Girton and Newnham have rendered intellectual sympathy also possible. In our day it is best for a man to be married, and men must give up the tyranny in married life which was once so dear to them, and which, we are afraid, lingers still, here and there.

'Do you wish to be my wife, Mabel?' said a little boy. 'Yes,' incautiously answered Mabel. 'Then pull off my boots.'

On marriage vows our author has, too, very sensible views and very amusing stories. He tells of a nervous bridegroom who, confusing the baptismal and marriage ceremonies, replied when asked if he consented to take the bride for his wife: 'I renounce them all'; of a Hampshire rustic who, when giving the ring, said solemnly to the bride: 'With my body I thee wash up, and with all my hurdle goods I thee and thou'; of another who when asked whether he would take his partner to be his wedded wife, replied with shameful indecision: 'Yes, I'm willin'; but I'd a sight rather have her sister'; and of a Scotch lady who, on the occasion of her daughter's wedding, was asked by an old friend whether she might congratulate her on the event, and answered: 'Yes, yes, upon the whole it is very satisfactory; it is true Jeannie hates her gudeman, but then there's always a something!' Indeed, the good stories contained in this book are quite endless and make it very pleasant reading, while the good advice is on all points admirable.

Most young married people nowadays start in life with a dreadful collection of ormolu inkstands covered with sham onyxes, or with a perfect museum of salt-cellars. We strongly recommend this book as one of the best of wedding presents. It is a complete handbook to an earthly Paradise, and its author may be regarded as the Murray of matrimony and the Baedeker of bliss.

How to be Happy though Married: Being a Handbook to Marriage.
By a Graduate in the University of Matrimony. (T. Fisher Unwin.)

TO READ OR NOT TO READ

(Pall Mall Gazette, February 8, 1886.)

Books, I fancy, may be conveniently divided into three classes:

1. Books to read, such as Cicero's Letters, Suetonius, Vasari's Lives of the Painters, the Autobiography of Benvenuto Cellini, Sir John Mandeville, Marco Polo, St. Simon's Memoirs, Mommsen, and (till we get a better one) Grote's History of Greece.

2. Books to re-read, such as Plato and Keats: in the sphere of poetry, the masters not the minstrels; in the sphere of philosophy, the seers not the savants.

3. Books not to read at all, such as Thomson's Seasons, Rogers's Italy, Paley's Evidences, all the Fathers except St. Augustine, all John Stuart Mill except the essay on Liberty, all Voltaire's plays without any exception, Butler's Analogy, Grant's Aristotle, Hume's England, Lewes's History of Philosophy, all argumentative books and all books that try to prove anything.

The third class is by far the most important. To tell people what to read is, as a rule, either useless or harmful; for, the appreciation of literature is a question of temperament not of teaching; to Parnassus there is no primer and nothing that one can learn is ever worth learning. But to tell people what not to read is a very different matter, and I venture to recommend it as a mission to the University Extension Scheme.

Indeed, it is one that is eminently needed in this age of ours, an age that reads so much, that it has no time to admire, and writes so much, that it has no time to think. Whoever will select out of the chaos of our modern curricula 'The Worst Hundred Books,' and publish a list of them, will confer on the rising generation a real and lasting benefit.

After expressing these views I suppose I should not offer any suggestions at all with regard to 'The Best Hundred Books,' but I hope you will allow me the pleasure of being inconsistent, as I am anxious to put in a claim for a book that has been strangely omitted by most of the excellent judges who have contributed to your columns. I mean the Greek Anthology. The beautiful poems contained in this collection seem to me to hold the same position with regard to Greek dramatic literature as do the delicate little figurines of Tanagra to the Phidian marbles, and to be quite as necessary for the complete understanding of the Greek spirit.

I am also amazed to find that Edgar Allan Poe has been passed over. Surely this marvellous lord of rhythmic expression deserves a place? If, in order to make room for him, it be necessary to elbow out some one else, I should elbow out Southey, and I think that Baudelaire might be most advantageously substituted for Keble.

No doubt, both in the Curse of Kehama and in the Christian Year there are poetic qualities of a certain kind, but absolute catholicity of taste is not without its dangers. It is only an auctioneer who should admire all schools of art.

THE LETTERS OF A GREAT WOMAN
(Pall Mall Gazette, March 6, 1886.)

Of the many collections of letters that have appeared in this century few, if any, can rival for fascination of style and variety of incident the letters of George Sand which have recently been translated into English by M. Ledos de Beaufort. They extend over a space of more than sixty years, from 1812 to 1876, in fact, and comprise the first letters of Aurore Dupin, a child of eight years old, as well as the last letters of George Sand, a woman of seventy-two.

The very early letters, those of the child and of the young married woman, possess, of course, merely a psychological interest; but from 1831, the date of Madame Dudevant's separation from her husband and her first entry into Paris life, the interest becomes universal, and the literary and political history of France is mirrored in every page.

For George Sand was an indefatigable correspondent; she longs in one of her letters, it is true, for 'a planet where reading and writing are absolutely unknown,' but still she had a real pleasure in letter-writing. Her greatest delight was the communication of ideas, and she is always in the heart of the battle. She discusses pauperism with Louis Napoleon in his prison at Ham, and liberty with Armand Barbes in his dungeon at Vincennes; she writes to Lamennais on philosophy, to Mazzini on socialism, to Lamartine on democracy, and to Ledru-Rollin on justice. Her letters reveal to us not merely the life of a great novelist but the soul of a great woman, of a woman who was one with all the noblest movements of her day and whose sympathy with humanity was boundless absolutely. For the aristocracy of intellect she had always the deepest veneration, but the democracy of suffering touched her more. She preached the regeneration of mankind, not with the noisy ardour of the paid advocate, but with the enthusiasm of the true evangelist. Of all the artists of this century she was the most altruistic; she felt every one's misfortunes except her own. Her faith never left her; to the end of her life, as she tells us, she was able to believe without illusions. But the people disappointed her a little. She saw that they followed persons not principles, and for 'the great man theory' George Sand had no respect. 'Proper names are the enemies of principles' is one of her aphorisms.

So from 1850 her letters are more distinctly literary. She discusses modern realism with Flaubert, and play-writing with Dumas fils; and protests with passionate vehemence against the doctrine of L'art pour l'art. 'Art for the sake of itself is an idle sentence,' she writes; 'art for the sake of truth, for the sake of what is beautiful and good, that is the creed I seek.' And in a delightful letter to M. Charles Poncy she repeats the same idea very charmingly. 'People say that birds sing for the sake of singing, but I doubt it. They sing their loves and happiness, and in that they are in keeping with nature. But man must

30

do something more, and poets only sing in order to move people and to make them think.' She wanted M. Poncy to be the poet of the people and, if good advice were all that had been needed, he would certainly have been the Burns of the workshop. She drew out a delightful scheme for a volume to be called Songs of all Trades and saw the possibilities of making handicrafts poetic. Perhaps she valued good intentions in art a little too much, and she hardly understood that art for art's sake is not meant to express the final cause of art but is merely a formula of creation; but, as she herself had scaled Parnassus, we must not quarrel at her bringing Proletarianism with her. For George Sand must be ranked among our poetic geniuses. She regarded the novel as still within the domain of poetry. Her heroes are not dead photographs; they are great possibilities. Modern novels are dissections; hers are dreams. 'I make popular types,' she writes, 'such as I do no longer see, but such as they should and might be.' For realism, in M. Zola's acceptation of the word, she had no admiration. Art to her was a mirror that transfigured truths but did not represent realities. Hence she could not understand art without personality. 'I am aware,' she writes to Flaubert, 'that you are opposed to the exposition of personal doctrine in literature. Are you right? Does not your opposition proceed rather from a want of conviction than from a principle of æsthetics? If we have any philosophy in our brain it must needs break forth in our writings. But you, as soon as you handle literature, you seem anxious, I know not why, to be another man, the one who must disappear, who annihilates himself and is no more. What a singular mania! What a deficient taste! The worth of our productions depends entirely on our own. Besides, if we withhold our own opinions respecting the personages we create, we naturally leave the reader in uncertainty as to the opinion he should himself form of them. That amounts to wishing not to be understood, and the result of this is that the reader gets weary of us and leaves us.'

She herself, however, may be said to have suffered from too dominant a personality, and this was the reason of the failure of most of her plays.

Of the drama in the sense of disinterested presentation she had no idea, and what is the strength and life-blood of her novels is the weakness of her dramatic works. But in the main she was right. Art without personality

31

is impossible. And yet the aim of art is not to reveal personality, but to please. This she hardly recognized in her æsthetics, though she realized it in her work. On literary style she has some excellent remarks. She dislikes the extravagances of the romantic school and sees the beauty of simplicity. 'Simplicity,' she writes, 'is the most difficult thing to secure in this world: it is the last limit of experience and the last effort of genius.' She hated the slang and argot of Paris life, and loved the words used by the peasants in the provinces. 'The provinces,' she remarks, 'preserve the tradition of the original tongue and create but few new words. I feel much respect for the language of the peasantry; in my estimation it is the more correct.'

She thought Flaubert too much preoccupied with the sense of form, and makes these excellent observations to him—perhaps her best piece of literary criticism. 'You consider the form as the aim, whereas it is but the effect. Happy expressions are only the outcome of emotion and emotion itself proceeds from a conviction. We are only moved by that which we ardently believe in.' Literary schools she distrusted. Individualism was to her the keystone of art as well as of life. 'Do not belong to any school: do not imitate any model,' is her advice. Yet she never encouraged eccentricity. 'Be correct,' she writes to Eugène Pelletan, 'that is rarer than being eccentric, as the time goes. It is much more common to please by bad taste than to receive the cross of honour.'

On the whole, her literary advice is sound and healthy. She never shrieks and she never sneers. She is the incarnation of good sense. And the whole collection of her letters is a perfect treasure-house of suggestions both on art and on politics.

Letters of George Sand. Translated and edited by Raphael Ledos de Beaufort. (Ward and Downey.)

BÉRANGER IN ENGLAND

(Pall Mall Gazette, April 21, 1886.)

A philosophic politician once remarked that the best possible form of government is an absolute monarchy tempered by street ballads.

Without at all agreeing with this aphorism we still cannot but regret that the new democracy does not use poetry as a means for the expression of political opinion. The Socialists, it is true, have been heard singing the later poems of Mr. William Morris, but the street ballad is really dead in England. The fact is that most modern poetry is so artificial in its form, so individual in its essence and so literary in its style, that the people as a body are little moved by it, and when they have grievances against the capitalist or the aristocrat they prefer strikes to sonnets and rioting to rondels.

Possibly, Mr. William Toynbee's pleasant little volume of translations from Béranger may be the herald of a new school. Béranger had all the qualifications for a popular poet. He wrote to be sung more than to be read; he preferred the Pont Neuf to Parnassus; he was patriotic as well as romantic, and humorous as well as humane. Translations of poetry as a rule are merely misrepresentations, but the muse of Béranger is so simple and naïve that she can wear our English dress with ease and grace, and Mr. Toynbee has kept much of the mirth and music of the original. Here and there, undoubtedly, the translation could be improved upon; 'rapiers' for instance is an abominable rhyme to 'forefathers'; 'the hated arms of Albion' in the same poem is a very feeble rendering of 'le léopard de l'Anglais,' and such a verse as

'Mid France's miracles of art,

   Rare trophies won from art's own land,

I've lived to see with burning heart

   The fog-bred poor triumphant stand,

reproduces very inadequately the charm of the original:

Dans nos palais, où, près de la victoire,

   Brillaient les arts, doux fruits des beaux climats,

J'ai vu du Nord les peuplades sans gloire,

   De leurs manteaux secouer les frimas.

33

On the whole, however, Mr. Toynbee's work is good; Les Champs, for example, is very well translated, and so are the two delightful poems Rosette and Ma République; and there is a good deal of spirit in Le Marquis de Carabas:

> Whom have we here in conqueror's rôle?
>
> Our grand old marquis, bless his soul!
>
> Whose grand old charger (mark his bone!)
>
> Has borne him back to claim his own.
>
> Note, if you please, the grand old style
>
> In which he nears his grand old pile;
>
> With what an air of grand old state
>
> He waves that blade immaculate!
>
> Hats off, hats off, for my lord to pass,
>
> The grand old Marquis of Carabas!—

though 'that blade immaculate' has hardly got the sting of 'un sabre innocent'; and in the fourth verse of the same poem, 'Marquise, you'll have the bed-chamber' does not very clearly convey the sense of the line 'La Marquise a le tabouret.' Béranger is not nearly well enough known in England, and though it is always better to read a poet in the original, still translations have their value as echoes have their music.

A Selection from the Songs of De Béranger in English Verse. By
William Toynbee. (Kegan Paul.)

THE POETRY OF THE PEOPLE

(Pall Mall Gazette, May 13, 1886.)

The Countess Martinengo deserves well of all poets, peasants and publishers. Folk-lore is so often treated nowadays merely from the point of view of the comparative mythologist, that it is really delightful to come across a book that deals with the subject simply as literature. For the Folk-tale is the father of all fiction as the Folk-song is the mother of all poetry; and in the games, the tales and the ballads of primitive people it is easy to see the germs of such perfected forms of art as the drama, the novel and the epic. It is, of course, true that the highest expression of life is to be found not in the popular songs, however poetical, of any nation, but in the great masterpieces of self-conscious Art; yet it is pleasant sometimes to leave the summit of Parnassus to look at the wildflowers in the valley, and to turn from the lyre of Apollo to listen to the reed of Pan. We can still listen to it. To this day, the vineyard dressers of Calabria will mock the passer-by with satirical verses as they used to do in the old pagan days, and the peasants of the olive woods of Provence answer each other in amœbæan strains. The Sicilian shepherd has not yet thrown his pipe aside, and the children of modern Greece sing the swallow-song through the villages in spring-time, though Theognis is more than two thousand years dead. Nor is this popular poetry merely the rhythmic expression of joy and sorrow; it is in the highest degree imaginative; and taking its inspiration directly from nature it abounds in realistic metaphor and in picturesque and fantastic imagery. It must, of course, be admitted that there is a conventionality of nature as there is a conventionality of art, and that certain forms of utterance are apt to become stereotyped by too constant use; yet, on the whole, it is impossible not to recognize in the Folk-songs that the Countess Martinengo has brought together one strong dominant note of fervent and flawless sincerity. Indeed, it is only in the more terrible dramas of the Elizabethan age that we can find any parallel to the Corsican voceri with their shrill intensity of passion, their awful frenzies of grief and hate. And yet, ardent as the feeling is, the form is nearly always beautiful. Now and then, in the poems of the extreme South one meets with a curious crudity of realism, but, as a rule, the sense of beauty prevails.

Some of the Folk-poems in this book have all the lightness and loveliness of lyrics, all of them have that sweet simplicity of pure song by which mirth finds its own melody and mourning its own music, and even where there are conceits of thought and expression they are conceits born of fancy not of affectation. Herrick himself might have envied that wonderful love-song of

Provence:

> If thou wilt be the falling dew
>
> And fall on me alway,
>
> Then I will be the white, white rose
>
> On yonder thorny spray.
>
> If thou wilt be the white, white rose
>
> On yonder thorny spray,
>
> Then I will be the honey-bee
>
> And kiss thee all the day.
>
> If thou wilt be the honey-bee
>
> And kiss me all the day,
>
> Then I will be in yonder heaven
>
> The star of brightest ray.
>
> If thou wilt be in yonder heaven
>
> The star of brightest ray,
>
> Then I will be the dawn, and we
>
> Shall meet at break of day.

How charming also is this lullaby by which the Corsican mother sings her babe to sleep!

> Gold and pearls my vessel lade,
>
> Silk and cloth the cargo be,
>
> All the sails are of brocade
>
> Coming from beyond the sea;
>
> And the helm of finest gold,

Made a wonder to behold.

Fast awhile in slumber lie;

Sleep, my child, and hushaby.

After you were born full soon,

You were christened all aright;

Godmother she was the moon,

Godfather the sun so bright.

All the stars in heaven told

Wore their necklaces of gold.

Fast awhile in slumber lie;

Sleep, my child, and hushaby.

Or this from Roumania:

Sleep, my daughter, sleep an hour;

Mother's darling gilliflower.

Mother rocks thee, standing near,

She will wash thee in the clear

Waters that from fountains run,

To protect thee from the sun.

Sleep, my darling, sleep an hour,

Grow thou as the gilliflower.

As a tear-drop be thou white,

As a willow tall and slight;

Gentle as the ring-doves are,

And be lovely as a star!

We hardly know what poems are sung to English babies, but we hope they are as beautiful as these two. Blake might have written them.

The Countess Martinengo has certainly given us a most fascinating book. In a volume of moderate dimensions, not too long to be tiresome nor too brief to be disappointing, she has collected together the best examples of modern Folk-songs, and with her as a guide the lazy reader lounging in his armchair may wander from the melancholy pine-forests of the North to Sicily's orange-groves and the pomegranate gardens of Armenia, and listen to the singing of those to whom poetry is a passion, not a profession, and whose art, coming from inspiration and not from schools, if it has the limitations, at least has also the loveliness of its origin, and is one with blowing grasses and the flowers of the field.

Essays in the Study of Folk-Songs. By the Countess Evelyn Martinengo Césaresco. (Redway.)

THE CENCI

(Dramatic Review, May 15, 1886.)

The production of The Cenci last week at the Grand Theatre, Islington, may be said to have been an era in the literary history of this century, and the Shelley Society deserves the highest praise and warmest thanks of all for having given us an opportunity of seeing Shelley's play under the conditions he himself desired for it. For The Cenci was written absolutely with a view to theatric presentation, and had Shelley's own wishes been carried out it would have been produced during his lifetime at Covent Garden, with Edmund Kean and Miss O'Neill in the principal parts. In working out his conception, Shelley had studied very carefully the æsthetics of dramatic art. He saw that the essence of the drama is disinterested presentation, and that the characters must not be merely mouthpieces for splendid poetry but must be living subjects for terror and for pity. 'I have endeavoured,' he says, 'as nearly as possible to represent the characters as they probably were, and have sought to

38

avoid the error of making them actuated by my own conception of right or wrong, false or true: thus under a thin veil converting names and actions of the sixteenth century into cold impersonations of my own mind. . . .

'I have avoided with great care the introduction of what is commonly called mere poetry, and I imagine there will scarcely be found a detached simile or a single isolated description, unless Beatrice's description of the chasm appointed for her father's murder should be judged to be of that nature.'

He recognized that a dramatist must be allowed far greater freedom of expression than what is conceded to a poet. 'In a dramatic composition,' to use his own words, 'the imagery and the passion should interpenetrate one another, the former being reserved simply for the full development and illustration of the latter. Imagination is as the immortal God which should assume flesh for the redemption of mortal passion. It is thus that the most remote and the most familiar imagery may alike be fit for dramatic purposes when employed in the illustration of strong feeling, which raises what is low, and levels to the apprehension that which is lofty, casting over all the shadow of its own greatness. In other respects I have written more carelessly, that is, without an over-fastidious and learned choice of words. In this respect I entirely agree with those modern critics who assert that in order to move men to true sympathy we must use the familiar language of men.'

He knew that if the dramatist is to teach at all it must be by example, not by precept.

'The highest moral purpose,' he remarks, 'aimed at in the highest species of the drama, is the teaching the human heart, through its sympathies and antipathies, the knowledge of itself; in proportion to the possession of which knowledge every human being is wise, just, sincere, tolerant and kind. If dogmas can do more it is well: but a drama is no fit place for the enforcement of them.' He fully realizes that it is by a conflict between our artistic sympathies and our moral judgment that the greatest dramatic effects are produced. 'It is in the restless and anatomizing casuistry with which men seek the justification of Beatrice, yet feel that she has done what needs justification; it is in the superstitious horror with which they contemplate alike her wrongs and their revenge, that the dramatic character of what she did and suffered consists.'

In fact no one has more clearly understood than Shelley the mission of the dramatist and the meaning of the drama.

BALZAC IN ENGLISH

(Pall Mall Gazette, September 13, 1886.)

Many years ago, in a number of All the Year Round, Charles Dickens complained that Balzac was very little read in England, and although since then the public has become more familiar with the great masterpieces of French fiction, still it may be doubted whether the Comédie Humaine is at all appreciated or understood by the general run of novel readers. It is really the greatest monument that literature has produced in our century, and M. Taine hardly exaggerates when he says that, after Shakespeare, Balzac is our most important magazine of documents on human nature. Balzac's aim, in fact, was to do for humanity what Buffon had done for the animal creation. As the naturalist studied lions and tigers, so the novelist studied men and women. Yet he was no mere reporter. Photography and procès-verbal were not the essentials of his method. Observation gave him the facts of life, but his genius converted facts into truths, and truths into truth. He was, in a word, a marvellous combination of the artistic temperament with the scientific spirit. The latter he bequeathed to his disciples; the former was entirely his own. The distinction between such a book as M. Zola's L'Assommoir and such a book as Balzac's Illusions Perdues is the distinction between unimaginative realism and imaginative reality. 'All Balzac's characters,' said Baudelaire, 'are gifted with the same ardour of life that animated himself. All his fictions are as deeply coloured as dreams. Every mind is a weapon loaded to the muzzle with will. The very scullions have genius.' He was, of course, accused of being immoral. Few writers who deal directly with life escape that charge. His answer to the accusation was characteristic and conclusive. 'Whoever contributes his stone to the edifice of ideas,' he wrote, 'whoever proclaims an abuse, whoever sets his mark upon an evil to be abolished, always passes

40

for immoral. If you are true in your portraits, if, by dint of daily and nightly toil, you succeed in writing the most difficult language in the world, the word immoral is thrown in your face.' The morals of the personages of the Comédie Humaine are simply the morals of the world around us. They are part of the artist's subject-matter; they are not part of his method. If there be any need of censure it is to life, not to literature, that it should be given. Balzac, besides, is essentially universal. He sees life from every point of view. He has no preferences and no prejudices. He does not try to prove anything. He feels that the spectacle of life contains its own secret. 'Il crée un monde et se tait.'

And what a world it is! What a panorama of passions! What a pell-mell of men and women! It was said of Trollope that he increased the number of our acquaintances without adding to our visiting list; but after the Comédie Humaine one begins to believe that the only real people are the people who never existed. Lucien de Rubempré, le Père Goriot, Ursule Mirouët, Marguerite Claës, the Baron Hulot, Madame Marneffe, le Cousin Pons, De Marsay—all bring with them a kind of contagious illusion of life. They have a fierce vitality about them: their existence is fervent and fiery-coloured; we not merely feel for them but we see them—they dominate our fancy and defy scepticism. A steady course of Balzac reduces our living friends to shadows, and our acquaintances to the shadows of shades. Who would care to go out to an evening party to meet Tomkins, the friend of one's boyhood, when one can sit at home with Lucien de Rubempré? It is pleasanter to have the entrée to Balzac's society than to receive cards from all the duchesses in Mayfair.

In spite of this, there are many people who have declared the Comédie Humaine to be indigestible. Perhaps it is: but then what about truffles? Balzac's publisher refused to be disturbed by any such criticism as that. 'Indigestible, is it?' he exclaimed with what, for a publisher, was rare good sense. 'Well, I should hope so; who ever thinks of a dinner that isn't?'

Balzac's Novels in English. *The Duchesse de Langeais and Other Stories; César Birotteau.* (Routledge and Sons.)

BEN JONSON

(Pall Mall Gazette, September 20, 1886.)

As for Mr. Symonds' estimate of Jonson's genius, it is in many points quite excellent. He ranks him with the giants rather than with the gods, with those who compel our admiration by their untiring energy and huge strength of intellectual muscle, not with those 'who share the divine gifts of creative imagination and inevitable instinct.' Here he is right. Pelion more than Parnassus was Jonson's home. His art has too much effort about it, too much definite intention. His style lacks the charm of chance. Mr. Symonds is right also in the stress he lays on the extraordinary combination in Jonson's work of the most concentrated realism with encyclopædic erudition. In Jonson's comedies London slang and learned scholarship go hand in hand. Literature was as living a thing to him as life itself. He used his classical lore not merely to give form to his verse, but to give flesh and blood to the persons of his plays. He could build up a breathing creature out of quotations. He made the poets of Greece and Rome terribly modern, and introduced them to the oddest company. His very culture is an element in his coarseness. There are moments when one is tempted to liken him to a beast that has fed off books.

We cannot, however, agree with Mr. Symonds when he says that Jonson 'rarely touched more than the outside of character,' that his men and women are 'the incarnations of abstract properties rather than living human beings,' that they are in fact mere 'masqueraders and mechanical puppets.' Eloquence is a beautiful thing but rhetoric ruins many a critic, and Mr. Symonds is essentially rhetorical. When, for instance, he tells us that 'Jonson made masks,' while 'Dekker and Heywood created souls,' we feel that he is asking us to accept a crude judgment for the sake of a smart antithesis. It is, of course, true that we do not find in Jonson the same growth of character that we find in Shakespeare, and we may admit that most of the characters in Jonson's plays are, so to speak, ready-made. But a ready-made character is not necessarily either mechanical or wooden, two epithets Mr. Symonds uses constantly in his criticism.

We cannot tell, and Shakespeare himself does not tell us, why Iago is evil, why Regan and Goneril have hard hearts, or why Sir Andrew Aguecheek is a fool. It is sufficient that they are what they are, and that nature gives warrant for their existence. If a character in a play is lifelike, if we recognize it as true to nature, we have no right to insist on the author explaining its genesis to us. We must accept it as it is: and in the hands of a good dramatist mere presentation can take the place of analysis, and indeed is often a more dramatic method, because a more direct one. And Jonson's characters are true to nature. They are in no sense abstractions; they are types. Captain Bobadil and Captain Tucca, Sir John Daw and Sir Amorous La Foole, Volpone and Mosca, Subtle and Sir Epicure Mammon, Mrs. Purecraft and the Rabbi Busy are all creatures of flesh and blood, none the less lifelike because they are labelled. In this point Mr. Symonds seems to us unjust towards Jonson.

We think, also, that a special chapter might have been devoted to Jonson as a literary critic. The creative activity of the English Renaissance is so great that its achievements in the sphere of criticism are often overlooked by the student. Then, for the first time, was language treated as an art. The laws of expression and composition were investigated and formularized. The importance of words was recognized. Romanticism, Realism and Classicism fought their first battles. The dramatists are full of literary and art criticisms, and amused the public with slashing articles on one another in the form of plays.

'English Worthies.' Edited by Andrew Lang. *Ben Jonson*. By John Addington Symonds. (Longmans, Green and Co.)

MR. SYMONDS' HISTORY OF THE RENAISSANCE

(Pall Mall Gazette, November 10, 1886.)

Mr. Symonds has at last finished his history of the Italian Renaissance. The two volumes just published deal with the intellectual and moral conditions in Italy during the seventy years of the sixteenth century which followed the coronation of Charles the Fifth at Bologna, an era to which Mr. Symonds gives the name of the Catholic Reaction, and they contain a most interesting and valuable account of the position of Spain in the Italian peninsula, the conduct of the Tridentine Council, the specific organization of the Holy Office and the Company of Jesus, and the state of society upon which those forces were brought to bear. In his previous volumes Mr. Symonds had regarded the past rather as a picture to be painted than as a problem to be solved. In these two last volumes, however, he shows a clearer appreciation of the office of history. The art of the picturesque chronicler is completed by something like the science of the true historian, the critical spirit begins to manifest itself, and life is not treated as a mere spectacle, but the laws of its evolution and progress are investigated also. We admit that the desire to represent life at all costs under dramatic conditions still accompanies Mr. Symonds, and that he hardly realizes that what seems romance to us was harsh reality to those who were engaged in it. Like most dramatists, also, he is more interested in the psychological exceptions than in the general rule. He has something of Shakespeare's sovereign contempt of the masses. The people stir him very little, but he is fascinated by great personalities. Yet it is only fair to remember that the age itself was one of exaggerated individualism, and that literature had not yet become a mouthpiece for the utterances of humanity. Men appreciated the aristocracy of intellect, but with the democracy of suffering they had no sympathy. The cry from the brickfields had still to be heard. Mr. Symonds' style, too, has much improved. Here and there, it is true, we come across traces of the old manner, as in the apocalyptic vision of the seven devils that entered Italy with the Spaniard, and the description of the Inquisition as a Belial-Moloch, a 'hideous idol whose face was blackened with soot from burning human flesh.' Such a sentence, also, as 'over the Dead Sea of social putrefaction floated the sickening oil of Jesuitical hypocrisy,' reminds us that rhetoric has not yet lost its charms for Mr. Symonds. Still, on the whole, the style shows far more reserve, balance and sobriety, than can be found in the earlier volumes where violent antithesis forms the predominant characteristic, and accuracy is often sacrificed to an adjective.

Amongst the most interesting chapters of the book are those on the Inquisition, on Sarpi, the great champion of the severance of Church from State, and on Giordano Bruno. Indeed, the story of Bruno's life, from his visit to London and Oxford, his sojourn in Paris and wanderings through

Germany, down to his betrayal at Venice and martyrdom at Rome, is most powerfully told, and the estimate of the value of his philosophy and the relation he holds to modern science, is at once just and appreciative. The account also of Ignatius Loyola and the rise of the Society of Jesus is extremely interesting, though we cannot think that Mr. Symonds is very happy in his comparison of the Jesuits to 'fanatics laying stones upon a railway' or 'dynamiters blowing up an emperor or a corner of Westminster Hall.' Such a judgment is harsh and crude in expression and more suitable to the clamour of the Protestant Union than to the dignity of the true historian. Mr. Symonds, however, is rarely deliberately unfair, and there is no doubt but that his work on the Catholic Reaction is a most valuable contribution to modern history—so valuable, indeed, that in the account he gives of the Inquisition in Venice it would be well worth his while to bring the picturesque fiction of the text into some harmony with the plain facts of the footnote.

On the poetry of the sixteenth century Mr. Symonds has, of course, a great deal to say, and on such subjects he always writes with ease, grace, and delicacy of perception. We admit that we weary sometimes of the continual application to literature of epithets appropriate to plastic and pictorial art. The conception of the unity of the arts is certainly of great value, but in the present condition of criticism it seems to us that it would be more useful to emphasize the fact that each art has its separate method of expression. The essay on Tasso, however, is delightful reading, and the position the poet holds towards modern music and modern sentiment is analysed with much subtlety. The essay on Marino also is full of interest. We have often wondered whether those who talk so glibly of Euphuism and Marinism in literature have ever read either Euphues or the Adone. To the latter they can have no better guide than Mr. Symonds, whose description of the poem is most fascinating. Marino, like many greater men, has suffered much from his disciples, but he himself was a master of graceful fancy and of exquisite felicity of phrase; not, of course, a great poet but certainly an artist in poetry and one to whom language is indebted. Even those conceits that Mr. Symonds feels bound to censure have something charming about them. The continual use of periphrases is undoubtedly a grave fault in style, yet who but a pedant would really quarrel with such periphrases as sirena de' boschi for the nightingale, or

45

il novello Edimione for Galileo?

From the poets Mr. Symonds passes to the painters: not those great artists of Florence and Venice of whom he has already written, but the Eclectics of Bologna, the Naturalists of Naples and Rome. This chapter is too polemical to be pleasant. The one on music is much better, and Mr. Symonds gives us a most interesting description of the gradual steps by which the Italian genius passed from poetry and painting to melody and song, till the whole of Europe thrilled with the marvel and mystery of this new language of the soul. Some small details should perhaps be noticed. It is hardly accurate, for instance, to say that Monteverde's Orfeo was the first form of the recitative-Opera, as Peri's Dafne and Euridice and Cavaliere's Rappresentazione preceded it by some years, and it is somewhat exaggerated to say that 'under the regime of the Commonwealth the national growth of English music received a check from which it never afterwards recovered,' as it was with Cromwell's auspices that the first English Opera was produced, thirteen years before any Opera was regularly established in Paris. The fact that England did not make such development in music as Italy and Germany did, must be ascribed to other causes than 'the prevalence of Puritan opinion.'

These, however, are minor points. Mr. Symonds is to be warmly congratulated on the completion of his history of the Renaissance in Italy. It is a most wonderful monument of literary labour, and its value to the student of Humanism cannot be doubted. We have often had occasion to differ from Mr. Symonds on questions of detail, and we have more than once felt it our duty to protest against the rhetoric and over-emphasis of his style, but we fully recognize the importance of his work and the impetus he has given to the study of one of the vital periods of the world's history. Mr. Symonds' learning has not made him a pedant; his culture has widened not narrowed his sympathies, and though he can hardly be called a great historian, yet he will always occupy a place in English literature as one of the remarkable men of letters in the nineteenth century.

Renaissance in Italy: The Catholic Reaction. In Two Parts. By John Addington Symonds. (Smith, Elder and Co.)

MR. MORRIS'S ODYSSEY

(Pall Mall Gazette, April 26, 1887.)

Of all our modern poets, Mr. William Morris is the one best qualified by nature and by art to translate for us the marvellous epic of the wanderings of Odysseus. For he is our only true story-singer since Chaucer; if he is a Socialist, he is also a Saga-man; and there was a time when he was never wearied of telling us strange legends of gods and men, wonderful tales of chivalry and romance. Master as he is of decorative and descriptive verse, he has all the Greek's joy in the visible aspect of things, all the Greek's sense of delicate and delightful detail, all the Greek's pleasure in beautiful textures and exquisite materials and imaginative designs; nor can any one have a keener sympathy with the Homeric admiration for the workers and the craftsmen in the various arts, from the stainers in white ivory and the embroiderers in purple and gold, to the weaver sitting by the loom and the dyer dipping in the vat, the chaser of shield and helmet, the carver of wood or stone. And to all this is added the true temper of high romance, the power to make the past as real to us as the present, the subtle instinct to discern passion, the swift impulse to portray life.

It is no wonder the lovers of Greek literature have so eagerly looked forward to Mr. Morris's version of the Odyssean epic, and now that the first volume has appeared, it is not extravagant to say that of all our English translations this is the most perfect and the most satisfying. In spite of Coleridge's well-known views on the subject, we have always held that Chapman's Odyssey is immeasurably inferior to his Iliad, the mere difference of metre alone being sufficient to set the former in a secondary place; Pope's Odyssey, with its glittering rhetoric and smart antithesis, has nothing of the grand manner of the original; Cowper is dull, and Bryant dreadful, and Worsley too full of Spenserian prettinesses; while excellent though Messrs. Butcher and Lang's version undoubtedly is in many respects, still, on the whole, it gives us merely the facts of the Odyssey without providing anything of its artistic effect. Avia's translation even, though better than almost all its predecessors in the same field, is not worthy of taking rank beside Mr. Morris's, for here we have a true work of art, a rendering not merely of language into language, but of poetry

47

into poetry, and though the new spirit added in the transfusion may seem to many rather Norse than Greek, and, perhaps at times, more boisterous than beautiful, there is yet a vigour of life in every line, a splendid ardour through each canto, that stirs the blood while one reads like the sound of a trumpet, and that, producing a physical as well as a spiritual delight, exults the senses no less than it exalts the soul. It may be admitted at once that, here and there, Mr. Morris has missed something of the marvellous dignity of the Homeric verse, and that, in his desire for rushing and ringing metre, he has occasionally sacrificed majesty to movement, and made stateliness give place to speed; but it is really only in such blank verse as Milton's that this effect of calm and lofty music can be attained, and in all other respects blank verse is the most inadequate medium for reproducing the full flow and fervour of the Greek hexameter. One merit, at any rate, Mr. Morris's version entirely and absolutely possesses. It is, in no sense of the word, literary; it seems to deal immediately with life itself, and to take from the reality of things its own form and colour; it is always direct and simple, and at its best has something of the 'large utterance of the early gods.'

As for individual passages of beauty, nothing could be better than the wonderful description of the house of the Phœacian king, or the whole telling of the lovely legend of Circe, or the manner in which the pageant of the pale phantoms in Hades is brought before our eyes. Perhaps the huge epic humour of the escape from the Cyclops is hardly realized, but there is always a linguistic difficulty about rendering this fascinating story into English, and where we are given so much poetry we should not complain about losing a pun; and the exquisite idyll of the meeting and parting with the daughter of Alcinous is really delightfully told. How good, for instance, is this passage taken at random from the Sixth Book:

> *But therewith unto the handmaids goodly Odysseus spake:*
>
> *'Stand off I bid you, damsels, while the work in hand I take,*
>
> *And wash the brine from my shoulders, and sleek them all around.*
>
> *Since verily now this long while sweet oil they have not found.*
>
> *But before you nought will I wash me, for shame I have indeed,*

Amidst of fair-tressed damsels to be all bare of weed.'

So he spake and aloof they gat them, and thereof they told the may,

But Odysseus with the river from his body washed away

The brine from his back and shoulders wrought broad and mightily,

And from his head was he wiping the foam of the untilled sea;

But when he had thoroughly washed him, and the oil about him had shed,

He did upon the raiment the gift of the maid unwed.

But Athene, Zeus-begotten, dealt with him in such wise

That bigger yet was his seeming, and mightier to all eyes,

With the hair on his head crisp curling as the bloom of the daffodil.

And as when the silver with gold is o'erlaid by a man of skill,

Yea, a craftsman whom Hephæstus and Pallas Athene have taught

To be master over masters, and lovely work he hath wrought;

So she round his head and his shoulders shed grace abundantly.

It may be objected by some that the line

With the hair on his head crisp curling as the bloom of the daffodil,

is a rather fanciful version of

ουλας ηκε κομας, ὑακινθίνω ανθει ομοιασ

and it certainly seems probable that the allusion is to the dark colour of the hero's hair; still, the point is not one of much importance, though it may be worth noting that a similar expression occurs in Ogilby's superbly illustrated translation of the Odyssey, published in 1665, where Charles ii.'s Master of the Revels in Ireland gives the passage thus:

Minerva renders him more tall and fair,

Curling in rings like daffodils his hair.

No anthology, however, can show the true merit of Mr. Morris's translation, whose real merit does not depend on stray beauties, nor is revealed by chance selections, but lies in the absolute rightness and coherence of the whole, in its purity and justice of touch, its freedom from affectation and commonplace, its harmony of form and matter. It is sufficient to say that this is a poet's version of a poet, and for such surely we should be thankful. In these latter days of coarse and vulgar literature, it is something to have made the great sea-epic of the South native and natural to our northern isle, something to have shown that our English speech may be a pipe through which Greek lips can blow, something to have taught Nausicaa to speak the same language as Perdita.

> *The Odyssey of Homer.* Done into English Verse by William
> Morris, author of *The Earthly Paradise.* In two volumes. Volume I.
> (Reeves and Turner.)

For review of Volume II. see *Mr. Morris's Completion of the Odyssey,* page 65.

RUSSIAN NOVELISTS

(Pall Mall Gazette, May 2, 1887.)

Of the three great Russian novelists of our time Tourgenieff is by far the finest artist. He has that spirit of exquisite selection, that delicate choice of detail, which is the essence of style; his work is entirely free from any personal intention; and by taking existence at its most fiery-coloured moments he can distil into a few pages of perfect prose the moods and passions of many lives.

Count Tolstoi's method is much larger, and his field of vision more extended. He reminds us sometimes of Paul Veronese, and, like that great painter, can crowd, without over-crowding, the giant canvas on which he works. We may not at first gain from his works that artistic unity of impression which is Tourgenieff's chief charm, but once that we have mastered the details the whole seems to have the grandeur and the simplicity of an epic. Dostoieffski differs widely from both his rivals. He is not so

50

fine an artist as Tourgenieff, for he deals more with the facts than with the effects of life; nor has he Tolstoi's largeness of vision and epic dignity; but he has qualities that are distinctively and absolutely his own, such as a fierce intensity of passion and concentration of impulse, a power of dealing with the deepest mysteries of psychology and the most hidden springs of life, and a realism that is pitiless in its fidelity, and terrible because it is true. Some time ago we had occasion to draw attention to his marvellous novel Crime and Punishment, where in the haunt of impurity and vice a harlot and an assassin meet together to read the story of Dives and Lazarus, and the outcast girl leads the sinner to make atonement for his sin; nor is the book entitled Injury and Insult at all inferior to that great masterpiece. Mean and ordinary though the surroundings of the story may seem, the heroine Natasha is like one of the noble victims of Greek tragedy; she is Antigone with the passion of Phædra, and it is impossible to approach her without a feeling of awe. Greek also is the gloom of Nemesis that hangs over each character, only it is a Nemesis that does not stand outside of life, but is part of our own nature and of the same material as life itself. Aleósha, the beautiful young lad whom Natasha follows to her doom, is a second Tito Melema, and has all Tito's charm and grace and fascination. Yet he is different. He would never have denied Baldassare in the Square at Florence, nor lied to Romola about Tessa. He has a magnificent, momentary sincerity, a boyish unconsciousness of all that life signifies, an ardent enthusiasm for all that life cannot give. There is nothing calculating about him. He never thinks evil, he only does it. From a psychological point of view he is one of the most interesting characters of modern fiction, as from an artistic he is one of the most attractive. As we grow to know him he stirs strange questions for us, and makes us feel that it is not the wicked only who do wrong, nor the bad alone who work evil.

And by what a subtle objective method does Dostoieffski show us his characters! He never tickets them with a list nor labels them with a description. We grow to know them very gradually, as we know people whom we meet in society, at first by little tricks of manner, personal appearance, fancies in dress, and the like; and afterwards by their deeds and words; and even then they constantly elude us, for though Dostoieffski may lay bare for us the secrets of their nature, yet he never explains his personages away; they are

51

always surprising us by something that they say or do, and keep to the end the eternal mystery of life.

Irrespective of its value as a work of art, this novel possesses a deep autobiographical interest also, as the character of Vania, the poor student who loves Natasha through all her sin and shame, is Dostoieffski's study of himself. Goethe once had to delay the completion of one of his novels till experience had furnished him with new situations, but almost before he had arrived at manhood Dostoieffski knew life in its most real forms; poverty and suffering, pain and misery, prison, exile, and love, were soon familiar to him, and by the lips of Vania he has told his own story. This note of personal feeling, this harsh reality of actual experience, undoubtedly gives the book something of its strange fervour and terrible passion, yet it has not made it egotistic; we see things from every point of view, and we feel, not that fiction has been trammelled by fact, but that fact itself has become ideal and imaginative. Pitiless, too, though Dostoieffski is in his method as an artist, as a man he is full of human pity for all, for those who do evil as well as for those who suffer it, for the selfish no less than for those whose lives are wrecked for others and whose sacrifice is in vain. Since Adam Bede and Le Père Goriot no more powerful novel has been written than Insult and Injury.

> *Injury and Insult.* By Fedor Dostoieffski. Translated from the
> Russian by Frederick Whishaw. (Vizetelly and Co.)

MR. PATER'S IMAGINARY PORTRAITS

(Pall Mall Gazette, June 11, 1887.)

To convey ideas through the medium of images has always been the aim of those who are artists as well as thinkers in literature, and it is to a desire to give a sensuous environment to intellectual concepts that we owe Mr. Pater's last volume. For these Imaginary or, as we should prefer to call them, Imaginative Portraits of his, form a series of philosophic studies in which the philosophy is tempered by personality, and the thought shown under varying conditions of mood and manner, the very permanence of each principle gaining something through the change and colour of the life through which it finds expression. The most fascinating of all these pictures is undoubtedly that of Sebastian Van Storck. The account of Watteau is perhaps a little too fanciful, and the description of him as one who was 'always a seeker after something in the world, that is there in no satisfying measure, or not at all,' seems to us more applicable to him who saw Mona Lisa sitting among the rocks than the gay and debonair peintre des fêtes galantes. But Sebastian, the grave young Dutch philosopher, is charmingly drawn. From the first glimpse we get of him, skating over the water-meadows with his plume of squirrel's tail and his fur muff, in all the modest pleasantness of boyhood, down to his strange death in the desolate house amid the sands of the Helder, we seem to see him, to know him, almost to hear the low music of his voice. He is a dreamer, as the common phrase goes, and yet he is poetical in this sense, that his theorems shape life for him, directly. Early in youth he is stirred by a fine saying of Spinoza, and sets himself to realize the ideal of an intellectual disinterestedness, separating himself more and more from the transient world of sensation, accident and even affection, till what is finite and relative becomes of no interest to him, and he feels that as nature is but a thought of his, so he himself is but a passing thought of God. This conception, of the power of a mere metaphysical abstraction over the mind of one so fortunately endowed for the reception of the sensible world, is exceedingly delightful, and Mr. Pater has never written a more subtle psychological study, the fact that Sebastian dies in an attempt to save the life of a little child giving to the whole story a touch of poignant pathos and sad irony.

Denys l'Auxerrois is suggested by a figure found, or said to be found, on some old tapestries in Auxerre, the figure of a 'flaxen and flowery creature, sometimes well-nigh naked among the vine-leaves, sometimes muffled in skins against the cold, sometimes in the dress of a monk, but always with a strong impress of real character and incident from the veritable streets' of the town itself. From this strange design Mr. Pater has fashioned a curious mediæval myth of the return of Dionysus among men, a myth steeped in colour and passion and old romance, full of wonder and full of worship, Denys himself being half animal and half god, making the world mad with a new ecstasy of living, stirring the artists simply by his visible presence, drawing the marvel of music from reed and pipe, and slain at last in a stage-play by those who had loved him. In its rich affluence of imagery this story is like a picture by Mantegna, and indeed Mantegna might have suggested the description of the pageant in which Denys rides upon a gaily-painted chariot, in soft silken raiment and, for head-dress, a strange elephant scalp with gilded tusks.

If Denys l'Auxerrois symbolizes the passion of the senses and Sebastian Van Storck the philosophic passion, as they certainly seem to do, though no mere formula or definition can adequately express the freedom and variety of the life that they portray, the passion for the imaginative world of art is the basis of the story of Duke Carl of Rosenmold. Duke Carl is not unlike the late King of Bavaria, in his love of France, his admiration for the Grand Monarque and his fantastic desire to amaze and to bewilder, but the resemblance is possibly only a chance one. In fact Mr. Pater's young hero is the precursor of the Aufklärung of the last century, the German precursor of Herder and Lessing and Goethe himself, and finds the forms of art ready to his hand without any national spirit to fill them or make them vital and responsive. He too dies, trampled to death by the soldiers of the country he so much admired, on the night of his marriage with a peasant girl, the very failure of his life lending him a certain melancholy grace and dramatic interest.

On the whole, then, this is a singularly attractive book. Mr. Pater is an intellectual impressionist. He does not weary us with any definite doctrine or seek to suit life to any formal creed. He is always looking for exquisite moments and, when he has found them, he analyses them with delicate and delightful art and then passes on, often to the opposite pole of thought or feeling, knowing that every mood has its own quality and charm and is justified by its mere existence. He has taken the sensationalism of Greek philosophy and made it a new method of art criticism. As for his style, it is curiously ascetic. Now and then, we come across phrases with a strange sensuousness of expression, as when he tells us how Denys l'Auxerrois, on his return from a long journey, 'ate flesh for the first time, tearing the hot, red morsels with his delicate fingers in a kind of wild greed,' but such passages are rare. Asceticism is the keynote of Mr. Pater's prose; at times it is almost

54

too severe in its self-control and makes us long for a little more freedom. For indeed, the danger of such prose as his is that it is apt to become somewhat laborious. Here and there, one is tempted to say of Mr. Pater that he is 'a seeker after something in language, that is there in no satisfying measure, or not at all.' The continual preoccupation with phrase and epithet has its drawbacks as well as its virtues. And yet, when all is said, what wonderful prose it is, with its subtle preferences, its fastidious purity, its rejection of what is common or ordinary! Mr. Pater has the true spirit of selection, the true art of omission. If he be not among the greatest prose writers of our literature he is, at least, our greatest artist in prose; and though it may be admitted that the best style is that which seems an unconscious result rather than a conscious aim, still in these latter days when violent rhetoric does duty for eloquence and vulgarity usurps the name of nature, we should be grateful for a style that deliberately aims at perfection of form, that seeks to produce its effect by artistic means and sets before itself an ideal of grave and chastened beauty.

Imaginary Portraits. By Walter Pater, M.A., Fellow of Brasenose
College, Oxford. (Macmillan and Co.)

A GERMAN PRINCESS

(Woman's World, November 1887.)

The Princess Christian's translation of the Memoirs of Wilhelmine, Margravine of Baireuth, is a most fascinating and delightful book. The Margravine and her brother, Frederick the Great, were, as the Princess herself points out in an admirably written introduction, 'among the first of those questioning minds that strove after spiritual freedom' in the last century. 'They had studied,' says the Princess, 'the English philosophers, Newton, Locke, and Shaftesbury, and were roused to enthusiasm by the writings of Voltaire and Rousseau. Their whole lives bore the impress of the influence of French thought on the burning questions of the day. In the eighteenth century began that great struggle of philosophy against tyranny and worn-out abuses which culminated in the French Revolution. The noblest minds were engaged in the struggle, and, like most reformers, they pushed their conclusions to extremes, and too often lost sight of the need of a due proportion in things. The Margravine's influence on the intellectual development of her country is untold. She formed at Baireuth a centre of culture and learning which had before been undreamt of in Germany.'

The historical value of these Memoirs is, of course, well known. Carlyle speaks of them as being 'by far the best authority' on the early life of Frederick the Great. But considered merely as the autobiography of a clever and charming woman, they are no less interesting, and even those who care nothing for eighteenth-century politics, and look upon history itself as an unattractive form of fiction, cannot fail to be fascinated by the Margravine's wit, vivacity and humour, by her keen powers of observation, and by her brilliant and assertive egotism. Not that her life was by any means a happy one. Her father, to quote the Princess Christian, 'ruled his family with the same harsh despotism with which he ruled his country, taking pleasure in making his power felt by all in the most galling manner,' and the Margravine and her brother 'had much to suffer, not only from his ungovernable temper, but also from the real privations to which they were subjected.' Indeed, the picture the Margravine gives of the King is quite extraordinary. 'He despised all learning,' she writes, 'and wished me to occupy myself with nothing but needlework and household duties or details. Had he found me writing or reading, he would probably have whipped me.' He 'considered music a capital offence, and maintained that every one should devote himself to one object: men to the military service, and women to their household duties. Science and the arts he counted among the "seven deadly sins."' Sometimes he took to religion, 'and then,' says the Margravine, 'we lived like trappists, to the great grief of my brother and myself. Every afternoon the King preached a sermon, to which we had to listen as attentively as if it proceeded from an Apostle. My brother and I were often seized with such an intense sense of the ridiculous that we burst out laughing, upon which an apostolic curse was poured out on our heads, which we had to accept with a show of humility and penitence.' Economy and soldiers were his only topics of conversation; his chief social amusement was to make his guests intoxicated; and as for his temper, the accounts the Margravine gives of it would be almost incredible if they were not amply corroborated from other sources. Suetonius has written of the strange madness that comes on kings, but even in his melodramatic chronicles there is hardly anything that rivals what the Margravine has to tell us. Here is one of her pictures of family life at a Royal Court in the last century, and it is not by any means the worst scene she describes:

> On one occasion, when his temper was more than usually bad, he told the Queen that he had received letters from Anspach, in which the Margrave announced his arrival at Berlin for the beginning of May. He was coming there for the purpose of marrying my sister, and one of his ministers would arrive previously with the betrothal ring. My father asked my sister whether she were pleased at this prospect, and how she would arrange her household. Now my sister had always made a point of telling him whatever came into her head, even the greatest home-truths, and he had never taken her outspokenness amiss. On this occasion, therefore, relying on former experience, she answered him as follows: 'When I have a house of my own, I shall take care to have a well-appointed dinner-table, better than yours is, and if I have children of my own, I shall not plague them as you do yours, and force them to eat things they thoroughly dislike!'

> 'What is amiss with my dinner-table?' the King enquired, getting very red in the face.

> 'You ask what is the matter with it,' my sister replied; 'there is not enough on it for us to eat, and what there is cabbage and carrots, which we detest.' Her first answer had already angered my father, but now he gave vent to his fury. But instead of punishing my sister he poured it all on my mother, my brother, and myself. To begin with he threw his plate at my brother's head, who would have been struck had he not got out of the way; a second one he threw at me, which I also happily escaped; then torrents of abuse followed these first signs of hostility. He reproached the Queen with having brought up her children so badly. 'You will curse your mother,' he said to my brother, 'for having made you such a good-for-nothing creature.' . . . As my brother and I passed near him to leave the room, he hit out at us with his crutch. Happily we escaped the blow, for it would certainly have struck us down, and

we at last escaped without harm.

Yet, as the Princess Christian remarks, 'despite the almost cruel treatment Wilhelmine received from her father, it is noticeable that throughout her memoirs she speaks of him with the greatest affection. She makes constant reference to his "good heart"'; and says that his faults 'were more those of temper than of nature.' Nor could all the misery and wretchedness of her home life dull the brightness of her intellect. What would have made others morbid, made her satirical. Instead of weeping over her own personal tragedies, she laughs at the general comedy of life. Here, for instance, is her description of Peter the Great and his wife, who arrived at Berlin in 1718:

> The Czarina was small, broad, and brown-looking, without the slightest dignity or appearance. You had only to look at her to detect her low origin. She might have passed for a German actress, she had decked herself out in such a manner. Her dress had been bought second-hand, and was trimmed with some dirty looking silver embroidery; the bodice was trimmed with precious stones, arranged in such a manner as to represent the double eagle. She wore a dozen orders; and round the bottom of her dress hung quantities of relics and pictures of saints, which rattled when she walked, and reminded one of a smartly harnessed mule. The orders too made a great noise, knocking against each other.

> The Czar, on the other hand, was tall and well grown, with a handsome face, but his expression was coarse, and impressed one with fear. He wore a simple sailor's dress. His wife, who spoke German very badly, called her court jester to her aid, and spoke Russian with her. This poor creature was a Princess Gallizin, who had been obliged to undertake this sorry office to save her life, as she had been mixed up in a conspiracy against the Czar, and had twice been flogged with the knout!

* * * * *

> The following day [the Czar] visited all the sights of Berlin, amongst others the very curious collection of coins and antiques. Amongst these last named was a statue, representing a heathen god. It was anything

but attractive, but was the most valuable in the collection. The Czar admired it very much, and insisted on the Czarina kissing it. On her refusing, he said to her in bad German that she should lose her head if she did not at once obey him. Being terrified at the Czar's anger she immediately complied with his orders without the least hesitation. The Czar asked the King to give him this and other statues, a request which he could not refuse. The same thing happened about a cupboard, inlaid with amber. It was the only one of its kind, and had cost King Frederick I. an enormous sum, and the consternation was general on its having to be sent to Petersburg.

This barbarous Court happily left after two days. The Queen rushed at once to Monbijou, which she found in a state resembling that of the fall of Jerusalem. I never saw such a sight. Everything was destroyed, so that the Queen was obliged to rebuild the whole house.

Nor are the Margravine's descriptions of her reception as a bride in the principality of Baireuth less amusing. Hof was the first town she came to, and a deputation of nobles was waiting there to welcome her. This is her account of them:

Their faces would have frightened little children, and, to add to their beauty, they had arranged their hair to resemble the wigs that were then in fashion. Their dresses clearly denoted the antiquity of their families, as they were composed of heirlooms, and were cut accordingly, so that most of them did not fit. In spite of their costumes being the 'Court Dresses,' the gold and silver trimmings were so black that you had a difficulty in making out of what they were made. The manners of these nobles suited their faces and their clothes. They might have passed for peasants. I could scarcely restrain my laughter when I first beheld these strange figures. I spoke to each in turn, but none of them understood what I said, and their replies sounded to me like Hebrew, because the dialect of the Empire is quite different from that spoken in Brandenburg.

The clergy also presented themselves. These were totally different creatures. Round their necks they wore great ruffs, which resembled washing baskets. They spoke very slowly, so that I might be able to understand them better. They said the most foolish things, and it was only with much difficulty that I was able to prevent myself from laughing. At last I got rid of all these people, and we sat down to dinner. I tried my best to converse with those at table, but it was useless. At last I touched on agricultural topics, and then they began to thaw. I was at once informed of all their different farmsteads and herds of cattle. An almost interesting discussion took place as to whether the oxen in the upper part of the country were fatter than those in the lowlands.

* * * * *

I was told that as the next day was Sunday, I must spend it at Hof, and listen to a sermon. Never before had I heard such a sermon! The clergyman began by giving us an account of all the marriages that had taken place from Adam's time to that of Noah. We were spared no detail, so that the gentlemen all laughed and the poor ladies blushed. The dinner went off as on the previous day. In the afternoon all the ladies came to pay me their respects. Gracious heavens! What ladies, too! They were all as ugly as the gentlemen, and their head-dresses were so curious that swallows might have built their nests in them.

As for Baireuth itself, and its petty Court, the picture she gives of it is exceedingly curious. Her father-in-law, the reigning Margrave, was a narrow-minded mediocrity, whose conversation 'resembled that of a sermon read aloud for the purpose of sending the listener to sleep,' and he had only two topics, Telemachus, and Amelot de la Houssaye's Roman History. The Ministers, from Baron von Stein, who always said 'yes' to everything, to Baron von Voit, who always said 'no,' were not by any means an intellectual set of men. 'Their chief amusement,' says the Margravine, 'was drinking from morning till night,' and horses and cattle were all they talked about. The palace itself was shabby, decayed and dirty. 'I was like a lamb among wolves,' cries the poor Margravine; 'I was settled in a strange country, at a Court which more resembled a peasant's farm, surrounded by coarse, bad, dangerous, and tiresome people.'

Yet her esprit never deserted her. She is always clever, witty, and entertaining. Her stories about the endless squabbles over precedence are extremely amusing. The society of her day cared very little for good manners, knew, indeed, very little about them, but all questions of etiquette were of vital importance, and the Margravine herself, though she saw the shallowness of the whole system, was far too proud not to assert her rights when circumstances demanded it, as the description she gives of her visit to the Empress of Germany shows very clearly. When this meeting was first proposed, the Margravine declined positively to entertain the idea. 'There was no precedent,' she writes, 'of a King's daughter and the Empress having met, and I did not know to what rights I ought to lay claim.' Finally, however, she is induced to consent, but she lays down three conditions for her reception:

> I desired first of all that the Empress's Court should receive me at the foot of the stairs, secondly, that she should meet me at the door of her bedroom, and, thirdly, that she should offer me an armchair to sit on.

* * * * *

> They disputed all day over the conditions I had made. The two first were granted me, but all that could be obtained with respect to the third was, that the Empress would use quite a small armchair, whilst she gave me a chair.

> Next day I saw this Royal personage. I own that had I been in her place I would have made all the rules of etiquette and ceremony the excuse for not being obliged to appear. The Empress was small and stout, round as a ball, very ugly, and without dignity or manner. Her mind corresponded to her body. She was terribly bigoted, and spent her whole day praying. The old and ugly are generally the Almighty's portion. She received me trembling all over, and was so upset that she could not say a word.

> After some silence I began the conversation in French. She answered me in her Austrian dialect that she could not speak in that language, and begged I would speak in German. The conversation did not last long, for the Austrian and low Saxon tongues are so different from each

other that to those acquainted with only one the other is unintelligible. This is what happened to us. A third person would have laughed at our misunderstandings, for we caught only a word here and there, and had to guess the rest. The poor Empress was such a slave to etiquette that she would have thought it high treason had she spoken to me in a foreign language, though she understood French quite well.

Many other extracts might be given from this delightful book, but from the few that have been selected some idea can be formed of the vivacity and picturesqueness of the Margravine's style. As for her character, it is very well summed up by the Princess Christian, who, while admitting that she often appears almost heartless and inconsiderate, yet claims that, 'taken as a whole, she stands out in marked prominence among the most gifted women of the eighteenth century, not only by her mental powers, but by her goodness of heart, her self-sacrificing devotion, and true friendship.' An interesting sequel to her Memoirs would be her correspondence with Voltaire, and it is to be hoped that we may shortly see a translation of these letters from the same accomplished pen to which we owe the present volume. [63]

Memoirs of Wilhelmine Margravine of Baireuth. Translated
and edited by Her Royal Highness Princess Christian of Schleswig-
Holstein, Princess of Great Britain and Ireland. (David Stott.)

A VILLAGE TRAGEDY

One of the most powerful and pathetic novels that has recently appeared is A Village Tragedy by Margaret L. Woods. To find any parallel to this lurid little story, one must go to Dostoieffski or to Guy de Maupassant. Not that Mrs. Woods can be said to have taken either of these two great masters of fiction as her model, but there is something in her work that recalls their method; she has not a little of their fierce intensity, their terrible concentration, their passionless yet poignant objectivity; like them, she seems to allow life to suggest its own mode of presentation; and, like them, she recognizes that a frank acceptance of the facts of life is the true basis of all modern imitative art. The scene of Mrs. Woods's story lies in one of the villages near Oxford; the characters are very few in number, and the plot is extremely simple. It is a romance of modern Arcadia—a tale of the love of a farm-labourer for a girl who, though slightly above him in social station and education, is yet herself also a servant on a farm. True Arcadians they are, both of them, and their ignorance and isolation serve only to intensify the tragedy that gives the story its title. It is the fashion nowadays to label literature, so, no doubt, Mrs. Woods's novel will be spoken of as 'realistic.' Its realism, however, is the realism of the artist, not of the reporter; its tact of treatment, subtlety of perception, and fine distinction of style, make it rather a poem than a procès-verbal; and though it lays bare to us the mere misery of life, it suggests something of life's mystery also. Very delicate, too, is the handling of external Nature. There are no formal guide-book descriptions of scenery, nor anything of what Byron petulantly called 'twaddling about trees,' but we seem to breathe the atmosphere of the country, to catch the exquisite scent of the beanfields, so familiar to all who have ever wandered through the Oxfordshire lanes in June; to hear the birds singing in the thicket, and the sheep-bells tinkling from the hill.

Characterization, that enemy of literary form, is such an essential part of the method of the modern writer of fiction, that Nature has almost become to the novelist what light and shade are to the painter—the one permanent element of style; and if the power of A Village Tragedy be due to its portrayal of human life, no small portion of its charm comes from its Theocritean setting.

A Village Tragedy. By Margaret L. Woods. (Bentley and Son.)

MR. MORRIS'S COMPLETION OF THE ODYSSEY

(Pall Mall Gazette, November 24, 1887.)

Mr. Morris's second volume brings the great romantic epic of Greek literature to its perfect conclusion, and although there can never be an ultimate translation of either Iliad or Odyssey, as each successive age is sure to find pleasure in rendering the two poems in its own manner and according to

63

its own canons of taste, still it is not too much to say that Mr. Morris's version will always be a true classic amongst our classical translations. It is not, of course, flawless. In our notice of the first volume we ventured to say that Mr. Morris was sometimes far more Norse than Greek, nor does the volume that now lies before us make us alter that opinion. The particular metre, also, selected by Mr. Morris, although admirably adapted to express 'the strong-winged music of Homer,' as far as its flow and freedom are concerned, misses something of its dignity and calm. Here, it must be admitted, we feel a distinct loss, for there is in Homer not a little of Milton's lofty manner, and if swiftness be an essential of the Greek hexameter, stateliness is one of its distinguishing qualities in Homer's hands. This defect, however, if we must call it a defect, seems almost unavoidable, as for certain metrical reasons a majestic movement in English verse is necessarily a slow movement; and, after all that can be said is said, how really admirable is this whole translation! If we set aside its noble qualities as a poem and look on it purely from the scholar's point of view, how straightforward it is, how honest and direct! Its fidelity to the original is far beyond that of any other verse-translation in our literature, and yet it is not the fidelity of a pedant to his text but rather the fine loyalty of poet to poet.

When Mr. Morris's first volume appeared many of the critics complained that his occasional use of archaic words and unusual expressions robbed his version of the true Homeric simplicity. This, however, is not a very felicitous criticism, for while Homer is undoubtedly simple in his clearness and largeness of vision, his wonderful power of direct narration, his wholesome sanity, and the purity and precision of his method, simple in language he undoubtedly is not. What he was to his contemporaries we have, of course, no means of judging, but we know that the Athenian of the fifth century b.c. found him in many places difficult to understand, and when the creative age was succeeded by the age of criticism and Alexandria began to take the place of Athens as the centre of culture for the Hellenistic world, Homeric dictionaries and glossaries seem to have been constantly published. Indeed, Athenæus tells us of a wonderful Byzantine blue-stocking, a précieuse from the Propontis, who wrote a long hexameter poem, called Mnemosyne, full of ingenious commentaries on difficulties in Homer, and in fact, it is evident that, as far as the language is concerned, such a phrase as 'Homeric simplicity' would have rather amazed an ancient Greek. As for Mr. Morris's tendency to emphasize the etymological meaning of words, a point commented on with somewhat flippant severity in a recent number of Macmillan's Magazine, here Mr. Morris seems to us to be in complete accord, not merely with the spirit of Homer, but with the spirit of all early poetry. It is quite true that language is apt to degenerate into a system of almost algebraic symbols, and the modern city-man who takes a ticket for Blackfriars Bridge, naturally never thinks of the Dominican monks who once had their monastery by Thames-side, and after whom the spot is named. But in earlier times it was not so. Men were then keenly conscious of the real meaning of words, and early poetry, especially, is full of this feeling, and, indeed, may be said to owe to it no small portion of its poetic power and charm. These old words, then, and this old use of words which we find in Mr. Morris's Odyssey can be amply justified upon historical grounds, and as for their artistic effect, it is quite excellent. Pope tried to put Homer into the ordinary language of his day, with what result we know only too well; but Mr. Morris, who uses his archaisms with the tact of a true artist, and to whom indeed they seem to come absolutely naturally, has succeeded in giving to his version by their aid that touch, not of 'quaintness,' for Homer is never quaint, but of old-world romance and old-world beauty, which we moderns find so pleasurable, and to which the Greeks themselves were so keenly sensitive.

As for individual passages of special merit, Mr. Morris's translation is no robe of rags sewn with purple patches for critics to sample. Its real value lies in the absolute rightness and coherence of the whole, in the grand architecture of the swift, strong verse, and in the fact that the standard is not merely high but everywhere sustained. It is impossible, however, to resist the temptation of quoting Mr. Morris's rendering of that famous passage in the twenty-third book of the epic, in which Odysseus eludes the trap laid for him by Penelope, whose very faith in the certainty of her husband's return makes her sceptical of his identity when he stands before her; an instance, by the way, of Homer's wonderful psychological knowledge of human nature, as it is always the dreamer himself who is most surprised when his dream comes true.

Thus she spake to prove her husband; but Odysseus, grieved at heart,

Spake thus unto his bed-mate well-skilled in gainful art:

'O woman, thou sayest a word exceeding grievous to me!

Who hath otherwhere shifted my bedstead? full hard for him should it be,

For as deft as he were, unless soothly a very God come here,

Who easily, if he willed it, might shift it otherwhere.

But no mortal man is living, how strong soe'er in his youth,

Who shall lightly hale it elsewhere, since a mighty wonder forsooth

Is wrought in that fashioned bedstead, and I wrought it, and I alone.

In the close grew a thicket of olive, a long-leaved tree full-grown,

That flourished and grew goodly as big as a pillar about,

So round it I built my bride-room, till I did the work right out

With ashlar stone close-fitting; and I roofed it overhead,

And thereto joined doors I made me, well-fitting in their stead.

Then I lopped away the boughs of the long-leafed olive-tree,

And, shearing the bole from the root up full well and cunningly,

I planed it about with the brass, and set the rule thereto,

And shaping thereof a bed-post, with the wimble I bored it through.

So beginning, I wrought out the bedstead, and finished it utterly,

And with gold enwrought it about, and with silver and ivory,

And stretched on it a thong of oxhide with the purple dye made bright.

Thus then the sign I have shown thee; nor, woman, know I aright

If my bed yet bideth steadfast, or if to another place

> *Some man hath moved it, and smitten the olive-bole from its base.'*

These last twelve books of the Odyssey have not the same marvel of romance, adventure and colour that we find in the earlier part of the epic. There is nothing in them that we can compare to the exquisite idyll of Nausicaa or to the Titanic humour of the episode in the Cyclops' cave. Penelope has not the glamour of Circe, and the song of the Sirens may sound sweeter than the whizz of the arrows of Odysseus as he stands on the threshold of his hall. Yet, for sheer intensity of passionate power, for concentration of intellectual interest and for masterly dramatic construction, these latter books are quite unequalled. Indeed, they show very clearly how it was that, as Greek art developed, the epos passed into the drama. The whole scheme of the argument, the return of the hero in disguise, his disclosure of himself to his son, his terrible vengeance on his enemies and his final recognition by his wife, reminds us of the plot of more than one Greek play, and shows us what the great Athenian poet meant when he said that his own dramas were merely scraps from Homer's table. In rendering this splendid poem into English verse, Mr. Morris has done our literature a service that can hardly be over-estimated, and it is pleasant to think that, even should the classics be entirely excluded from our educational systems, the English boy will still be able to know something of Homer's delightful tales, to catch an echo of his grand music and to wander with the wise Odysseus round 'the shores of old romance.'

> *The Odyssey of Homer.* Done into English Verse by William
> Morris, Author of *The Earthly Paradise*. Volume II. (Reeves and
> Turner.)

MRS. SOMERVILLE

(Pall Mall Gazette, November 30, 1887.)

Phyllis Browne's Life of Mrs. Somerville forms part of a very interesting little series, called 'The World's Workers'—a collection of short biographies catholic enough to include personalities so widely different as Turner and

Richard Cobden, Handel and Sir Titus Salt, Robert Stephenson and Florence Nightingale, and yet possessing a certain definite aim. As a mathematician and a scientist, the translator and popularizer of La Mécanique Céleste, and the author of an important book on physical geography, Mrs. Somerville is, of course, well known. The scientific bodies of Europe covered her with honours; her bust stands in the hall of the Royal Society, and one of the Women's Colleges at Oxford bears her name. Yet, considered simply in the light of a wife and a mother, she is no less admirable; and those who consider that stupidity is the proper basis for the domestic virtues, and that intellectual women must of necessity be helpless with their hands, cannot do better than read Phyllis Browne's pleasant little book, in which they will find that the greatest woman-mathematician of any age was a clever needlewoman, a good housekeeper, and a most skilful cook. Indeed, Mrs. Somerville seems to have been quite renowned for her cookery. The discoverers of the North-West Passage christened an island 'Somerville,' not as a tribute to the distinguished mathematician, but as a recognition of the excellence of some orange marmalade which the distinguished mathematician had prepared with her own hands and presented to the ships before they left England; and to the fact that she was able to make currant jelly at a very critical moment she owed the affection of some of her husband's relatives, who up to that time had been rather prejudiced against her on the ground that she was merely an unpractical Blue-stocking.

Nor did her scientific knowledge ever warp or dull the tenderness and humanity of her nature. For birds and animals she had always a great love. We hear of her as a little girl watching with eager eyes the swallows as they built their nests in summer or prepared for their flight in the autumn; and when snow was on the ground she used to open the windows to let the robins hop in and pick crumbs on the breakfast-table. On one occasion she went with her father on a tour in the Highlands, and found on her return that a pet goldfinch, which had been left in the charge of the servants, had been neglected by them and had died of starvation. She was almost heart-broken at the event, and in writing her Recollections, seventy years after, she mentioned it and said that, as she wrote, she felt deep pain. Her chief pet in her old age was a mountain sparrow, which used to perch on her arm and go to sleep there while she was writing. One day the sparrow fell into the water-jug and was drowned, to the great grief of its mistress who could hardly be consoled for its loss, though later on we hear of a beautiful paroquet taking the place of le moineau d'Uranie, and becoming Mrs. Somerville's constant companion. She was also very energetic, Phyllis Browne tells us, in trying to get a law passed in the Italian Parliament for the protection of animals, and said once, with reference to this subject, 'We English cannot boast of humanity so long as our sportsmen find pleasure in shooting down tame pigeons as they fly terrified out of a cage'—a remark with which I entirely agree. Mr. Herbert's Bill for the protection of land birds gave her immense pleasure, though, to quote her own words, she was 'grieved to find that "the lark, which at heaven's gate sings," is thought unworthy of man's protection'; and she took a great fancy to a gentleman who, on being told of the number of singing birds that is eaten in Italy—nightingales, goldfinches, and robins—exclaimed in horror, 'What! robins! our household birds! I would as soon eat a child!' Indeed, she believed to some extent in the immortality of animals on the ground that, if animals have no future, it would seem as if some were created for uncompensated misery—an idea which does not seem to me to be either extravagant or fantastic, though it must be admitted that the optimism on which it is based receives absolutely no support from science.

On the whole, Phyllis Browne's book is very pleasant reading. Its only fault is that it is far too short, and this is a fault so rare in modern literature that it almost amounts to a distinction. However, Phyllis Browne has managed to crowd into the narrow limits at her disposal a great many interesting anecdotes. The picture she gives of Mrs. Somerville working away at her translation of Laplace in the same room with her children is very charming, and reminds one of what is told of George Sand; there is an amusing account of Mrs. Somerville's visit to the widow of the young Pretender, the Countess of Albany, who, after talking with her for some time, exclaimed, 'So you don't speak Italian. You must have had a very bad education'! And this story about the Waverley Novels may possibly be new to some of my readers:

A very amusing circumstance in connection with Mrs. Somerville's acquaintance with Sir Walter arose out of the childish inquisitiveness of Woronzow Greig, Mrs. Somerville's little boy.

During the time Mrs. Somerville was visiting Abbotsford the Waverley Novels were appearing, and were creating a great sensation; yet even Scott's intimate friends did not know that he was the author; he enjoyed keeping the affair a mystery. But little Woronzow discovered what he was about. One day when Mrs. Somerville was talking about a novel that had just been published, Woronzow said, 'I knew all these stories long ago, for Mr. Scott writes on the dinner-table; when he has finished he puts the green cloth with the papers in a corner of the dining-room, and when he goes out Charlie Scott and I read the stories.'

Phyllis Browne remarks that this incident shows 'that persons who want to keep a secret ought to be very careful when children are about'; but the story seems to me to be far too charming to require any moral of the kind.

Bound up in the same volume is a Life of Miss Mary Carpenter, also written by Phyllis Browne. Miss Carpenter does not seem to me to have the charm and fascination of Mrs. Somerville. There is always something about her that is formal, limited, and precise. When she was about two years old she insisted on being called 'Doctor Carpenter' in the nursery; at the age of twelve she is described by a friend as a sedate little girl, who always spoke like a book; and before she entered on her educational schemes she wrote down a solemn dedication of herself to the service of humanity. However, she was one of the practical, hardworking saints of the nineteenth century, and it is no doubt quite right that the saints should take themselves very seriously. It is only fair also to remember that her work of rescue and reformation was carried on under great difficulties. Here, for instance, is the picture Miss Cobbe gives us of one of the Bristol night-schools:

It was a wonderful spectacle to see Mary Carpenter sitting patiently before the large school gallery in St. James's Back, teaching, singing, and praying with the wild street-boys, in spite of endless interruptions caused by such proceedings as shooting marbles at any object behind her, whistling, stamping, fighting, shrieking out 'Amen' in the middle of a prayer, and sometimes rising en masse and tearing like a troop of bisons in hob-nailed shoes down from the gallery, round the great schoolroom, and down the stairs, and into the street. These irrepressible outbreaks she bore with infinite good humour.

Her own account is somewhat pleasanter, and shows that 'the troop of bisons in hob-nailed shoes' was not always so barbarous.

> I had taken to my class on the preceding week some specimens of ferns neatly gummed on white paper. . . . This time I took a piece of coalshale, with impressions of ferns, to show them. . . . I told each to examine the specimen, and tell me what he thought it was. W. gave so bright a smile that I saw he knew; none of the others could tell; he said they were ferns, like what I showed them last week, but he thought they were chiselled on the stone. Their surprise and pleasure were great when I explained the matter to them.

> The history of Joseph: they all found a difficulty in realizing that this had actually occurred. One asked if Egypt existed now, and if people lived in it. When I told them that buildings now stood which had been erected about the time of Joseph, one said that it was impossible, as they must have fallen down ere this. I showed them the form of a pyramid, and they were satisfied. One asked if all books were true.

> The story of Macbeth impressed them very much. They knew the name of Shakespeare, having seen his name over a public-house.

> A boy defined conscience as 'a thing a gentleman hasn't got, who, when a boy finds his purse and gives it back to him, doesn't give the boy sixpence.'

> Another boy was asked, after a Sunday evening lecture on 'Thankfulness,' what pleasure he enjoyed most in the course of a year. He replied candidly, 'Cock-fightin', ma'am; there's a pit up by the "Black Boy" as is worth anythink in Brissel.'

There is something a little pathetic in the attempt to civilize the rough street-boy by means of the refining influence of ferns and fossils, and it is difficult to help feeling that Miss Carpenter rather over-estimated the value of elementary education. The poor are not to be fed upon facts. Even Shakespeare and the Pyramids are not sufficient; nor is there much use in giving them the results of culture, unless we also give them those conditions under which culture can be realized. In these cold, crowded cities of the North, the proper basis for morals, using the word in its wide Hellenic signification, is to be found in architecture, not in books.

Still, it would be ungenerous not to recognize that Mary Carpenter gave to the children of the poor not merely her learning, but her love. In early life, her biographer tells us, she had longed for the happiness of being a wife and a mother; but later she became content that her affection could be freely given to all who needed it, and the verse in the prophecies, 'I have given thee children whom thou hast not borne,' seemed to her to indicate what was to be her true mission. Indeed, she rather inclined to Bacon's opinion, that unmarried people do the best public work. 'It is quite striking,' she says in one of her letters, 'to observe how much the useful power and influence of woman has developed of late years. Unattached ladies, such as widows and unmarried women, have quite ample work to do in the world for the good of others to absorb all their powers. Wives and mothers have a very noble work given them by God, and want no more.' The whole passage is extremely interesting, and the phrase 'unattached ladies' is quite delightful, and reminds one of Charles Lamb.

> *Mrs. Somerville and Mary Carpenter.* By Phyllis Browne, Author
> of *What Girls Can Do, etc.* (Cassell and Co.)

ARISTOTLE AT AFTERNOON TEA

(Pall Mall Gazette, December 16, 1887.)

In society, says Mr. Mahaffy, every civilized man and woman ought to feel it their duty to say something, even when there is hardly anything to be said, and, in order to encourage this delightful art of brilliant chatter, he has published a social guide without which no débutante or dandy should ever dream of going out to dine. Not that Mr. Mahaffy's book can be said to be, in any sense of the word, popular. In discussing this important subject of conversation, he has not merely followed the scientific method of Aristotle which is, perhaps, excusable, but he has adopted the literary style of Aristotle for which no excuse is possible. There is, also, hardly a single anecdote, hardly a single illustration, and the reader is left to put the Professor's abstract rules into practice, without either the examples or the warnings of history to encourage or to dissuade him in his reckless career. Still, the book can be warmly recommended to all who propose to substitute the vice of verbosity for the stupidity of silence. It fascinates in spite of its form and pleases in spite of its pedantry, and is the nearest approach, that we know of, in modern literature to meeting Aristotle at an afternoon tea.

As regards physical conditions, the only one that is considered by Mr. Mahaffy as being absolutely essential to a good conversationalist, is the possession of a musical voice. Some learned writers have been of opinion that a slight stammer often gives peculiar zest to conversation, but Mr. Mahaffy rejects this view and is extremely severe on every eccentricity from a native brogue to an artificial catchword. With his remarks on the latter point, the meaningless repetition of phrases, we entirely agree. Nothing can be more irritating than the scientific person who is always saying 'Exactly so,' or the commonplace person who ends every sentence with 'Don't you know?' or the pseudo-artistic person who murmurs 'Charming, charming,' on the smallest-provocation. It is, however, with the mental and moral qualifications for conversation that Mr. Mahaffy specially deals. Knowledge he, naturally, regards as an absolute essential, for, as he most justly observes, 'an ignorant man is seldom agreeable, except as a butt.' Upon the other hand, strict accuracy should be avoided. 'Even a consummate liar,' says Mr. Mahaffy, is a better ingredient in a company than 'the scrupulously truthful man, who weighs every statement, questions every fact, and corrects every inaccuracy.' The liar at any rate recognizes that recreation, not instruction, is the aim of conversation, and is a far more civilized being than the blockhead who loudly expresses his disbelief in a story which is told simply for the amusement of the company. Mr. Mahaffy, however, makes an exception in favour of the eminent specialist and tells us that intelligent questions addressed to an astronomer, or a pure mathematician, will elicit many curious facts which will pleasantly beguile the time. Here, in the interest of Society, we feel bound to enter a formal protest. Nobody, even in the provinces, should ever be allowed to ask an intelligent question about pure mathematics across a dinner-table. A question of this kind is quite as bad as inquiring suddenly about the state of a man's soul, a sort of coup which, as Mr. Mahaffy remarks elsewhere, 'many pious people have actually thought a decent introduction to a conversation.'

As for the moral qualifications of a good talker, Mr. Mahaffy, following the example of his great master, warns us against any disproportionate excess of virtue. Modesty, for instance, may easily become a social vice, and to be continually apologizing for one's ignorance or stupidity is a grave injury to conversation, for, 'what we want to learn from each member is his free opinion on the subject in hand, not his own estimate of the value of that opinion.' Simplicity, too, is not without its dangers. The enfant terrible, with his shameless love of truth, the raw country-bred girl who always says what she means, and the plain, blunt man who makes a point of speaking his mind on every possible occasion, without ever considering whether he has a mind at all, are the fatal examples of what simplicity leads to. Shyness may be a form of vanity, and reserve a development of pride, and as for sympathy, what can be more detestable than the man, or woman, who insists on agreeing with everybody, and so makes 'a discussion, which implies differences in opinion,' absolutely impossible? Even the unselfish listener is apt to become a bore. 'These silent people,' says Mr. Mahaffy, 'not only take all they can get in Society for nothing, but they take it without the smallest gratitude, and have the audacity afterwards to censure those who have laboured for their amusement.' Tact, which is an exquisite sense of the symmetry of things, is, according to Mr. Mahaffy, the highest and best of all the moral conditions for conversation. The man of tact, he most wisely remarks, 'will instinctively avoid jokes about Blue Beard' in the company of a woman who is a man's third wife; he will never be guilty of talking like a book, but will rather avoid too careful an attention to grammar and the rounding of periods; he will cultivate the art of graceful interruption, so as to prevent a subject being worn threadbare by the aged or the inexperienced; and should he be desirous of telling a story, he will look round and consider each member of the party, and if there be a single stranger present will forgo the pleasure of anecdotage rather than make the social mistake of hurting even one of the guests. As for prepared or premeditated art, Mr. Mahaffy has a great contempt for it and tells us of a certain college don (let us hope not at Oxford or Cambridge) who always carried a jest-book in his pocket and had to refer to it when he wished to make a repartee. Great wits, too, are often very cruel, and great humorists often very vulgar, so it will be better to try and 'make good conversation without any large help from these brilliant but dangerous gifts.'

In a tête-à-tête one should talk about persons, and in general Society about things. The state of the weather is always an excusable exordium, but it is convenient to have a paradox or heresy on the subject always ready so as to direct the conversation into other channels. Really domestic people are almost invariably bad talkers as their very virtues in home life have dulled their interest in outer things. The very best mothers will insist on chattering of their babies and prattling about infant education. In fact, most women do not take sufficient interest in politics, just as most men are deficient in general reading. Still, anybody can be made to talk, except the very obstinate, and even a commercial traveller may be drawn out and become quite interesting. As for Society small talk, it is impossible, Mr. Mahaffy tells us, for any sound theory of conversation to depreciate gossip, 'which is perhaps the main factor in agreeable talk throughout Society.' The retailing of small personal points about great people always gives pleasure, and if one is not fortunate enough to be an Arctic traveller or an escaped Nihilist, the best thing one can do is to relate some anecdote of 'Prince Bismarck, or King Victor Emmanuel, or Mr. Gladstone.' In the case of meeting a genius and a Duke at dinner, the good talker will try to raise himself to the level of the former and to bring the latter down to his own level. To succeed among one's social superiors one must have no hesitation in contradicting them. Indeed, one should make bold criticisms and introduce a bright and free tone into a Society whose grandeur and extreme respectability make it, Mr. Mahaffy remarks, as pathetically as inaccurately, 'perhaps somewhat dull.' The best conversationalists are those whose ancestors have been bilingual, like the French and Irish, but the art of conversation is really within the reach of almost every one, except those who are morbidly truthful, or whose high moral worth requires to be sustained by a permanent gravity of demeanour and a general dullness of mind.

These are the broad principles contained in Mr. Mahaffy's clever little book, and many of them will, no doubt, commend themselves to our readers. The maxim, 'If you find the company dull, blame yourself,' seems to us somewhat optimistic, and we have no sympathy at all with the professional storyteller who is really a great bore at a dinner-table; but Mr. Mahaffy is quite right in insisting that no bright social intercourse is possible without equality, and it is no objection to his book to say that it will not teach people how to talk cleverly. It is not logic that makes men reasonable, nor the science of ethics that makes men good, but it is always useful to analyse, to formularize and to investigate. The only thing to be regretted in the volume is the arid and jejune character of the style. If Mr. Mahaffy would only write as he talks, his book would be much pleasanter reading.

The Principles of the Art of Conversation: A Social Essay. By J. P. Mahaffy. (Macmillan and Co.)

EARLY CHRISTIAN ART IN IRELAND

(Pall Mall Gazette, December 17, 1887.)

The want of a good series of popular handbooks on Irish art has long been felt, the works of Sir William Wilde, Petrie and others being somewhat too elaborate for the ordinary student; so we are glad to notice the appearance, under the auspices of the Committee of Council on Education, of Miss Margaret Stokes's useful little volume on the early Christian art of her country. There is, of course, nothing particularly original in Miss Stokes's book, nor can she be said to be a very attractive or pleasing writer, but it is unfair to look for originality in primers, and the charm of the illustrations fully atones for the somewhat heavy and pedantic character of the style.

This early Christian art of Ireland is full of interest to the artist, the archæologist and the historian. In its rudest forms, such as the little iron hand-bell, the plain stone chalice and the rough wooden staff, it brings us back to the simplicity of the primitive Christian Church, while to the period of its highest development we owe the great masterpieces of Celtic metal-work. The stone chalice is now replaced by the chalice of silver and gold; the

76

iron bell has its jewel-studded shrine, and the rough staff its gorgeous casing; rich caskets and splendid bindings preserve the holy books of the Saints and, instead of the rudely carved symbol of the early missionaries, we have such beautiful works of art as the processional cross of Cong Abbey. Beautiful this cross certainly is with its delicate intricacy of ornamentation, its grace of proportion and its marvel of mere workmanship, nor is there any doubt about its history. From the inscriptions on it, which are corroborated by the annals of Innisfallen and the book of Clonmacnoise, we learn that it was made for King Turlough O'Connor by a native artist under the superintendence of Bishop O'Duffy, its primary object being to enshrine a portion of the true cross that was sent to the king in 1123. Brought to Cong some years afterwards, probably by the archbishop, who died there in 1150, it was concealed at the time of the Reformation, but at the beginning of the present century was still in the possession of the last abbot, and at his death it was purchased by Professor MacCullagh and presented by him to the museum of the Royal Irish Academy. This wonderful work is alone well worth a visit to Dublin, but not less lovely is the chalice of Ardagh, a two-handled silver cup, absolutely classical in its perfect purity of form, and decorated with gold and amber and crystal and with varieties of cloisonné and champlevé enamel. There is no mention of this cup, or of the so-called Tara brooch, in ancient Irish history. All that we know of them is that they were found accidentally, the former by a boy who was digging potatoes near the old Rath of Ardagh, the latter by a poor child who picked it up near the seashore. They both, however, belong probably to the tenth century.

Of all these works, as well as of the bell shrines, book-covers, sculptured crosses and illuminated designs in manuscripts, excellent pictures are given in Miss Stokes's handbook. The extremely interesting Fiachal Phadrig, or shrine of St. Patrick's tooth, might have been figured and noted as an interesting example of the survival of ornament, and one of the old miniatures of the scribe or Evangelist writing would have given an additional interest to the chapter on Irish MSS. On the whole, however, the book is wonderfully well illustrated, and the ordinary art student will be able to get some useful suggestions from it. Indeed, Miss Stokes, echoing the aspirations of many of the great Irish archæologists, looks forward to the revival of a native Irish school in architecture, sculpture, metal-work and painting. Such an aspiration is, of course, very laudable, but there is always a danger of these revivals being merely artificial reproductions, and it may be questioned whether the peculiar forms of Irish ornamentation could be made at all expressive of the modern spirit. A recent writer on house decoration has gravely suggested that the British householder should take his meals in a Celtic dining-room adorned with a dado of Ogham inscriptions, and such wicked proposals may serve as a warning to all who fancy that the reproduction of a form necessarily implies a revival of the spirit that gave the form life and meaning, and who fail to recognize the difference between art and anachronisms. Miss Stokes's proposal for an ark-shaped church in which the mural painter is to repeat the arcades and 'follow the architectural compositions of the grand pages of the Eusebian canons in the Book of Kells,' has, of course, nothing grotesque about it, but it is not probable that the artistic genius of the Irish people will, even when 'the land has rest,' find in such interesting imitations its healthiest or best expression. Still, there are certain elements of beauty in ancient Irish art that the modern artist would do well to study. The value of the intricate illuminations in the Book of Kells, as far as their adaptability to modern designs and modern material goes, has been very much overrated, but in the ancient Irish torques, brooches, pins, clasps and the like, the modern goldsmith will find a rich and, comparatively speaking, an untouched field; and now that the Celtic spirit has become the leaven of our politics, there is no reason why it should not contribute something to our decorative art. This result, however, will not be obtained by a patriotic misuse of old designs, and even the most enthusiastic Home Ruler must not be allowed to decorate his dining-room with a dado of Oghams.

Early Christian Art in Ireland. By Margaret Stokes. (Published for the Committee of Council on Education by Chapman and Hall.)

MADAME RISTORI

(Woman's World, January 1888.)

Madame Ristori's Etudes et Souvenirs is one of the most delightful books on the stage that has appeared since Lady Martin's charming volume on the Shakespearian heroines. It is often said that actors leave nothing behind them but a barren name and a withered wreath; that they subsist simply upon the applause of the moment; that they are ultimately doomed to the oblivion of old play-bills; and that their art, in a word, dies with them, and shares their own mortality. 'Chippendale, the cabinet-maker,' says the clever author of Obiter Dicta, 'is more potent than Garrick the actor. The vivacity of the latter no longer charms (save in Boswell); the chairs of the former still render rest impossible in a hundred homes.' This view, however, seems to me to be exaggerated. It rests on the assumption that acting is simply a mimetic art, and takes no account of its imaginative and intellectual basis. It is quite true, of course, that the personality of the player passes away, and with it that pleasure-giving power by virtue of which the arts exist. Yet the artistic method of a great actor survives. It lives on in tradition, and becomes part of the science of a school. It has all the intellectual life of a principle. In England, at the present moment, the influence of Garrick on our actors is far stronger than that of Reynolds on our painters of portraits, and if we turn to France it is easy to discern the tradition of Talma, but where is the tradition of David?

Madame Ristori's memoirs, then, have not merely the charm that always attaches to the autobiography of a brilliant and beautiful woman, but have also a definite and distinct artistic value. Her analysis of the character of Lady Macbeth, for instance, is full of psychological interest, and shows us that the subtleties of Shakespearian criticism are not necessarily confined to those who have views on weak endings and rhyming tags, but may also be suggested by the art of acting itself. The author of Obiter Dicta seeks to deny to actors all critical insight and all literary appreciation. The actor, he tells us, is art's slave, not her child, and lives entirely outside literature, 'with its words for ever on his lips, and none of its truths engraven on his heart.' But this seems to me to be a harsh and reckless generalization. Indeed, so far from agreeing with it, I would be inclined to say that the mere artistic process of acting, the translation of literature back again into life, and the presentation of thought under the conditions of action, is in itself a critical method of a very high order; nor do I think that a study of the careers of our great English actors will really sustain the charge of want of literary appreciation. It may be true that actors pass too quickly away from the form, in order to get at the feeling that gives the form beauty and colour, and that, where the literary critic studies the language, the actor looks simply for the life; and yet, how well the great actors have appreciated that marvellous music of words, which in Shakespeare, at any rate, is so vital an element of poetic power, if, indeed, it be not equally so in the case of all who have any claim to be regarded as true poets. 'The sensual life of verse,' says Keats, in a dramatic criticism published in the Champion, 'springs warm from the lips of Kean, and to one learned in Shakespearian hieroglyphics, learned in the spiritual portion of those lines to which Kean adds a sensual grandeur, his tongue must seem to have robbed the Hybla bees and left them honeyless.' This particular feeling, of which Keats speaks, is familiar to all who have heard Salvini, Sarah Bernhardt, Ristori, or any of the great artists of our day, and it is a feeling that one cannot, I think, gain merely by reading the passage to oneself. For my own part, I must confess that it was not until I heard Sarah Bernhardt in Phèdre that I absolutely realized the sweetness of the music of Racine. As for Mr. Birrell's statement that actors have the words of literature for ever on their lips, but none of its truths engraved on their hearts, all that one can say is that, if it be true, it is a defect which actors share with the majority of literary critics.

The account Madame Ristori gives of her own struggles, voyages and adventures, is very pleasant reading indeed. The child of poor actors, she made her first appearance when she was three months old, being brought on in a hamper as a New Year's gift to a selfish old gentleman who would not forgive his daughter for having married for love. As, however, she began to cry long before the hamper was opened, the comedy became a farce, to the immense amusement of the public. She next appeared in a mediæval melodrama, being then three years of age, and was so terrified at the machinations of the villain that she ran away at the most critical moment. However, her stage-fright seems to have disappeared, and we find her playing Silvio Pellico's Francesca da Rimini at fifteen, and at eighteen making her début as Marie Stuart. At this time the naturalism of the French method was gradually displacing the artificial elocution and academic poses of the Italian school of acting. Madame Ristori seems to have tried to combine simplicity with style, and the passion of nature with the self-restraint of the artist. 'J'ai voulu fondre les deux manières,' she tells us, 'car je sentais que toutes choses étant susceptibles de progrès, l'art dramatique aussi était appelé à subir des transformations.' The natural development, however, of the Italian drama was almost arrested by the ridiculous censorship of plays then existing in each town under Austrian or Papal rule. The slightest allusion to the sentiment of nationality or the spirit of freedom was prohibited. Even the word patria was regarded as treasonable, and Madame Ristori tells us an amusing story of the indignation of a censor who was asked to license a play, in which a dumb man returns home after an absence of many years, and on his entrance upon the stage makes gestures expressive of his joy in seeing his native land once more. 'Gestures of this kind,' said the censor, 'are obviously of a very revolutionary tendency, and cannot possibly be allowed. The only gestures that I could think of permitting would be gestures expressive of a dumb man's delight in scenery generally.' The stage directions were accordingly altered, and the word 'landscape' substituted for 'native land'! Another censor was extremely severe on an unfortunate poet who had used the expression 'the beautiful Italian sky,' and explained to him that 'the beautiful Lombardo-Venetian sky' was the proper official expression to use. Poor Gregory in Romeo and Juliet had to be rechristened, because Gregory is a name dear to the Popes; and the

> Here I have a pilot's thumb,
>
> Wrecked as homeward he did come,

of the first witch in Macbeth was ruthlessly struck out as containing an obvious allusion to the steersman of St. Peter's bark. Finally, bored and bothered by the political and theological Dogberrys of the day, with their inane prejudices, their solemn stupidity, and their entire ignorance of the conditions necessary for the growth of sane and healthy art, Madame Ristori made up her mind to leave the stage. She, however, was extremely anxious to appear once before a Parisian audience, Paris being at that time the centre of dramatic activity, and after some consideration left Italy for France in the year 1855. There she seems to have been a great success, particularly in the part of Myrrha; classical without being cold, artistic without being academic, she brought to the interpretation of the character of Alfieri's great heroine the colour-element of passion, the form-element of style. Jules Janin was loud in his praises, the Emperor begged Ristori to join the troupe of the Comédie Française, and Rachel, with the strange narrow jealousy of her nature, trembled for her laurels. Myrrha was followed by Marie Stuart, and Marie Stuart by Medea. In the latter part Madame Ristori excited the greatest enthusiasm. Ary Scheffer designed her costumes for her; and the Niobe that stands in the Uffizi Gallery at Florence, suggested to Madame Ristori her famous pose in the scene with the children. She would not consent, however, to remain in France, and we find her subsequently playing in almost every country in the world from Egypt to Mexico, from Denmark to Honolulu. Her representations of classical plays seem to have been always immensely admired. When she played at Athens, the King offered to arrange for a performance in the beautiful old theatre of Dionysos, and during her tour in Portugal she produced Medea before the University of Coimbra. Her description of the latter engagement is extremely interesting. On her arrival at the University, she was received by the entire body of the undergraduates, who still wear a costume almost mediæval in character. Some of them came on the stage in the course of the play as the handmaidens of Creusa, hiding their black beards beneath heavy veils, and as soon as they had finished their parts they took their places gravely among the audience, to Madame Ristori's horror, still in their Greek dress, but with their veils thrown back and smoking long cigars. 'Ce n'est pas la première fois,' she says, 'que j'ai dû empêcher, par un effort de volonté, la tragédie de se terminer en farce.' Very interesting, also, is her account of the production of Montanelli's Camma, and she tells an amusing story of the arrest of the author by the French police on the charge of murder, in consequence of a telegram she sent to him in which the words 'body of the victim' occurred. Indeed, the whole book is full of cleverly written stories, and admirable criticisms on dramatic art. I have quoted from the French version, which happens to be the one that lies before me, but whether in French or Italian the book is one of the most fascinating autobiographies that has appeared for some time, even in an age like ours when literary egotism has been brought to such an exquisite pitch of perfection.

Etudes et Souvenirs. By Madame Ristori. (Paul Ollendorff.)

ENGLISH POETESSES

(Queen, December 8, 1888.)

England has given to the world one great poetess, Elizabeth Barrett Browning. By her side Mr. Swinburne would place Miss Christina Rossetti, whose New Year hymn he describes as so much the noblest of sacred poems in our language, that there is none which comes near it enough to stand second. 'It is a hymn,' he tells us, 'touched as with the fire, and bathed as in the light of sunbeams, tuned as to chords and cadences of refluent sea-music beyond reach of harp and organ, large echoes of the serene and sonorous tides of heaven.' Much as I admire Miss Rossetti's work, her subtle choice of words, her rich imagery, her artistic naïveté, wherein curious notes of strangeness and simplicity are fantastically blended together, I cannot but think that Mr. Swinburne has, with noble and natural loyalty, placed her on too lofty a pedestal. To me, she is simply a very delightful artist in poetry. This is indeed something so rare that when we meet it we cannot fail to love it, but it is not everything. Beyond it and above it are higher and more sunlit heights of song, a larger vision, and an ampler air, a music at once more passionate and more profound, a creative energy that is born of the spirit, a winged rapture that is born of the soul, a force and fervour of mere utterance that has all the wonder of the prophet, and not a little of the consecration of the priest.

Mrs. Browning is unapproachable by any woman who has ever touched lyre or blown through reed since the days of the great Æolian poetess. But Sappho, who to the antique world was a pillar of flame, is to us but a pillar of shadow. Of her poems, burnt with other most precious work by Byzantine Emperor and by Roman Pope, only a few fragments remain. Possibly they lie mouldering in the scented darkness of an Egyptian tomb, clasped in the withered hand of some long-dead lover. Some Greek monk at Athos may even now be poring over an ancient manuscript, whose crabbed characters conceal lyric or ode by her whom the Greeks spoke of as 'the Poetess' just as they termed Homer 'the Poet,' who was to them the tenth Muse, the flower of the Graces, the child of Erôs, and the pride of Hellas—Sappho, with the sweet voice, the bright, beautiful eyes, the dark hyacinth coloured hair. But, practically, the work of the marvellous singer of Lesbos is entirely lost to us.

We have a few rose-leaves out of her garden, that is all. Literature nowadays survives marble and bronze, but in the old days, in spite of the Roman poet's noble boast, it was not so. The fragile clay vases of the Greeks still keep for us pictures of Sappho, delicately painted in black and red and white; but of her song we have only the echo of an echo.

Of all the women of history, Mrs. Browning is the only one that we could name in any possible or remote conjunction with Sappho.

Sappho was undoubtedly a far more flawless and perfect artist. She stirred the whole antique world more than Mrs. Browning ever stirred our modern age. Never had Love such a singer. Even in the few lines that remain to us the passion seems to scorch and burn. But, as unjust Time, who has crowned her with the barren laurels of fame, has twined with them the dull poppies of oblivion, let us turn from the mere memory of a poetess to one whose song still remains to us as an imperishable glory to our literature; to her who heard the cry of the children from dark mine and crowded factory, and made England weep over its little ones; who, in the feigned sonnets from the Portuguese, sang of the spiritual mystery of Love, and of the intellectual gifts that Love brings to the soul; who had faith in all that is worthy, and enthusiasm for all that is great, and pity for all that suffers; who wrote the Vision of Poets and Casa Guidi Windows and Aurora Leigh.

As one, to whom I owe my love of poetry no less than my love of country, said of her:

> Still on our ears
>
> The clear 'Excelsior' from a woman's lip
>
> Rings out across the Apennines, although
>
> The woman's brow lies pale and cold in death
>
> With all the mighty marble dead in Florence.
>
> For while great songs can stir the hearts of men,

Spreading their full vibrations through the world

In ever-widening circles till they reach

The Throne of God, and song becomes a prayer,

And prayer brings down the liberating strength

That kindles nations to heroic deeds,

She lives—the great-souled poetess who saw

From Casa Guidi windows Freedom dawn

On Italy, and gave the glory back

In sunrise hymns to all Humanity!

She lives indeed, and not alone in the heart of Shakespeare's England, but in the heart of Dante's Italy also. To Greek literature she owed her scholarly culture, but modern Italy created her human passion for Liberty. When she crossed the Alps she became filled with a new ardour, and from that fine, eloquent mouth, that we can still see in her portraits, broke forth such a noble and majestic outburst of lyrical song as had not been heard from woman's lips for more than two thousand years. It is pleasant to think that an English poetess was to a certain extent a real factor in bringing about that unity of Italy that was Dante's dream, and if Florence drove her great singer into exile, she at least welcomed within her walls the later singer that England had sent to her.

If one were asked the chief qualities of Mrs. Browning's work, one would say, as Mr. Swinburne said of Byron's, its sincerity and its strength. Faults it, of course, possesses. 'She would rhyme moon to table,' used to be said of her in jest; and certainly no more monstrous rhymes are to be found in all literature than some of those we come across in Mrs. Browning's poems. But her ruggedness was never the result of carelessness. It was deliberate, as her letters to Mr. Horne show very clearly. She refused to sandpaper her muse. She disliked facile smoothness and artificial polish. In her very rejection of art she was an artist. She intended to produce a certain effect by certain means, and she succeeded; and her indifference to complete assonance in rhyme often gives a splendid richness to her verse, and brings into it a pleasurable element of surprise.

In philosophy she was a Platonist, in politics an Opportunist. She attached herself to no particular party. She loved the people when they were king-like, and kings when they showed themselves to be men. Of the real value and motive of poetry she had a most exalted idea. 'Poetry,' she says, in the preface of one of her volumes, 'has been as serious a thing to me as life itself; and life has been a very serious thing. There has been no playing at skittles for me in either. I never mistook pleasure for the final cause of poetry, nor leisure for the hour of the poet. I have done my work so far, not as mere hand and head work apart from the personal being, but as the completest expression of that being to which I could attain.'

It certainly is her completest expression, and through it she realizes her fullest perfection. 'The poet,' she says elsewhere, 'is at once richer and poorer than he used to be; he wears better broadcloth, but speaks no more oracles.' These words give us the keynote to her view of the poet's mission. He was to utter Divine oracles, to be at once inspired prophet and holy priest; and as such we may, I think, without exaggeration, conceive her. She was a Sibyl delivering a message to the world, sometimes through stammering lips, and once at least with blinded eyes, yet always with the true fire and fervour of lofty and unshaken faith, always with the great raptures of a spiritual nature, the high ardours of an impassioned soul. As we read her best poems we feel that, though Apollo's shrine be empty and the bronze tripod overthrown, and the vale of Delphi desolate, still the Pythia is not dead. In our own age she has sung for us, and this land gave her new birth. Indeed, Mrs. Browning is the wisest of the Sibyls, wiser even than that mighty figure whom Michael Angelo has painted on the roof of the Sistine Chapel at Rome, poring over the scroll of mystery, and trying to decipher the secrets of Fate; for she realized that, while knowledge is power, suffering is part of knowledge.

To her influence, almost as much as to the higher education of women, I would be inclined to attribute the really remarkable awakening of woman's song that characterizes the latter half of our century in England. No country has ever had so many poetesses at once. Indeed, when one remembers that the Greeks had only nine muses, one is sometimes apt to fancy that we have too many. And yet the work done by women in the sphere of poetry is really of a very high standard of excellence. In England we have always been prone to underrate the value of tradition in literature. In our eagerness to find a new voice and a fresh mode of music, we have forgotten how beautiful Echo may be. We look first for individuality and personality, and these are, indeed, the chief characteristics of the masterpieces of our literature, either in prose or verse; but deliberate culture and a study of the best models, if united to an artistic temperament and a nature susceptible of exquisite impressions, may produce much that is admirable, much that is worthy of praise. It would be quite impossible to give a complete catalogue of all the women who since Mrs. Browning's day have tried lute and lyre. Mrs. Pfeiffer, Mrs. Hamilton King, Mrs. Augusta Webster, Graham Tomson, Miss Mary Robinson, Jean Ingelow, Miss May Kendall, Miss Nesbit, Miss May Probyn, Mrs. Craik, Mrs. Meynell, Miss Chapman, and many others have done really good work in poetry, either in the grave Dorian mode of thoughtful and intellectual verse, or in the light and graceful forms of old French song, or in the romantic manner of antique ballad, or in that 'moment's monument,' as Rossetti called it, the intense and concentrated sonnet. Occasionally one is tempted to wish that the quick, artistic faculty that women undoubtedly possess developed itself somewhat more in prose and somewhat less in verse. Poetry is for our highest moods, when we wish to be with the gods, and in our poetry nothing but the very best should satisfy us; but prose is for our daily bread, and the lack of good prose is one of the chief blots on our culture. French prose, even in the hands of the most ordinary writers, is always readable, but English prose is detestable. We have a few, a very few, masters, such as they are. We have Carlyle, who should not be imitated; and Mr. Pater, who, through the subtle perfection of his form, is inimitable absolutely; and Mr. Froude, who is useful; and Matthew Arnold, who is a model; and Mr. George Meredith, who is a warning; and Mr. Lang, who is the divine amateur; and Mr. Stevenson, who is the humane artist; and Mr. Ruskin, whose rhythm and colour and fine rhetoric and marvellous music of words are entirely unattainable. But the general prose that one reads in magazines and in newspapers is terribly dull and cumbrous, heavy in movement and uncouth or exaggerated in expression. Possibly some day our women of letters will apply themselves more definitely to prose.

Their light touch, and exquisite ear, and delicate sense of balance and proportion would be of no small service to us. I can fancy women bringing a new manner into our literature.

However, we have to deal here with women as poetesses, and it is interesting to note that, though Mrs. Browning's influence undoubtedly contributed very largely to the development of this new song-movement, if I may so term it, still there seems to have been never a time during the last three hundred years when the women of this kingdom did not cultivate, if not the art, at least the habit, of writing poetry.

Who the first English poetess was I cannot say. I believe it was the Abbess Juliana Berners, who lived in the fifteenth century; but I have no doubt that Mr. Freeman would be able at a moment's notice to produce some wonderful Saxon or Norman poetess, whose works cannot be read without a glossary, and even with its aid are completely unintelligible. For my own part, I am content with the Abbess Juliana, who wrote enthusiastically about hawking; and after her I would mention Anne Askew, who in prison and on the eve of her fiery martyrdom wrote a ballad that has, at any rate, a pathetic and historical interest. Queen Elizabeth's 'most sweet and sententious ditty' on Mary Stuart is highly praised by Puttenham, a contemporary critic, as an example of 'Exargasia, or the Gorgeous in Literature,' which somehow seems a very suitable epithet for such a great Queen's poems. The term she applies to the unfortunate Queen of Scots, 'the daughter of debate,' has, of course, long since passed into literature. The Countess of Pembroke, Sir Philip Sidney's sister, was much admired as a poetess in her day.

In 1613 the 'learned, virtuous, and truly noble ladie,' Elizabeth Carew, published a Tragedie of Marian, the Faire Queene of Jewry, and a few years later the 'noble ladie Diana Primrose' wrote A Chain of Pearl, which is a panegyric on the 'peerless graces' of Gloriana. Mary Morpeth, the friend and admirer of Drummond of Hawthornden; Lady Mary Wroth, to whom

Ben Jonson dedicated The Alchemist; and the Princess Elizabeth, the sister of Charles I., should also be mentioned.

After the Restoration women applied themselves with still greater ardour to the study of literature and the practice of poetry. Margaret, Duchess of Newcastle, was a true woman of letters, and some of her verses are extremely pretty and graceful. Mrs. Aphra Behn was the first Englishwoman who adopted literature as a regular profession. Mrs. Katharine Philips, according to Mr. Gosse, invented sentimentality. As she was praised by Dryden, and mourned by Cowley, let us hope she may be forgiven. Keats came across her poems at Oxford when he was writing Endymion, and found in one of them 'a most delicate fancy of the Fletcher kind'; but I fear nobody reads the Matchless Orinda now. Of Lady Winchelsea's Nocturnal Reverie Wordsworth said that, with the exception of Pope's Windsor Forest, it was the only poem of the period intervening between Paradise Lost and Thomson's Seasons that contained a single new image of external nature. Lady Rachel Russell, who may be said to have inaugurated the letter-writing literature of England; Eliza Haywood, who is immortalized by the badness of her work, and has a niche in The Dunciad; and the Marchioness of Wharton, whose poems Waller said he admired, are very remarkable types, the finest of them being, of course, the first named, who was a woman of heroic mould and of a most noble dignity of nature.

Indeed, though the English poetesses up to the time of Mrs. Browning cannot be said to have produced any work of absolute genius, they are certainly interesting figures, fascinating subjects for study. Amongst them we find Lady Mary Wortley Montague, who had all the caprice of Cleopatra, and whose letters are delightful reading; Mrs. Centlivre, who wrote one brilliant comedy; Lady Anne Barnard, whose Auld Robin Gray was described by Sir Walter Scott as 'worth all the dialogues Corydon and Phillis have together spoken from the days of Theocritus downwards,' and is certainly a very beautiful and touching poem; Esther Vanhomrigh and Hester Johnson, the Vanessa and the Stella of Dean Swift's life; Mrs. Thrale, the friend of the great lexicographer; the worthy Mrs. Barbauld; the excellent Miss Hannah More; the industrious Joanna Baillie; the admirable Mrs. Chapone, whose

Ode to Solitude always fills me with the wildest passion for society, and who will at least be remembered as the patroness of the establishment at which Becky Sharp was educated; Miss Anna Seward, who was called 'The Swan of Lichfield'; poor L. E. L. whom Disraeli described in one of his clever letters to his sister as 'the personification of Brompton—pink satin dress, white satin shoes, red cheeks, snub nose, and her hair à la Sappho'; Mrs. Ratcliffe, who introduced the romantic novel, and has consequently much to answer for; the beautiful Duchess of Devonshire, of whom Gibbon said that she was 'made for something better than a Duchess'; the two wonderful sisters, Lady Dufferin and Mrs. Norton; Mrs. Tighe, whose Psyche Keats read with pleasure; Constantia Grierson, a marvellous blue-stocking in her time; Mrs. Hemans; pretty, charming 'Perdita,' who flirted alternately with poetry and the Prince Regent, played divinely in the Winter's Tale, was brutally attacked by Gifford, and has left us a pathetic little poem on a Snowdrop; and Emily Brontë, whose poems are instinct with tragic power, and seem often on the verge of being great.

Old fashions in literature are not so pleasant as old fashions in dress. I like the costume of the age of powder better than the poetry of the age of Pope. But if one adopts the historical standpoint—and this is, indeed, the only standpoint from which we can ever form a fair estimate of work that is not absolutely of the highest order—we cannot fail to see that many of the English poetesses who preceded Mrs. Browning were women of no ordinary talent, and that if the majority of them looked upon poetry simply as a department of belles lettres, so in most cases did their contemporaries. Since Mrs. Browning's day our woods have become full of singing birds, and if I venture to ask them to apply themselves more to prose and less to song, it is not that I like poetical prose, but that I love the prose of poets.

VENUS OR VICTORY

(Pall Mall Gazette, February 24, 1888.)

There are certain problems in archæology that seem to possess a real romantic interest, and foremost among these is the question of the so-called

Venus of Melos. Who is she, this marble mutilated goddess whom Gautier loved, to whom Heine bent his knee? What sculptor wrought her, and for what shrine? Whose hands walled her up in that rude niche where the Melian peasant found her? What symbol of her divinity did she carry? Was it apple of gold or shield of bronze? Where is her city and what was her name among gods and men? The last writer on this fascinating subject is Mr. Stillman, who in a most interesting book recently published in America, claims that the work of art in question is no sea-born and foam-born Aphrodite, but the very Victory Without Wings that once stood in the little chapel outside the gates of the Acropolis at Athens. So long ago as 1826, that is to say six years after the discovery of the statue, the Venus hypothesis was violently attacked by Millingen, and from that time to this the battle of the archæologists has never ceased. Mr. Stillman, who fights, of course, under Millingen's banner, points out that the statue is not of the Venus type at all, being far too heroic in character to correspond to the Greek conception of Aphrodite at any period of their artistic development, but that it agrees distinctly with certain well-known statues of Victory, such as the celebrated 'Victory of Brescia.' The latter is in bronze, is later, and has the wings, but the type is unmistakable, and though not a reproduction it is certainly a recollection of the Melian statue. The representation of Victory on the coin of Agathocles is also obviously of the Melian type, and in the museum of Naples is a terra-cotta Victory in almost the identical action and drapery. As for Dumont d'Urville's statement that, when the statue was discovered, one hand held an apple and the other a fold of the drapery, the latter is obviously a mistake, and the whole evidence on the subject is so contradictory that no reliance can be placed on the statement made by the French Consul and the French naval officers, none of whom seems to have taken the trouble to ascertain whether the arm and hand now in the Louvre were really found in the same niche as the statue at all. At any rate, these fragments seem to be of extremely inferior workmanship, and they are so imperfect that they are quite worthless as data for measure or opinion. So far, Mr. Stillman is on old ground. His real artistic discovery is this. In working about the Acropolis of Athens, some years ago, he photographed among other sculptures the mutilated Victories in the Temple of Nikè Apteros, the 'Wingless Victory,' the little Ionic temple in which stood that statue of Victory of which it was said that 'the Athenians made her without wings that she might never leave Athens.' Looking over the photographs afterwards, when the impression of the comparatively diminutive size had passed, he was struck with the close resemblance of the type to that of the Melian statue. Now, this resemblance is so striking that it cannot be questioned by any one who has an eye for form. There are the same large heroic proportions, the same ampleness of physical development, and the same treatment of drapery, and there is also that perfect spiritual kinship which, to any true antiquarian, is one of the most valuable modes of evidence. Now it is generally admitted on both sides that the Melian statue is probably Attic in its origin, and belongs certainly to the period between Phidias and Praxiteles, that is to say, to the age of Scopas, if it be not actually the work of Scopas himself; and as it is to Scopas that these bas-reliefs have been always attributed, the similarity of style can, on Mr. Stillman's hypothesis, be easily accounted for.

As regards the appearance of the statue in Melos, Mr. Stillman points out that Melos belonged to Athens as late as she had any Greek allegiance, and that it is probable that the statue was sent there for concealment on the occasion of some siege or invasion. When this took place, Mr. Stillman does not pretend to decide with any degree of certainty, but it is evident that it must have been subsequent to the establishment of the Roman hegemony, as the brickwork of the niche in which the statue was found is clearly Roman in character, and before the time of Pausanias and Pliny, as neither of these antiquaries mentions the statue. Accepting, then, the statue as that of the Victory Without Wings, Mr. Stillman agrees with Millingen in supposing that in her left hand she held a bronze shield, the lower rim of which rested on the left knee where some marks of the kind are easily recognizable, while with her right hand she traced, or had just finished tracing, the names of the great heroes of Athens. Valentin's objection, that if this were so the left thigh would incline outwards so as to secure a balance, Mr. Stillman meets partly by the analogy of the Victory of Brescia and partly by the evidence of Nature herself; for he has had a model photographed in the same position as the statue and holding a shield in the manner he proposes in his restoration. The result is precisely the contrary to that which Valentin assumes. Of course, Mr.

Stillman's solution of the whole matter must not be regarded as an absolutely scientific demonstration. It is simply an induction in which a kind of artistic instinct, not communicable or equally valuable to all people, has had the greatest part, but to this mode of interpretation archæologists as a class have been far too indifferent; and it is certain that in the present case it has given us a theory which is most fruitful and suggestive.

The little temple of Nikè Apteros has had, as Mr. Stillman reminds us, a destiny unique of its kind. Like the Parthenon, it was standing little more than two hundred years ago, but during the Turkish occupation it was razed, and its stones all built into the great bastion which covered the front of the Acropolis and blocked up the staircase to the Propylæa. It was dug out and restored, nearly every stone in its place, by two German architects during the reign of Otho, and it stands again just as Pausanias described it on the spot where old Ægeus watched for the return of Theseus from Crete. In the distance are Salamis and Ægina, and beyond the purple hills lies Marathon. If the Melian statue be indeed the Victory Without Wings, she had no unworthy shrine.

There are some other interesting essays in Mr. Stillman's book on the wonderful topographical knowledge of Ithaca displayed in the Odyssey, and discussions of this kind are always interesting as long as there is no attempt to represent Homer as the ordinary literary man; but the article on the Melian statue is by far the most important and the most delightful. Some people will, no doubt, regret the possibility of the disappearance of the old name, and as Venus not as Victory will still worship the stately goddess, but there are others who will be glad to see in her the image and ideal of that spiritual enthusiasm to which Athens owed her liberty, and by which alone can liberty be won.

On the Track of Ulysses; together with an Excursion in Quest of the So-called Venus of Melos. By W. J. Stillman. (Houghton, Mifflin and Co., Boston.)

M. CARO ON GEORGE SAND

(Pall Mall Gazette, April 14, 1888.)

The biography of a very great man from the pen of a very ladylike writer—this is the best description we can give of M. Caro's Life of George Sand. The late Professor of the Sorbonne could chatter charmingly about culture, and had all the fascinating insincerity of an accomplished phrase-maker; being an extremely superior person he had a great contempt for Democracy and its doings, but he was always popular with the Duchesses of the Faubourg, as there was nothing in history or in literature that he could not explain away for their edification; having never done anything remarkable he was naturally elected a member of the Academy, and he always remained loyal to the traditions of that thoroughly respectable and thoroughly pretentious institution. In fact, he was just the sort of man who should never have attempted to write a Life of George Sand or to interpret George Sand's genius. He was too feminine to appreciate the grandeur of that large womanly nature, too much of a dilettante to realize the masculine force of that strong and ardent mind. He never gets at the secret of George Sand, and never brings us near to her wonderful personality. He looks on her simply as a littérateur, as a writer of pretty stories of country life and of charming, if somewhat exaggerated, romances. But George Sand was much more than this. Beautiful as are such books as Consuelo and Mauprat, François le Champi and La Mare au Diable, yet in none of them is she adequately expressed, by none of them is she adequately revealed. As Mr. Matthew Arnold said, many years ago, 'We do not know George Sand unless we feel the spirit which goes through her work as a whole.' With this spirit, however, M. Caro has no sympathy. Madame Sand's doctrines are antediluvian, he tells us, her philosophy is quite dead and her ideas of social regeneration are Utopian, incoherent and absurd. The best thing for us to do is to forget these silly dreams and to read Teverino and Le Secrétaire Intime. Poor M. Caro! This spirit, which he treats with such airy flippancy, is the very leaven of modern life. It is remoulding the world for us and fashioning our age anew. If it is antediluvian, it is so because the deluge is yet to come; if it is Utopian, then Utopia must be added to our geographies. To what curious straits M. Caro is driven by his violent

94

prejudices may be estimated by the fact that he tries to class George Sand's novels with the old Chansons de geste, the stories of adventure characteristic of primitive literatures; whereas in using fiction as a vehicle of thought, and romance as a means of influencing the social ideals of her age, George Sand was merely carrying out the traditions of Voltaire and Rousseau, of Diderot and of Chateaubriand. The novel, says M. Caro, must be allied either to poetry or to science. That it has found in philosophy one of its strongest allies seems not to have occurred to him. In an English critic such a view might possibly be excusable. Our greatest novelists, such as Fielding, Scott and Thackeray, cared little for the philosophy of their age. But coming, as it does, from a French critic, the statement seems to show a strange want of recognition of one of the most important elements of French fiction. Nor, even in the narrow limits that he has imposed upon himself, can M. Caro be said to be a very fortunate or felicitous critic. To take merely one instance out of many, he says nothing of George Sand's delightful treatment of art and the artist's life. And yet how exquisitely does she analyse each separate art and present it to us in its relation to life! In Consuelo she tells us of music; in Horace of authorship; in Le Château des Désertes of acting; in Les Maîtres Mosaïstes of mosaic work; in Le Château de Pictordu of portrait painting; and in La Daniella of the painting of landscape. What Mr. Ruskin and Mr. Browning have done for England she did for France. She invented an art literature. It is unnecessary, however, to discuss any of M. Caro's minor failings, for the whole effect of the book, so far as it attempts to portray for us the scope and character of George Sand's genius, is entirely spoiled by the false attitude assumed from the beginning, and though the dictum may seem to many harsh and exclusive, we cannot help feeling that an absolute incapacity for appreciating the spirit of a great writer is no qualification for writing a treatise on the subject.

As for Madame Sand's private life, which is so intimately connected with her art (for, like Goethe, she had to live her romances before she could write them), M. Caro says hardly anything about it. He passes it over with a modesty that almost makes one blush, and for fear of wounding the susceptibilities of those grandes dames whose passions M. Paul Bourget analyses with such subtlety, he transforms her mother, who was a typical French grisette, into 'a very amiable and spirituelle milliner'! It must be admitted that Joseph Surface himself could hardly show greater tact and delicacy, though we ourselves must plead guilty to preferring Madame Sand's own description of her as an 'enfant du vieux pavé de Paris.'

> *George Sand.* By the late Elmé Marie Caro. Translated by
> Gustave Masson, B.A., Assistant Master, Harrow School. 'Great
> French Writers' Series. (Routledge and Sons.)

A FASCINATING BOOK

(Woman's World, November 1888.)

Mr. Alan Cole's carefully-edited translation of M. Lefébure's history of Embroidery and Lace is one of the most fascinating books that has appeared on this delightful subject. M. Lefébure is one of the administrators of the Musée des Arts Décoratifs at Paris, besides being a lace manufacturer; and his work has not merely an important historical value, but as a handbook of technical instruction it will be found of the greatest service by all needle-women. Indeed, as the translator himself points out, M. Lefébure's book suggests the question whether it is not rather by the needle and the bobbin, than by the brush, the graver or the chisel, that the influence of woman should assert itself in the arts. In Europe, at any rate, woman is sovereign in the domain of art-needlework, and few men would care to dispute with her the right of using those delicate implements so intimately associated with the dexterity of her nimble and slender fingers; nor is there any reason why the productions of embroidery should not, as Mr. Alan Cole suggests, be placed on the same level with those of painting, engraving and sculpture, though there must always be a great difference between those purely decorative arts that glorify their own material and the more imaginative arts in which the material is, as it were, annihilated, and absorbed into the creation of a new form. In the beautifying of modern houses it certainly must be admitted—indeed, it should be more generally recognized than it is—that rich embroidery on hangings and curtains, portières, couches and the like, produces a far more decorative and far more artistic effect than can be gained from our somewhat wearisome English practice of covering the walls with pictures and engravings; and the almost complete disappearance of embroidery from dress has robbed modern costume of one of the chief elements of grace and fancy.

That, however, a great improvement has taken place in English embroidery during the last ten or fifteen years cannot, I think, be denied. It is shown, not merely in the work of individual artists, such as Mrs. Holiday, Miss May Morris and others, but also in the admirable productions of the South Kensington School of Embroidery (the best—indeed, the only real good—school that South Kensington has produced). It is pleasant to note on turning over the leaves of M. Lefébure's book, that in this we are merely carrying out certain old traditions of Early English art. In the seventh century, St. Ethelreda, first abbess of the monastery of Ely, made an offering to St. Cuthbert of a sacred ornament she had worked with gold and precious stones, and the cope and maniple of St. Cuthbert, which are preserved at Durham, are considered to be specimens of opus Anglicanum. In the year 800, the Bishop of Durham allotted the income of a farm of two hundred acres for life to an embroideress named Eanswitha, in consideration of her keeping in repair the vestments of the clergy in his diocese. The battle standard of King Alfred was embroidered by Danish Princesses; and the Anglo-Saxon Gudric gave Alcuid a piece of land, on condition that she instructed his daughter in needle-work. Queen Mathilda bequeathed to the Abbey of the Holy Trinity at Caen a tunic embroidered at Winchester by the wife of one Alderet; and when William presented himself to the English nobles, after the Battle of Hastings, he wore a mantle covered with Anglo-Saxon embroideries, which is probably, M. Lefébure suggests, the same as that mentioned in the inventory of the Bayeux Cathedral, where, after the entry relating to the broderie à telle (representing the conquest of England), two mantles are described—one of King William, 'all of gold, powdered with crosses and blossoms of gold, and edged along the lower border with an orphrey of figures.' The most splendid example of the opus Anglicanum now in existence is, of course, the Syon cope at the South Kensington Museum; but English work seems to have been celebrated all over the Continent. Pope Innocent iv. so admired the splendid vestments worn by the English clergy in 1246, that he ordered similar articles from Cistercian monasteries in England. St. Dunstan, the artistic English monk, was known as a designer for embroideries; and the stole of St. Thomas à Becket is still preserved in the cathedral at Sens, and shows us the interlaced scroll-forms used by Anglo-Saxon MS. illuminators.

How far this modern artistic revival of rich and delicate embroidery will bear fruit depends, of course, almost entirely on the energy and study that women are ready to devote to it; but I think that it must be admitted that all our decorative arts in Europe at present have, at least, this element of strength—that they are in immediate relationship with the decorative arts of Asia. Wherever we find in European history a revival of decorative art, it has, I fancy, nearly always been due to Oriental influence and contact with Oriental nations. Our own keenly intellectual art has more than once been ready to sacrifice real decorative beauty either to imitative presentation or to ideal motive. It has taken upon itself the burden of expression, and has sought to interpret the secrets of thought and passion. In its marvellous truth of presentation it has found its strength, and yet its weakness is there also. It is never with impunity that an art seeks to mirror life. If Truth has her revenge upon those who do not follow her, she is often pitiless to her worshippers. In Byzantium the two arts met—Greek art, with its intellectual sense of form, and its quick sympathy with humanity; Oriental art, with its gorgeous materialism, its frank rejection of imitation, its wonderful secrets of craft and colour, its splendid textures, its rare metals and jewels, its marvellous and priceless traditions. They had, indeed, met before, but in Byzantium they were married; and the sacred tree of the Persians, the palm of Zoroaster, was embroidered on the hem of the garments of the Western world. Even the Iconoclasts, the Philistines of theological history, who, in one of those strange outbursts of rage against Beauty that seem to occur only amongst European nations, rose up against the wonder and magnificence of the new art, served merely to distribute its secrets more widely; and in the Liber Pontificalis, written in 687 by Athanasius, the librarian, we read of an influx into Rome of gorgeous embroideries, the work of men who had arrived from Constantinople and from Greece. The triumph of the Mussulman gave the decorative art of Europe a new departure—that very principle of their religion that forbade the actual representation of any object in nature being of the greatest artistic service to them, though it was not, of course, strictly

98

carried out. The Saracens introduced into Sicily the art of weaving silken and golden fabrics; and from Sicily the manufacture of fine stuffs spread to the North of Italy, and became localized in Genoa, Florence, Venice, and other towns. A still greater art-movement took place in Spain under the Moors and Saracens, who brought over workmen from Persia to make beautiful things for them. M. Lefébure tells us of Persian embroidery penetrating as far as Andalusia; and Almeria, like Palermo, had its Hôtel des Tiraz, which rivalled the Hôtel des Tiraz at Bagdad, tiraz being the generic name for ornamental tissues and costumes made with them. Spangles (those pretty little discs of gold, silver, or polished steel, used in certain embroidery for dainty glinting effects) were a Saracenic invention; and Arabic letters often took the place of letters in the Roman characters for use in inscriptions upon embroidered robes and Middle Age tapestries, their decorative value being so much greater. The book of crafts by Etienne Boileau, provost of the merchants in 1258–1268, contains a curious enumeration of the different craft-guilds of Paris, among which we find 'the tapiciers, or makers of the tapis sarrasinois (or Saracen cloths), who say that their craft is for the service only of churches, or great men like kings and counts'; and, indeed, even in our own day, nearly all our words descriptive of decorative textures and decorative methods point to an Oriental origin. What the inroads of the Mohammedans did for Sicily and Spain, the return of the Crusaders did for the other countries of Europe. The nobles who left for Palestine clad in armour, came back in the rich stuffs of the East; and their costumes, pouches (aumônières sarrasinoises), and caparisons excited the admiration of the needle-workers of the West. Matthew Paris says that at the sacking of Antioch, in 1098, gold, silver and priceless costumes were so equally distributed among the Crusaders, that many who the night before were famishing and imploring relief, suddenly found themselves overwhelmed with wealth; and Robert de Clair tells us of the wonderful fêtes that followed the capture of Constantinople. The thirteenth century, as M. Lefébure points out, was conspicuous for an increased demand in the West for embroidery. Many Crusaders made offerings to churches of plunder from Palestine; and St. Louis, on his return from the first Crusade, offered thanks at St. Denis to God for mercies bestowed on him during his six years' absence and travel, and presented some richly embroidered stuffs to be used on great occasions as coverings to the reliquaries containing the relics of holy martyrs. European embroidery, having thus become possessed of new materials and wonderful methods, developed on its own intellectual and imitative lines, inclining, as it went on, to the purely pictorial, and seeking to rival painting, and to produce landscapes and figure-subjects with elaborate perspective and subtle aerial effects. A fresh Oriental influence, however, came through the Dutch and the Portuguese, and the famous Compagnie des Grandes Indes; and M. Lefébure gives an illustration of a door-hanging now in the Cluny Museum, where we find the French fleurs-de-lys intermixed with Indian ornament. The hangings of Madame de Maintenon's room at Fontainebleau, which were embroidered at St. Cyr, represent Chinese scenery upon a jonquil-yellow ground.

Clothes were sent out ready cut to the East to be embroidered, and many of the delightful coats of the period of Louis xv. and Louis xvi. owe their dainty decoration to the needles of Chinese artists. In our own day the influence of the East is strongly marked. Persia has sent us her carpets for patterns, and Cashmere her lovely shawls, and India her dainty muslins finely worked with gold thread palmates, and stitched over with iridescent beetles' wings. We are beginning now to dye by Oriental methods, and the silk robes of China and Japan have taught us new wonders of colour-combination, and new subtleties of delicate design. Whether we have yet learned to make a wise use of what we have acquired is less certain. If books produce an effect, this book of M. Lefébure should certainly make us study with still deeper interest the whole question of embroidery, and by those who already work with their needles it will be found full of most fertile suggestion and most admirable advice.

Even to read of the marvellous works of embroidery that were fashioned in bygone ages is pleasant. Time has kept a few fragments of Greek embroidery of the fourth century b.c. for us. One is figured in M. Lefébure's book—a chain-stitch embroidery of yellow flax upon a mulberry-coloured worsted material, with graceful spirals and palmetto-patterns: and another, a tapestried cloth powdered with ducks, was reproduced in the Woman's World some months ago for an article by Mr. Alan Cole. [115] Now and then we

100

find in the tomb of some dead Egyptian a piece of delicate work. In the treasury at Ratisbon is preserved a specimen of Byzantine embroidery on which the Emperor Constantine is depicted riding on a white palfrey, and receiving homage from the East and West. Metz has a red silk cope wrought with great eagles, the gift of Charlemagne, and Bayeux the needle-wrought epic of Queen Matilda. But where is the great crocus-coloured robe, wrought for Athena, on which the gods fought against the giants? Where is the huge velarium that Nero stretched across the Colosseum at Rome, on which was represented the starry sky, and Apollo driving a chariot drawn by steeds? How one would like to see the curious table-napkins wrought for Heliogabalus, on which were displayed all the dainties and viands that could be wanted for a feast; or the mortuary-cloth of King Chilperic, with its three hundred golden bees; or the fantastic robes that excited the indignation of the Bishop of Pontus, and were embroidered with 'lions, panthers, bears, dogs, forests, rocks, hunters—all, in fact, that painters can copy from nature.' Charles of Orleans had a coat, on the sleeves of which were embroidered the verses of a song beginning 'Madame, je suis tout joyeux,' the musical accompaniment of the words being wrought in gold thread, and each note, of square shape in those days, formed with four pearls. [116] The room prepared in the palace at Rheims for the use of Queen Joan of Burgundy was decorated with 'thirteen hundred and twenty-one papegauts (parrots) made in broidery and blazoned with the King's arms, and five hundred and sixty-one butterflies, whose wings were similarly ornamented with the Queen's arms—the whole worked in fine gold.' Catherine de Medicis had a mourning-bed made for her 'of black velvet embroidered with pearls and powdered with crescents and suns.' Its curtains were of damask, 'with leafy wreaths and garlands figured upon a gold and silver ground, and fringed along the edges with broideries of pearls,' and it stood in a room hung with rows of the Queen's devices in cut black velvet on cloth of silver. Louis xiv. had gold-embroidered caryatides fifteen feet high in his apartment. The state bed of Sobieski, King of Poland, was made of Smyrna gold brocade embroidered in turquoises and pearls, with verses from the Koran; its supports were of silver-gilt, beautifully chased and profusely set with enamelled and jewelled medallions. He had taken it from the Turkish camp before Vienna, and the standard of Mahomet had stood under it. The Duchess de la Ferté wore a dress of reddish-brown velvet, the skirt of which, adjusted in graceful folds, was held up by big butterflies made of Dresden china; the front was a tablier of cloth of silver, upon which was embroidered an orchestra of musicians arranged in a pyramidal group, consisting of a series of six ranks of performers, with beautiful instruments wrought in raised needle-work. 'Into the night go one and all,' as Mr. Henley sings in his charming Ballade of Dead Actors.

Many of the facts related by M. Lefébure about the embroiderers' guilds are also extremely interesting. Etienne Boileau, in his book of crafts, to which I have already alluded, tells us that a member of the guild was prohibited from using gold of less value than 'eight sous (about 6s.) the skein; he was bound to use the best silk, and never to mix thread with silk, because that made the work false and bad.' The test or trial piece prescribed for a worker who was the son of a master-embroiderer was 'a single figure, a sixth of the natural size, to be shaded in gold'; whilst one not the son of a master was required to produce 'a complete incident with many figures.' The book of crafts also mentions 'cutters-out and stencillers and illuminators' amongst those employed in the industry of embroidery. In 1551 the Parisian Corporation of Embroiderers issued a notice that 'for the future, the colouring in representations of nude figures and faces should be done in three or four gradations of carnation-dyed silk, and not, as formerly, in white silks.' During the fifteenth century every household of any position retained the services of an embroiderer by the year. The preparation of colours also, whether for painting or for dyeing threads and textile fabrics, was a matter which, M. Lefébure points out, received close attention from the artists of the Middle Ages. Many undertook long journeys to obtain the more famous recipes, which they filed, subsequently adding to and correcting them as experience dictated. Nor were great artists above making and supplying designs for embroidery. Raphael made designs for Francis i., and Boucher for Louis xv.; and in the Ambras collection at Vienna is a superb set of sacerdotal robes from designs by the brothers Van Eyck and their pupils. Early in the sixteenth century books of embroidery designs were produced, and their success was so great that in a few years French, German, Italian, Flemish, and English publishers spread broadcast books of design made by their best engravers. In the same century, in order to give the designers opportunity of studying directly from nature, Jean Robin opened a garden with conservatories, in which he cultivated strange varieties of plants then but little known in our latitudes. The rich brocades and brocadelles of the time are characterized by the introduction of large flowery patterns, with pomegranates and other fruits with fine foliage.

The second part of M. Lefébure's book is devoted to the history of lace, and though some may not find it quite as interesting as the earlier portion it will more than repay perusal; and those who still work in this delicate and fanciful art will find many valuable suggestions in it, as well as a large number of exceedingly beautiful designs. Compared to embroidery, lace seems comparatively modern. M. Lefébure and Mr. Alan Cole tell us that there is no reliable or documentary evidence to prove the existence of lace before the fifteenth century. Of course in the East, light tissues, such as gauzes, muslins, and nets, were made at very early times, and were used as veils and scarfs after the manner of subsequent laces, and women enriched them with some sort of embroidery, or varied the openness of them by here and there drawing out threads. The threads of fringes seem also to have been plaited and knotted together, and the borders of one of the many fashions of Roman toga were of open reticulated weaving. The Egyptian Museum at the Louvre has a curious network embellished with glass beads; and the monk Reginald, who took part in opening the tomb of St. Cuthbert at Durham in the twelfth century, writes that the Saint's shroud had a fringe of linen threads an inch long, surmounted by a border, 'worked upon the threads,' with representations of birds and pairs of beasts, there being between each such pair a branching tree, a survival of the palm of Zoroaster, to which I have before alluded. Our authors, however, do not in these examples recognize lace, the production of which involves more refined and artistic methods, and postulates a combination of skill and varied execution carried to a higher degree of perfection. Lace, as we know it, seems to have had its origin in the habit of embroidering linen. White embroidery on linen has, M. Lefébure remarks, a cold and monotonous aspect; that with coloured threads is brighter and gayer in effect, but is apt to fade in frequent washing; but white embroidery relieved by open spaces in, or shapes cut from, the linen ground, is possessed of an entirely new charm; and from a sense of this the birth may be traced of an art in the result of which happy contrasts are effected between ornamental details of close texture and others of open-work.

Soon, also, was suggested the idea that, instead of laboriously withdrawing threads from stout linen, it would be more convenient to introduce a needle-made pattern into an open network ground, which was called a lacis. Of this kind of embroidery many specimens are extant. The Cluny Museum possesses a linen cap said to have belonged to Charles v.; and an alb of linen drawn-thread work, supposed to have been made by Anne of Bohemia (1527), is preserved in the cathedral at Prague. Catherine de Medicis had a bed draped with squares of réseuil, or lacis, and it is recorded that 'the girls and servants of her household consumed much time in making squares of réseuil.' The interesting pattern-books for open-ground embroidery, of which the first was published in 1527 by Pierre Quinty, of Cologne, supply us with the means of tracing the stages in the transition from white thread embroidery to needle-point lace. We meet in them with a style of needle-work which differs from embroidery in not being wrought upon a stuff foundation. It is, in fact, true lace, done, as it were, 'in the air,' both ground and pattern being entirely produced by the lace-maker.

The elaborate use of lace in costume was, of course, largely stimulated by the fashion of wearing ruffs, and their companion cuffs or sleeves. Catherine de Medicis induced one Frederic Vinciolo to come from Italy and make ruffs and gadrooned collars, the fashion of which she started in France; and Henry iii. was so punctilious over his ruffs that he would iron and goffer his cuffs and collars himself rather than see their pleats limp and out of shape. The pattern-books also gave a great impulse to the art. M. Lefébure mentions German books with patterns of eagles, heraldic emblems, hunting scenes, and plants and leaves belonging to Northern vegetation; and Italian books, in which the motifs consist of oleander blossoms, and elegant wreaths and scrolls, landscapes with mythological scenes, and hunting episodes, less realistic than the Northern ones, in which appear fauns, and nymphs or amorini shooting arrows. With regard to these patterns, M. Lefébure notices a curious fact. The oldest painting in which lace is depicted is that of a lady, by Carpaccio, who died about 1523. The cuffs of the lady are edged with a narrow lace, the

104

pattern of which reappears in Vecellio's Corona, a book not published until 1591. This particular pattern was, therefore, in use at least eighty years before it got into circulation with other published patterns.

It was not, however, till the seventeenth century that lace acquired a really independent character and individuality, and M. Duplessis states that the production of the more noteworthy of early laces owes more to the influence of men than to that of women. The reign of Louis xiv. witnessed the production of the most stately needle-point laces, the transformation of Venetian point, and the growth of Points d'Alençon, d'Argentan, de Bruxelles and d'Angleterre.

The king, aided by Colbert, determined to make France the centre, if possible, for lace manufacture, sending for this purpose both to Venice and to Flanders for workers. The studio of the Gobelins supplied designs. The dandies had their huge rabatos or bands falling from beneath the chin over the breast, and great prelates, like Bossuet and Fénelon, wore their wonderful albs and rochets. It is related of a collar made at Venice for Louis xiv. that the lace-workers, being unable to find sufficiently fine horse-hair, employed some of their own hairs instead, in order to secure that marvellous delicacy of work which they aimed at producing.

In the eighteenth century, Venice, finding that laces of lighter texture were sought after, set herself to make rose-point; and at the Court of Louis xv. the choice of lace was regulated by still more elaborate etiquette. The Revolution, however, ruined many of the manufactures. Alençon survived, and Napoleon encouraged it, and endeavoured to renew the old rules about the necessity of wearing point-lace at Court receptions. A wonderful piece of lace, powdered over with devices of bees, and costing 40,000 francs, was ordered. It was begun for the Empress Josephine, but in the course of its making her escutcheons were replaced by those of Marie Louise.

M. Lefébure concludes his interesting history by stating very clearly his attitude towards machine-made lace. 'It would be an obvious loss to art,' he says, 'should the making of lace by hand become extinct, for machinery, as skilfully devised as possible, cannot do what the hand does.' It can give us 'the results of processes, not the creations of artistic handicraft.' Art is absent 'where formal calculation pretends to supersede emotion'; it is absent 'where no trace can be detected of intelligence guiding handicraft, whose hesitancies even possess peculiar charm . . . cheapness is never commendable in respect of things which are not absolute necessities; it lowers artistic standard.' These are admirable remarks, and with them we take leave of this fascinating book, with its delightful illustrations, its charming anecdotes, its excellent advice. Mr. Alan Cole deserves the thanks of all who are interested in art for bringing this book before the public in so attractive and so inexpensive a form.

Embroidery and Lace: Their Manufacture and History from the Remotest Antiquity to the Present Day. Translated and enlarged by Alan S. Cole from the French of Ernest Lefébure. (Grevel and Co.)

HENLEY'S POEMS

(Woman's World, December 1888.)

'If I were king,' says Mr. Henley, in one of his most modest rondeaus,

'Art should aspire, yet ugliness be dear;

Beauty, the shaft, should speed with wit for feather;

And love, sweet love, should never fall to sere,

If I were king.'

And these lines contain, if not the best criticism of his own work, certainly a very complete statement of his aim and motive as a poet. His little Book of Verses reveals to us an artist who is seeking to find new methods of expression and has not merely a delicate sense of beauty and a brilliant, fantastic wit, but a real passion also for what is horrible, ugly, or grotesque. No doubt, everything that is worthy of existence is worthy also of art—at least, one would like to think so—but while echo or mirror can repeat for us a beautiful thing, to render artistically a thing that is ugly requires the most exquisite alchemy of form, the most subtle magic of transformation. To me there is more of the cry of Marsyas than of the singing of Apollo in the earlier poems of Mr. Henley's volume, In Hospital: Rhymes and Rhythms, as he calls them. But it is impossible to deny their power. Some of them are like bright, vivid pastels; others like charcoal drawings, with dull blacks and murky whites; others like etchings with deeply-bitten lines, and abrupt contrasts, and clever colour-suggestions. In fact, they are like anything and everything, except perfected poems—that they certainly are not. They are still in the twilight. They are preludes, experiments, inspired jottings in a note-book, and should be heralded by a design of 'Genius Making Sketches.' Rhyme gives architecture as well as melody to verse; it gives that delightful sense of limitation which in all the arts is so pleasurable, and is, indeed, one of the secrets of perfection; it will whisper, as a French critic has said, 'things unexpected and charming, things with strange and remote relations to each other,' and bind them together in indissoluble bonds of beauty; and in his constant rejection of rhyme, Mr. Henley seems to me to have abdicated half his power. He is a roi en exil who has thrown away some of the strings of his lute; a poet who has forgotten the fairest part of his kingdom.

However, all work criticizes itself. Here is one of Mr. Henley's inspired jottings. According to the temperament of the reader, it will serve either as a model or as the reverse:

> As with varnish red and glistening
>
> Dripped his hair; his feet were rigid;
>
> Raised, he settled stiffly sideways:
>
> You could see the hurts were spinal.
>
> He had fallen from an engine,
>
> And been dragged along the metals.
>
> It was hopeless, and they knew it;
>
> So they covered him, and left him.
>
> As he lay, by fits half sentient,

Inarticulately moaning,

With his stockinged feet protruded

Sharp and awkward from the blankets,

To his bed there came a woman,

Stood and looked and sighed a little,

And departed without speaking,

As himself a few hours after.

I was told she was his sweetheart.

They were on the eve of marriage.

She was quiet as a statue,

But her lip was gray and writhen.

In this poem, the rhythm and the music, such as it is, are obvious—perhaps a little too obvious. In the following I see nothing but ingeniously printed prose. It is a description—and a very accurate one—of a scene in a hospital ward. The medical students are supposed to be crowding round the doctor. What I quote is only a fragment, but the poem itself is a fragment:

So shows the ring

Seen, from behind, round a conjuror

Doing his pitch in the street.

High shoulders, low shoulders, broad shoulders, narrow ones,

Round, square, and angular, serry and shove;

While from within a voice,

Gravely and weightily fluent,

Sounds; and then ceases; and suddenly

(Look at the stress of the shoulders!)

Out of a quiver of silence,

Over the hiss of the spray,

Comes a low cry, and the sound

Of breath quick intaken through teeth

Clenched in resolve. And the master

Breaks from the crowd, and goes,

Wiping his hands,

To the next bed, with his pupils

Flocking and whispering behind him.

Now one can see.

Case Number One

Sits (rather pale) with his bedclothes

Stripped up, and showing his foot

(Alas, for God's image!)

Swaddled in wet white lint

Brilliantly hideous with red.

Théophile Gautier once said that Flaubert's style was meant to be read, and his own style to be looked at. Mr. Henley's unrhymed rhythms form very dainty designs, from a typographical point of view. From the point of view of literature, they are a series of vivid, concentrated impressions, with a keen grip of fact, a terrible actuality, and an almost masterly power of picturesque presentation. But the poetic form—what of that?

Well, let us pass to the later poems, to the rondels and rondeaus, the sonnets and quatorzains, the echoes and the ballades. How brilliant and fanciful this is! The Toyokuni colour-print that suggested it could not be more delightful. It seems to have kept all the wilful fantastic charm of the original:

Was I a Samurai renowned,

Two-sworded, fierce, immense of bow?

A histrion angular and profound?

A priest? a porter?—Child, although

I have forgotten clean, I know

That in the shade of Fujisan,

What time the cherry-orchards blow,

I loved you once in old Japan.

As here you loiter, flowing-gowned

And hugely sashed, with pins a-row

Your quaint head as with flamelets crowned,

Demure, inviting—even so,

When merry maids in Miyako

To feel the sweet o' the year began,

And green gardens to overflow,

I loved you once in old Japan.

Clear shine the hills; the rice-fields round

Two cranes are circling; sleepy and slow,

A blue canal the lake's blue bound

Breaks at the bamboo bridge; and lo!

Touched with the sundown's spirit and glow,

I see you turn, with flirted fan,

Against the plum-tree's bloomy snow . . .

I loved you once in old Japan!

ENVOY.

Dear, 'twas a dozen lives ago

But that I was a lucky man

The Toyokuni here will show:

I loved you—once—in old Japan!

This rondel, too—how light it is, and graceful!—

We'll to the woods and gather may

Fresh from the footprints of the rain.

We'll to the woods, at every vein

To drink the spirit of the day.

The winds of spring are out at play,

The needs of spring in heart and brain.

We'll to the woods and gather may

Fresh from the footprints of the rain.

The world's too near her end, you say?

Hark to the blackbird's mad refrain!

It waits for her, the vast Inane?

Then, girls, to help her on the way

We'll to the woods and gather may.

111

There are fine verses, also, scattered through this little book; some of them very strong, as—

> Out of the night that covers me,
>
> Black as the pit from pole to pole,
>
> I thank whatever gods may be
>
> For my unconquerable soul.
>
> It matters not how strait the gate,
>
> How charged with punishments the scroll,
>
> I am the master of my fate:
>
> I am the captain of my soul.

Others with a true touch of romance, as—

> Or ever the knightly years were gone
>
> With the old world to the grave,
>
> I was a king in Babylon,
>
> And you were a Christian slave.

And here and there we come across such felicitous phrases as—

> In the sand
>
> The gold prow-griffin claws a hold,

or—

> The spires
>
> Shine and are changed,

and many other graceful or fanciful lines, even 'the green sky's minor thirds' being perfectly right in its place, and a very refreshing bit of affectation in a volume where there is so much that is natural.

However, Mr. Henley is not to be judged by samples. Indeed, the most attractive thing in the book is no single poem that is in it, but the strong humane personality that stands behind both flawless and faulty work alike, and looks out through many masks, some of them beautiful, and some grotesque, and not a few misshapen. In the case with most of our modern poets, when we have analysed them down to an adjective, we can go no further, or we care to go no further; but with this book it is different. Through these reeds and pipes blows the very breath of life. It seems as if one could put one's hand upon the singer's heart and count its pulsations. There is something wholesome, virile and sane about the man's soul. Anybody can be reasonable, but to be sane is not common; and sane poets are as rare as blue lilies, though they may not be quite so delightful.

> Let the great winds their worst and wildest blow,
>
> Or the gold weather round us mellow slow;
>
> We have fulfilled ourselves, and we can dare,
>
> And we can conquer, though we may not share
>
> In the rich quiet of the afterglow,
>
> What is to come,

is the concluding stanza of the last rondeau—indeed, of the last poem in the collection, and the high, serene temper displayed in these lines serves at once as keynote and keystone to the book. The very lightness and slightness of so much of the work, its careless moods and casual fancies, seem to suggest a nature that is not primarily interested in art—a nature, like Sordello's, passionately enamoured of life, one to which lyre and lute are things of less importance. From this mere joy of living, this frank delight in experience for its own sake, this lofty indifference, and momentary unregretted ardours, come all the faults and all the beauties of the volume. But there is this difference between them—the faults are deliberate, and the result of much study; the beauties have the air of fascinating impromptus. Mr. Henley's healthy, if sometimes misapplied, confidence in the myriad suggestions of life gives him his charm. He is made to sing along the highways, not to sit down and write. If he took himself more seriously, his work would become trivial.

A Book of Verses. By William Ernest Henley. (David Nutt.)

SOME LITERARY LADIES

(Woman's World, January 1889.)

In a recent article on English Poetesses, I ventured to suggest that our women of letters should turn their attention somewhat more to prose and somewhat less to poetry. Women seem to me to possess just what our literature wants—a light touch, a delicate hand, a graceful mode of treatment, and an unstudied felicity of phrase. We want some one who will do for our prose what Madame de Sévigné did for the prose of France. George Eliot's style was far too cumbrous, and Charlotte Brontë's too exaggerated. However, one must not forget that amongst the women of England there have been some charming letter-writers, and certainly no book can be more delightful reading than Mrs. Ross's Three Generations of English Women, which has recently appeared. The three Englishwomen whose memoirs and correspondence Mrs. Ross has so admirably edited are Mrs. John Taylor, Mrs. Sarah Austin, and Lady Duff Gordon, all of them remarkable personalities, and two of them women of brilliant wit and European reputation. Mrs. Taylor belonged to that great Norwich family about whom the Duke of Sussex remarked that they reversed the ordinary saying that it takes nine tailors to make a man, and was for many years one of the most distinguished figures in the famous society of her native town. Her only daughter married John Austin, the great authority on jurisprudence, and her salon in Paris was the centre of the intellect and culture of her day. Lucie Duff Gordon, the only child of John and Sarah Austin, inherited the talents of her parents. A beauty, a femme d'esprit, a traveller, and clever writer, she charmed and fascinated her age, and her premature death in Egypt was really a loss to our literature. It is to her daughter that we owe this delightful volume of memoirs.

First we are introduced to Mrs. Ross's great-grandmother, Mrs. Taylor, who 'was called, by her intimate friends, "Madame Roland of Norwich," from her likeness to the portraits of the handsome and unfortunate Frenchwoman.' We hear of her darning her boy's grey worsted stockings while holding her own with Southey and Brougham, and dancing round the Tree of Liberty

114

with Dr. Parr when the news of the fall of the Bastille was first known. Amongst her friends were Sir James Mackintosh, the most popular man of the day, 'to whom Madame de Staël wrote, "Il n'y a pas de société sans vous." "C'est très ennuyeux de dîner sans vous; la société ne va pas quand vous n'êtes pas là";' Sir James Smith, the botanist; Crabb Robinson; the Gurneys; Mrs. Barbauld; Dr. Alderson and his charming daughter, Amelia Opie; and many other well-known people. Her letters are extremely sensible and thoughtful. 'Nothing at present,' she says in one of them, 'suits my taste so well as Susan's Latin lessons, and her philosophical old master. . . . When we get to Cicero's discussions on the nature of the soul, or Virgil's fine descriptions, my mind is filled up. Life is either a dull round of eating, drinking, and sleeping, or a spark of ethereal fire just kindled. . . . The character of girls must depend upon their reading as much as upon the company they keep. Besides the intrinsic pleasure to be derived from solid knowledge, a woman ought to consider it as her best resource against poverty.' This is a somewhat caustic aphorism: 'A romantic woman is a troublesome friend, as she expects you to be as impudent as herself, and is mortified at what she calls coldness and insensibility.' And this is admirable: 'The art of life is not to estrange oneself from society, and yet not to pay too dear for it.' This, too, is good: 'Vanity, like curiosity, is wanted as a stimulus to exertion; indolence would certainly get the better of us if it were not for these two powerful principles'; and there is a keen touch of humour in the following: 'Nothing is so gratifying as the idea that virtue and philanthropy are becoming fashionable.' Dr. James Martineau, in a letter to Mrs. Ross, gives us a pleasant picture of the old lady returning from market 'weighted by her huge basket, with the shank of a leg of mutton thrust out to betray its contents,' and talking divinely about philosophy, poets, politics, and every intellectual topic of the day. She was a woman of admirable good sense, a type of Roman matron, and quite as careful as were the Roman matrons to keep up the purity of her native tongue.

Mrs. Taylor, however, was more or less limited to Norwich. Mrs. Austin was for the world. In London, Paris, and Germany, she ruled and dominated society, loved by every one who knew her. 'She is "My best and brightest" to Lord Jeffrey; "Dear, fair and wise" to Sydney Smith; "My great ally" to Sir James Stephen; "Sunlight through waste weltering chaos" to Thomas Carlyle (while he needed her aid); "La petite mère du genre humain" to Michael Chevalier; "Liebes Mütterlein" to John Stuart Mill; and "My own Professorin" to Charles Buller, to whom she taught German, as well as to the sons of Mr. James Mill.' Jeremy Bentham, when on his deathbed, gave her a ring with his portrait and some of his hair let in behind. 'There, my dear,' he said, 'it is the only ring I ever gave a woman.' She corresponded with Guizot, Barthelemy de St. Hilaire, the Grotes, Dr. Whewell, the Master of Trinity, Nassau Senior, the Duchesse d'Orléans, Victor Cousin, and many other distinguished people. Her translation of Ranke's History of the Popes is admirable; indeed, all her literary work was thoroughly well done, and her edition of her husband's Province of Jurisprudence deserves the very highest praise. Two people more unlike than herself and her husband it would have been difficult to find. He was habitually grave and despondent; she was brilliantly handsome, fond of society, in which she shone, and 'with an almost superabundance of energy and animal spirits,' Mrs. Ross tells us. She married him because she thought him perfect, but he never produced the work of which he was worthy, and of which she knew him to be worthy. Her estimate of him in the preface to the Jurisprudence is wonderfully striking and simple. 'He was never sanguine. He was intolerant of any imperfection. He was always under the control of severe love of truth. He lived and died a poor man.' She was terribly disappointed in him, but she loved him. Some years after his death, she wrote to M. Guizot:

> In the intervals of my study of his works I read his letters to me—forty-five years of love-letters, the last as tender and passionate as the first. And how full of noble sentiments! The midday of our lives was clouded and stormy, full of cares and disappointments; but the sunset was bright and serene—as bright as the morning, and more serene. Now it is night with me, and must remain so till the dawn of another day. I am always alone—that is, I live with him.

The most interesting letters in the book are certainly those to M. Guizot, with whom she maintained the closest intellectual friendship; but there is hardly one of them that does not contain something clever, or thoughtful, or witty, while those addressed to her, in turn, are very interesting. Carlyle writes her letters full of lamentations, the wail of a Titan in pain, superbly exaggerated for literary effect.

> Literature, one's sole craft and staff of life, lies broken in abeyance; what room for music amid the braying of innumerable jackasses, the howling of innumerable hyænas whetting the tooth to eat them up? Alas for it! it is a sick disjointed time; neither shall we ever mend it; at best let us hope to mend ourselves. I declare I sometimes think of throwing down the Pen altogether as a worthless weapon; and leading out a colony of these poor starving Drudges to the waste places of their old Mother Earth, when for sweat of their brow bread will rise for them; it were perhaps the worthiest service that at this moment could be rendered our old world to throw open for it the doors of the New. Thither must they come at last, 'bursts of eloquence' will do nothing; men are starving and will try many things before they die. But poor I, ach Gott! I am no Hengist or Alaric; only a writer of Articles in bad prose; stick to thy last, O Tutor; the Pen is not worthless, it is omnipotent to those who have Faith.

Henri Beyle (Stendhal), the great, I am often tempted to think the greatest of French novelists, writes her a charming letter about nuances. 'It seems to me,' he says, 'that except when they read Shakespeare, Byron, or Sterne, no Englishman understands "nuances"; we adore them. A fool says to a woman "I love you"; the words mean nothing, he might as well say "Olli Batachor"; it is the nuance which gives force to the meaning.' In 1839 Mrs. Austin writes to Victor Cousin: 'I have seen young Gladstone, a distinguished Tory who wants to re-establish education based on the Church in quite a Catholic form'; and we find her corresponding with Mr. Gladstone on the subject of education. 'If you are strong enough to provide motives and checks,' she says to him, 'you may do two blessed acts—reform your clergy and teach your people. As it is, how few of them conceive what it is to teach a people'! Mr. Gladstone replies at great length, and in many letters, from which we may quote this passage:

> You are for pressing and urging the people to their profit against their inclination: so am I. You set little value upon all merely technical instruction, upon all that fails to touch the inner nature of man: so do

I. And here I find ground of union broad and deep-laid. . . .

I more than doubt whether your idea, namely that of raising man to social sufficiency and morality, can be accomplished, except through the ancient religion of Christ; . . . or whether, the principles of eclecticism are legitimately applicable to the Gospel; or whether, if we find ourselves in a state of incapacity to work through the Church, we can remedy the defect by the adoption of principles contrary to hers. . . .

But indeed I am most unfit to pursue the subject; private circumstances of no common interest are upon me, as I have become very recently engaged to Miss Glynne, and I hope your recollections will enable you in some degree to excuse me.

Lord Jeffrey has a very curious and suggestive letter on popular education, in which he denies, or at least doubts, the effect of this education on morals. He, however, supports it on the ground 'that it will increase the enjoyment of individuals,' which is certainly a very sensible claim. Humboldt writes to her about an old Indian language which was preserved by a parrot, the tribe who spoke it having been exterminated, and about 'young Darwin,' who had just published his first book. Here are some extracts from her own letters:

I heard from Lord Lansdowne two or three days ago. . . . I think he is ce que nous avons de mieux. He wants only the energy that great ambition gives. He says, 'We shall have a parliament of railway kings' . . . what can be worse than that?—The deification of money by a whole people. As Lord Brougham says, we have no right to give ourselves pharisaical airs. I must give you a story sent to me. Mrs. Hudson, the railway queen, was shown a bust of Marcus Aurelius at Lord Westminster's, on which she said, 'I suppose that is not the present Marquis.' To goûter this, you must know that the extreme vulgar (hackney coachmen, etc.) in England pronounce 'marquis' very like 'Marcus.'

Dec. 17th.—Went to Savigny's. Nobody was there but W. Grimm and his wife and a few men. Grimm told me he had received two volumes of Norwegian fairy-tales, and that they were delightful. Talking of them, I said, 'Your children appear to be the happiest in the world; they live in the midst of fairy-tales.' 'Ah,' said he, 'I must tell you about that. When we were at Göttingen, somebody spoke to my little son about his father's Mährchen. He had read them but never thought of their being mine. He came running to me, and said with an offended air, "Father, they say you wrote those fairy-tales; surely you never invented such silly rubbish?" He thought it below my dignity.'

Savigny told a Volksmährchen too:

'St. Anselm was grown old and infirm, and lay on the ground among thorns and thistles. Der liebe Gott said to him, "You are very badly lodged there; why don't you build yourself a house?" "Before I take the trouble," said Anselm, "I should like to know how long I have to live." "About thirty years," said Der liebe Gott. "Oh, for so short a time," replied he, "it's not worth while," and turned himself round among the thistles.'

Dr. Franck told me a story of which I had never heard before. Voltaire had for some reason or other taken a grudge against the prophet Habakkuk, and affected to find in him things he never wrote. Somebody took the Bible and began to demonstrate to him that he was mistaken. 'C'est égal,' he said impatiently, 'Habakkuk était capable de tout!'

Oct. 30, 1853.

I am not in love with the Richtung (tendency) of our modern novelists. There is abundance of talent; but writing a pretty, graceful, touching, yet pleasing story is the last thing our writers nowadays think of. Their novels are party pamphlets on political or social questions, like Sybil, or Alton Locke, or Mary Barton, or Uncle Tom; or they are the most minute and painful dissections of the least agreeable and beautiful parts of our nature, like those of Miss Brontë—Jane Eyre and Villette; or they are a kind of martyrology, like Mrs. Marsh's Emilia Wyndham, which makes you almost doubt whether any torments the heroine would have earned by being naughty could exceed those she incurred by her virtue.

Where, oh! where is the charming, humane, gentle spirit that dictated the Vicar of Wakefield—the spirit which Goethe so justly calls versöhnend (reconciling), with all the weaknesses and woes of humanity? . . . Have you read Thackeray's Esmond? It is a curious and very successful attempt to imitate the style of our old novelists. . . . Which of Mrs. Gore's novels are translated? They are very clever, lively, worldly, bitter, disagreeable, and entertaining. . . . Miss Austen's—are they translated? They are not new, and are Dutch paintings of every-day people—very clever, very true, very unæsthetic, but amusing. I have not seen Ruth, by Mrs. Gaskell. I hear it much admired—and blamed. It is one of the many proofs of the desire women now have to friser questionable topics, and to poser insoluble moral problems. George Sand has turned their heads in that direction. I think a few broad scenes or hearty jokes à la Fielding were very harmless in comparison. They confounded nothing. . . .

The Heir of Redcliffe I have not read. . . . I am not worthy of superhuman flights of virtue—in a novel. I want to see how people act and suffer who are as good-for-nothing as I am myself. Then I have the sinful pretension to be amused, whereas all our novelists want to reform us, and to show us what a hideous place this world is: Ma foi, je ne le sais que trop, without their help.

The Head of the Family has some merits. . . . But there is too much affliction and misery and frenzy. The heroine is one of those creatures now so common (in novels), who remind me of a poor bird tied to a stake (as was once the cruel sport of boys) to be 'shyed' at (i.e. pelted) till it died; only our gentle lady-writers at the end of all untie the poor battered bird, and assure us that it is never the worse for all the blows it has had—nay, the better—and that now, with its broken wings and torn feathers and bruised body, it is going to be quite happy. No, fair ladies, you know that it is not so—resigned, if you please, but make me no shams of happiness out of such wrecks.

In politics Mrs. Austin was a philosophical Tory. Radicalism she detested, and she and most of her friends seem to have regarded it as moribund. 'The

Radical party is evidently effete,' she writes to M. Victor Cousin; the probable 'leader of the Tory party' is Mr. Gladstone. 'The people must be instructed, must be guided, must be, in short, governed,' she writes elsewhere; and in a letter to Dr. Whewell, she says that the state of things in France fills 'me with the deepest anxiety on one point,—the point on which the permanency of our institutions and our salvation as a nation turn. Are our higher classes able to keep the lead of the rest? If they are, we are safe; if not, I agree with my poor dear Charles Buller—our turn must come. Now Cambridge and Oxford must really look to this.' The belief in the power of the Universities to stem the current of democracy is charming. She grew to regard Carlyle as 'one of the dissolvents of the age—as mischievous as his extravagances will let him be'; speaks of Kingsley and Maurice as 'pernicious'; and talks of John Stuart Mill as a 'demagogue.' She was no doctrinaire. 'One ounce of education demanded is worth a pound imposed. It is no use to give the meat before you give the hunger.' She was delighted at a letter of St. Hilaire's, in which he said, 'We have a system and no results; you have results and no system.' Yet she had a deep sympathy with the wants of the people. She was horrified at something Babbage told her of the population of some of the manufacturing towns who are worked out before they attain to thirty years of age. 'But I am persuaded that the remedy will not, cannot come from the people,' she adds. Many of her letters are concerned with the question of the higher education of women. She discusses Buckle's lecture on 'The Influence of Women upon the Progress of Knowledge,' admits to M. Guizot that women's intellectual life is largely coloured by the emotions, but adds: 'One is not precisely a fool because one's opinions are greatly influenced by one's affections. The opinions of men are often influenced by worse things.' Dr. Whewell consults her about lecturing women on Plato, being slightly afraid lest people should think it ridiculous; Comte writes her elaborate letters on the relation of women to progress; and Mr. Gladstone promises that Mrs. Gladstone will carry out at Hawarden the suggestions contained in one of her pamphlets. She was always very practical, and never lost her admiration for plain sewing.

All through the book we come across interesting and amusing things. She gets St. Hilaire to order a large, sensible bonnet for her in Paris, which was at once christened the 'Aristotelian,' and was supposed to be the only useful bonnet in England. Grote has to leave Paris after the coup d'état, he tells her, because he cannot bear to see the establishment of a Greek tyrant. Alfred de Vigny, Macaulay, John Stirling, Southey, Alexis de Tocqueville, Hallam, and Jean Jacques Ampère all contribute to these pleasant pages. She seems to have inspired the warmest feelings of friendship in those who knew her. Guizot writes to her: 'Madame de Staël used to say that the best thing in the world was a serious Frenchman. I turn the compliment, and say that the best thing in the world is an affectionate Englishman. How much more an Englishwoman! Given equal qualities, a woman is always more charming than a man.'

Lucie Austin, afterwards Lady Duff Gordon, was born in 1821. Her chief playfellow was John Stuart Mill, and Jeremy Bentham's garden was her playground. She was a lovely, romantic child, who was always wanting the flowers to talk to her, and used to invent the most wonderful stories about animals, of whom she was passionately fond. In 1834 Mrs. Austin decided on leaving England, and Sydney Smith wrote his immortal letter to the little girl:

Lucie, Lucie, my dear child, don't tear your frock: tearing frocks is not of itself a proof of genius. But write as your mother writes, act as your mother acts: be frank, loyal, affectionate, simple, honest, and then integrity or laceration of frock is of little import. And Lucie, dear child, mind your arithmetic. You know in the first sum of yours I ever saw there was a mistake. You had carried two (as a cab is licensed to do), and you ought, dear Lucie, to have carried but one. Is this a trifle? What would life be without arithmetic but a scene of horrors? You are going to Boulogne, the city of debts, peopled by men who have never understood arithmetic. By the time you return, I shall probably have received my first paralytic stroke, and shall have lost all recollection of you. Therefore I now give you my parting advice—don't marry anybody who has not a tolerable understanding and a thousand a year. And God bless you, dear child.

At Boulogne she sat next Heine at table d'hôte. 'He heard me speak

German to my mother, and soon began to talk to me, and then said, "When you go back to England, you can tell your friends that you have seen Heinrich Heine." I replied, "And who is Heinrich Heine?" He laughed heartily and took no offence at my ignorance; and we used to lounge on the end of the pier together, where he told me stories in which fish, mermaids, water-sprites and a very funny old French fiddler with a poodle were mixed up in the most fanciful manner, sometimes humorous, and very often pathetic, especially when the water-sprites brought him greetings from the "Nord See." He was . . . so kind to me and so sarcastic to every one else.' Twenty years afterwards the little girl whose 'braune Augen' Heine had celebrated in his charming poem Wenn ick an deinem Hause, used to go and see the dying poet in Paris. 'It does one good,' he said to her, 'to see a woman who does not carry about a broken heart, to be mended by all sorts of men, like the women here, who do not see that a total want of heart is their real failing.' On another occasion he said to her: 'I have now made peace with the whole world, and at last also with God, who sends thee to me as a beautiful angel of death: I shall certainly soon die.' Lady Duff Gordon said to him: 'Poor Poet, do you still retain such splendid illusions, that you transform a travelling Englishwoman into Azrael? That used not to be the case, for you always disliked us.' He answered: 'Yes, I do not know what possessed me to dislike the English, . . . it really was only petulance; I never hated them, indeed, I never knew them. I was only once in England, but knew no one, and found London very dreary, and the people and the streets odious. But England has revenged herself well; she has sent me most excellent friends—thyself and Milnes, that good Milnes.'

There are delightful letters from Dicky Doyle here, with the most amusing drawings, one of the present Sir Robert Peel as he made his maiden speech in the House being excellent; and the various descriptions of Hassan's performances are extremely amusing. Hassan was a black boy, who had been turned away by his master because he was going blind, and was found by Lady Duff Gordon one night sitting on her doorstep. She took care of him, and had him cured, and he seems to have been a constant source of delight to every one. On one occasion, 'when Prince Louis Napoleon (the late Emperor of the French) came in unexpectedly, he gravely said: "Please, my lady, I ran out and bought twopennyworth of sprats for the Prince, and for the honour

123

of the house."' Here is an amusing letter from Mrs. Norton:

> MY DEAR LUCIE,—We have never thanked you for the red Pots, which no early Christian should be without, and which add that finishing stroke to the splendour of our demesne, which was supposed to depend on a roc's egg, in less intelligent times. We have now a warm Pompeian appearance, and the constant contemplation of these classical objects favours the beauty of the facial line; for what can be deducted from the great fact, apparent in all the states of antiquity, that straight noses were the ancient custom, but the logical assumption that the constant habit of turning up the nose at unsightly objects—such as the National Gallery and other offensive and obtrusive things—has produced the modern divergence from the true and proper line of profile? I rejoice to think that we ourselves are exempt. I attribute this to our love of Pompeian Pots (on account of the beauty and distinction of this Pot's shape I spell it with a big P), which has kept us straight in a world of crookedness. The pursuit of profiles under difficulties—how much more rare than a pursuit of knowledge! Talk of setting good examples before our children! Bah! let us set good Pompeian Pots before our children, and when they grow up they will not depart from them.

Lady Duff Gordon's Letters from the Cape, and her brilliant translation of The Amber Witch, are, of course, well known. The latter book was, with Lady Wilde's translation of Sidonia the Sorceress, my favourite romantic reading when a boy. Her letters from Egypt are wonderfully vivid and picturesque. Here is an interesting bit of art criticism:

> Sheykh Yoosuf laughed so heartily over a print in an illustrated paper from a picture of Hilton's of Rebekah at the well, with the old 'wekeel' of 'Sidi Ibraheem' (Abraham's chief servant) kneeling before the girl he was sent to fetch, like an old fool without his turban, and Rebekah and the other girls in queer fancy dresses, and the camels with snouts like pigs. 'If the painter could not go into "Es Sham" to see how the Arab really look,' said Sheykh Yoosuf, 'why did he not paint a well in England, with girls like English peasants—at least it would have looked natural to English people? and the wekeel would not seem so

like a madman if he had taken off a hat!' I cordially agree with Yoosuf's art criticism. Fancy pictures of Eastern things are hopelessly absurd.

Mrs. Ross has certainly produced a most fascinating volume, and her book is one of the books of the season. It is edited with tact and judgment.

Three Generations of English Women. Memoirs and Correspondence of Susannah Taylor, Sarah Austin, and Lady Duff Gordon. By Janet Ross, author of Italian Sketches, Land of Manfred, etc. (Fisher Unwin.)

POETRY AND PRISON

(Pall Mall Gazette, January 3, 1889.)

Prison has had an admirable effect on Mr. Wilfrid Blunt as a poet. The Love Sonnets of Proteus, in spite of their clever Musset-like modernities and their swift brilliant wit, were but affected or fantastic at best. They were simply the records of passing moods and moments, of which some were sad and others sweet, and not a few shameful. Their subject was not of high or serious import. They contained much that was wilful and weak. In Vinculis, upon the other hand, is a book that stirs one by its fine sincerity of purpose, its lofty and impassioned thought, its depth and ardour of intense feeling. 'Imprisonment,' says Mr. Blunt in his preface, 'is a reality of discipline most useful to the modern soul, lapped as it is in physical sloth and self-indulgence. Like a sickness or a spiritual retreat it purifies and ennobles; and the soul emerges from it stronger and more self-contained.' To him, certainly, it has been a mode of purification. The opening sonnets, composed in the bleak cell of Galway Gaol, and written down on the flyleaves of the prisoner's prayer-book, are full of things nobly conceived and nobly uttered, and show that though Mr. Balfour may enforce 'plain living' by his prison regulations, he cannot prevent 'high thinking' or in any way limit or constrain the freedom of a man's soul. They are, of course, intensely personal in expression. They could not fail to be so. But the personality that they reveal has nothing petty or ignoble about it. The petulant cry of the shallow egoist which was the chief

125

characteristic of the Love Sonnets of Proteus is not to be found here. In its place we have wild grief and terrible scorn, fierce rage and flame-like passion. Such a sonnet as the following comes out of the very fire of heart and brain:

God knows, 'twas not with a fore-reasoned plan

I left the easeful dwellings of my peace,

And sought this combat with ungodly Man,

And ceaseless still through years that do not cease

Have warred with Powers and Principalities.

My natural soul, ere yet these strifes began,

Was as a sister diligent to please

And loving all, and most the human clan.

God knows it. And He knows how the world's tears

Touched me. And He is witness of my wrath,

How it was kindled against murderers

Who slew for gold, and how upon their path

I met them. Since which day the World in arms

Strikes at my life with angers and alarms.

And this sonnet has all the strange strength of that despair which is but the prelude to a larger hope:

I thought to do a deed of chivalry,

An act of worth, which haply in her sight

Who was my mistress should recorded be

And of the nations. And, when thus the fight

Faltered and men once bold with faces white

126

Turned this and that way in excuse to flee,

I only stood, and by the foeman's might

Was overborne and mangled cruelly.

Then crawled I to her feet, in whose dear cause

I made this venture, and 'Behold,' I said,

'How I am wounded for thee in these wars.'

But she, 'Poor cripple, would'st thou I should wed

A limbless trunk?' and laughing turned from me.

Yet she was fair, and her name 'Liberty.'

The sonnet beginning

A prison is a convent without God—

Poverty, Chastity, Obedience

Its precepts are:

is very fine; and this, written just after entering the gaol, is powerful:

Naked I came into the world of pleasure,

And naked come I to this house of pain.

Here at the gate I lay down my life's treasure,

My pride, my garments and my name with men.

The world and I henceforth shall be as twain,

No sound of me shall pierce for good or ill

These walls of grief. Nor shall I hear the vain

Laughter and tears of those who love me still.

Within, what new life waits me! Little ease,

Cold lying, hunger, nights of wakefulness,

Harsh orders given, no voice to soothe or please,

Poor thieves for friends, for books rules meaningless;

This is the grave—nay, hell. Yet, Lord of Might,

Still in Thy light my spirit shall see light.

But, indeed, all the sonnets are worth reading, and The Canon of Aughrim, the longest poem in the book, is a most masterly and dramatic description of the tragic life of the Irish peasant. Literature is not much indebted to Mr. Balfour for his sophistical Defence of Philosophic Doubt, which is one of the dullest books we know, but it must be admitted that by sending Mr. Blunt to gaol he has converted a clever rhymer into an earnest and deep-thinking poet. The narrow confines of a prison cell seem to suit the 'sonnet's scanty plot of ground,' and an unjust imprisonment for a noble cause strengthens as well as deepens the nature.

In Vinculis. By Wilfrid Scawen Blunt, Author of *The Wind and
the Whirlwind, The Love Sonnets of Proteus, etc. etc.* (Kegan Paul.)

THE GOSPEL ACCORDING TO WALT WHITMAN
(Pall Mall Gazette, January 25, 1889.)

'No one will get to my verses who insists upon viewing them as a literary performance . . . or as aiming mainly towards art and æstheticism.' 'Leaves of Grass . . . has mainly been the outcropping of my own emotional and other personal nature—an attempt, from first to last, to put a Person, a human being (myself, in the latter half of the Nineteenth Century in America,) freely, fully and truly on record. I could not find any similar personal record in current literature that satisfied me.' In these words Walt Whitman gives us the true attitude we should adopt towards his work, having, indeed, a much saner view of the value and meaning of that work than either his eloquent admirers or noisy detractors can boast of possessing. His last book, November Boughs, as he calls it, published in the winter of the old man's life, reveals to us, not

128

indeed a soul's tragedy, for its last note is one of joy and hope, and noble and unshaken faith in all that is fine and worthy of such faith, but certainly the drama of a human soul, and puts on record with a simplicity that has in it both sweetness and strength the record of his spiritual development, and of the aim and motive both of the manner and the matter of his work. His strange mode of expression is shown in these pages to have been the result of deliberate and self-conscious choice. The 'barbaric yawp' which he sent over 'the roofs of the world' so many years ago, and which wrung from Mr. Swinburne's lip such lofty panegyric in song and such loud clamorous censure in prose, appears here in what will be to many an entirely new light. For in his very rejection of art Walt Whitman is an artist. He tried to produce a certain effect by certain means and he succeeded. There is much method in what many have termed his madness, too much method, indeed, some may be tempted to fancy.

In the story of his life, as he tells it to us, we find him at the age of sixteen beginning a definite and philosophical study of literature:

> Summers and falls, I used to go off, sometimes for a week at a stretch, down in the country, or to Long Island's seashores—there, in the presence of outdoor influences, I went over thoroughly the Old and New Testaments, and absorb'd (probably to better advantage for me than in any library or indoor room—it makes such difference where you read) Shakspere, Ossian, the best translated versions I could get of Homer, Eschylus, Sophocles, the old German Nibelungen, the ancient Hindoo poems, and one or two other masterpieces, Dante's among them. As it happen'd, I read the latter mostly in an old wood. The Iliad . . . I read first thoroughly on the peninsula of Orient, northeast end of Long Island, in a shelter'd hollow of rock and sand, with the sea on each side. (I have wonder'd since why I was not overwhelm'd by those mighty masters. Likely because I read them, as described, in the full presence of Nature, under the sun, with the far-spreading landscapes and vistas, or the sea rolling in.)

Edgar Allan Poe's amusing bit of dogmatism that, for our occasions and our day, 'there can be no such thing as a long poem,' fascinated him. 'The same thought had been haunting my mind before,' he said, 'but Poe's argument . . . work'd the sum out, and proved it to me,' and the English translation of the Bible seems to have suggested to him the possibility of a poetic form which, while retaining the spirit of poetry, would still be free from the trammels of rhyme and of a definite metrical system. Having thus, to a certain degree, settled upon what one might call the 'technique' of Whitmanism, he began to brood upon the nature of that spirit which was to give life to the strange form. The central point of the poetry of the future seemed to him to be necessarily 'an identical body and soul, a personality,' in fact, which personality, he tells us frankly, 'after many considerations and ponderings I deliberately settled should be myself.' However, for the true creation and revealing of this personality, at first only dimly felt, a new stimulus was needed. This came from the Civil War. After describing the many dreams and passions of his boyhood and early manhood, he goes on to say:

> These, however, and much more might have gone on and come to naught (almost positively would have come to naught,) if a sudden, vast, terrible, direct and indirect stimulus for new and national declamatory expression had not been given to me. It is certain, I say, that although I had made a start before, only from the occurrence of the Secession War, and what it show'd me as by flashes of lightning, with the emotional depths it sounded and arous'd (of course, I don't mean in my own heart only, I saw it just as plainly in others, in millions)—that only from the strong flare and provocation of that war's sights and scenes the final reasons-for-being of an autochthonic and passionate song definitely came forth.

> I went down to the war fields of Virginia . . . lived thenceforward in camp—saw great battles and the days and nights afterward—partook of all the fluctuations, gloom, despair, hopes again arous'd, courage evoked—death readily risk'd—the cause, too—along and filling those agonistic and lurid following years . . . the real parturition years . . . of this henceforth homogeneous Union. Without those three or four years and the experiences they gave, Leaves of Grass would not now be existing.

130

Having thus obtained the necessary stimulus for the quickening and awakening of the personal self, some day to be endowed with universality, he sought to find new notes of song, and, passing beyond the mere passion for expression, he aimed at 'Suggestiveness' first.

I round and finish little, if anything; and could not, consistently with my scheme. The reader will have his or her part to do, just as much as I have had mine. I seek less to state or display any theme or thought, and more to bring you, reader, into the atmosphere of the theme or thought—there to pursue your own flight.

Another 'impetus-word' is Comradeship, and other 'word-signs' are Good Cheer, Content and Hope. Individuality, especially, he sought for:

I have allow'd the stress of my poems from beginning to end to bear upon American individuality and assist it—not only because that is a great lesson in Nature, amid all her generalizing laws, but as counterpoise to the leveling tendencies of Democracy—and for other reasons. Defiant of ostensible literary and other conventions, I avowedly chant 'the great pride of man in himself,' and permit it to be more or less a motif of nearly all my verse. I think this pride is indispensable to an American. I think it not inconsistent with obedience, humility, deference, and self-questioning.

A new theme also was to be found in the relation of the sexes, conceived in a natural, simple and healthy form, and he protests against poor Mr. William Rossetti's attempt to Bowdlerise and expurgate his song.

From another point of view Leaves of Grass is avowedly the song of Sex and Amativeness, and even Animality—though meanings that do not usually go along with these words are behind all, and will duly emerge; and all are sought to be lifted into a different light and atmosphere. Of this feature, intentionally palpable in a few lines, I shall only say the espousing principle of those lines so gives breath to my whole scheme that the bulk of the pieces might as well have been left unwritten were those lines omitted. . . .

Universal as are certain facts and symptoms of communities . . . there is nothing so rare in modern conventions and poetry as their normal recognizance. Literature is always calling in the doctor for consultation and confession, and always giving evasions and swathing suppressions in place of that 'heroic nudity' on which only a genuine diagnosis . . . can be built. And in respect to editions of Leaves of Grass in time to come (if there should be such) I take occasion now to confirm those lines with the settled convictions and deliberate renewals of thirty years, and to hereby prohibit, as far as word of mine can do so, any elision of them.

But beyond all these notes and moods and motives is the lofty spirit of a grand and free acceptance of all things that are worthy of existence. He desired, he says, 'to formulate a poem whose every thought or fact should directly or indirectly be or connive at an implicit belief in the wisdom, health, mystery, beauty of every process, every concrete object, every human or other existence, not only consider'd from the point of view of all, but of each.' His two final utterances are that 'really great poetry is always . . . the result of a national spirit, and not the privilege of a polish'd and select few'; and that 'the strongest and sweetest songs yet remain to be sung.'

Such are the views contained in the opening essay A Backward Glance O'er Travel'd Roads, as he calls it; but there are many other essays in this fascinating volume, some on poets such as Burns and Lord Tennyson, for whom Walt Whitman has a profound admiration; some on old actors and singers, the elder Booth, Forrest, Alboni and Mario being his special favourites; others on the native Indians, on the Spanish element in American nationality, on Western slang, on the poetry of the Bible, and on Abraham Lincoln. But Walt Whitman is at his best when he is analysing his own work and making schemes for the poetry of the future. Literature, to him, has a distinctly social aim. He seeks to build up the masses by 'building up grand individuals.' And yet literature itself must be preceded by noble forms of life. 'The best literature is always the result of something far greater than itself—not the hero but the portrait of the hero. Before there can be recorded history or poem there must be the transaction.' Certainly, in Walt Whitman's views there is a largeness of vision, a healthy sanity and a fine ethical purpose. He is not to be placed with the professional littérateurs of his country, Boston novelists, New York poets and the like. He stands apart, and the chief value of his work is in its prophecy, not in its performance. He has begun a prelude to larger themes. He is the herald to a new era. As a man he is the precursor of a fresh type. He is a factor in the heroic and spiritual evolution of the human being. If Poetry has passed him by, Philosophy will take note of him.

November Boughs. By Walt Whitman. (Alexander Gardner.)

IRISH FAIRY TALES

(Woman's World, February 1889.)

'The various collectors of Irish folk-lore,' says Mr. W. B. Yeats in his charming little book *Fairy and Folk Tales of the Irish Peasantry*, 'have, from our point of view, one great merit, and from the point of view of others, one great fault.'

They have made their work literature rather than science, and told us of the Irish peasantry rather than of the primitive religion of mankind, or whatever else the folk-lorists are on the gad after. To be considered scientists they should have tabulated all their tales in forms like grocers' bills—item the fairy king, item the queen. Instead of this they have caught the very voice of the people, the very pulse of life, each giving what was most noticed in his day. Croker and Lover, full of the ideas of harum-scarum Irish gentility, saw everything humorized. The impulse of the Irish literature of their time came from a class that did not—mainly for political reasons—take the populace seriously, and imagined the country as a humorist's Arcadia; its passion, its gloom, its tragedy, they knew nothing of. What they did was not wholly false; they merely magnified an irresponsible type, found oftenest among boatmen, carmen, and gentlemen's servants, into the type of a whole nation, and created the stage Irishman. The writers of 'Forty-eight, and the famine combined, burst their bubble. Their work had the dash as well as the shallowness of an ascendant and idle class, and in

Croker is touched everywhere with beauty—a gentle Arcadian beauty. Carleton, a peasant born, has in many of his stories, . . . more especially in his ghost stories, a much more serious way with him, for all his humour. Kennedy, an old bookseller in Dublin, who seems to have had a something of genuine belief in the fairies, comes next in time. He has far less literary faculty, but is wonderfully accurate, giving often the very words the stories were told in. But the best book since Croker is Lady Wilde's Ancient Legends. The humour has all given way to pathos and tenderness. We have here the innermost heart of the Celt in the moments he has grown to love through years of persecution, when, cushioning himself about with dreams, and hearing fairy-songs in the twilight, he ponders on the soul and on the dead. Here is the Celt, only it is the Celt dreaming.

Into a volume of very moderate dimensions, and of extremely moderate price, Mr. Yeats has collected together the most characteristic of our Irish folklore stories, grouping them together according to subject. First come The Trooping Fairies. The peasants say that these are 'fallen angels who were not good enough to be saved, nor bad enough to be lost'; but the Irish antiquarians see in them 'the gods of pagan Ireland,' who, 'when no longer worshipped and fed with offerings, dwindled away in the popular imagination, and now are only a few spans high.' Their chief occupations are feasting, fighting, making love, and playing the most beautiful music. 'They have only one industrious person amongst them, the lepra-caun—the shoemaker.' It is his duty to repair their shoes when they wear them out with dancing. Mr. Yeats tells us that 'near the village of Ballisodare is a little woman who lived amongst them seven years. When she came home she had no toes—she had danced them off.' On May Eve, every seventh year, they fight for the harvest, for the best ears of grain belong to them. An old man informed Mr. Yeats that he saw them fight once, and that they tore the thatch off a house. 'Had any one else been near they would merely have seen a great wind whirling everything into the air as it passed.' When the wind drives the leaves and straws before it, 'that is the fairies, and the peasants take off their hats and say "God bless them."' When they are gay, they sing. Many of the most beautiful tunes of Ireland 'are only their music, caught up by eavesdroppers.' No prudent

134

peasant would hum The Pretty Girl Milking the Cow near a fairy rath, 'for they are jealous, and do not like to hear their songs on clumsy mortal lips.' Blake once saw a fairy's funeral. But this, as Mr. Yeats points out, must have been an English fairy, for the Irish fairies never die; they are immortal.

Then come The Solitary Fairies, amongst whom we find the little Lepracaun mentioned above. He has grown very rich, as he possesses all the treasure-crocks buried in war-time. In the early part of this century, according to Croker, they used to show in Tipperary a little shoe forgotten by the fairy shoemaker. Then there are two rather disreputable little fairies—the Cluricaun, who gets intoxicated in gentlemen's cellars, and the Red Man, who plays unkind practical jokes. 'The Fear-Gorta (Man of Hunger) is an emaciated phantom that goes through the land in famine time, begging an alms and bringing good luck to the giver.' The Water-sheerie is 'own brother to the English Jack-o'-Lantern.' 'The Leanhaun Shee (fairy mistress) seeks the love of mortals. If they refuse, she must be their slave; if they consent, they are hers, and can only escape by finding another to take their place. The fairy lives on their life, and they waste away. Death is no escape from her. She is the Gaelic muse, for she gives inspiration to those she persecutes. The Gaelic poets die young, for she is restless, and will not let them remain long on earth.' The Pooka is essentially an animal spirit, and some have considered him the forefather of Shakespeare's 'Puck.' He lives on solitary mountains, and among old ruins 'grown monstrous with much solitude,' and 'is of the race of the nightmare.' 'He has many shapes—is now a horse, . . . now a goat, now an eagle. Like all spirits, he is only half in the world of form.' The banshee does not care much for our democratic levelling tendencies; she loves only old families, and despises the parvenu or the nouveau riche. When more than one banshee is present, and they wail and sing in chorus, it is for the death of some holy or great one. An omen that sometimes accompanies the banshee is '. . . an immense black coach, mounted by a coffin, and drawn by headless horses driven by a Dullahan.' A Dullahan is the most terrible thing in the world. In 1807 two of the sentries stationed outside St. James's Park saw one climbing the railings, and died of fright. Mr. Yeats suggests that they are possibly 'descended from that Irish giant who swam across the Channel with his head in his teeth.'

Then come the stories of ghosts, of saints and priests, and of giants. The ghosts live in a state intermediary between this world and the next. They are held there by some earthly longing or affection, or some duty unfulfilled, or anger against the living; they are those who are too good for hell, and too bad for heaven. Sometimes they 'take the forms of insects, especially of butterflies.' The author of the Parochial Survey of Ireland 'heard a woman say to a child who was chasing a butterfly, "How do you know it is not the soul of your grandfather?" On November eve they are abroad, and dance with the fairies.' As for the saints and priests, 'there are no martyrs in the stories.' That ancient chronicler Giraldus Cambrensis 'taunted the Archbishop of Cashel, because no one in Ireland had received the crown of martyrdom. "Our people may be barbarous," the prelate answered, "but they have never lifted their hands against God's saints; but now that a people have come amongst us who know how to make them (it was just after the English invasion), we shall have martyrs plentifully."' The giants were the old pagan heroes of Ireland, who grew bigger and bigger, just as the gods grew smaller and smaller. The fact is they did not wait for offerings; they took them vi et armis.

Some of the prettiest stories are those that cluster round Tír-na-n-Og. This is the Country of the Young, 'for age and death have not found it; neither tears nor loud laughter have gone near it.' 'One man has gone there and returned. The bard, Oisen, who wandered away on a white horse, moving on the surface of the foam with his fairy Niamh, lived there three hundred years, and then returned looking for his comrades. The moment his foot touched the earth his three hundred years fell on him, and he was bowed double, and his beard swept the ground. He described his sojourn in the Land of Youth to Patrick before he died.' Since then, according to Mr. Yeats, 'many have seen it in many places; some in the depths of lakes, and have heard rising therefrom a vague sound of bells; more have seen it far off on the horizon, as they peered out from the western cliffs. Not three years ago a fisherman imagined that he saw it.'

Mr. Yeats has certainly done his work very well. He has shown great critical capacity in his selection of the stories, and his little introductions are charmingly written. It is delightful to come across a collection of purely imaginative work, and Mr. Yeats has a very quick instinct in finding out the best and the most beautiful things in Irish folklore.

I am also glad to see that he has not confined himself entirely to prose, but has included Allingham's lovely poem on The Fairies:

Up the airy mountain,

Down the rushy glen,

We daren't go a-hunting

For fear of little men;

Wee folk, good folk,

Trooping all together;

Green jacket, red cap,

And white owl's feather!

Down along the rocky shore

Some make their home,

They live on crispy pancakes

Of yellow tide-foam;

Some in the reeds

Of the black mountain lake,

With frogs for their watch-dogs

All night awake.

High on the hill-top

The old King sits;

He is now so old and gray

He's nigh lost his wits.

With a bridge of white mist

Columbkill he crosses,

On his stately journeys

From Slieveleague to Rosses;

Or going up with music,

On cold starry nights,

To sup with the Queen

Of the gay Northern Lights.

All lovers of fairy tales and folklore should get this little book. The Horned Women, The Priest's Soul, [157] and Teig O'Kane, are really marvellous in their way; and, indeed, there is hardly a single story that is not worth reading and thinking over.

Fairy and Folk Tales of the Irish Peasantry. Edited and Selected by
W. B. Yeats. (Walter Scott.)

MR. W. B. YEATS
(Woman's World, March 1889.)

'*The Wanderings of Oisin and Other Poems is*, I believe, the first volume of poems that Mr. Yeats has published, and it is certainly full of promise. It must be admitted that many of the poems are too fragmentary, too incomplete. They read like stray scenes out of unfinished plays, like things only half remembered, or, at best, but dimly seen. But the architectonic power of construction, the power to build up and make perfect a harmonious whole, is nearly always the latest, as it certainly is the highest, development of the artistic temperament. It is somewhat unfair to expect it in early work. One quality Mr. Yeats has in a marked degree, a quality that is not common in the work of our minor poets, and is therefore all the more welcome to us—I mean the romantic temper. He is essentially Celtic, and his verse, at its best, is Celtic also. Strongly influenced by Keats, he seems to study how to 'load every rift with ore,' yet is more fascinated by the beauty of words than by the beauty of metrical music. The spirit that dominates the whole book is perhaps more valuable than any individual poem or particular passage, but this from The Wanderings of Oisin is worth quoting. It describes the ride to the Island of Forgetfulness:

> *And the ears of the horse went sinking away in the hollow light,*
>
> > *For, as drift from a sailor slow drowning the gleams of the world and the sun,*
>
> *Ceased on our hands and faces, on hazel and oak leaf, the light,*
>
> > *And the stars were blotted above us, and the whole of the world was one;*
>
> *Till the horse gave a whinny; for cumbrous with stems of the hazel and oak,*
>
> > *Of hollies, and hazels, and oak-trees, a valley was sloping away*
>
> *From his hoofs in the heavy grasses, with monstrous slumbering folk,*
>
> > *Their mighty and naked and gleaming bodies heaped loose where they lay.*
>
> *More comely than man may make them, inlaid with silver and gold,*
>
> > *Were arrow and shield and war-axe, arrow and spear and blade,*
>
> *And dew-blanched horns, in whose hollows a child of three years old*
>
> > *Could sleep on a couch of rushes, round and about them laid.*

And this, which deals with the old legend of the city lying under the waters of a lake, is strange and interesting:

> The maker of the stars and worlds
>
> > Sat underneath the market cross,
>
> And the old men were walking, walking,
>
> > And little boys played pitch-and-toss.

'The props,' said He, 'of stars and worlds

   Are prayers of patient men and good.

The boys, the women, and old men,

   Listening, upon their shadows stood.

A grey professor passing cried,

   'How few the mind's intemperance rule!

What shallow thoughts about deep things!

   The world grows old and plays the fool.'

The mayor came, leaning his left ear—

   There were some talking of the poor—

And to himself cried, 'Communist!'

   And hurried to the guardhouse door.

The bishop came with open book,

   Whispering along the sunny path;

There was some talking of man's God,

   His God of stupor and of wrath.

The bishop murmured, 'Atheist!

   How sinfully the wicked scoff!'

And sent the old men on their way,

   And drove the boys and women off.

The place was empty now of people;

   A cock came by upon his toes;

An old horse looked across the fence,

And rubbed along the rail his nose.

The maker of the stars and worlds

To His own house did Him betake,

And on that city dropped a tear,

And now that city is a lake.

Mr. Yeats has a great deal of invention, and some of the poems in his book, such as Mosada, Jealousy, and The Island of Statues, are very finely conceived. It is impossible to doubt, after reading his present volume, that he will some day give us work of high import. Up to this he has been merely trying the strings of his instrument, running over the keys.

The Wanderings of Oisin and Other Poems. By W. B. Yeats.
(Kegan Paul.)

MR. YEATS'S WANDERINGS OF OISIN

(Pall Mall Gazette, July 12, 1889.)

Books of poetry by young writers are usually promissory notes that are never met. Now and then, however, one comes across a volume that is so far above the average that one can hardly resist the fascinating temptation of recklessly prophesying a fine future for its author. Such a book Mr. Yeats's Wanderings of Oisin certainly is. Here we find nobility of treatment and nobility of subject-matter, delicacy of poetic instinct and richness of imaginative resource. Unequal and uneven much of the work must be admitted to be. Mr. Yeats does not try to 'out-baby' Wordsworth, we are glad to say; but he occasionally succeeds in 'out-glittering' Keats, and, here and there, in his book we come across strange crudities and irritating conceits. But when he is at his best he is very good. If he has not the grand simplicity of epic treatment, he has at least something of the largeness of vision that belongs to the epical temper. He does not rob of their stature the great heroes

141

of Celtic mythology. He is very naïve and very primitive and speaks of his giants with the air of a child. Here is a characteristic passage from the account of Oisin's return from the Island of Forgetfulness:

And I rode by the plains of the sea's edge, where all is barren and grey,

Grey sands on the green of the grasses and over the dripping trees,

Dripping and doubling landward, as though they would hasten away

Like an army of old men longing for rest from the moan of the seas.

Long fled the foam-flakes around me, the winds fled out of the vast,

Snatching the bird in secret, nor knew I, embosomed apart,

When they froze the cloth on my body like armour riveted fast,

For Remembrance, lifting her leanness, keened in the gates of my heart.

Till fattening the winds of the morning, an odour of new-mown hay

Came, and my forehead fell low, and my tears like berries fell down;

Later a sound came, half lost in the sound of a shore far away,

From the great grass-barnacle calling, and later the shore-winds brown.

If I were as I once was, the gold hooves crushing the sand and the shells,

Coming forth from the sea like the morning with red lips murmuring a song,

Not coughing, my head on my knees, and praying, and wroth with the bells,

I would leave no Saint's head on his body, though spacious his lands were and strong.

Making way from the kindling surges, I rode on a bridle-path,

Much wondering to see upon all hands, of wattle and woodwork made,

Thy bell-mounted churches, and guardless the sacred cairn and the earth,

And a small and feeble populace stooping with mattock and spade.

In one or two places the music is faulty, the construction is sometimes too involved, and the word 'populace' in the last line is rather infelicitous; but, when all is said, it is impossible not to feel in these stanzas the presence of the true poetic spirit.

The Wanderings of Oisin and other Poems. By W. B. Yeats. (Kegan Paul.)

MR. WILLIAM MORRIS'S LAST BOOK

(Pall Mall Gazette, March 2, 1889.)

Mr. Morris's last book is a piece of pure art workmanship from beginning to end, and the very remoteness of its style from the common language and ordinary interests of our day gives to the whole story a strange beauty and an unfamiliar charm. It is written in blended prose and verse, like the mediæval 'cante-fable,' and tells the tale of the House of the Wolfings in its struggles against the legionaries of Rome then advancing into Northern Germany. It is a kind of Saga, and the language in which the folk-epic, as we may call it, is set forth recalls the antique dignity and directness of our English tongue four centuries ago. From an artistic point of view it may be described as an attempt to return by a self-conscious effort to the conditions of an earlier and a fresher age. Attempts of this kind are not uncommon in the history of art. From some such feeling came the Pre-Raphaelite movement of our own day and the archaistic movement of later Greek sculpture. When the result is beautiful the method is justified, and no shrill insistence upon a supposed necessity for absolute modernity of form can prevail against the value of work that has the incomparable excellence of style. Certainly, Mr. Morris's work possesses this excellence. His fine harmonies and rich cadences create in the reader that spirit by which alone can its own spirit be interpreted, awake in him something of the temper of romance and, by taking him out of his own age, place him in a truer and more vital relation to the great masterpieces of all time. It is a bad thing for an age to be always looking in art for its own reflection. It is well that, now and then, we are given work that is nobly imaginative in its method and purely artistic in its aim. As we read Mr. Morris's story with its fine alternations of verse and prose, its decorative and descriptive beauties, its wonderful handling of romantic and adventurous themes, we cannot but feel that we are as far removed from the ignoble fiction as we are from the ignoble facts of our own day. We breathe a purer air, and have dreams of a time when life had a kind of poetical quality of its own, and was simple and stately and complete.

The tragic interest of The House of the Wolfings centres round the figure of Thiodolf, the great hero of the tribe. The goddess who loves him gives him, as he goes to battle against the Romans, a magical hauberk on which rests this strange fate: that he who wears it shall save his own life and destroy the life of his land. Thiodolf, finding out this secret, brings the hauberk back to the Wood-Sun, as she is called, and chooses death for himself rather than the ruin of his cause, and so the story ends.

But Mr. Morris has always preferred romance to tragedy, and set the development of action above the concentration of passion. His story is like some splendid old tapestry crowded with stately images and enriched with delicate and delightful detail. The impression it leaves on us is not of a single central figure dominating the whole, but rather of a magnificent design to which everything is subordinated, and by which everything becomes of enduring import. It is the whole presentation of the primitive life that really fascinates. What in other hands would have been mere archæology is here transformed by quick artistic instinct and made wonderful for us, and human and full of high interest. The ancient world seems to have come to life again for our pleasure.

Of a work so large and so coherent, completed with no less perfection than it is conceived, it is difficult by mere quotation to give any adequate idea. This, however, may serve as an example of its narrative power. The passage describes the visit of Thiodolf to the Wood-Sun:

The moonlight lay in a great flood on the grass without, and the dew

144

was falling in the coldest hour of the night, and the earth smelled sweetly: the whole habitation was asleep now, and there was no sound to be known as the sound of any creature, save that from the distant meadow came the lowing of a cow that had lost her calf, and that a white owl was flitting about near the eaves of the Roof with her wild cry that sounded like the mocking of merriment now silent. Thiodolf turned toward the wood, and walked steadily through the scattered hazel-trees, and thereby into the thick of the beech-trees, whose boles grew smooth and silver-grey, high and close-set: and so on and on he went as one going by a well-known path, though there was no path, till all the moonlight was quenched under the close roof of the beech-leaves, though yet for all the darkness, no man could go there and not feel that the roof was green above him. Still he went on in despite of the darkness, till at last there was a glimmer before him, that grew greater till he came unto a small wood-lawn whereon the turf grew again, though the grass was but thin, because little sunlight got to it, so close and thick were the tall trees round about it. . . . Nought looked Thiodolf either at the heavens above, or the trees, as he strode from off the husk-strewn floor of the beech wood on to the scanty grass of the lawn, but his eyes looked straight before him at that which was amidmost of the lawn: and little wonder was that; for there on a stone chair sat a woman exceeding fair, clad in glittering raiment, her hair lying as pale in the moonlight on the grey stone as the barley acres in the August night before the reaping-hook goes in amongst them. She sat there as though she were awaiting some one, and he made no stop nor stay, but went straight up to her, and took her in his arms, and kissed her mouth and her eyes, and she him again; and then he sat himself down beside her.

As an example of the beauty of the verse we would take this from the song of the Wood-Sun. It at least shows how perfectly the poetry harmonizes with the prose, and how natural the transition is from the one to the other:

In many a stead Doom dwelleth, nor sleepeth day nor night:

The rim of the bowl she kisseth, and beareth the chambering light

When the kings of men wend happy to the bride-bed from the board.

It is little to say that she wendeth the edge of the grinded sword,

When about the house half builded she hangeth many a day;

The ship from the strand she shoveth, and on his wonted way

By the mountain hunter fareth where his foot ne'er failed before:

She is where the high bank crumbles at last on the river's shore:

The mower's scythe she whetteth; and lulleth the shepherd to sleep

Where the deadly ling-worm wakeneth in the desert of the sheep.

Now we that come of the God-kin of her redes for ourselves we wot,

But her will with the lives of men-folk and their ending know we not.

So therefore I bid thee not fear for thyself of Doom and her deed.

But for me: and I bid thee hearken to the helping of my need.

Or else—Art thou happy in life, or lusteth thou to die

In the flower of thy days, when thy glory and thy longing bloom on high?

The last chapter of the book in which we are told of the great feast made for the dead is so finely written that we cannot refrain from quoting this passage:

> Now was the glooming falling upon the earth; but the Hall was bright within even as the Hall-Sun had promised. Therein was set forth the Treasure of the Wolfings; fair cloths were hung on the walls, goodly broidered garments on the pillars: goodly brazen cauldrons and fair-carven chests were set down in nooks where men could see them well, and vessels of gold and silver were set all up and down the tables of the feast. The pillars also were wreathed with flowers, and flowers hung garlanded from the walls over the precious hangings; sweet gums and spices were burning in fair-wrought censers of brass, and so many candles were alight under the Roof, that scarce had it looked more

ablaze when the Romans had litten the faggots therein for its burning amidst the hurry of the Morning Battle.

There then they fell to feasting, hallowing in the high-tide of their return with victory in their hands: and the dead corpses of Thiodolf and Otter, clad in precious glittering raiment, looked down on them from the High-seat, and the kindreds worshipped them and were glad; and they drank the Cup to them before any others, were they Gods or men.

In days of uncouth realism and unimaginative imitation, it is a high pleasure to welcome work of this kind. It is a work in which all lovers of literature cannot fail to delight.

A Tale of the House of the Wolfings and all the Kindreds of the Mark. Written in Prose and in Verse by William Morris. (Reeves and Turner.)

SOME LITERARY NOTES

(Woman's World, April 1889.)

'In modern life,' said Matthew Arnold once, 'you cannot well enter a monastery; but you can enter the Wordsworth Society.' I fear that this will sound to many a somewhat uninviting description of this admirable and useful body, whose papers and productions have been recently published by Professor Knight, under the title of Wordsworthiana. 'Plain living and high thinking' are not popular ideals. Most people prefer to live in luxury, and to think with the majority. However, there is really nothing in the essays and addresses of the Wordsworth Society that need cause the public any unnecessary alarm; and it is gratifying to note that, although the society is still in the first blush of enthusiasm, it has not yet insisted upon our admiring Wordsworth's inferior work. It praises what is worthy of praise, reverences what should be reverenced, and explains what does not require explanation. One paper is quite delightful; it is from the pen of Mr. Rawnsley, and deals with such reminiscences of Wordsworth as still linger among the peasantry of Westmoreland. Mr. Rawnsley grew up, he tells us, in the immediate vicinity of the present Poet-Laureate's old home in Lincolnshire, and had been struck with the swiftness with which,

> As year by year the labourer tills
>
> His wonted glebe, or lops the glades,

the memories of the poet of the Somersby Wold had 'faded from off the circle of the hills'—had, indeed, been astonished to note how little real interest was taken in him or his fame, and how seldom his works were met with in the houses of the rich or poor in the very neighbourhood. Accordingly, when he came to reside in the Lake Country, he endeavoured to find out what of Wordsworth's memory among the men of the Dales still lingered on—how far he was still a moving presence among them—how far his works had made their way into the cottages and farmhouses of the valleys. He also tried to discover how far the race of Westmoreland and Cumberland farm-folk—the 'Matthews' and the 'Michaels' of the poet, as described by him—were real or fancy pictures, or how far the characters of the Dalesmen had been altered in any remarkable manner by tourist influences during the thirty-two years that have passed since the Lake poet was laid to rest.

With regard to the latter point, it will be remembered that Mr. Ruskin, writing in 1876, said that 'the Border peasantry, painted with absolute fidelity by Scott and Wordsworth,' are, as hitherto, a scarcely injured race; that in his fields at Coniston he had men who might have fought with Henry v. at Agincourt without being distinguished from any of his knights; that he could take his tradesmen's word for a thousand pounds, and need never latch his garden gate; and that he did not fear molestation, in wood or on moor, for his girl guests. Mr. Rawnsley, however, found that a certain beauty had vanished which the simple retirement of old valley days fifty years ago gave to the men among whom Wordsworth lived. 'The strangers,' he says, 'with their gifts of gold, their vulgarity, and their requirements, have much to answer for.' As for their impressions of Wordsworth, to understand them one must understand the vernacular of the Lake District. 'What was Mr. Wordsworth like in personal appearance?' said Mr. Rawnsley once to an old retainer, who still lives not far from Rydal Mount. 'He was a ugly-faäced man, and a meän-liver,' was the answer; but all that was really meant was that he was a man of marked features, and led a very simple life in matters of food and raiment. Another old man, who believed that Wordsworth 'got most of his poetry out of Hartley,' spoke of the poet's wife as 'a very onpleasant woman, very onpleasant indeed. A close-fisted woman, that's what she was.' This, however, seems to have been merely a tribute to Mrs. Wordsworth's admirable housekeeping qualities.

The first person interviewed by Mr. Rawnsley was an old lady who had been once in service at Rydal Mount, and was, in 1870, a lodging-house keeper at Grasmere. She was not a very imaginative person, as may be gathered from the following anecdote:—Mr. Rawnsley's sister came in from a late evening walk, and said, 'O Mrs. D---, have you seen the wonderful sunset?' The good lady turned sharply round and, drawing herself to her full height, as if mortally offended, answered: 'No, miss; I'm a tidy cook, I know, and "they say" a decentish body for a landlady, but I don't knaw nothing about sunsets or them sort of things, they've never been in my line.' Her reminiscence of Wordsworth was as worthy of tradition as it was explanatory, from her point of view, of the method in which Wordsworth composed, and was helped in his labours by his enthusiastic sister. 'Well, you know,' she said, 'Mr. Wordsworth went humming and booing about, and she, Miss Dorothy, kept close behint him, and she picked up the bits as he let 'em fall, and tak' 'em down, and put 'em together on paper for him. And you may be very well sure as how she didn't understand nor make sense out of 'em, and I doubt that he didn't know much about them either himself, but, howivver, there's a great many folk as do, I dare say.' Of Wordsworth's habit of talking to himself, and composing aloud, we hear a great deal. 'Was Mr. Wordsworth a sociable man?' asked Mr. Rawnsley of a Rydal farmer. 'Wudsworth, for a' he had noa pride nor nowt,' was the answer, 'was a man who was quite one to hissel, ye kna. He was not a man as folks could crack wi', nor not a man as could crack wi' folks. But there was another thing as kep' folk off, he had a ter'ble girt deep voice, and ye might see his faace agaan for long enuff. I've knoan folks, village lads and lasses, coming over by old road above, which runs from Grasmere to Rydal, flayt a'most to death there by Wishing Gaate to hear the girt voice a groanin' and mutterin' and thunderin' of a still evening. And he had a way of standin' quite still by the rock there in t' path under Rydal, and folks could hear sounds like a wild beast coming from the rocks, and childer were scared fit to be dead a'most.'

Wordsworth's description of himself constantly recurs to one:

And who is he with modest looks,

And clad in sober russet gown?

He murmurs by the running brooks,

A music sweeter than their own;

He is retired as noontide dew,

Or fountain in a noonday grove.

But the corroboration comes in strange guise. Mr. Rawnsley asked one of the Dalesmen about Wordsworth's dress and habits. This was the reply: 'Wudsworth wore a Jem Crow, never seed him in a boxer in my life,—a Jem Crow and an old blue cloak was his rig, and as for his habits, he had noan; niver knew him with a pot i' his hand, or a pipe i' his mouth. But he was a greät skater, for a' that—noan better in these parts—why, he could cut his own naäme upo' the ice, could Mr. Wudsworth.' Skating seems to have been Wordsworth's one form of amusement. He was 'over feckless i' his hands'—could not drive or ride—'not a bit of fish in him,' and 'nowt of a mountaineer.' But he could skate. The rapture of the time when, as a boy, on Esthwaite's frozen lake, he had

wheeled about,

Proud and exulting like an untired horse

That cares not for his home, and, shod with steel,

Had hissed along the polished ice,

was continued, Mr. Rawnsley tells us, into manhood's later day; and Mr. Rawnsley found many proofs that the skill the poet had gained, when

Not seldom from the uproar he retired,

Into a silent bay, or sportively

Glanced sideways, leaving the tumultuous throng

To cut across the reflex of a star,

was of such a kind as to astonish the natives among whom he dwelt. The recollection of a fall he once had, when his skate caught on a stone, still lingers in the district. A boy had been sent to sweep the snow from the White Moss Tarn for him. 'Did Mr. Wudsworth gie ye owt?' he was asked, when he returned from his labour. 'Na, but I seed him tumlle, though!' was the answer. 'He was a ter'ble girt skater, was Wudsworth now,' says one of Mr. Rawnsley's informants; 'he would put one hand i' his breast (he wore a frill shirt i' them days), and t' other hand i' his waistband, same as shepherds does to keep their hands warm, and he would stand up straight and sway and swing away grandly.'

Of his poetry they did not think much, and whatever was good in it they ascribed to his wife, his sister, and Hartley Coleridge. He wrote poetry, they said, 'because he couldn't help it—because it was his hobby'—for sheer love, and not for money. They could not understand his doing work 'for nowt,' and held his occupation in somewhat light esteem because it did not bring in 'a deal o' brass to the pocket.' 'Did you ever read his poetry, or see any books about in the farmhouses?' asked Mr. Rawnsley. The answer was curious: 'Ay, ay, time or two. But ya're weel aware there's potry and potry. There's potry wi' a li'le bit pleasant in it, and potry sic as a man can laugh at or the childer understand, and some as takes a deal of mastery to make out what's said, and a deal of Wudsworth's was this sort, ye kna. You could tell fra the man's faace his potry would niver have no laugh in it. His potry was quite different work from li'le Hartley. Hartley 'ud goa running along beside o' the brooks and mak his, and goa in the first oppen door and write what he had got upo' paper. But Wudsworth's potry was real hard stuff, and bided a deal of makking, and he'd keep it in his head for long enough. Eh, but it's queer, mon, different ways folks hes of making potry now. . . . Not but what Mr. Wudsworth didn't stand very high, and was a well-spoken man enough.' The best criticism on Wordsworth that Mr. Rawnsley heard was this: 'He was an open-air man, and a great critic of trees.'

There are many useful and well-written essays in Professor Knight's

151

volume, but Mr. Rawnsley's is far the most interesting of all. It gives us a graphic picture of the poet as he appeared in outward semblance and manner to those about whom he wrote.

Wordsworthiana: A Selection from Papers read to the Wordsworth Society. Edited by William Knight. (Macmillan and Co.)

MR. SWINBURNE'S POEMS AND BALLADS (third series)
(Pall Mall Gazette, June 27, 1889.)

Mr. Swinburne once set his age on fire by a volume of very perfect and very poisonous poetry. Then he became revolutionary and pantheistic, and cried out against those that sit in high places both in heaven and on earth. Then he invented Marie Stuart and laid upon us the heavy burden of Bothwell. Then he retired to the nursery and wrote poems about children of a somewhat over-subtle character. He is now extremely patriotic, and manages to combine with his patriotism a strong affection for the Tory party. He has always been a great poet. But he has his limitations, the chief of which is, curiously enough, the entire lack of any sense of limit. His song is nearly always too loud for his subject. His magnificent rhetoric, nowhere more magnificent than in the volume that now lies before us, conceals rather than reveals. It has been said of him, and with truth, that he is a master of language, but with still greater truth it may be said that Language is his master. Words seem to dominate him. Alliteration tyrannizes over him. Mere sound often becomes his lord. He is so eloquent that whatever he touches becomes unreal.

Let us turn to the poem on the Armada:

The wings of the south-west wind are widened; the breath of his fervent lips,

More keen than a sword's edge, fiercer than fire, falls full on the plunging ships.

The pilot is he of the northward flight, their stay and their steersman he;

A helmsman clothed with the tempest, and girdled with strength to constrain

152

the sea.

And the host of them trembles and quails, caught fast in his hand as a bird in the toils:

For the wrath and the joy that fulfil him are mightier than man's, whom he slays and spoils.

And vainly, with heart divided in sunder, and labour of wavering will,

The lord of their host takes counsel with hope if haply their star shine still.

Somehow we seem to have heard all this before. Does it come from the fact that of all the poets who ever lived Mr. Swinburne is the one who is the most limited in imagery? It must be admitted that he is so. He has wearied us with his monotony. 'Fire' and the 'Sea' are the two words ever on his lips. We must confess also that this shrill singing—marvellous as it is—leaves us out of breath. Here is a passage from a poem called A Word with the Wind:

Be the sunshine bared or veiled, the sky superb or shrouded,

Still the waters, lax and languid, chafed and foiled,

Keen and thwarted, pale and patient, clothed with fire or clouded,

Vex their heart in vain, or sleep like serpents coiled.

Thee they look for, blind and baffled, wan with wrath and weary,

Blown for ever back by winds that rock the bird:

Winds that seamews breast subdue the sea, and bid the dreary

Waves be weak as hearts made sick with hope deferred.

Let the clarion sound from westward, let the south bear token

How the glories of thy godhead sound and shine:

Bid the land rejoice to see the land-wind's broad wings broken,

Bid the sea take comfort, bid the world be thine.

Verse of this kind may be justly praised for the sustained strength and vigour of its metrical scheme. Its purely technical excellence is extraordinary. But is it more than an oratorical tour de force? Does it really convey much? Does it charm? Could we return to it again and again with renewed pleasure? We think not. It seems to us empty.

Of course, we must not look to these poems for any revelation of human life. To be at one with the elements seems to be Mr. Swinburne's aim. He seeks to speak with the breath of wind and wave. The roar of the fire is ever in his ears. He puts his clarion to the lips of Spring and bids her blow, and the Earth wakes from her dreams and tells him her secret. He is the first lyric poet who has tried to make an absolute surrender of his own personality, and he has succeeded. We hear the song, but we never know the singer. We never even get near to him. Out of the thunder and splendour of words he himself says nothing. We have often had man's interpretation of Nature; now we have Nature's interpretation of man, and she has curiously little to say. Force and Freedom form her vague message. She deafens us with her clangours.

But Mr. Swinburne is not always riding the whirlwind and calling out of the depths of the sea. Romantic ballads in Border dialect have not lost their fascination for him, and this last volume contains some very splendid examples of this curious artificial kind of poetry. The amount of pleasure one gets out of dialect is a matter entirely of temperament. To say 'mither' instead of 'mother' seems to many the acme of romance. There are others who are not quite so ready to believe in the pathos of provincialism. There is, however, no doubt of Mr. Swinburne's mastery over the form, whether the form be quite legitimate or not. The Weary Wedding has the concentration and colour of a great drama, and the quaintness of its style lends it something of the power of a grotesque. The ballad of The Witch-Mother, a mediæval Medea who slays her children because her lord is faithless, is worth reading on account of its horrible simplicity. The Bride's Tragedy, with its strange refrain of

In, in, out and in,

Blows the wind and whirls the whin:

The Jacobite's Exile—

O lordly flow the Loire and Seine,

And loud the dark Durance:

But bonnier shine the braes of Tyne

Than a' the fields of France;

And the waves of Till that speak sae still

Gleam goodlier where they glance:

The Tyneside Widow and A Reiver's Neck-verse are all poems of fine imaginative power, and some of them are terrible in their fierce intensity of passion. There is no danger of English poetry narrowing itself to a form so limited as the romantic ballad in dialect. It is of too vital a growth for that. So we may welcome Mr. Swinburne's masterly experiments with the hope that things which are inimitable will not be imitated. The collection is completed by a few poems on children, some sonnets, a threnody on John William Inchbold, and a lovely lyric entitled The Interpreters.

In human thought have all things habitation;

Our days

Laugh, lower, and lighten past, and find no station

That stays.

But thought and faith are mightier things than time

Can wrong,

Made splendid once by speech, or made sublime

By song.

Remembrance, though the tide of change that rolls

Wax hoary,

Gives earth and heaven, for song's sake and the soul's,

Their glory.

Certainly, 'for song's sake' we should love Mr. Swinburne's work, cannot, indeed, help loving it, so marvellous a music-maker is he. But what of the soul? For the soul we must go elsewhere.

> *Poems and Ballads.* Third Series. By Algernon Charles
> Swinburne. (Chatto and Windus.)

A CHINESE SAGE

(Speaker, February 8, 1890.)

An eminent Oxford theologian once remarked that his only objection to modern progress was that it progressed forward instead of backward—a view that so fascinated a certain artistic undergraduate that he promptly wrote an essay upon some unnoticed analogies between the development of ideas and the movements of the common sea-crab. I feel sure the Speaker will not be suspected even by its most enthusiastic friends of holding this dangerous heresy of retrogression. But I must candidly admit that I have come to the conclusion that the most caustic criticism of modern life I have met with for some time is that contained in the writings of the learned Chuang Tzŭ, recently translated into the vulgar tongue by Mr. Herbert Giles, Her Majesty's Consul at Tamsui.

The spread of popular education has no doubt made the name of this great thinker quite familiar to the general public, but, for the sake of the few and the over-cultured, I feel it my duty to state definitely who he was, and to give a brief outline of the character of his philosophy.

Chuang Tzŭ, whose name must carefully be pronounced as it is not written, was born in the fourth century before Christ, by the banks of the Yellow River, in the Flowery Land; and portraits of the wonderful sage seated on the flying dragon of contemplation may still be found on the simple tea-trays and pleasing screens of many of our most respectable suburban households. The honest ratepayer and his healthy family have no doubt often mocked at the dome-like forehead of the philosopher, and laughed over the strange perspective of the landscape that lies beneath him. If they really knew

156

who he was, they would tremble. Chuang Tzŭ spent his life in preaching the great creed of Inaction, and in pointing out the uselessness of all useful things. 'Do nothing, and everything will be done,' was the doctrine which he inherited from his great master Lao Tzŭ. To resolve action into thought, and thought into abstraction, was his wicked transcendental aim. Like the obscure philosopher of early Greek speculation, he believed in the identity of contraries; like Plato, he was an idealist, and had all the idealist's contempt for utilitarian systems; he was a mystic like Dionysius, and Scotus Erigena, and Jacob Böhme, and held, with them and with Philo, that the object of life was to get rid of self-consciousness, and to become the unconscious vehicle of a higher illumination. In fact, Chuang Tzŭ may be said to have summed up in himself almost every mood of European metaphysical or mystical thought, from Heraclitus down to Hegel. There was something in him of the Quietist also; and in his worship of Nothing he may be said to have in some measure anticipated those strange dreamers of mediæval days who, like Tauler and Master Eckhart, adored the purum nihil and the Abyss. The great middle classes of this country, to whom, as we all know, our prosperity, if not our civilization, is entirely due, may shrug their shoulders over all this and ask, with a certain amount of reason, what is the identity of contraries to them, and why they should get rid of that self-consciousness which is their chief characteristic. But Chuang Tzŭ was something more than a metaphysician and an illuminist. He sought to destroy society, as we know it, as the middle classes know it; and the sad thing is that he combines with the passionate eloquence of a Rousseau the scientific reasoning of a Herbert Spencer. There is nothing of the sentimentalist in him. He pities the rich more than the poor, if he even pities at all, and prosperity seems to him as tragic a thing as suffering. He has nothing of the modern sympathy with failures, nor does he propose that the prizes should always be given on moral grounds to those who come in last in the race. It is the race itself that he objects to; and as for active sympathy, which has become the profession of so many worthy people in our own day, he thinks that trying to make others good is as silly an occupation as 'beating a drum in a forest in order to find a fugitive.' It is a mere waste of energy. That is all. While, as for a thoroughly sympathetic man, he is, in the eyes of Chuang Tzŭ, simply a man who is always trying to be somebody else, and so misses the only possible excuse for his own existence.

Yes; incredible as it may seem, this curious thinker looked back with a sigh of regret to a certain Golden Age when there were no competitive examinations, no wearisome educational systems, no missionaries, no penny dinners for the people, no Established Churches, no Humanitarian Societies, no dull lectures about one's duty to one's neighbour, and no tedious sermons about any subject at all. In those ideal days, he tells us, people loved each other without being conscious of charity, or writing to the newspapers about it. They were upright, and yet they never published books upon Altruism. As every man kept his knowledge to himself, the world escaped the curse of scepticism; and as every man kept his virtues to himself, nobody meddled in other people's business. They lived simple and peaceful lives, and were contented with such food and raiment as they could get. Neighbouring districts were in sight, and 'the cocks and dogs of one could be heard in the other,' yet the people grew old and died without ever interchanging visits. There was no chattering about clever men, and no laudation of good men. The intolerable sense of obligation was unknown. The deeds of humanity left no trace, and their affairs were not made a burden for prosperity by foolish historians.

In an evil moment the Philanthropist made his appearance, and brought with him the mischievous idea of Government. 'There is such a thing,' says Chuang Tzŭ, 'as leaving mankind alone: there has never been such a thing as governing mankind.' All modes of government are wrong. They are unscientific, because they seek to alter the natural environment of man; they are immoral because, by interfering with the individual, they produce the most aggressive forms of egotism; they are ignorant, because they try to spread education; they are self-destructive, because they engender anarchy. 'Of old,' he tells us, 'the Yellow Emperor first caused charity and duty to one's neighbour to interfere with the natural goodness of the heart of man. In consequence of this, Yao and Shun wore the hair off their legs in endeavouring to feed their people. They disturbed their internal economy in order to find room for artificial virtues. They exhausted their energies in framing laws, and they were failures.' Man's heart, our philosopher goes on to say, may be 'forced down or stirred up,' and in either case the issue is fatal. Yao made the people too happy, so they were not satisfied. Chieh made them too wretched, so they grew discontented. Then every one began to argue about the best way of tinkering up society. 'It is quite clear that something must be done,' they said to each other, and there was a general rush for knowledge. The results were so dreadful that the Government of the day had to bring in Coercion, and as a consequence of this 'virtuous men sought refuge in mountain caves, while rulers of state sat trembling in ancestral halls.' Then, when everything was in a state of perfect chaos, the Social Reformers got up on platforms, and preached salvation from the ills that they and their system had caused. The poor Social Reformers! 'They know not shame, nor what it is to blush,' is the verdict of Chuang Tzŭ upon them.

The economic question, also, is discussed by this almond-eyed sage at great length, and he writes about the curse of capital as eloquently as Mr. Hyndman. The accumulation of wealth is to him the origin of evil. It makes the strong violent, and the weak dishonest. It creates the petty thief, and puts him in a bamboo cage. It creates the big thief, and sets him on a throne of white jade. It is the father of competition, and competition is the waste, as well as the destruction, of energy. The order of nature is rest, repetition, and peace. Weariness and war are the results of an artificial society based upon capital; and the richer this society gets, the more thoroughly bankrupt it really is, for it has neither sufficient rewards for the good nor sufficient punishments for the wicked. There is also this to be remembered—that the prizes of the world degrade a man as much as the world's punishments. The age is rotten with its worship of success. As for education, true wisdom can neither be learnt nor taught. It is a spiritual state, to which he who lives in harmony with nature attains. Knowledge is shallow if we compare it with the extent of the unknown, and only the unknowable is of value. Society produces rogues, and education makes one rogue cleverer than another. That is the only result of School Boards. Besides, of what possible philosophic importance can education be, when it serves simply to make each man differ from his neighbour? We arrive ultimately at a chaos of opinions, doubt everything, and fall into the vulgar habit of arguing; and it is only the intellectually lost who ever argue. Look at Hui Tzu. 'He was a man of many ideas. His work

159

would fill five carts. But his doctrines were paradoxical.' He said that there were feathers in an egg, because there were feathers on a chicken; that a dog could be a sheep, because all names were arbitrary; that there was a moment when a swift-flying arrow was neither moving nor at rest; that if you took a stick a foot long, and cut it in half every day, you would never come to the end of it; and that a bay horse and a dun cow were three, because taken separately they were two, and taken together they were one, and one and two made up three. 'He was like a man running a race with his own shadow, and making a noise in order to drown the echo. He was a clever gadfly, that was all. What was the use of him?'

Morality is, of course, a different thing. It went out of fashion, says Chuang Tzŭ, when people began to moralize. Men ceased then to be spontaneous and to act on intuition. They became priggish and artificial, and were so blind as to have a definite purpose in life. Then came Governments and Philanthropists, those two pests of the age. The former tried to coerce people into being good, and so destroyed the natural goodness of man. The latter were a set of aggressive busybodies who caused confusion wherever they went. They were stupid enough to have principles, and unfortunate enough to act up to them. They all came to bad ends, and showed that universal altruism is as bad in its results as universal egotism. 'They tripped people up over charity, and fettered them with duties to their neighbours.' They gushed over music, and fussed over ceremonies. As a consequence of all this, the world lost its equilibrium, and has been staggering ever since.

Who, then, according to Chuang Tzŭ, is the perfect man? And what is his manner of life? The perfect man does nothing beyond gazing at the universe. He adopts no absolute position. 'In motion, he is like water. At rest, he is like a mirror. And, like Echo, he answers only when he is called upon.' He lets externals take care of themselves. Nothing material injures him; nothing spiritual punishes him. His mental equilibrium gives him the empire of the world. He is never the slave of objective existences. He knows that, 'just as the best language is that which is never spoken, so the best action is that which is never done.' He is passive, and accepts the laws of life. He rests in inactivity, and sees the world become virtuous of itself. He does not try to 'bring about his own good deeds.' He never wastes himself on effort. He is not troubled about moral distinctions. He knows that things are what they are, and that their consequences will be what they will be. His mind is the 'speculum of creation,' and he is ever at peace.

All this is of course excessively dangerous, but we must remember that Chuang Tzŭ lived more than two thousand years ago, and never had the opportunity of seeing our unrivalled civilization. And yet it is possible that, were he to come back to earth and visit us, he might have something to say to Mr. Balfour about his coercion and active misgovernment in Ireland; he might smile at some of our philanthropic ardours, and shake his head over many of our organized charities; the School Board might not impress him, nor our race for wealth stir his admiration; he might wonder at our ideals, and grow sad over what we have realized. Perhaps it is well that Chuang Tzŭ cannot return.

Meanwhile, thanks to Mr. Giles and Mr. Quaritch, we have his book to console us, and certainly it is a most fascinating and delightful volume. Chuang Tzŭ is one of the Darwinians before Darwin. He traces man from the germ, and sees his unity with nature. As an anthropologist he is excessively interesting, and he describes our primitive arboreal ancestor living in trees through his terror of animals stronger than himself, and knowing only one parent, the mother, with all the accuracy of a lecturer at the Royal Society. Like Plato, he adopts the dialogue as his mode of expression, 'putting words into other people's mouths,' he tells us, 'in order to gain breadth of view.' As a story-teller he is charming. The account of the visit of the respectable Confucius to the great Robber Chê is most vivid and brilliant, and it is impossible not to laugh over the ultimate discomfiture of the sage, the barrenness of whose moral platitudes is ruthlessly exposed by the successful brigand. Even in his metaphysics, Chuang Tzŭ is intensely humorous. He personifies his abstractions, and makes them act plays before us. The Spirit of the Clouds, when passing eastward through the expanse of air, happened to fall in with the Vital Principle. The latter was slapping his ribs and hopping about: whereupon the Spirit of the Clouds said, 'Who are you, old man, and what are you doing?' 'Strolling!' replied the Vital Principle, without stopping,

161

for all activities are ceaseless. 'I want to know something,' continued the Spirit of the Clouds. 'Ah!' cried the Vital Principle, in a tone of disapprobation, and a marvellous conversation follows, that is not unlike the dialogue between the Sphinx and the Chimera in Flaubert's curious drama. Talking animals, also, have their place in Chuang Tzŭ's parables and stories, and through myth and poetry and fancy his strange philosophy finds musical utterance.

Of course it is sad to be told that it is immoral to be consciously good, and that doing anything is the worst form of idleness. Thousands of excellent and really earnest philanthropists would be absolutely thrown upon the rates if we adopted the view that nobody should be allowed to meddle in what does not concern him. The doctrine of the uselessness of all useful things would not merely endanger our commercial supremacy as a nation, but might bring discredit upon many prosperous and serious-minded members of the shop-keeping classes. What would become of our popular preachers, our Exeter Hall orators, our drawing-room evangelists, if we said to them, in the words of Chuang Tzŭ, 'Mosquitoes will keep a man awake all night with their biting, and just in the same way this talk of charity and duty to one's neighbour drives us nearly crazy. Sirs, strive to keep the world to its own original simplicity, and, as the wind bloweth where it listeth, so let Virtue establish itself. Wherefore this undue energy?' And what would be the fate of governments and professional politicians if we came to the conclusion that there is no such thing as governing mankind at all? It is clear that Chuang Tzŭ is a very dangerous writer, and the publication of his book in English, two thousand years after his death, is obviously premature, and may cause a great deal of pain to many thoroughly respectable and industrious persons. It may be true that the ideal of self-culture and self-development, which is the aim of his scheme of life, and the basis of his scheme of philosophy, is an ideal somewhat needed by an age like ours, in which most people are so anxious to educate their neighbours that they have actually no time left in which to educate themselves. But would it be wise to say so? It seems to me that if we once admitted the force of any one of Chuang Tzŭ's destructive criticisms we should have to put some check on our national habit of self-glorification; and the only thing that ever consoles man for the stupid things he does is the praise he always gives himself for doing them. There may, however, be a few who have grown wearied of that strange modern tendency that sets enthusiasm to do the work of the intellect. To these, and such as these, Chuang Tzŭ will be welcome. But let them only read him. Let them not talk about him. He would be disturbing at dinner-parties, and impossible at afternoon teas, and his whole life was a protest against platform speaking. 'The perfect man ignores self; the divine man ignores action; the true sage ignores reputation.' These are the principles of Chuang Tzŭ.

> *Chuang Tzŭ: Mystic, Moralist, and Social Reformer.* Translated from the Chinese by Herbert A. Giles, H.B.M.'s Consul at Tamsui.
> (Bernard Quaritch.)

MR. PATER'S APPRECIATIONS

(Speaker, March 22, 1890.)

When I first had the privilege—and I count it a very high one—of meeting Mr. Walter Pater, he said to me, smiling, 'Why do you always write poetry? Why do you not write prose? Prose is so much more difficult.'

It was during my undergraduate days at Oxford; days of lyrical ardour and of studious sonnet-writing; days when one loved the exquisite intricacy and musical repetitions of the ballade, and the villanelle with its linked long-drawn echoes and its curious completeness; days when one solemnly sought to discover the proper temper in which a triolet should be written; delightful days, in which, I am glad to say, there was far more rhyme than reason.

I may frankly confess now that at the time I did not quite comprehend what Mr. Pater really meant; and it was not till I had carefully studied his beautiful and suggestive essays on the Renaissance that I fully realized what a wonderful self-conscious art the art of English prose-writing really is, or may be made to be. Carlyle's stormy rhetoric, Ruskin's winged and passionate eloquence, had seemed to me to spring from enthusiasm rather than from art. I do not think I knew then that even prophets correct their proofs. As for Jacobean prose, I thought it too exuberant; and Queen Anne prose appeared to me terribly bald, and irritatingly rational. But Mr. Pater's essays became

163

to me 'the golden book of spirit and sense, the holy writ of beauty.' They are still this to me. It is possible, of course, that I may exaggerate about them. I certainly hope that I do; for where there is no exaggeration there is no love, and where there is no love there is no understanding. It is only about things that do not interest one, that one can give a really unbiassed opinion; and this is no doubt the reason why an unbiassed opinion is always valueless.

But I must not allow this brief notice of Mr. Pater's new volume to degenerate into an autobiography. I remember being told in America that whenever Margaret Fuller wrote an essay upon Emerson the printers had always to send out to borrow some additional capital 'I's,' and I feel it right to accept this transatlantic warning.

Appreciations, in the fine Latin sense of the word, is the title given by Mr. Pater to his book, which is an exquisite collection of exquisite essays, of delicately wrought works of art—some of them being almost Greek in their purity of outline and perfection of form, others mediæval in their strangeness of colour and passionate suggestion, and all of them absolutely modern, in the true meaning of the term modernity. For he to whom the present is the only thing that is present, knows nothing of the age in which he lives. To realize the nineteenth century one must realize every century that has preceded it, and that has contributed to its making. To know anything about oneself, one must know all about others. There must be no mood with which one cannot sympathize, no dead mode of life that one cannot make alive. The legacies of heredity may make us alter our views of moral responsibility, but they cannot but intensify our sense of the value of Criticism; for the true critic is he who bears within himself the dreams and ideas and feelings of myriad generations, and to whom no form of thought is alien, no emotional impulse obscure.

Perhaps the most interesting, and certainly the least successful, of the essays contained in the present volume is that on Style. It is the most interesting because it is the work of one who speaks with the high authority that comes from the noble realization of things nobly conceived. It is the least successful, because the subject is too abstract. A true artist like Mr. Pater is most felicitous when he deals with the concrete, whose very limitations give him finer freedom, while they necessitate more intense vision. And yet

164

what a high ideal is contained in these few pages! How good it is for us, in these days of popular education and facile journalism, to be reminded of the real scholarship that is essential to the perfect writer, who, 'being a true lover of words for their own sake, a minute and constant observer of their physiognomy,' will avoid what is mere rhetoric, or ostentatious ornament, or negligent misuse of terms, or ineffective surplusage, and will be known by his tact of omission, by his skilful economy of means, by his selection and self-restraint, and perhaps above all by that conscious artistic structure which is the expression of mind in style. I think I have been wrong in saying that the subject is too abstract. In Mr. Pater's hands it becomes very real to us indeed, and he shows us how, behind the perfection of a man's style, must lie the passion of a man's soul.

As one passes to the rest of the volume, one finds essays on Wordsworth and on Coleridge, on Charles Lamb and on Sir Thomas Browne, on some of Shakespeare's plays and on the English kings that Shakespeare fashioned, on Dante Rossetti, and on William Morris. As that on Wordsworth seems to be Mr. Pater's last work, so that on the singer of the Defence of Guenevere is certainly his earliest, or almost his earliest, and it is interesting to mark the change that has taken place in his style. This change is, perhaps, at first sight not very apparent. In 1868 we find Mr. Pater writing with the same exquisite care for words, with the same studied music, with the same temper, and something of the same mode of treatment. But, as he goes on, the architecture of the style becomes richer and more complex, the epithet more precise and intellectual. Occasionally one may be inclined to think that there is, here and there, a sentence which is somewhat long, and possibly, if one may venture to say so, a little heavy and cumbersome in movement. But if this be so, it comes from those side-issues suddenly suggested by the idea in its progress, and really revealing the idea more perfectly; or from those felicitous after-thoughts that give a fuller completeness to the central scheme, and yet convey something of the charm of chance; or from a desire to suggest the secondary shades of meaning with all their accumulating effect, and to avoid, it may be, the violence and harshness of too definite and exclusive an opinion. For in matters of art, at any rate, thought is inevitably coloured by emotion, and so is fluid rather than fixed, and, recognizing its dependence upon the moods and upon the passion of fine moments, will not accept the rigidity of a scientific formula or a theological dogma. The critical pleasure, too, that we receive from tracing, through what may seem the intricacies of a sentence, the working of the constructive intelligence, must not be overlooked. As soon as we have realized the design, everything appears clear and simple. After a time, these long sentences of Mr. Pater's come to have the charm of an elaborate piece of music, and the unity of such music also.

I have suggested that the essay on Wordsworth is probably the most recent bit of work contained in this volume. If one might choose between so much that is good, I should be inclined to say it is the finest also. The essay on Lamb is curiously suggestive; suggestive, indeed, of a somewhat more tragic, more sombre figure, than men have been wont to think of in connection with the author of the Essays of Elia. It is an interesting aspect under which to regard Lamb, but perhaps he himself would have had some difficulty in recognizing the portrait given of him. He had, undoubtedly, great sorrows, or motives for sorrow, but he could console himself at a moment's notice for the real tragedies of life by reading any one of the Elizabethan tragedies, provided it was in a folio edition. The essay on Sir Thomas Browne is delightful, and has the strange, personal, fanciful charm of the author of the Religio Medici, Mr. Pater often catching the colour and accent and tone of whatever artist, or work of art, he deals with. That on Coleridge, with its insistence on the necessity of the cultivation of the relative, as opposed to the absolute spirit in philosophy and in ethics, and its high appreciation of the poet's true position in our literature, is in style and substance a very blameless work. Grace of expression and delicate subtlety of thought and phrase, characterize the essays on Shakespeare. But the essay on Wordsworth has a spiritual beauty of its own. It appeals, not to the ordinary Wordsworthian with his uncritical temper, and his gross confusion of ethical and æsthetical problems, but rather to those who desire to separate the gold from the dross, and to reach at the true Wordsworth through the mass of tedious and prosaic work that bears his name, and that serves often to conceal him from us. The presence of an alien element in Wordsworth's art is, of course, recognized by Mr. Pater, but he touches on it merely from the psychological point of view, pointing out how this quality of higher and lower moods gives the effect in his poetry

166

'of a power not altogether his own, or under his control'; a power which comes and goes when it wills, 'so that the old fancy which made the poet's art an enthusiasm, a form of divine possession, seems almost true of him.' Mr. Pater's earlier essays had their purpurei panni, so eminently suitable for quotation, such as the famous passage on Mona Lisa, and that other in which Botticelli's strange conception of the Virgin is so strangely set forth. From the present volume it is difficult to select any one passage in preference to another as specially characteristic of Mr. Pater's treatment. This, however, is worth quoting at length. It contains a truth eminently suitable for our age:

> That the end of life is not action but contemplation—being as distinct from doing—a certain disposition of the mind: is, in some shape or other, the principle of all the higher morality. In poetry, in art, if you enter into their true spirit at all, you touch this principle in a measure; these, by their sterility, are a type of beholding for the mere joy of beholding. To treat life in the spirit of art is to make life a thing in which means and ends are identified: to encourage such treatment, the true moral significance of art and poetry. Wordsworth, and other poets who have been like him in ancient or more recent times, are the masters, the experts, in this art of impassioned contemplation. Their work is not to teach lessons, or enforce rules, or even to stimulate us to noble ends, but to withdraw the thoughts for a while from the mere machinery of life, to fix them, with appropriate emotions, on the spectacle of those great facts in man's existence which no machinery affects, 'on the great and universal passions of men, the most general and interesting of their occupations, and the entire world of nature'—on 'the operations of the elements and the appearances of the visible universe, on storm and sunshine, on the revolutions of the seasons, on cold and heat, on loss of friends and kindred, on injuries and resentments, on gratitude and hope, on fear and sorrow.' To witness this spectacle with appropriate emotions is the aim of all culture; and of these emotions poetry like Wordsworth's is a great nourisher and stimulant. He sees nature full of sentiment and excitement; he sees men and women as parts of nature, passionate, excited, in strange grouping and connection with the grandeur and beauty of the natural world:—images, in his own words,

'of men suffering; amid awful forms and powers.'

Certainly the real secret of Wordsworth has never been better expressed. After having read and reread Mr. Pater's essay—for it requires re-reading—one returns to the poet's work with a new sense of joy and wonder, and with something of eager and impassioned expectation. And perhaps this might be roughly taken as the test or touchstone of the finest criticism.

Finally, one cannot help noticing the delicate instinct that has gone to fashion the brief epilogue that ends this delightful volume. The difference between the classical and romantic spirits in art has often, and with much over-emphasis, been discussed. But with what a light sure touch does Mr. Pater write of it! How subtle and certain are his distinctions! If imaginative prose be really the special art of this century, Mr. Pater must rank amongst our century's most characteristic artists. In certain things he stands almost alone. The age has produced wonderful prose styles, turbid with individualism, and violent with excess of rhetoric. But in Mr. Pater, as in Cardinal Newman, we find the union of personality with perfection. He has no rival in his own sphere, and he has escaped disciples. And this, not because he has not been imitated, but because in art so fine as his there is something that, in its essence, is inimitable.

> *Appreciations, with an Essay on Style.* By Walter Pater, Fellow of
> Brasenose College. (Macmillan and Co.)

SENTENTIAE

(Extracted from Reviews)

Perhaps he will write poetry some day. If he does we would earnestly appeal to him to give up calling a cock 'proud chanticleer.' Few synonyms are so depressing.

A young writer can gain more from the study of a literary poet than from the study of a lyrist.

I have seen many audiences more interesting than the actors, and have often heard better dialogue in the foyer than I have on the stage.

The Dramatic College might take up the education of spectators as well as that of players, and teach people that there is a proper moment for the throwing of flowers as well as a proper method.

Life remains eternally unchanged; it is art which, by presenting it to us under various forms, enables us to realize its many-sided mysteries, and to catch the quality of its most fiery-coloured moments. The originality, I mean, which we ask from the artist, is originality of treatment, not of subject. It is only the unimaginative who ever invents. The true artist is known by the use he makes of what he annexes, and he annexes everything.

If I ventured on a bit of advice, which I feel most reluctant to do, it would be to the effect that while one should always study the method of a great artist, one should never imitate his manner. The manner of an artist is essentially individual, the method of an artist is absolutely universal. The first is personality, which no one should copy; the second is perfection, which all should aim at.

A critic who posed as an authority on field sports assured me that no one ever went out hunting when roses were in full bloom. Personally, that is exactly the season I would select for the chase, but then I know more about flowers than I do about foxes, and like them much better.

The nineteenth century may be a prosaic age, but we fear that, if we are to judge by the general run of novels, it is not an age of prose.

Perhaps in this century we are too altruistic to be really artistic.

I am led to hope that the University will some day have a theatre of its own, and that proficiency in scene-painting will be regarded as a necessary qualification for the Slade Professorship. On the stage, literature returns to life and archæology becomes art. A fine theatre is a temple where all the muses may meet, a second Parnassus.

It would be sad indeed if the many volumes of poems that are every year published in London found no readers but the authors themselves and the authors' relations; and the real philanthropist should recognize it as part of his duties to buy every new book of verse that appears.

A fifteen-line sonnet is as bad a monstrosity as a sonnet in dialogue.

Antiquarian books, as a rule, are extremely dull reading. They give us facts without form, science without style, and learning without life.

The Roman patron, in fact, kept the Roman poet alive, and we fancy that many of our modern bards rather regret the old system. Better, surely, the humiliation of the sportula than the indignity of a bill for printing! Better to accept a country-house as a gift than to be in debt to one's landlady! On the whole, the patron was an excellent institution, if not for poetry at least for the poets; . . . every poet longs for a Mæcenas.

The two things the Greeks valued most in actors were grace of gesture and music of voice. Indeed, to gain these virtues their actors used to subject themselves to a regular course of gymnastics and a particular regime of diet, health being to the Greeks not merely a quality of art, but a condition of its production.

One should not be too severe on English novels: they are the only relaxation of the intellectually unemployed.

Most modern novels are more remarkable for their crime than for their culture.

Not that a tramp's mode of life is at all unsuited to the development of the poetic faculty. Far from it! He, if any one, should possess that freedom of mood which is so essential to the artist, for he has no taxes to pay and no relations to worry him. The man who possesses a permanent address, and whose name is to be found in the Directory, is necessarily limited and localized. Only the tramp has absolute liberty of living. Was not Homer himself a vagrant, and did not Thespis go about in a caravan?

In art as in life the law of heredity holds good. On est toujours fils de quelqu'un.

He has succeeded in studying a fine poet without stealing from him—a very difficult thing to do.

Morocco is a sort of paradox among countries, for though it lies westward of Piccadilly, yet it is purely Oriental in character, and though it is but three hours' sail from Europe, yet it makes you feel (to use the forcible expression of an American writer) as if you had been taken up by the scruff of the neck and set down in the Old Testament.

As children themselves are the perfect flowers of life, so a collection of the best poems written on children should be the most perfect of all anthologies.

No English poet has written of children with more love and grace and delicacy [than Herrick]. His Ode on the Birth of Our Saviour, his poem To His Saviour, A Child: A Present by a Child, his Graces for Children, and his many lovely epitaphs on children are all of them exquisite works of art, simple, sweet and sincere.

As the cross-benches form a refuge for those who have no minds to make up, so those who cannot make up their minds always take to Homeric studies. Many of our leaders have sulked in their tents with Achilles after some violent political crisis and, enraged at the fickleness of fortune, more than one has given up to poetry what was obviously meant for party.

There are two ways of misunderstanding a poem. One is to misunderstand it and the other to praise it for qualities it does not possess.

Most modern calendars mar the sweet simplicity of our lives by reminding us that each day that passes is the anniversary of some perfectly uninteresting event. It is true that such aphorisms as

> Graves are a *mother's dimples*
>
> When we complain,

or

> The primrose wears a constant smile,
>
> And captive takes the heart,

can hardly be said to belong to the very highest order of poetry, still, they are preferable, on the whole, to the date of Hannah More's birth, or of the burning down of Exeter Change, or of the opening of the Great Exhibition; and though it would be dangerous to make calendars the basis of Culture, we should all be much improved if we began each day with a fine passage of English poetry.

Even the most uninteresting poet cannot survive bad editing.

Prefixed to the Calendar is an introductory note . . . displaying that intimate acquaintance with Sappho's lost poems which is the privilege only of those who are not acquainted with Greek literature.

Mediocre critics are usually safe in their generalities; it is in their reasons and examples that they come so lamentably to grief.

All premature panegyrics bring their own punishment upon themselves.

No one survives being over-estimated.

Henry Wadsworth Longfellow was one of the first true men of letters America produced, and as such deserves a high place in any history of American civilization. To a land out of breath in its greed for gain he showed the example of a life devoted entirely to the study of literature; his lectures, though not by any means brilliant, were still productive of much good; he had a most charming and gracious personality, and he wrote some pretty poems. But his poems are not of the kind that call for intellectual analysis or for elaborate description or, indeed, for any serious discussion at all.

Though the Psalm of Life be shouted from Maine to California, that would not make it true poetry.

Longfellow has no imitators, for of echoes themselves there are no echoes and it is only style that makes a school.

Poe's marvellous lines To Helen, a poem as beautiful as a Greek gem and as musical as Apollo's lute.

Good novelists are much rarer than good sons, and none of us would part readily with Micawber and Mrs. Nickleby. Still, the fact remains

172

that a man who was affectionate and loving to his children, generous and warm-hearted to his friends, and whose books are the very bacchanalia of benevolence, pilloried his parents to make the groundlings laugh, and this fact every biographer of Dickens should face and, if possible, explain.

No age ever borrows the slang of its predecessor.

What we do not know about Shakespeare is a most fascinating subject, and one that would fill a volume, but what we do know about him is so meagre and inadequate that when it is collected together the result is rather depressing.

They show a want of knowledge that must be the result of years of study.

Rossetti's was a great personality, and personalities such as his do not easily survive shilling primers.

We are sorry to find an English dramatic critic misquoting Shakespeare, as we had always been of opinion that this was a privilege reserved specially for our English actors.

Biographies of this kind rob life of much of its dignity and its wonder, add to death itself a new terror, and make one wish that all art were anonymous.

A pillar of fire to the few who knew him, and of cloud to the many who knew him not, Dante Gabriel Rossetti lived apart from the gossip and tittle-tattle of a shallow age. He never trafficked with the merchants for his soul, nor brought his wares into the market-place for the idle to gape at. Passionate and romantic though he was, yet there was in his nature something of high austerity. He loved seclusion, and hated notoriety, and would have shuddered at the idea that within a few years after his death he was to make his appearance in a series of popular biographies, sandwiched between the author of Pickwick and the Great Lexicographer.

We sincerely hope that a few more novels like these will be published, as the public will then find out that a bad book is very dear at a shilling.

The only form of fiction in which real characters do not seem out of place is history. In novels they are detestable.

Shilling literature is always making demands on our credulity without ever appealing to our imagination.

Pathology is rapidly becoming the basis of sensational literature, and in art, as in politics, there is a great future for monsters.

It is only mediocrities and old maids who consider it a grievance to be misunderstood.

As truly religious people are resigned to everything, even to mediocre poetry, there is no reason at all why Madame Guyon's verses should not be popular with a large section of the community.

A simile committing suicide is always a depressing spectacle.

Such novels as Scamp are possibly more easy to write than they are to read.

We have no doubt that when Bailey wrote to Lord Houghton that common-sense and gentleness were Keats's two special characteristics the worthy Archdeacon meant extremely well, but we prefer the real Keats, with his passionate wilfulness, his fantastic moods and his fine inconsistence. Part of Keats's charm as a man is his fascinating incompleteness.

The Apostolic dictum, that women should not be suffered to teach, is no longer applicable to a society such as ours, with its solidarity of interests, its recognition of natural rights, and its universal education, however suitable it may have been to the Greek cities under Roman rule. Nothing in the United States struck me more than the fact that the remarkable intellectual progress of that country is very largely due to the efforts of American women, who edit many of the most powerful magazines and newspapers, take part in the discussion of every question of public interest, and exercise an important influence upon the growth and tendencies of literature and art. Indeed, the women of America are the one class in the community that enjoys that leisure which is so necessary for culture. The men are, as a rule, so absorbed in business, that the task of bringing some element of form into the chaos of daily life is left almost entirely to the opposite sex, and an eminent Bostonian once assured me that in the twentieth century the whole culture of his country would be in petticoats. By that time, however, it is probable that the dress of the two sexes will be assimilated, as similarity of costume always follows similarity of pursuits.

The aim of social comedy, in Menander no less than in Sheridan, is to mirror the manners, not to reform the morals, of its day, and the censure of the Puritan, whether real or affected, is always out of place in literary criticism, and shows a want of recognition of the essential distinction between art and life. After all, it is only the Philistine who thinks of blaming Jack Absolute for his deception, Bob Acres for his cowardice, and Charles Surface for his extravagance, and there is very little use in airing one's moral sense at the expense of one's artistic appreciation.

The Æneid bears almost the same relation to the Iliad that the Idylls of the King do to the old Celtic romances of Arthur. Like them it is full of felicitous modernisms, of exquisite literary echoes and of delicate and delightful pictures; as Lord Tennyson loves England so did Virgil love Rome; the pageants of history and the purple of empire are equally dear to both poets; but neither of them has the grand simplicity or the large humanity of the early singers, and, as a hero, Æneas is no less a failure than Arthur.

There is always a certain amount of danger in any attempt to cultivate impossible virtues.

As far as the serious presentation of life is concerned, what we require is more imaginative treatment, greater freedom from theatric language and theatric convention. It may be questioned, also, whether the consistent reward of virtue and punishment of wickedness be really the healthiest ideal for an art that claims to mirror nature.

True originality is to be found rather in the use made of a model than in the rejection of all models and masters. Dans l'art comme dans la nature on est toujours fils de quelqu'un, and we should not quarrel with the reed if it whispers to us the music of the lyre. A little child once asked me if it was the nightingale who taught the linnets how to sing.

In France they have had one great genius, Balzac, who invented the modern method of looking at life; and one great artist, Flaubert, who is the impeccable master of style; and to the influence of these two men we may trace almost all contemporary French fiction. But in England we have had no schools worth speaking of. The fiery torch lit by the Brontës has not been passed on to other hands; Dickens has influenced only journalism; Thackeray's delightful superficial philosophy, superb narrative power, and clever social satire have found no echoes; nor has Trollope left any direct successors behind him—a fact which is not much to be regretted, however, as, admirable though Trollope undoubtedly is for rainy afternoons and tedious railway journeys, from the point of view of literature he is merely the perpetual curate of Pudlington Parva.

George Meredith's style is chaos illumined by brilliant flashes of lightning. As a writer he has mastered everything, except language; as a novelist he can do everything, except tell a story; as an artist he is everything, except articulate. Too strange to be popular, too individual to have imitators, the author of Richard Feverel stands absolutely alone. It is easy to disarm criticism, but he has disarmed the disciple. He gives us his philosophy through the medium of wit, and is never so pathetic as when he is humorous. To turn truth into a paradox is not difficult, but George Meredith makes all his paradoxes truths, and no Theseus can thread his labyrinth, no Œdipus solve his secret.

The most perfect and the most poisonous of all modern French poets once remarked that a man can live for three days without bread, but that no one can live for three days without poetry. This, however, can hardly be said to be a popular view, or one that commends itself to that curiously uncommon quality which is called common-sense. I fancy that most people, if they do not actually prefer a salmis to a sonnet, certainly like their culture to repose on a basis of good cookery.

A cynical critic once remarked that no great poet is intelligible and no little poet worth understanding, but that otherwise poetry is an admirable thing. This, however, seems to us a somewhat harsh view of the subject. Little poets are an extremely interesting study. The best of them have often some new beauty to show us, and though the worst of them may bore yet they rarely brutalize.

It is a curious thing that when minor poets write choruses to a play they should always consider it necessary to adopt the style and language of a bad translator. We fear that Mr. Bohn has much to answer for.

In one sonnet he makes a distinct attempt to be original and the result is extremely depressing.

> Earth wears her grandest robe, by autumn spun,
>
> *Like some stout matron who of youth has run*
>
> *The course, . . .*

is the most dreadful simile we have ever come across even in poetry. Mr. Griffiths should beware of originality. Like beauty, it is a fatal gift.

There is a wide difference between the beautiful Tuscan city and the sea-city of the Adriatic. Florence is a city full of memories of the great figures of the past. The traveller cannot pass along her streets without treading in the very traces of Dante, without stepping on soil made memorable by footprints never to be effaced. The greatness of the surroundings, the palaces, churches, and frowning mediæval castles in the midst of the city, are all thrown into the background by the greatness, the individuality, the living power and vigour of the men who are their originators, and at the same time their inspiring soul. But when we turn to Venice the effect is very different. We do not think of the makers of that marvellous city, but rather of what they made. The idealized image of Venice herself meets us everywhere. The mother is not overshadowed by the too great glory of any of her sons. In her records the city is everything—the republic, the worshipped ideal of a community in which every man for the common glory seems to have been willing to sink his own. We know that Dante stood within the red walls of the arsenal, and saw the galleys making and mending, and the pitch flaming up to heaven; Petrarch came to visit the great Mistress of the Sea, taking refuge there, 'in this city, true home of the human race,' from trouble, war and pestilence outside; and Byron, with his facile enthusiasms and fervent eloquence, made his home for a time in one of the stately, decaying palaces; but with these exceptions no great poet has ever associated himself with the life of Venice. She had architects, sculptors and painters, but no singer of her own.

To realize the popularity of the great poets one should turn to the minor poets and see whom they follow, what master they select, whose music they echo.

Ordinary theology has long since converted its gold into lead, and words and phrases that once touched the heart of the world have become wearisome and meaningless through repetition. If Theology desires to move us, she must re-write her formulas.

It takes a great artist to be thoroughly modern. Nature is always a little behind the age.

Mr. Nash, who styles himself 'a humble soldier in the army of Faith,' expresses a hope that his book may 'invigorate devotional feeling, especially among the young, to whom verse is perhaps more attractive than to their elders,' but we should be sorry to think that people of any age could admire such a paraphrase as the following:

> Foxes have holes in which to slink for rest,
>
> The birds of air find shelter in the nest;
>
> But He, the Son of Man and Lord of all,
>
> Has no abiding place His own to call.

It is a curious fact that the worst work is always done with the best intentions, and that people are never so trivial as when they take themselves very seriously.

Mr. Foster is an American poet who has read Hawthorne, which is wise of him, and imitated Longfellow, which is not quite so commendable.

Andiatoroctè is the title of a volume of poems by the Rev. Clarence Walworth, of Albany, N.Y. It is a word borrowed from the Indians, and should, we think, be returned to them as soon as possible. The most curious poem of the book is called Scenes at the Holy Home:

> Jesus and Joseph at work! Hurra!
>
> Sight never to see again,

A prentice Deity plies the saw,

While the Master ploughs with the plane.

Poems of this kind were popular in the Middle Ages when the cathedrals of every Christian country served as its theatres. They are anachronisms now, and it is odd that they should come to us from the United States. In matters of this kind we should have some protection.

As for the triolets, and the rondels, and the careful study of metrical subtleties, these things are merely the signs of a desire for perfection in small things and of the recognition of poetry as an art. They have had certainly one good result—they have made our minor poets readable, and have not left us entirely at the mercy of geniuses.

Poetry has many modes of music; she does not blow through one pipe alone. Directness of utterance is good, but so is the subtle recasting of thought into a new and delightful form. Simplicity is good, but complexity, mystery, strangeness, symbolism, obscurity even, these have their value. Indeed, properly speaking, there is no such thing as Style; there are merely styles, that is all.

Writers of poetical prose are rarely good poets.

Poetry may be said to need far more self-restraint than prose. Its conditions are more exquisite. It produces its effects by more subtle means. It must not be allowed to degenerate into mere rhetoric or mere eloquence. It is, in one sense, the most self-conscious of all the arts, as it is never a means to an end but always an end in itself.

It may be difficult for a poet to find English synonyms for Asiatic expressions, but even if it were impossible it is none the less a poet's duty to find them. As it is, Sir Edwin Arnold has translated Sa'di and some one must translate Sir Edwin Arnold.

Lounging in the open air is not a bad school for poets, but it largely depends on the lounger.

People are so fond of giving away what they do not want themselves, that charity is largely on the increase. But with this kind of charity I have not much sympathy. If one gives away a book, it should be a charming book—so charming, that one regrets having given it.

Mr. Whistler, for some reason or other, always adopted the phraseology of the minor prophets. Possibly it was in order to emphasize his well-known claims to verbal inspiration, or perhaps he thought with Voltaire that Habakkuk était capable de tout, and wished to shelter himself under the shield of a definitely irresponsible writer none of whose prophecies, according to the French philosopher, has ever been fulfilled. The idea was clever enough at the beginning, but ultimately the manner became monotonous. The spirit of the Hebrews is excellent but their mode of writing is not to be imitated, and no amount of American jokes will give it that modernity which is essential to a good literary style. Admirable as are Mr. Whistler's fireworks on canvas, his fireworks in prose are abrupt, violent and exaggerated.

'The decisive events of the world,' as has been well said, 'take place in the intellect,' and as for Board-schools, academic ceremonies, hospital wards and the like, they may be well left to the artists of the illustrated papers, who do them admirably and quite as well as they need be done. Indeed, the pictures of contemporary events, Royal marriages, naval reviews and things of this kind that appear in the Academy every year, are always extremely bad; while the very same subjects treated in black and white in the Graphic or the London News are excellent. Besides, if we want to understand the history of a nation through the medium of art, it is to the imaginative and ideal arts that we have to go and not to the arts that are definitely imitative. The visible aspect of life no longer contains for us the secret of life's spirit.

The difficulty under which the novelists of our day labour seems to me to be this: if they do not go into society, their books are unreadable; and if they do go into society, they have no time left for writing.

I must confess that most modern mysticism seems to me to be simply a method of imparting useless knowledge in a form that no one can understand. Allegory, parable, and vision have their high artistic uses, but their philosophical and scientific uses are very small.

180

The object of most modern fiction is not to give pleasure to the artistic instinct, but rather to portray life vividly for us, to draw attention to social anomalies, and social forms of injustice. Many of our novelists are really pamphleteers, reformers masquerading as story-tellers, earnest sociologists seeking to mend as well as to mirror life.

The book is certainly characteristic of an age so practical and so literary as ours, an age in which all social reforms have been preceded and have been largely influenced by fiction.

Mr. Stopford Brooke said some time ago that Socialism and the socialistic spirit would give our poets nobler and loftier themes for song, would widen their sympathies and enlarge the horizon of their vision, and would touch, with the fire and fervour of a new faith, lips that had else been silent, hearts that but for this fresh gospel had been cold. What Art gains from contemporary events is always a fascinating problem and a problem that is not easy to solve. It is, however, certain that Socialism starts well equipped. She has her poets and her painters, her art lecturers and her cunning designers, her powerful orators and her clever writers. If she fails it will not be for lack of expression. If she succeeds her triumph will not be a triumph of mere brute force.

Socialism is not going to allow herself to be trammelled by any hard and fast creed or to be stereotyped into an iron formula. She welcomes many and multiform natures. She rejects none and has room for all. She has the attraction of a wonderful personality and touches the heart of one and the brain of another, and draws this man by his hatred and injustice, and his neighbour by his faith in the future, and a third, it may be, by his love of art or by his wild worship of a lost and buried past. And all of this is well. For, to make men Socialists is nothing, but to make Socialism human is a great thing.

The Reformation gained much from the use of popular hymn-tunes, and the Socialists seem determined to gain by similar means a similar hold upon the people. However, they must not be too sanguine about the result. The walls of Thebes rose up to the sound of music, and Thebes was a very dull city indeed.

We really must protest against Mr. Matthews' efforts to confuse the poetry of Piccadilly with the poetry of Parnassus. To tell us, for instance, that Mr. Austin Dobson's verse 'has not the condensed clearness nor the incisive vigor of Mr. Locker's' is really too bad even for Transatlantic criticism. Nobody who lays claim to the slightest knowledge of literature and the forms of literature should ever bring the two names into conjunction.

Mr. Dobson has produced work that is absolutely classical in its exquisite beauty of form. Nothing more artistically perfect in its way than the Lines to a Greek Girl has been written in our time. This little poem will be remembered in literature as long as Thyrsis is remembered, and Thyrsis will never be forgotten. Both have that note of distinction that is so rare in these days of violence, exaggeration and rhetoric. Of course, to suggest, as Mr. Matthews does, that Mr. Dobson's poems belong to 'the literature of power' is ridiculous. Power is not their aim, nor is it their effect. They have other qualities, and in their own delicately limited sphere they have no contemporary rivals; they have none even second to them.

The heroine is a sort of well-worn Becky Sharp, only much more beautiful than Becky, or at least than Thackeray's portraits of her, which, however, have always seemed to me rather ill-natured. I feel sure that Mrs. Rawdon Crawley was extremely pretty, and I have never understood how it was that Thackeray could caricature with his pencil so fascinating a creation of his pen.

A critic recently remarked of Adam Lindsay Gordon that through him Australia had found her first fine utterance in song. This, however, is an amiable error. There is very little of Australia in Gordon's poetry. His heart and mind and fancy were always preoccupied with memories and dreams of England and such culture as England gave him. He owed nothing to the land of his adoption. Had he stayed at home he would have done much better work.

That Australia, however, will some day make amends by producing a poet of her own we cannot doubt, and for him there will be new notes to sound and new wonders to tell of.

The best that we can say of him is that he wrote imperfectly in Australia those poems that in England he might have made perfect.

Judges, like the criminal classes, have their lighter moments.

There seems to be some curious connection between piety and poor rhymes.

The South African poets, as a class, are rather behind the age. They seem to think that 'Aurora' is a very novel and delightful epithet for the dawn. On the whole they depress us.

The only original thing in the volume is the description of Mr. Robert Buchanan's 'grandeur of mind.' This is decidedly new.

Dr. Cockle tells us that Müllner's Guilt and The Ancestress of Grillparzer are the masterpieces of German fate-tragedy. His translation of the first of these two masterpieces does not make us long for any further acquaintance with the school. Here is a specimen from the fourth act of the fate-tragedy.

SCENE VIII.

ELVIRA.　　　HUGO.

ELVIRA (*after long silence, leaving the harp, steps to Hugo, and seeks his gaze*).

HUGO (*softly*). Though I made sacrifice of thy sweet life, the Father has forgiven. Can the wife—forgive?

ELVIRA (*on his breast*). She can!

HUGO (*with all the warmth of love*). Dear wife!

ELVIRA (*after a pause, in deep sorrow*). Must it be so, beloved one?

HUGO (*sorry to have betrayed himself*). What?

The Renaissance had for its object the development of great personalities. The perfect freedom of the temperament in matters of art, the perfect freedom of the intellect in intellectual matters, the full development of the individual, were the things it aimed at. As we study its history we find it full of great anarchies. It solved no political or social problems; it did not seek to solve

183

them. The ideal of the 'Grand Siècle,' and of Richelieu, in whom the forces of that great age were incarnate, was different. The ideas of citizenship, of the building up of a great nation, of the centralization of forces, of collective action, of ethnic unity of purpose, came before the world.

The creation of a formal tradition upon classical lines is never without its danger, and it is sad to find the provincial towns of France, once so varied and individual in artistic expression, writing to Paris for designs and advice. And yet, through Colbert's great centralizing scheme of State supervision and State aid, France was the one country in Europe, and has remained the one country in Europe, where the arts are not divorced from industry.

Hawthorne re-created for us the America of the past with the incomparable grace of a very perfect artist, but Mr. Bret Harte's emphasized modernity has, in its own sphere, won equal, or almost equal, triumphs.

It is pleasant to come across a heroine [Bret Harte's Cressy] who is not identified with any great cause, and represents no important principle, but is simply a wonderful nymph from American backwoods, who has in her something of Artemis, and not a little of Aphrodite.

It is always a pleasure to come across an American poet who is not national, and who tries to give expression to the literature that he loves rather than to the land in which he lives. The Muses care so little for geography!

Blue-books are generally dull reading, but Blue-books on Ireland have always been interesting. They form the record of one of the great tragedies of modern Europe. In them England has written down her indictment against herself and has given to the world the history of her shame. If in the last century she tried to govern Ireland with an insolence that was intensified by race hatred and religious prejudice, she has sought to rule her in this century with a stupidity that is aggravated by good intentions.

Like most penmen he [Froude] overrates the power of the sword. Where England has had to struggle she has been wise. Where physical strength has been on her side, as in Ireland, she has been made unwieldy by that strength. Her own strong hands have blinded her. She has had force but no direction.

184

There are some who will welcome with delight the idea of solving the Irish question by doing away with the Irish people. There are others who will remember that Ireland has extended her boundaries, and that we have now to reckon with her not merely in the Old World but in the New.

Plastic simplicity of outline may render for us the visible aspect of life; it is different when we come to deal with those secrets which self-consciousness alone contains, and which self-consciousness itself can but half reveal. Action takes place in the sunlight, but the soul works in the dark. There is something curiously interesting in the marked tendency of modern poetry to become obscure. Many critics, writing with their eyes fixed on the masterpieces of past literature, have ascribed this tendency to wilfulness and to affectation. Its origin is rather to be found in the complexity of the new problems, and in the fact that self-consciousness is not yet adequate to explain the contents of the Ego. In Mr. Browning's poems, as in life itself, which has suggested, or rather necessitated, the new method, thought seems to proceed not on logical lines, but on lines of passion. The unity of the individual is being expressed through its inconsistencies and its contradictions. In a strange twilight man is seeking for himself, and when he has found his own image, he cannot understand it. Objective forms of art, such as sculpture and the drama, sufficed one for the perfect presentation of life; they can no longer so suffice.

As he is not a genius he, naturally, behaves admirably on every occasion.

Certainly dialect is dramatic. It is a vivid method of re-creating a past that never existed. It is something between 'A Return to Nature' and 'A Return to the Glossary.' It is so artificial that it is really naïve. From the point of view of mere music, much may be said for it. Wonderful diminutives lend new notes of tenderness to the song. There are possibilities of fresh rhymes, and in search for a fresh rhyme poets may be excused if they wander from the broad highroad of classical utterance into devious byways and less-trodden paths. Sometimes one is tempted to look on dialect as expressing simply the pathos of provincialisms, but there is more in it than mere mispronunciation. With that revival of an antique form, often comes the revival of an antique spirit. Through limitations that are sometimes uncouth, and always narrow, comes Tragedy herself; and though she may stammer in her utterance, and deck herself in cast-off weeds and trammelling raiment, still we must hold ourselves in readiness to accept her, so rare are her visits to us now, so rare her presence in an age that demands a happy ending from every play, and that sees in the theatre merely a source of amusement.

There is a great deal to be said in favour of reading a novel backwards. The last page is, as a rule, the most interesting, and when one begins with the catastrophe or the dénoûment one feels on pleasant terms of equality with the author. It is like going behind the scenes of a theatre. One is no longer taken in, and the hairbreadth escapes of the hero and the wild agonies of the heroine leave one absolutely unmoved.

He has every form of sincerity except the sincerity of the artist, a defect that he shares with most of our popular writers.

On the whole Primavera is a pleasant little book, and we are glad to welcome it. It is charmingly 'got up,' and undergraduates might read it with advantage during lecture hours.

Footnotes:

[2] Reverently some well-meaning persons have placed a marble slab on the wall of the cemetery with a medallion-profile of Keats on it and some mediocre lines of poetry. The face is ugly, and rather hatchet-shaped, with thick sensual lips, and is utterly unlike the poet himself, who was very beautiful to look upon. 'His countenance,' says a lady who saw him at one of Hazlitt's lectures, 'lives in my mind as one of singular beauty and brightness; it had the expression as if he had been looking on some glorious sight.' And this is the idea which Severn's picture of him gives. Even Haydon's rough pen-and-ink sketch of him is better than this 'marble libel,' which I hope will soon be taken down. I think the best representation of the poet would be a coloured bust, like that of the young Rajah of Koolapoor at Florence, which is a lovely and lifelike work of art.

[5] 'Make' is of course a mere printer's error for 'mock,' and was subsequently corrected by Lord Houghton. The sonnet as given in The Garden of Florence reads 'orbs for 'those.'

[63] The Margravine of Baireuth and Voltaire. (David Stott, 1888.)

[115] September 1888.

[116] See The Picture of Dorian Gray, chapter xi., page 222.

[157] From Lady Wilde' Ancient Legends of Ireland.

A WOMAN OF NO
IMPORTANCE: A PLAY

TO

GLADYS

COUNTESS DE GREY

[MARCHIONESS OF RIPON]

THE PERSONS OF THE PLAY

LORD ILLINGWORTH

SIR JOHN PONTEFRACT

LORD ALFRED RUFFORD

MR. KELVIL, M.P.

THE VEN. ARCHDEACON DAUBENY, D.D.

GERALD ARBUTHNOT

FARQUHAR, BUTLER

FRANCIS, FOOTMAN

LADY HUNSTANTON

LADY CAROLINE PONTEFRACT

LADY STUTFIELD

MRS. ALLONBY

MISS HESTER WORSLEY

ALICE, MAID

MRS. ARBUTHNOT

THE SCENES OF THE PLAY

ACT I. *The Terrace at Hunstanton Chase.*

ACT II. *The Drawing-room at Hunstanton Chase.*

ACT III. *The Hall at Hunstanton Chase.*

ACT IV. *Sitting-room in Mrs. Arbuthnot's House at Wrockley.*

TIME: *The Present.*

PLACE: *The Shires.*

The action of the play takes place within twenty-four hours.

LONDON: HAYMARKET THEATRE

Lessee and Manager: Mr. H Beerbohm Tree

April 19th, 1893

Lord Illingworth	*Mr. Tree.*
Sir John Pontefract	*Mr. E. Holman Clark.*
Lord Alfred Rufford	*Mr. Ernest Lawford.*
Mr. Kelvil, M.P.	*Mr. Charles Allan.*
The Ven. Archdeacon Daubeny, D.D.	*Mr. Kemble.*
Gerald Arbuthnot	*Mr. Terry.*
Farquhar (Butler)	*Mr. Hay.*
Francis (Footman)	*Mr. Montague.*
Lady Hunstanton	*Miss Rose Leclercq.*
Lady Caroline Pontefract	*Miss Le Thière.*
Lady Stutfield	*Miss Blanche Horlock.*
Mrs. Allonby	*Mrs. Tree.*
Miss Hester Worsley	*Miss Julia Neilson.*
Alice (Maid)	*Miss Kelly.*
Mrs. Arbuthnot	*Mrs. Bernard-Beere.*

FIRST ACT

SCENE

Lawn in front of the terrace at Hunstanton.

[Sir John and Lady Caroline Pontefract, Miss Worsley, on chairs under large yew tree.]

Lady Caroline. I believe this is the first English country house you have stayed at, Miss Worsley?

Hester. Yes, Lady Caroline.

Lady Caroline. You have no country houses, I am told, in America?

Hester. We have not many.

Lady Caroline. Have you any country? What we should call country?

Hester. [Smiling.] We have the largest country in the world, Lady Caroline. They used to tell us at school that some of our states are as big as France and England put together.

Lady Caroline. Ah! you must find it very draughty, I should fancy. [To Sir John.] John, you should have your muffler. What is the use of my always knitting mufflers for you if you won't wear them?

Sir John. I am quite warm, Caroline, I assure you.

Lady Caroline. I think not, John. Well, you couldn't come to a more charming place than this, Miss Worsley, though the house is excessively damp, quite unpardonably damp, and dear Lady Hunstanton is sometimes a little lax about the people she asks down here. [To Sir John.] Jane mixes too much. Lord Illingworth, of course, is a man of high distinction. It is a privilege to meet him. And that member of Parliament, Mr. Kettle—

Sir John. Kelvil, my love, Kelvil.

Lady Caroline. He must be quite respectable. One has never heard his name before in the whole course of one's life, which speaks volumes for a man, nowadays. But Mrs. Allonby is hardly a very suitable person.

Hester. I dislike Mrs. Allonby. I dislike her more than I can say.

Lady Caroline. I am not sure, Miss Worsley, that foreigners like yourself should cultivate likes or dislikes about the people they are invited to meet. Mrs. Allonby is very well born. She is a niece of Lord Brancaster's. It is said, of course, that she ran away twice before she was married. But you know how unfair people often are. I myself don't believe she ran away more than once.

Hester. Mr. Arbuthnot is very charming.

Lady Caroline. Ah, yes! the young man who has a post in a bank. Lady Hunstanton is most kind in asking him here, and Lord Illingworth seems to have taken quite a fancy to him. I am not sure, however, that Jane is right in taking him out of his position. In my young days, Miss Worsley, one never met any one in society who worked for their living. It was not considered the thing.

Hester. In America those are the people we respect most.

Lady Caroline. I have no doubt of it.

Hester. Mr. Arbuthnot has a beautiful nature! He is so simple, so sincere. He has one of the most beautiful natures I have ever come across. It is a privilege to meet him.

Lady Caroline. It is not customary in England, Miss Worsley, for a young lady to speak with such enthusiasm of any person of the opposite sex. English women conceal their feelings till after they are married. They show them then.

Hester. Do you, in England, allow no friendship to exist between a young man and a young girl?

[Enter Lady Hunstanton, followed by Footman with shawls and a cushion.]

Lady Caroline. We think it very inadvisable. Jane, I was just saying

198

what a pleasant party you have asked us to meet. You have a wonderful power of selection. It is quite a gift.

Lady Hunstanton. Dear Caroline, how kind of you! I think we all do fit in very nicely together. And I hope our charming American visitor will carry back pleasant recollections of our English country life. [To Footman.] The cushion, there, Francis. And my shawl. The Shetland. Get the Shetland. [Exit Footman for shawl.]

[Enter Gerald Arbuthnot.]

Gerald. Lady Hunstanton, I have such good news to tell you. Lord Illingworth has just offered to make me his secretary.

Lady Hunstanton. His secretary? That is good news indeed, Gerald. It means a very brilliant future in store for you. Your dear mother will be delighted. I really must try and induce her to come up here to-night. Do you think she would, Gerald? I know how difficult it is to get her to go anywhere.

Gerald. Oh! I am sure she would, Lady Hunstanton, if she knew Lord Illingworth had made me such an offer.

[Enter Footman with shawl.]

Lady Hunstanton. I will write and tell her about it, and ask her to come up and meet him. [To Footman.] Just wait, Francis. [Writes letter.]

Lady Caroline. That is a very wonderful opening for so young a man as you are, Mr. Arbuthnot.

Gerald. It is indeed, Lady Caroline. I trust I shall be able to show myself worthy of it.

Lady Caroline. I trust so.

Gerald. [To Hester.] You have not congratulated me yet, Miss Worsley.

Hester. Are you very pleased about it?

Gerald. Of course I am. It means everything to me—things that were out of the reach of hope before may be within hope's reach now.

Hester. Nothing should be out of the reach of hope. Life is a hope.

Lady Hunstanton. I fancy, Caroline, that Diplomacy is what Lord Illingworth is aiming at. I heard that he was offered Vienna. But that may not be true.

Lady Caroline. I don't think that England should be represented abroad by an unmarried man, Jane. It might lead to complications.

Lady Hunstanton. You are too nervous, Caroline. Believe me, you are too nervous. Besides, Lord Illingworth may marry any day. I was in hopes he would have married lady Kelso. But I believe he said her family was too large. Or was it her feet? I forget which. I regret it very much. She was made to be an ambassador's wife.

Lady Caroline. She certainly has a wonderful faculty of remembering people's names, and forgetting their faces.

Lady Hunstanton. Well, that is very natural, Caroline, is it not? [To Footman.] Tell Henry to wait for an answer. I have written a line to your dear mother, Gerald, to tell her your good news, and to say she really must come to dinner.

[Exit Footman.]

Gerald. That is awfully kind of you, Lady Hunstanton. [To Hester.] Will you come for a stroll, Miss Worsley?

Hester. With pleasure. [Exit with Gerald.]

Lady Hunstanton. I am very much gratified at Gerald Arbuthnot's good fortune. He is quite a protégé of mine. And I am particularly pleased that Lord Illingworth should have made the offer of his own accord without my suggesting anything. Nobody likes to be asked favours. I remember poor Charlotte Pagden making herself quite unpopular one season, because she had a French governess she wanted to recommend to every one.

Lady Caroline. I saw the governess, Jane. Lady Pagden sent her to me. It was before Eleanor came out. She was far too good-looking to be in any respectable household. I don't wonder Lady Pagden was so anxious to get rid of her.

Lady Hunstanton. Ah, that explains it.

Lady Caroline. John, the grass is too damp for you. You had better go and put on your overshoes at once.

Sir John. I am quite comfortable, Caroline, I assure you.

Lady Caroline. You must allow me to be the best judge of that, John. Pray do as I tell you.

[Sir John gets up and goes off.]

Lady Hunstanton. You spoil him, Caroline, you do indeed!

[Enter Mrs. Allonby and Lady Stutfield.]

[To Mrs. Allonby.] Well, dear, I hope you like the park. It is said to be well timbered.

Mrs. Allonby. The trees are wonderful, Lady Hunstanton.

Lady Stutfield. Quite, quite wonderful.

Mrs. Allonby. But somehow, I feel sure that if I lived in the country for six months, I should become so unsophisticated that no one would take the slightest notice of me.

Lady Hunstanton. I assure you, dear, that the country has not that effect at all. Why, it was from Melthorpe, which is only two miles from here, that Lady Belton eloped with Lord Fethersdale. I remember the occurrence perfectly. Poor Lord Belton died three days afterwards of joy, or gout. I forget which. We had a large party staying here at the time, so we were all very much interested in the whole affair.

Mrs. Allonby. I think to elope is cowardly. It's running away from danger. And danger has become so rare in modern life.

Lady Caroline. As far as I can make out, the young women of the present day seem to make it the sole object of their lives to be always playing with fire.

Mrs. Allonby. The one advantage of playing with fire, Lady Caroline, is that one never gets even singed. It is the people who don't know how to play with it who get burned up.

Lady Stutfield. Yes; I see that. It is very, very helpful.

Lady Hunstanton. I don't know how the world would get on with such a theory as that, dear Mrs. Allonby.

Lady Stutfield. Ah! The world was made for men and not for women.

Mrs. Allonby. Oh, don't say that, Lady Stutfield. We have a much better time than they have. There are far more things forbidden to us than are forbidden to them.

Lady Stutfield. Yes; that is quite, quite true. I had not thought of that.

[Enter Sir John and Mr. Kelvil.]

Lady Hunstanton. Well, Mr. Kelvil, have you got through your work?

Kelvil. I have finished my writing for the day, Lady Hunstanton. It has been an arduous task. The demands on the time of a public man are very heavy nowadays, very heavy indeed. And I don't think they meet with adequate recognition.

Lady Caroline. John, have you got your overshoes on?

Sir John. Yes, my love.

Lady Caroline. I think you had better come over here, John. It is more sheltered.

Sir John. I am quite comfortable, Caroline.

Lady Caroline. I think not, John. You had better sit beside me. [Sir John rises and goes across.]

Lady Stutfield. And what have you been writing about this morning,

Mr. Kelvil?

Kelvil. On the usual subject, Lady Stutfield. On Purity.

Lady Stutfield. That must be such a very, very interesting thing to write about.

Kelvil. It is the one subject of really national importance, nowadays, Lady Stutfield. I purpose addressing my constituents on the question before Parliament meets. I find that the poorer classes of this country display a marked desire for a higher ethical standard.

Lady Stutfield. How quite, quite nice of them.

Lady Caroline. Are you in favour of women taking part in politics, Mr. Kettle?

Sir John. Kelvil, my love, Kelvil.

Kelvil. The growing influence of women is the one reassuring thing in our political life, Lady Caroline. Women are always on the side of morality, public and private.

Lady Stutfield. It is so very, very gratifying to hear you say that.

Lady Hunstanton. Ah, yes!—the moral qualities in women—that is the important thing. I am afraid, Caroline, that dear Lord Illingworth doesn't value the moral qualities in women as much as he should.

[Enter Lord Illingworth.]

Lady Stutfield. The world says that Lord Illingworth is very, very wicked.

Lord Illingworth. But what world says that, Lady Stutfield? It must be the next world. This world and I are on excellent terms. [Sits down beside Mrs. Allonby.]

Lady Stutfield. Every one I know says you are very, very wicked.

Lord Illingworth. It is perfectly monstrous the way people go about, nowadays, saying things against one behind one's back that are absolutely and entirely true.

Lady Hunstanton.   Dear Lord Illingworth is quite hopeless, Lady Stutfield. I have given up trying to reform him. It would take a Public Company with a Board of Directors and a paid Secretary to do that. But you have the secretary already, Lord Illingworth, haven't you? Gerald Arbuthnot has told us of his good fortune; it is really most kind of you.

Lord Illingworth.   Oh, don't say that, Lady Hunstanton. Kind is a dreadful word. I took a great fancy to young Arbuthnot the moment I met him, and he'll be of considerable use to me in something I am foolish enough to think of doing.

Lady Hunstanton.   He is an admirable young man. And his mother is one of my dearest friends. He has just gone for a walk with our pretty American. She is very pretty, is she not?

Lady Caroline.   Far too pretty. These American girls carry off all the good matches. Why can't they stay in their own country? They are always telling us it is the Paradise of women.

Lord Illingworth.   It is, Lady Caroline. That is why, like Eve, they are so extremely anxious to get out of it.

Lady Caroline.   Who are Miss Worsley's parents?

Lord Illingworth.   American women are wonderfully clever in concealing their parents.

Lady Hunstanton.   My dear Lord Illingworth, what do you mean? Miss Worsley, Caroline, is an orphan. Her father was a very wealthy millionaire or philanthropist, or both, I believe, who entertained my son quite hospitably, when he visited Boston. I don't know how he made his money, originally.

Kelvil.   I fancy in American dry goods.

Lady Hunstanton.   What are American dry goods?

Lord Illingworth.   American novels.

Lady Hunstanton.   How very singular! . . . Well, from whatever source her large fortune came, I have a great esteem for Miss Worsley. She dresses exceedingly well. All Americans do dress well. They get their clothes in Paris.

Mrs. Allonby. They say, Lady Hunstanton, that when good Americans die they go to Paris.

Lady Hunstanton. Indeed? And when bad Americans die, where do they go to?

Lord Illingworth. Oh, they go to America.

Kelvil. I am afraid you don't appreciate America, Lord Illingworth. It is a very remarkable country, especially considering its youth.

Lord Illingworth. The youth of America is their oldest tradition. It has been going on now for three hundred years. To hear them talk one would imagine they were in their first childhood. As far as civilisation goes they are in their second.

Kelvil. There is undoubtedly a great deal of corruption in American politics. I suppose you allude to that?

Lord Illingworth. I wonder.

Lady Hunstanton. Politics are in a sad way everywhere, I am told. They certainly are in England. Dear Mr. Cardew is ruining the country. I wonder Mrs. Cardew allows him. I am sure, Lord Illingworth, you don't think that uneducated people should be allowed to have votes?

Lord Illingworth. I think they are the only people who should.

Kelvil. Do you take no side then in modern politics, Lord Illingworth?

Lord Illingworth. One should never take sides in anything, Mr. Kelvil. Taking sides is the beginning of sincerity, and earnestness follows shortly afterwards, and the human being becomes a bore. However, the House of Commons really does very little harm. You can't make people good by Act of Parliament,—that is something.

Kelvil. You cannot deny that the House of Commons has always shown great sympathy with the sufferings of the poor.

Lord Illingworth. That is its special vice. That is the special vice of the age. One should sympathise with the joy, the beauty, the colour of life. The less said about life's sores the better, Mr. Kelvil.

Kelvil. Still our East End is a very important problem.

Lord Illingworth. Quite so. It is the problem of slavery. And we are trying to solve it by amusing the slaves.

Lady Hunstanton. Certainly, a great deal may be done by means of cheap entertainments, as you say, Lord Illingworth. Dear Dr. Daubeny, our rector here, provides, with the assistance of his curates, really admirable recreations for the poor during the winter. And much good may be done by means of a magic lantern, or a missionary, or some popular amusement of that kind.

Lady Caroline. I am not at all in favour of amusements for the poor, Jane. Blankets and coals are sufficient. There is too much love of pleasure amongst the upper classes as it is. Health is what we want in modern life. The tone is not healthy, not healthy at all.

Kelvil. You are quite right, Lady Caroline.

Lady Caroline. I believe I am usually right.

Mrs. Allonby. Horrid word 'health.'

Lord Illingworth. Silliest word in our language, and one knows so well the popular idea of health. The English country gentleman galloping after a fox—the unspeakable in full pursuit of the uneatable.

Kelvil. May I ask, Lord Illingworth, if you regard the House of Lords as a better institution than the House of Commons?

Lord Illingworth. A much better institution, of course. We in the House of Lords are never in touch with public opinion. That makes us a civilised body.

Kelvil. Are you serious in putting forward such a view?

Lord Illingworth. Quite serious, Mr. Kelvil. [To Mrs. Allonby.] Vulgar habit that is people have nowadays of asking one, after one has given them an idea, whether one is serious or not. Nothing is serious except passion. The intellect is not a serious thing, and never has been. It is an instrument on which one plays, that is all. The only serious form of intellect I know is the British intellect. And on the British intellect the illiterates play the drum.

Lady Hunstanton. What are you saying, Lord Illingworth, about the drum?

Lord Illingworth. I was merely talking to Mrs. Allonby about the leading articles in the London newspapers.

Lady Hunstanton. But do you believe all that is written in the newspapers?

Lord Illingworth. I do. Nowadays it is only the unreadable that occurs. [Rises with Mrs. Allonby.]

Lady Hunstanton. Are you going, Mrs. Allonby?

Mrs. Allonby. Just as far as the conservatory. Lord Illingworth told me this morning that there was an orchid there as beautiful as the seven deadly sins.

Lady Hunstanton. My dear, I hope there is nothing of the kind. I will certainly speak to the gardener.

[Exit Mrs. Allonby and Lord Illingworth.]

Lady Caroline. Remarkable type, Mrs. Allonby.

Lady Hunstanton. She lets her clever tongue run away with her sometimes.

Lady Caroline. Is that the only thing, Jane, Mrs. Allonby allows to run away with her?

Lady Hunstanton. I hope so, Caroline, I am sure.

[Enter Lord Alfred.]

Dear Lord Alfred, do join us. [Lord Alfred sits down beside Lady Stutfield.]

Lady Caroline. You believe good of every one, Jane. It is a great fault.

Lady Stutfield. Do you really, really think, Lady Caroline, that one should believe evil of every one?

Lady Caroline. I think it is much safer to do so, Lady Stutfield. Until, of course, people are found out to be good. But that requires a great deal of investigation nowadays.

Lady Stutfield. But there is so much unkind scandal in modern life.

Lady Caroline. Lord Illingworth remarked to me last night at dinner that the basis of every scandal is an absolutely immoral certainty.

Kelvil. Lord Illingworth is, of course, a very brilliant man, but he seems to me to be lacking in that fine faith in the nobility and purity of life which is so important in this century.

Lady Stutfield. Yes, quite, quite important, is it not?

Kelvil. He gives me the impression of a man who does not appreciate the beauty of our English home-life. I would say that he was tainted with foreign ideas on the subject.

Lady Stutfield. There is nothing, nothing like the beauty of home-life, is there?

Kelvil. It is the mainstay of our moral system in England, Lady Stutfield. Without it we would become like our neighbours.

Lady Stutfield. That would be so, so sad, would it not?

Kelvil. I am afraid, too, that Lord Illingworth regards woman simply as a toy. Now, I have never regarded woman as a toy. Woman is the intellectual helpmeet of man in public as in private life. Without her we should forget the true ideals. [Sits down beside Lady Stutfield.]

Lady Stutfield. I am so very, very glad to hear you say that.

Lady Caroline. You a married man, Mr. Kettle?

Sir John. Kelvil, dear, Kelvil.

Kelvil. I am married, Lady Caroline.

Lady Caroline. Family?

Kelvil. Yes.

Lady Caroline. How many?

Kelvil. Eight.

[Lady Stutfield turns her attention to Lord Alfred.]

Lady Caroline. Mrs. Kettle and the children are, I suppose, at the seaside? [Sir John shrugs his shoulders.]

Kelvil. My wife is at the seaside with the children, Lady Caroline.

Lady Caroline. You will join them later on, no doubt?

Kelvil. If my public engagements permit me.

Lady Caroline. Your public life must be a great source of gratification to Mrs. Kettle.

Sir John. Kelvil, my love, Kelvil.

Lady Stutfield. [To Lord Alfred.] How very, very charming those gold-tipped cigarettes of yours are, Lord Alfred.

Lord Alfred. They are awfully expensive. I can only afford them when I'm in debt.

Lady Stutfield. It must be terribly, terribly distressing to be in debt.

Lord Alfred. One must have some occupation nowadays. If I hadn't my debts I shouldn't have anything to think about. All the chaps I know are in debt.

Lady Stutfield. But don't the people to whom you owe the money give you a great, great deal of annoyance?

[Enter Footman.]

Lord Alfred. Oh, no, they write; I don't.

Lady Stutfield. How very, very strange.

Lady Hunstanton. Ah, here is a letter, Caroline, from dear Mrs. Arbuthnot. She won't dine. I am so sorry. But she will come in the evening. I am very pleased indeed. She is one of the sweetest of women. Writes a beautiful hand, too, so large, so firm. [Hands letter to Lady Caroline.]

Lady Caroline. [Looking at it.] A little lacking in femininity, Jane. Femininity is the quality I admire most in women.

Lady Hunstanton. [Taking back letter and leaving it on table.] Oh! she is very feminine, Caroline, and so good too. You should hear what the Archdeacon says of her. He regards her as his right hand in the parish. [Footman speaks to her.] In the Yellow Drawing-room. Shall we all go in? Lady Stutfield, shall we go in to tea?

Lady Stutfield. With pleasure, Lady Hunstanton. [They rise and proceed to go off. Sir John offers to carry Lady Stutfield's cloak.]

Lady Caroline. John! If you would allow your nephew to look after Lady Stutfield's cloak, you might help me with my workbasket.

[Enter Lord Illingworth and Mrs. Allonby.]

Sir John. Certainly, my love. [Exeunt.]

Mrs. Allonby. Curious thing, plain women are always jealous of their husbands, beautiful women never are!

Lord Illingworth. Beautiful women never have time. They are always so occupied in being jealous of other people's husbands.

Mrs. Allonby. I should have thought Lady Caroline would have grown tired of conjugal anxiety by this time! Sir John is her fourth!

Lord Illingworth. So much marriage is certainly not becoming. Twenty

210

years of romance make a woman look like a ruin; but twenty years of marriage make her something like a public building.

Mrs. Allonby. Twenty years of romance! Is there such a thing?

Lord Illingworth. Not in our day. Women have become too brilliant. Nothing spoils a romance so much as a sense of humour in the woman.

Mrs. Allonby. Or the want of it in the man.

Lord Illingworth. You are quite right. In a Temple every one should be serious, except the thing that is worshipped.

Mrs. Allonby. And that should be man?

Lord Illingworth. Women kneel so gracefully; men don't.

Mrs. Allonby. You are thinking of Lady Stutfield!

Lord Illingworth. I assure you I have not thought of Lady Stutfield for the last quarter of an hour.

Mrs. Allonby. Is she such a mystery?

Lord Illingworth. She is more than a mystery—she is a mood.

Mrs. Allonby. Moods don't last.

Lord Illingworth. It is their chief charm.

[Enter Hester and Gerald.]

Gerald. Lord Illingworth, every one has been congratulating me, Lady Hunstanton and Lady Caroline, and . . . every one. I hope I shall make a good secretary.

Lord Illingworth. You will be the pattern secretary, Gerald. [Talks to him.]

Mrs. Allonby. You enjoy country life, Miss Worsley?

Hester. Very much indeed.

Mrs. Allonby. Don't find yourself longing for a London dinner-party?

Hester. I dislike London dinner-parties.

Mrs. Allonby. I adore them. The clever people never listen, and the stupid people never talk.

Hester. I think the stupid people talk a great deal.

Mrs. Allonby. Ah, I never listen!

Lord Illingworth. My dear boy, if I didn't like you I wouldn't have made you the offer. It is because I like you so much that I want to have you with me.

[Exit Hester with Gerald.]

Charming fellow, Gerald Arbuthnot!

Mrs. Allonby. He is very nice; very nice indeed. But I can't stand the American young lady.

Lord Illingworth. Why?

Mrs. Allonby. She told me yesterday, and in quite a loud voice too, that she was only eighteen. It was most annoying.

Lord Illingworth. One should never trust a woman who tells one her real age. A woman who would tell one that, would tell one anything.

Mrs. Allonby. She is a Puritan besides—

Lord Illingworth. Ah, that is inexcusable. I don't mind plain women being Puritans. It is the only excuse they have for being plain. But she is decidedly pretty. I admire her immensely. [Looks steadfastly at Mrs. Allonby.]

Mrs. Allonby. What a thoroughly bad man you must be!

Lord Illingworth. What do you call a bad man?

Mrs. Allonby. The sort of man who admires innocence.

Lord Illingworth. And a bad woman?

Mrs. Allonby. Oh! the sort of woman a man never gets tired of.

Lord Illingworth. You are severe—on yourself.

Mrs. Allonby. Define us as a sex.

Lord Illingworth. Sphinxes without secrets.

Mrs. Allonby. Does that include the Puritan women?

Lord Illingworth. Do you know, I don't believe in the existence of Puritan women? I don't think there is a woman in the world who would not be a little flattered if one made love to her. It is that which makes women so irresistibly adorable.

Mrs. Allonby. You think there is no woman in the world who would object to being kissed?

Lord Illingworth. Very few.

Mrs. Allonby. Miss Worsley would not let you kiss her.

Lord Illingworth. Are you sure?

Mrs. Allonby. Quite.

Lord Illingworth. What do you think she'd do if I kissed her?

Mrs. Allonby. Either marry you, or strike you across the face with her glove. What would you do if she struck you across the face with her glove?

Lord Illingworth. Fall in love with her, probably.

Mrs. Allonby. Then it is lucky you are not going to kiss her!

Lord Illingworth. Is that a challenge?

Mrs. Allonby. It is an arrow shot into the air.

Lord Illingworth. Don't you know that I always succeed in whatever I try?

Mrs. Allonby. I am sorry to hear it. We women adore failures. They lean on us.

Lord Illingworth. You worship successes. You cling to them.

Mrs. Allonby. We are the laurels to hide their baldness.

Lord Illingworth. And they need you always, except at the moment of triumph.

Mrs. Allonby. They are uninteresting then.

Lord Illingworth. How tantalising you are! [A pause.]

Mrs. Allonby. Lord Illingworth, there is one thing I shall always like you for.

Lord Illingworth. Only one thing? And I have so many bad qualities.

Mrs. Allonby. Ah, don't be too conceited about them. You may lose them as you grow old.

Lord Illingworth. I never intend to grow old. The soul is born old but grows young. That is the comedy of life.

Mrs. Allonby. And the body is born young and grows old. That is life's tragedy.

Lord Illingworth. Its comedy also, sometimes. But what is the mysterious reason why you will always like me?

Mrs. Allonby. It is that you have never made love to me.

Lord Illingworth. I have never done anything else.

Mrs. Allonby. Really? I have not noticed it.

Lord Illingworth. How fortunate! It might have been a tragedy for both of us.

Mrs. Allonby. We should each have survived.

Lord Illingworth. One can survive everything nowadays, except death, and live down anything except a good reputation.

Mrs. Allonby. Have you tried a good reputation?

Lord Illingworth. It is one of the many annoyances to which I have never been subjected.

Mrs. Allonby. It may come.

Lord Illingworth. Why do you threaten me?

Mrs. Allonby. I will tell you when you have kissed the Puritan.

[Enter Footman.]

Francis. Tea is served in the Yellow Drawing-room, my lord.

Lord Illingworth. Tell her ladyship we are coming in.

Francis. Yes, my lord.

[Exit.]

Lord Illingworth. Shall we go in to tea?

Mrs. Allonby. Do you like such simple pleasures?

Lord Illingworth. I adore simple pleasures. They are the last refuge of the complex. But, if you wish, let us stay here. Yes, let us stay here. The Book of Life begins with a man and a woman in a garden.

Mrs. Allonby. It ends with Revelations.

Lord Illingworth. You fence divinely. But the button has come of your foil.

Mrs. Allonby. I have still the mask.

Lord Illingworth. It makes your eyes lovelier.

Mrs. Allonby. Thank you. Come.

Lord Illingworth. [Sees Mrs. Arbuthnot's letter on table, and takes it up and looks at envelope.] What a curious handwriting! It reminds me of the handwriting of a woman I used to know years ago.

Mrs. Allonby. Who?

Lord Illingworth. Oh! no one. No one in particular. A woman of no

importance. [Throws letter down, and passes up the steps of the terrace with
Mrs. Allonby. They smile at each other.]

Act Drop.

SECOND ACT

SCENE

Drawing-room at Hunstanton, after dinner, lamps lit. Door L.C. Door R.C.

[Ladies seated on sofas.]

Mrs. Allonby. What a comfort it is to have got rid of the men for a little!

Lady Stutfield. Yes; men persecute us dreadfully, don't they?

Mrs. Allonby. Persecute us? I wish they did.

Lady Hunstanton. My dear!

Mrs. Allonby. The annoying thing is that the wretches can be perfectly happy without us. That is why I think it is every woman's duty never to leave them alone for a single moment, except during this short breathing space after dinner; without which I believe we poor women would be absolutely worn to shadows.

[Enter Servants with coffee.]

Lady Hunstanton. Worn to shadows, dear?

Mrs. Allonby. Yes, Lady Hunstanton. It is such a strain keeping men up to the mark. They are always trying to escape from us.

Lady Stutfield. It seems to me that it is we who are always trying to escape from them. Men are so very, very heartless. They know their power and use it.

Lady Caroline. [Takes coffee from Servant.] What stuff and nonsense all this about men is! The thing to do is to keep men in their proper place.

Mrs. Allonby. But what is their proper place, Lady Caroline?

Lady Caroline. Looking after their wives, Mrs. Allonby.

Mrs. Allonby. [Takes coffee from Servant.] Really? And if they're not married?

Lady Caroline. If they are not married, they should be looking after a wife. It's perfectly scandalous the amount of bachelors who are going about society. There should be a law passed to compel them all to marry within twelve months.

Lady Stutfield. [Refuses coffee.] But if they're in love with some one who, perhaps, is tied to another?

Lady Caroline. In that case, Lady Stutfield, they should be married off in a week to some plain respectable girl, in order to teach them not to meddle with other people's property.

Mrs. Allonby. I don't think that we should ever be spoken of as other people's property. All men are married women's property. That is the only true definition of what married women's property really is. But we don't belong to any one.

Lady Stutfield. Oh, I am so very, very glad to hear you say so.

Lady Hunstanton. But do you really think, dear Caroline, that legislation would improve matters in any way? I am told that, nowadays, all the married men live like bachelors, and all the bachelors like married men.

Mrs. Allonby. I certainly never know one from the other.

Lady Stutfield. Oh, I think one can always know at once whether a man has home claims upon his life or not. I have noticed a very, very sad expression in the eyes of so many married men.

Mrs. Allonby. Ah, all that I have noticed is that they are horribly tedious when they are good husbands, and abominably conceited when they are not.

Lady Hunstanton. Well, I suppose the type of husband has completely changed since my young days, but I'm bound to state that poor dear Hunstanton was the most delightful of creatures, and as good as gold.

Mrs. Allonby. Ah, my husband is a sort of promissory note; I'm tired of meeting him.

218

Lady Caroline. But you renew him from time to time, don't you?

Mrs. Allonby. Oh no, Lady Caroline. I have only had one husband as yet. I suppose you look upon me as quite an amateur.

Lady Caroline. With your views on life I wonder you married at all.

Mrs. Allonby. So do I.

Lady Hunstanton. My dear child, I believe you are really very happy in your married life, but that you like to hide your happiness from others.

Mrs. Allonby. I assure you I was horribly deceived in Ernest.

Lady Hunstanton. Oh, I hope not, dear. I knew his mother quite well. She was a Stratton, Caroline, one of Lord Crowland's daughters.

Lady Caroline. Victoria Stratton? I remember her perfectly. A silly fair-haired woman with no chin.

Mrs. Allonby. Ah, Ernest has a chin. He has a very strong chin, a square chin. Ernest's chin is far too square.

Lady Stutfield. But do you really think a man's chin can be too square? I think a man should look very, very strong, and that his chin should be quite, quite square.

Mrs. Allonby. Then you should certainly know Ernest, Lady Stutfield. It is only fair to tell you beforehand he has got no conversation at all.

Lady Stutfield. I adore silent men.

Mrs. Allonby. Oh, Ernest isn't silent. He talks the whole time. But he has got no conversation. What he talks about I don't know. I haven't listened to him for years.

Lady Stutfield. Have you never forgiven him then? How sad that seems! But all life is very, very sad, is it not?

Mrs. Allonby. Life, Lady Stutfield, is simply a mauvais quart d'heure made up of exquisite moments.

Lady Stutfield. Yes, there are moments, certainly. But was it something very, very wrong that Mr. Allonby did? Did he become angry with you, and say anything that was unkind or true?

Mrs. Allonby. Oh dear, no. Ernest is invariably calm. That is one of the reasons he always gets on my nerves. Nothing is so aggravating as calmness. There is something positively brutal about the good temper of most modern men. I wonder we women stand it as well as we do.

Lady Stutfield. Yes; men's good temper shows they are not so sensitive as we are, not so finely strung. It makes a great barrier often between husband and wife, does it not? But I would so much like to know what was the wrong thing Mr. Allonby did.

Mrs. Allonby. Well, I will tell you, if you solemnly promise to tell everybody else.

Lady Stutfield. Thank you, thank you. I will make a point of repeating it.

Mrs. Allonby. When Ernest and I were engaged, he swore to me positively on his knees that he had never loved any one before in the whole course of his life. I was very young at the time, so I didn't believe him, I needn't tell you. Unfortunately, however, I made no enquiries of any kind till after I had been actually married four or five months. I found out then that what he had told me was perfectly true. And that sort of thing makes a man so absolutely uninteresting.

Lady Hunstanton. My dear!

Mrs. Allonby. Men always want to be a woman's first love. That is their clumsy vanity. We women have a more subtle instinct about things. What we like is to be a man's last romance.

Lady Stutfield. I see what you mean. It's very, very beautiful.

Lady Hunstanton. My dear child, you don't mean to tell me that you won't forgive your husband because he never loved any one else? Did you ever hear such a thing, Caroline? I am quite surprised.

220

Lady Caroline. Oh, women have become so highly educated, Jane, that nothing should surprise us nowadays, except happy marriages. They apparently are getting remarkably rare.

Mrs. Allonby. Oh, they're quite out of date.

Lady Stutfield. Except amongst the middle classes, I have been told.

Mrs. Allonby. How like the middle classes!

Lady Stutfield. Yes—is it not?—very, very like them.

Lady Caroline. If what you tell us about the middle classes is true, Lady Stutfield, it redounds greatly to their credit. It is much to be regretted that in our rank of life the wife should be so persistently frivolous, under the impression apparently that it is the proper thing to be. It is to that I attribute the unhappiness of so many marriages we all know of in society.

Mrs. Allonby. Do you know, Lady Caroline, I don't think the frivolity of the wife has ever anything to do with it. More marriages are ruined nowadays by the common sense of the husband than by anything else. How can a woman be expected to be happy with a man who insists on treating her as if she were a perfectly rational being?

Lady Hunstanton. My dear!

Mrs. Allonby. Man, poor, awkward, reliable, necessary man belongs to a sex that has been rational for millions and millions of years. He can't help himself. It is in his race. The History of Woman is very different. We have always been picturesque protests against the mere existence of common sense. We saw its dangers from the first.

Lady Stutfield. Yes, the common sense of husbands is certainly most, most trying. Do tell me your conception of the Ideal Husband. I think it would be so very, very helpful.

Mrs. Allonby. The Ideal Husband? There couldn't be such a thing. The institution is wrong.

Lady Stutfield. The Ideal Man, then, in his relations to us.

Lady Caroline. He would probably be extremely realistic.

Mrs. Caroline. The Ideal Man! Oh, the Ideal Man should talk to us as if we were goddesses, and treat us as if we were children. He should refuse all our serious requests, and gratify every one of our whims. He should encourage us to have caprices, and forbid us to have missions. He should always say much more than he means, and always mean much more than he says.

Lady Hunstanton. But how could he do both, dear?

Mrs. Allonby. He should never run down other pretty women. That would show he had no taste, or make one suspect that he had too much. No; he should be nice about them all, but say that somehow they don't attract him.

Lady Stutfield. Yes, that is always very, very pleasant to hear about other women.

Mrs. Allonby. If we ask him a question about anything, he should give us an answer all about ourselves. He should invariably praise us for whatever qualities he knows we haven't got. But he should be pitiless, quite pitiless, in reproaching us for the virtues that we have never dreamed of possessing. He should never believe that we know the use of useful things. That would be unforgiveable. But he should shower on us everything we don't want.

Lady Caroline. As far as I can see, he is to do nothing but pay bills and compliments.

Mrs. Allonby. He should persistently compromise us in public, and treat us with absolute respect when we are alone. And yet he should be always ready to have a perfectly terrible scene, whenever we want one, and to become miserable, absolutely miserable, at a moment's notice, and to overwhelm us with just reproaches in less than twenty minutes, and to be positively violent at the end of half an hour, and to leave us for ever at a quarter to eight, when we have to go and dress for dinner. And when, after that, one has seen him for really the last time, and he has refused to take back the little things he has given one, and promised never to communicate with one again, or to write one any foolish letters, he should be perfectly broken-hearted, and telegraph

222

to one all day long, and send one little notes every half-hour by a private hansom, and dine quite alone at the club, so that every one should know how unhappy he was. And after a whole dreadful week, during which one has gone about everywhere with one's husband, just to show how absolutely lonely one was, he may be given a third last parting, in the evening, and then, if his conduct has been quite irreproachable, and one has behaved really badly to him, he should be allowed to admit that he has been entirely in the wrong, and when he has admitted that, it becomes a woman's duty to forgive, and one can do it all over again from the beginning, with variations.

Lady Hunstanton. How clever you are, my dear! You never mean a single word you say.

Lady Stutfield. Thank you, thank you. It has been quite, quite entrancing. I must try and remember it all. There are such a number of details that are so very, very important.

Lady Caroline. But you have not told us yet what the reward of the Ideal Man is to be.

Mrs. Allonby. His reward? Oh, infinite expectation. That is quite enough for him.

Lady Stutfield. But men are so terribly, terribly exacting, are they not?

Mrs. Allonby. That makes no matter. One should never surrender.

Lady Stutfield. Not even to the Ideal Man?

Mrs. Allonby. Certainly not to him. Unless, of course, one wants to grow tired of him.

Lady Stutfield. Oh! . . . yes. I see that. It is very, very helpful. Do you think, Mrs. Allonby, I shall ever meet the Ideal Man? Or are there more than one?

Mrs. Allonby. There are just four in London, Lady Stutfield.

Lady Hunstanton. Oh, my dear!

Mrs. Allonby. [Going over to her.] What has happened? Do tell me.

223

Lady Hunstanton [in a low voice] I had completely forgotten that the American young lady has been in the room all the time. I am afraid some of this clever talk may have shocked her a little.

Mrs. Allonby. Ah, that will do her so much good!

Lady Hunstanton. Let us hope she didn't understand much. I think I had better go over and talk to her. [Rises and goes across to Hester Worsley.] Well, dear Miss Worsley. [Sitting down beside her.] How quiet you have been in your nice little corner all this time! I suppose you have been reading a book? There are so many books here in the library.

Hester. No, I have been listening to the conversation.

Lady Hunstanton. You mustn't believe everything that was said, you know, dear.

Hester. I didn't believe any of it

Lady Hunstanton. That is quite right, dear.

Hester. [Continuing.] I couldn't believe that any women could really hold such views of life as I have heard to-night from some of your guests. [An awkward pause.]

Lady Hunstanton. I hear you have such pleasant society in America. Quite like our own in places, my son wrote to me.

Hester. There are cliques in America as elsewhere, Lady Hunstanton. But true American society consists simply of all the good women and good men we have in our country.

Lady Hunstanton. What a sensible system, and I dare say quite pleasant too. I am afraid in England we have too many artificial social barriers. We don't see as much as we should of the middle and lower classes.

Hester. In America we have no lower classes.

Lady Hunstanton. Really? What a very strange arrangement!

Mrs. Allonby. What is that dreadful girl talking about?

224

Lady Stutfield. She is painfully natural, is she not?

Lady Caroline. There are a great many things you haven't got in America, I am told, Miss Worsley. They say you have no ruins, and no curiosities.

Mrs. Allonby. [To Lady Stutfield.] What nonsense! They have their mothers and their manners.

Hester. The English aristocracy supply us with our curiosities, Lady Caroline. They are sent over to us every summer, regularly, in the steamers, and propose to us the day after they land. As for ruins, we are trying to build up something that will last longer than brick or stone. [Gets up to take her fan from table.]

Lady Hunstanton. What is that, dear? Ah, yes, an iron Exhibition, is it not, at that place that has the curious name?

Hester. [Standing by table.] We are trying to build up life, Lady Hunstanton, on a better, truer, purer basis than life rests on here. This sounds strange to you all, no doubt. How could it sound other than strange? You rich people in England, you don't know how you are living. How could you know? You shut out from your society the gentle and the good. You laugh at the simple and the pure. Living, as you all do, on others and by them, you sneer at self-sacrifice, and if you throw bread to the poor, it is merely to keep them quiet for a season. With all your pomp and wealth and art you don't know how to live—you don't even know that. You love the beauty that you can see and touch and handle, the beauty that you can destroy, and do destroy, but of the unseen beauty of life, of the unseen beauty of a higher life, you know nothing. You have lost life's secret. Oh, your English society seems to me shallow, selfish, foolish. It has blinded its eyes, and stopped its ears. It lies like a leper in purple. It sits like a dead thing smeared with gold. It is all wrong, all wrong.

Lady Stutfield. I don't think one should know of these things. It is not very, very nice, is it?

Lady Hunstanton. My dear Miss Worsley, I thought you liked English society so much. You were such a success in it. And you were so much admired by the best people. I quite forget what Lord Henry Weston said of you—but it was most complimentary, and you know what an authority he is on beauty.

Hester. Lord Henry Weston! I remember him, Lady Hunstanton. A man with a hideous smile and a hideous past. He is asked everywhere. No dinner-party is complete without him. What of those whose ruin is due to him? They are outcasts. They are nameless. If you met them in the street you would turn your head away. I don't complain of their punishment. Let all women who have sinned be punished.

[Mrs. Arbuthnot enters from terrace behind in a cloak with a lace veil over her head. She hears the last words and starts.]

Lady Hunstanton. My dear young lady!

Hester. It is right that they should be punished, but don't let them be the only ones to suffer. If a man and woman have sinned, let them both go forth into the desert to love or loathe each other there. Let them both be branded. Set a mark, if you wish, on each, but don't punish the one and let the other go free. Don't have one law for men and another for women. You are unjust to women in England. And till you count what is a shame in a woman to be an infamy in a man, you will always be unjust, and Right, that pillar of fire, and Wrong, that pillar of cloud, will be made dim to your eyes, or be not seen at all, or if seen, not regarded.

Lady Caroline. Might I, dear Miss Worsley, as you are standing up, ask you for my cotton that is just behind you? Thank you.

Lady Hunstanton. My dear Mrs. Arbuthnot! I am so pleased you have come up. But I didn't hear you announced.

Mrs. Allonby. Oh, I came straight in from the terrace, Lady Hunstanton, just as I was. You didn't tell me you had a party.

Lady Hunstanton. Not a party. Only a few guests who are staying in the house, and whom you must know. Allow me. [Tries to help her. Rings bell.] Caroline, this is Mrs. Arbuthnot, one of my sweetest friends. Lady

Caroline Pontefract, Lady Stutfield, Mrs. Allonby, and my young American friend, Miss Worsley, who has just been telling us all how wicked we are.

Hester. I am afraid you think I spoke too strongly, Lady Hunstanton. But there are some things in England—

Lady Hunstanton. My dear young lady, there was a great deal of truth, I dare say, in what you said, and you looked very pretty while you said it, which is much more important, Lord Illingworth would tell us. The only point where I thought you were a little hard was about Lady Caroline's brother, about poor Lord Henry. He is really such good company.

[Enter Footman.]

Take Mrs. Arbuthnot's things.

[Exit Footman with wraps.]

Hester. Lady Caroline, I had no idea it was your brother. I am sorry for the pain I must have caused you—I—

Lady Caroline. My dear Miss Worsley, the only part of your little speech, if I may so term it, with which I thoroughly agreed, was the part about my brother. Nothing that you could possibly say could be too bad for him. I regard Henry as infamous, absolutely infamous. But I am bound to state, as you were remarking, Jane, that he is excellent company, and he has one of the best cooks in London, and after a good dinner one can forgive anybody, even one's own relations.

Lady Hunstanton [to Miss Worsley] Now, do come, dear, and make friends with Mrs. Arbuthnot. She is one of the good, sweet, simple people you told us we never admitted into society. I am sorry to say Mrs. Arbuthnot comes very rarely to me. But that is not my fault.

Mrs. Allonby. What a bore it is the men staying so long after dinner! I expect they are saying the most dreadful things about us.

Lady Stutfield. Do you really think so?

Mrs. Allonby. I was sure of it.

Lady Stutfield. How very, very horrid of them! Shall we go onto the terrace?

Mrs. Allonby. Oh, anything to get away from the dowagers and the dowdies. [Rises and goes with Lady Stutfield to door L.C.] We are only going to look at the stars, Lady Hunstanton.

Lady Hunstanton. You will find a great many, dear, a great many. But don't catch cold. [To Mrs. Arbuthnot.] We shall all miss Gerald so much, dear Mrs. Arbuthnot.

Mrs. Arbuthnot. But has Lord Illingworth really offered to make Gerald his secretary?

Lady Hunstanton. Oh, yes! He has been most charming about it. He has the highest possible opinion of your boy. You don't know Lord Illingworth, I believe, dear.

Mrs. Arbuthnot. I have never met him.

Lady Hunstanton. You know him by name, no doubt?

Mrs. Arbuthnot. I am afraid I don't. I live so much out of the world, and see so few people. I remember hearing years ago of an old Lord Illingworth who lived in Yorkshire, I think.

Lady Hunstanton. Ah, yes. That would be the last Earl but one. He was a very curious man. He wanted to marry beneath him. Or wouldn't, I believe. There was some scandal about it. The present Lord Illingworth is quite different. He is very distinguished. He does—well, he does nothing, which I am afraid our pretty American visitor here thinks very wrong of anybody, and I don't know that he cares much for the subjects in which you are so interested, dear Mrs. Arbuthnot. Do you think, Caroline, that Lord Illingworth is interested in the Housing of the Poor?

Lady Caroline. I should fancy not at all, Jane.

Lady Hunstanton. We all have our different tastes, have we not? But Lord Illingworth has a very high position, and there is nothing he couldn't get if he chose to ask for it. Of course, he is comparatively a young man still, and he has only come to his title within—how long exactly is it, Caroline, since Lord Illingworth succeeded?

Lady Caroline. About four years, I think, Jane. I know it was the same year in which my brother had his last exposure in the evening newspapers.

Lady Hunstanton. Ah, I remember. That would be about four years ago. Of course, there were a great many people between the present Lord Illingworth and the title, Mrs. Arbuthnot. There was—who was there, Caroline?

Lady Caroline. There was poor Margaret's baby. You remember how anxious she was to have a boy, and it was a boy, but it died, and her husband died shortly afterwards, and she married almost immediately one of Lord Ascot's sons, who, I am told, beats her.

Lady Hunstanton. Ah, that is in the family, dear, that is in the family. And there was also, I remember, a clergyman who wanted to be a lunatic, or a lunatic who wanted to be a clergyman, I forget which, but I know the Court of Chancery investigated the matter, and decided that he was quite sane. And I saw him afterwards at poor Lord Plumstead's with straws in his hair, or something very odd about him. I can't recall what. I often regret, Lady Caroline, that dear Lady Cecilia never lived to see her son get the title.

Mrs. Arbuthnot. Lady Cecilia?

Lady Hunstanton. Lord Illingworth's mother, dear Mrs. Arbuthnot, was one of the Duchess of Jerningham's pretty daughters, and she married Sir Thomas Harford, who wasn't considered a very good match for her at the time, though he was said to be the handsomest man in London. I knew them all quite intimately, and both the sons, Arthur and George.

Mrs. Arbuthnot. It was the eldest son who succeeded, of course, Lady Hunstanton?

Lady Hunstanton. No, dear, he was killed in the hunting field. Or was it fishing, Caroline? I forget. But George came in for everything. I always tell him that no younger son has ever had such good luck as he has had.

Mrs. Arbuthnot. Lady Hunstanton, I want to speak to Gerald at once. Might I see him? Can he be sent for?

Lady Hunstanton. Certainly, dear. I will send one of the servants into the dining-room to fetch him. I don't know what keeps the gentlemen so long. [Rings bell.] When I knew Lord Illingworth first as plain George Harford, he was simply a very brilliant young man about town, with not a penny of money except what poor dear Lady Cecilia gave him. She was quite devoted to him. Chiefly, I fancy, because he was on bad terms with his father. Oh, here is the dear Archdeacon. [To Servant.] It doesn't matter.

[Enter Sir John and Doctor Daubeny. Sir John goes over to Lady Stutfield, Doctor Daubeny to Lady Hunstanton.]

The Archdeacon. Lord Illingworth has been most entertaining. I have never enjoyed myself more. [Sees Mrs. Arbuthnot.] Ah, Mrs. Arbuthnot.

Lady Hunstanton. [To Doctor Baubeny.] You see I have got Mrs. Arbuthnot to come to me at last.

The Archdeacon. That is a great honour, Lady Hunstanton. Mrs. Daubeny will be quite jealous of you.

Lady Hunstanton. Ah, I am so sorry Mrs. Daubeny could not come with you to-night. Headache as usual, I suppose.

The Archdeacon. Yes, Lady Hunstanton; a perfect martyr. But she is happiest alone. She is happiest alone.

Lady Caroline. [To her husband.] John! [Sir John goes over to his wife. Doctor Baubeny talks to Lady Hunstanton and Mrs. Arbuthnot.]

[Mrs. Arbuthnot watches Lord Illingworth the whole time. He has passed across the room without noticing her, and approaches Mrs. Allonby, who with Lady Stutfield is standing by the door looking on to the terrace.]

Lord Illingworth. How is the most charming woman in the world?

Mrs. Allonby. [Taking Lady Stutfield by the hand.] We are both quite

230

well, thank you, Lord Illingworth. But what a short time you have been in the dining-room! It seems as if we had only just left.

Lord Illingworth. I was bored to death. Never opened my lips the whole time. Absolutely longing to come in to you.

Mrs. Allonby. You should have. The American girl has been giving us a lecture.

Lord Illingworth. Really? All Americans lecture, I believe. I suppose it is something in their climate. What did she lecture about?

Mrs. Allonby. Oh, Puritanism, of course.

Lord Illingworth. I am going to convert her, am I not? How long do you give me?

Mrs. Allonby. A week.

Lord Illingworth. A week is more than enough.

[Enter Gerald and Lord Alfred.]

Gerald. [Going to Mrs. Arbuthnot.] Dear mother!

Mrs. Arbuthnot. Gerald, I don't feel at all well. See me home, Gerald. I shouldn't have come.

Gerald. I am so sorry, mother. Certainly. But you must know Lord Illingworth first. [Goes across room.]

Mrs. Arbuthnot. Not to-night, Gerald.

Gerald. Lord Illingworth, I want you so much to know my mother.

Lord Illingworth. With the greatest pleasure. [To Mrs. Allonby.] I'll be back in a moment. People's mothers always bore me to death. All women become like their mothers. That is their tragedy.

Mrs. Allonby. No man does. That is his.

Lord Illingworth. What a delightful mood you are in to-night! [Turns

231

round and goes across with Gerald to Mrs. Arbuthnot. When he sees her, he starts back in wonder. Then slowly his eyes turn towards Gerald.]

Gerald. Mother, this is Lord Illingworth, who has offered to take me as his private secretary. [Mrs. Arbuthnot bows coldly.] It is a wonderful opening for me, isn't it? I hope he won't be disappointed in me, that is all. You'll thank Lord Illingworth, mother, won't you?

Mrs. Arbuthnot. Lord Illingworth in very good, I am sure, to interest himself in you for the moment.

Lord Illingworth. [Putting his hand on Gerald's shoulder.] Oh, Gerald and I are great friends already, Mrs . . . Arbuthnot.

Mrs. Arbuthnot. There can be nothing in common between you and my son, Lord Illingworth.

Gerald. Dear mother, how can you say so? Of course Lord Illingworth is awfully clever and that sort of thing. There is nothing Lord Illingworth doesn't know.

Lord Illingworth. My dear boy!

Gerald. He knows more about life than any one I have ever met. I feel an awful duffer when I am with you, Lord Illingworth. Of course, I have had so few advantages. I have not been to Eton or Oxford like other chaps. But Lord Illingworth doesn't seem to mind that. He has been awfully good to me, mother.

Mrs. Arbuthnot. Lord Illingworth may change his mind. He may not really want you as his secretary.

Gerald. Mother!

Mrs. Arbuthnot. You must remember, as you said yourself, you have had so few advantages.

Mrs. Allonby. Lord Illingworth, I want to speak to you for a moment. Do come over.

Lord Illingworth. Will you excuse me, Mrs. Arbuthnot? Now, don't let your charming mother make any more difficulties, Gerald. The thing is quite settled, isn't it?

Gerald. I hope so. [Lord Illingworth goes across to Mrs. Arbuthnot.]

Mrs. Allonby. I thought you were never going to leave the lady in black velvet.

Lord Illingworth. She is excessively handsome. [Looks at Mrs. Arbuthnot.]

Lady Hunstanton. Caroline, shall we all make a move to the music-room? Miss Worsley is going to play. You'll come too, dear Mrs. Arbuthnot, won't you? You don't know what a treat is in store for you. [To Doctor Baubeny.] I must really take Miss Worsley down some afternoon to the rectory. I should so much like dear Mrs. Daubeny to hear her on the violin. Ah, I forgot. Dear Mrs. Daubeny's hearing is a little defective, is it not?

The Archdeacon. Her deafness is a great privation to her. She can't even hear my sermons now. She reads them at home. But she has many resources in herself, many resources.

Lady Hunstanton. She reads a good deal, I suppose?

The Archdeacon. Just the very largest print. The eyesight is rapidly going. But she's never morbid, never morbid.

Gerald. [To Lord Illingworth.] Do speak to my mother, Lord Illingworth, before you go into the music-room. She seems to think, somehow, you don't mean what you said to me.

Mrs. Allonby. Aren't you coming?

Lord Illingworth. In a few moments. Lady Hunstanton, if Mrs. Arbuthnot would allow me, I would like to say a few words to her, and we will join you later on.

Lady Hunstanton. Ah, of course. You will have a great deal to say to her, and she will have a great deal to thank you for. It is not every son who gets such an offer, Mrs. Arbuthnot. But I know you appreciate that, dear.

Lady Caroline. John!

Lady Hunstanton. Now, don't keep Mrs. Arbuthnot too long, Lord Illingworth. We can't spare her.

[Exit following the other guests. Sound of violin heard from music-room.]

Lord Illingworth. So that is our son, Rachel! Well, I am very proud of him. He in a Harford, every inch of him. By the way, why Arbuthnot, Rachel?

Mrs. Arbuthnot. One name is as good as another, when one has no right to any name.

Lord Illingworth. I suppose so—but why Gerald?

Mrs. Arbuthnot. After a man whose heart I broke—after my father.

Lord Illingworth. Well, Rachel, what in over is over. All I have got to say now in that I am very, very much pleased with our boy. The world will know him merely as my private secretary, but to me he will be something very near, and very dear. It is a curious thing, Rachel; my life seemed to be quite complete. It was not so. It lacked something, it lacked a son. I have found my son now, I am glad I have found him.

Mrs. Arbuthnot. You have no right to claim him, or the smallest part of him. The boy is entirely mine, and shall remain mine.

Lord Illingworth. My dear Rachel, you have had him to yourself for over twenty years. Why not let me have him for a little now? He is quite as much mine as yours.

Mrs. Arbuthnot. Are you talking of the child you abandoned? Of the child who, as far as you are concerned, might have died of hunger and of want?

Lord Illingworth. You forget, Rachel, it was you who left me. It was not I who left you.

Mrs. Arbuthnot. I left you because you refused to give the child a name.

234

Before my son was born, I implored you to marry me.

Lord Illingworth. I had no expectations then. And besides, Rachel, I wasn't much older than you were. I was only twenty-two. I was twenty-one, I believe, when the whole thing began in your father's garden.

Mrs. Arbuthnot. When a man is old enough to do wrong he should be old enough to do right also.

Lord Illingworth. My dear Rachel, intellectual generalities are always interesting, but generalities in morals mean absolutely nothing. As for saying I left our child to starve, that, of course, is untrue and silly. My mother offered you six hundred a year. But you wouldn't take anything. You simply disappeared, and carried the child away with you.

Mrs. Arbuthnot. I wouldn't have accepted a penny from her. Your father was different. He told you, in my presence, when we were in Paris, that it was your duty to marry me.

Lord Illingworth. Oh, duty is what one expects from others, it is not what one does oneself. Of course, I was influenced by my mother. Every man is when he is young.

Mrs. Arbuthnot. I am glad to hear you say so. Gerald shall certainly not go away with you.

Lord Illingworth. What nonsense, Rachel!

Mrs. Arbuthnot. Do you think I would allow my son—

Lord Illingworth. Our son.

Mrs. Arbuthnot. My son [Lord Illingworth shrugs his shoulders]—to go away with the man who spoiled my youth, who ruined my life, who has tainted every moment of my days? You don't realise what my past has been in suffering and in shame.

Lord Illingworth. My dear Rachel, I must candidly say that I think Gerald's future considerably more important than your past.

Mrs. Arbuthnot. Gerald cannot separate his future from my past.

Lord Illingworth. That is exactly what he should do. That is exactly what you should help him to do. What a typical woman you are! You talk sentimentally, and you are thoroughly selfish the whole time. But don't let us have a scene. Rachel, I want you to look at this matter from the common-sense point of view, from the point of view of what is best for our son, leaving you and me out of the question. What is our son at present? An underpaid clerk in a small Provincial Bank in a third-rate English town. If you imagine he is quite happy in such a position, you are mistaken. He is thoroughly discontented.

Mrs. Arbuthnot. He was not discontented till he met you. You have made him so.

Lord Illingworth. Of course, I made him so. Discontent is the first step in the progress of a man or a nation. But I did not leave him with a mere longing for things he could not get. No, I made him a charming offer. He jumped at it, I need hardly say. Any young man would. And now, simply because it turns out that I am the boy's own father and he my own son, you propose practically to ruin his career. That is to say, if I were a perfect stranger, you would allow Gerald to go away with me, but as he is my own flesh and blood you won't. How utterly illogical you are!

Mrs. Arbuthnot. I will not allow him to go.

Lord Illingworth. How can you prevent it? What excuse can you give to him for making him decline such an offer as mine? I won't tell him in what relations I stand to him, I need hardly say. But you daren't tell him. You know that. Look how you have brought him up.

Mrs. Arbuthnot. I have brought him up to be a good man.

Lord Illingworth. Quite so. And what is the result? You have educated him to be your judge if he ever finds you out. And a bitter, an unjust judge he will be to you. Don't be deceived, Rachel. Children begin by loving their parents. After a time they judge them. Rarely, if ever, do they forgive them.

Mrs. Arbuthnot. George, don't take my son away from me. I have had twenty years of sorrow, and I have only had one thing to love me, only one thing to love. You have had a life of joy, and pleasure, and success. You have been quite happy, you have never thought of us. There was no reason, according to your views of life, why you should have remembered us at all. Your meeting us was a mere accident, a horrible accident. Forget it. Don't come now, and rob me of . . . of all I have in the whole world. You are so rich in other things. Leave me the little vineyard of my life; leave me the walled-in garden and the well of water; the ewe-lamb God sent me, in pity or in wrath, oh! leave me that. George, don't take Gerald from me.

Lord Illingworth. Rachel, at the present moment you are not necessary to Gerald's career; I am. There is nothing more to be said on the subject.

Mrs. Arbuthnot. I will not let him go.

Lord Illingworth. Here is Gerald. He has a right to decide for himself.

[Enter Gerald.]

Gerald. Well, dear mother, I hope you have settled it all with Lord Illingworth?

Mrs. Arbuthnot. I have not, Gerald.

Lord Illingworth. Your mother seems not to like your coming with me, for some reason.

Gerald. Why, mother?

Mrs. Arbuthnot. I thought you were quite happy here with me, Gerald. I didn't know you were so anxious to leave me.

Gerald. Mother, how can you talk like that? Of course I have been quite happy with you. But a man can't stay always with his mother. No chap does. I want to make myself a position, to do something. I thought you would have been proud to see me Lord Illingworth's secretary.

Mrs. Arbuthnot. I do not think you would be suitable as a private secretary to Lord Illingworth. You have no qualifications.

Lord Illingworth. I don't wish to seem to interfere for a moment, Mrs.

237

Arbuthnot, but as far as your last objection is concerned, I surely am the best judge. And I can only tell you that your son has all the qualifications I had hoped for. He has more, in fact, than I had even thought of. Far more. [Mrs. Arbuthnot remains silent.] Have you any other reason, Mrs. Arbuthnot, why you don't wish your son to accept this post?

Gerald. Have you, mother? Do answer.

Lord Illingworth. If you have, Mrs. Arbuthnot, pray, pray say it. We are quite by ourselves here. Whatever it is, I need not say I will not repeat it.

Gerald. Mother?

Lord Illingworth. If you would like to be alone with your son, I will leave you. You may have some other reason you don't wish me to hear.

Mrs. Arbuthnot. I have no other reason.

Lord Illingworth. Then, my dear boy, we may look on the thing as settled. Come, you and I will smoke a cigarette on the terrace together. And Mrs. Arbuthnot, pray let me tell you, that I think you have acted very, very wisely.

[Exit with Gerald. Mrs. Arbuthnot is left alone. She stands immobile with a look of unutterable sorrow on her face.]

ACT DROP

THIRD ACT

SCENE

The Picture Gallery at Hunstanton. Door at back leading on to terrace.

[Lord Illingworth and Gerald, R.C. Lord Illingworth lolling on a sofa. Gerald in a chair.]

Lord Illingworth. Thoroughly sensible woman, your mother, Gerald. I knew she would come round in the end.

Gerald. My mother is awfully conscientious, Lord Illingworth, and I know she doesn't think I am educated enough to be your secretary. She is perfectly right, too. I was fearfully idle when I was at school, and I couldn't pass an examination now to save my life.

Lord Illingworth. My dear Gerald, examinations are of no value whatsoever. If a man is a gentleman, he knows quite enough, and if he is not a gentleman, whatever he knows is bad for him.

Gerald. But I am so ignorant of the world, Lord Illingworth.

Lord Illingworth. Don't be afraid, Gerald. Remember that you've got on your side the most wonderful thing in the world—youth! There is nothing like youth. The middle-aged are mortgaged to Life. The old are in life's lumber-room. But youth is the Lord of Life. Youth has a kingdom waiting for it. Every one is born a king, and most people die in exile, like most kings. To win back my youth, Gerald, there is nothing I wouldn't do—except take exercise, get up early, or be a useful member of the community.

Gerald. But you don't call yourself old, Lord Illingworth?

Lord Illingworth. I am old enough to be your father, Gerald.

Gerald. I don't remember my father; he died years ago.

Lord Illingworth. So Lady Hunstanton told me.

Gerald. It is very curious, my mother never talks to me about my father. I sometimes think she must have married beneath her.

Lord Illingworth. [Winces slightly.] Really? [Goes over and puts his hand on Gerald's shoulder.] You have missed not having a father, I suppose, Gerald?

Gerald. Oh, no; my mother has been so good to me. No one ever had such a mother as I have had.

Lord Illingworth. I am quite sure of that. Still I should imagine that most mothers don't quite understand their sons. Don't realise, I mean, that a son has ambitions, a desire to see life, to make himself a name. After all, Gerald, you couldn't be expected to pass all your life in such a hole as Wrockley, could you?

Gerald. Oh, no! It would be dreadful!

Lord Illingworth. A mother's love is very touching, of course, but it is often curiously selfish. I mean, there is a good deal of selfishness in it.

Gerald. [Slowly.] I suppose there is.

Lord Illingworth. Your mother is a thoroughly good woman. But good women have such limited views of life, their horizon is so small, their interests are so petty, aren't they?

Gerald. They are awfully interested, certainly, in things we don't care much about.

Lord Illingworth. I suppose your mother is very religious, and that sort of thing.

Gerald. Oh, yes, she's always going to church.

Lord Illingworth. Ah! she is not modern, and to be modern is the only thing worth being nowadays. You want to be modern, don't you, Gerald? You want to know life as it really is. Not to be put of with any old-fashioned theories about life. Well, what you have to do at present is simply to fit yourself for the best society. A man who can dominate a London dinner-table

240

can dominate the world. The future belongs to the dandy. It is the exquisites who are going to rule.

Gerald. I should like to wear nice things awfully, but I have always been told that a man should not think too much about his clothes.

Lord Illingworth. People nowadays are so absolutely superficial that they don't understand the philosophy of the superficial. By the way, Gerald, you should learn how to tie your tie better. Sentiment is all very well for the button-hole. But the essential thing for a necktie is style. A well-tied tie is the first serious step in life.

Gerald. [Laughing.] I might be able to learn how to tie a tie, Lord Illingworth, but I should never be able to talk as you do. I don't know how to talk.

Lord Illingworth. Oh! talk to every woman as if you loved her, and to every man as if he bored you, and at the end of your first season you will have the reputation of possessing the most perfect social tact.

Gerald. But it is very difficult to get into society isn't it?

Lord Illingworth. To get into the best society, nowadays, one has either to feed people, amuse people, or shock people—that is all!

Gerald. I suppose society is wonderfully delightful!

Lord Illingworth. To be in it is merely a bore. But to be out of it simply a tragedy. Society is a necessary thing. No man has any real success in this world unless he has got women to back him, and women rule society. If you have not got women on your side you are quite over. You might just as well be a barrister, or a stockbroker, or a journalist at once.

Gerald. It is very difficult to understand women, is it not?

Lord Illingworth. You should never try to understand them. Women are pictures. Men are problems. If you want to know what a woman really means—which, by the way, is always a dangerous thing to do—look at her, don't listen to her.

Gerald. But women are awfully clever, aren't they?

Lord Illingworth. One should always tell them so. But, to the philosopher, my dear Gerald, women represent the triumph of matter over mind—just as men represent the triumph of mind over morals.

Gerald. How then can women have so much power as you say they have?

Lord Illingworth. The history of women is the history of the worst form of tyranny the world has ever known. The tyranny of the weak over the strong. It is the only tyranny that lasts.

Gerald. But haven't women got a refining influence?

Lord Illingworth. Nothing refines but the intellect.

Gerald. Still, there are many different kinds of women, aren't there?

Lord Illingworth. Only two kinds in society: the plain and the coloured.

Gerald. But there are good women in society, aren't there?

Lord Illingworth. Far too many.

Gerald. But do you think women shouldn't be good?

Lord Illingworth. One should never tell them so, they'd all become good at once. Women are a fascinatingly wilful sex. Every woman is a rebel, and usually in wild revolt against herself.

Gerald. You have never been married, Lord Illingworth, have you?

Lord Illingworth. Men marry because they are tired; women because they are curious. Both are disappointed.

Gerald. But don't you think one can be happy when one is married?

Lord Illingworth. Perfectly happy. But the happiness of a married man, my dear Gerald, depends on the people he has not married.

Gerald. But if one is in love?

242

Lord Illingworth. One should always be in love. That is the reason one should never marry.

Gerald. Love is a very wonderful thing, isn't it?

Lord Illingworth. When one is in love one begins by deceiving oneself. And one ends by deceiving others. That is what the world calls a romance. But a really grande passion is comparatively rare nowadays. It is the privilege of people who have nothing to do. That is the one use of the idle classes in a country, and the only possible explanation of us Harfords.

Gerald. Harfords, Lord Illingworth?

Lord Illingworth. That is my family name. You should study the Peerage, Gerald. It is the one book a young man about town should know thoroughly, and it is the best thing in fiction the English have ever done. And now, Gerald, you are going into a perfectly new life with me, and I want you to know how to live. [Mrs. Arbuthnot appears on terrace behind.] For the world has been made by fools that wise men should live in it!

[Enter L.C. Lady Hunstanton and Dr. Daubeny.]

Lady Hunstanton. Ah! here you are, dear Lord Illingworth. Well, I suppose you have been telling our young friend, Gerald, what his new duties are to be, and giving him a great deal of good advice over a pleasant cigarette.

Lord Illingworth. I have been giving him the best of advice, Lady Hunstanton, and the best of cigarettes.

Lady Hunstanton. I am so sorry I was not here to listen to you, but I suppose I am too old now to learn. Except from you, dear Archdeacon, when you are in your nice pulpit. But then I always know what you are going to say, so I don't feel alarmed. [Sees Mrs. Arbuthnot.] Ah! dear Mrs. Arbuthnot, do come and join us. Come, dear. [Enter Mrs. Arbuthnot.] Gerald has been having such a long talk with Lord Illingworth; I am sure you must feel very much flattered at the pleasant way in which everything has turned out for him. Let us sit down. [They sit down.] And how is your beautiful embroidery going on?

Mrs. Arbuthnot. I am always at work, Lady Hunstanton.

Lady Hunstanton. Mrs. Daubeny embroiders a little, too, doesn't she?

The Archdeacon. She was very deft with her needle once, quite a Dorcas. But the gout has crippled her fingers a good deal. She has not touched the tambour frame for nine or ten years. But she has many other amusements. She is very much interested in her own health.

Lady Hunstanton. Ah! that is always a nice distraction, in it not? Now, what are you talking about, Lord Illingworth? Do tell us.

Lord Illingworth. I was on the point of explaining to Gerald that the world has always laughed at its own tragedies, that being the only way in which it has been able to bear them. And that, consequently, whatever the world has treated seriously belongs to the comedy side of things.

Lady Hunstanton. Now I am quite out of my depth. I usually am when Lord Illingworth says anything. And the Humane Society is most careless. They never rescue me. I am left to sink. I have a dim idea, dear Lord Illingworth, that you are always on the side of the sinners, and I know I always try to be on the side of the saints, but that is as far as I get. And after all, it may be merely the fancy of a drowning person.

Lord Illingworth. The only difference between the saint and the sinner is that every saint has a past, and every sinner has a future.

Lady Hunstanton. Ah! that quite does for me. I haven't a word to say. You and I, dear Mrs. Arbuthnot, are behind the age. We can't follow Lord Illingworth. Too much care was taken with our education, I am afraid. To have been well brought up is a great drawback nowadays. It shuts one out from so much.

Mrs. Arbuthnot. I should be sorry to follow Lord Illingworth in any of his opinions.

Lady Hunstanton. You are quite right, dear.

[Gerald shrugs his shoulders and looks irritably over at his mother.

Enter Lady Caroline.]

Lady Caroline. Jane, have you seen John anywhere?

Lady Hunstanton. You needn't be anxious about him, dear. He is with Lady Stutfield; I saw them some time ago, in the Yellow Drawing-room. They seem quite happy together. You are not going, Caroline? Pray sit down.

Lady Caroline. I think I had better look after John.

[Exit Lady Caroline.]

Lady Hunstanton. It doesn't do to pay men so much attention. And Caroline has really nothing to be anxious about. Lady Stutfield is very sympathetic. She is just as sympathetic about one thing as she is about another. A beautiful nature.

[Enter Sir John and Mrs. Allonby.]

Ah! here is Sir John! And with Mrs. Allonby too! I suppose it was Mrs. Allonby I saw him with. Sir John, Caroline has been looking everywhere for you.

Mrs. Allonby. We have been waiting for her in the Music-room, dear Lady Hunstanton.

Lady Hunstanton. Ah! the Music-room, of course. I thought it was the Yellow Drawing-room, my memory is getting so defective. [To the Archdeacon.] Mrs. Daubeny has a wonderful memory, hasn't she?

The Archdeacon. She used to be quite remarkable for her memory, but since her last attack she recalls chiefly the events of her early childhood. But she finds great pleasure in such retrospections, great pleasure.

[Enter Lady Stutfield and Mr. Kelvil.]

Lady Hunstanton. Ah! dear Lady Stutfield! and what has Mr. Kelvil been talking to you about?

Lady Stutfield. About Bimetallism, as well as I remember.

Lady Hunstanton. Bimetallism! Is that quite a nice subject? However,

I know people discuss everything very freely nowadays. What did Sir John talk to you about, dear Mrs. Allonby?

Mrs. Allonby. About Patagonia.

Lady Hunstanton. Really? What a remote topic! But very improving, I have no doubt.

Mrs. Allonby. He has been most interesting on the subject of Patagonia. Savages seem to have quite the same views as cultured people on almost all subjects. They are excessively advanced.

Lady Hunstanton. What do they do?

Mrs. Allonby. Apparently everything.

Lady Hunstanton. Well, it is very gratifying, dear Archdeacon, is it not, to find that Human Nature is permanently one.—On the whole, the world is the same world, is it not?

Lord Illingworth. The world is simply divided into two classes—those who believe the incredible, like the public—and those who do the improbable—

Mrs. Allonby. Like yourself?

Lord Illingworth. Yes; I am always astonishing myself. It is the only thing that makes life worth living.

Lady Stutfield. And what have you been doing lately that astonishes you?

Lord Illingworth. I have been discovering all kinds of beautiful qualities in my own nature.

Mrs. Allonby. Ah! don't become quite perfect all at once. Do it gradually!

Lord Illingworth. I don't intend to grow perfect at all. At least, I hope I shan't. It would be most inconvenient. Women love us for our defects. If we have enough of them, they will forgive us everything, even our gigantic intellects.

246

Mrs. Allonby. It is premature to ask us to forgive analysis. We forgive adoration; that is quite as much as should be expected from us.

[Enter Lord Alfred. He joins Lady Stutfield.]

Lady Hunstanton. Ah! we women should forgive everything, shouldn't we, dear Mrs. Arbuthnot? I am sure you agree with me in that.

Mrs. Arbuthnot. I do not, Lady Hunstanton. I think there are many things women should never forgive.

Lady Hunstanton. What sort of things?

Mrs. Arbuthnot. The ruin of another woman's life.

[Moves slowly away to back of stage.]

Lady Hunstanton. Ah! those things are very sad, no doubt, but I believe there are admirable homes where people of that kind are looked after and reformed, and I think on the whole that the secret of life is to take things very, very easily.

Mrs. Allonby. The secret of life is never to have an emotion that is unbecoming.

Lady Stutfield. The secret of life is to appreciate the pleasure of being terribly, terribly deceived.

Kelvil. The secret of life is to resist temptation, Lady Stutfield.

Lord Illingworth. There is no secret of life. Life's aim, if it has one, is simply to be always looking for temptations. There are not nearly enough. I sometimes pass a whole day without coming across a single one. It is quite dreadful. It makes one so nervous about the future.

Lady Hunstanton. [Shakes her fan at him.] I don't know how it is, dear Lord Illingworth, but everything you have said to-day seems to me excessively immoral. It has been most interesting, listening to you.

Lord Illingworth. All thought is immoral. Its very essence is destruction. If you think of anything, you kill it. Nothing survives being thought of.

Lady Hunstanton. I don't understand a word, Lord Illingworth. But I have no doubt it is all quite true. Personally, I have very little to reproach myself with, on the score of thinking. I don't believe in women thinking too much. Women should think in moderation, as they should do all things in moderation.

Lord Illingworth. Moderation is a fatal thing, Lady Hunstanton. Nothing succeeds like excess.

Lady Hunstanton. I hope I shall remember that. It sounds an admirable maxim. But I'm beginning to forget everything. It's a great misfortune.

Lord Illingworth. It is one of your most fascinating qualities, Lady Hunstanton. No woman should have a memory. Memory in a woman is the beginning of dowdiness. One can always tell from a woman's bonnet whether she has got a memory or not.

Lady Hunstanton. How charming you are, dear Lord Illingworth. You always find out that one's most glaring fault is one's most important virtue. You have the most comforting views of life.

[Enter Farquhar.]

Farquhar. Doctor Daubeny's carriage!

Lady Hunstanton. My dear Archdeacon! It is only half-past ten.

The Archdeacon. [Rising.] I am afraid I must go, Lady Hunstanton. Tuesday is always one of Mrs. Daubeny's bad nights.

Lady Hunstanton. [Rising.] Well, I won't keep you from her. [Goes with him towards door.] I have told Farquhar to put a brace of partridge into the carriage. Mrs. Daubeny may fancy them.

The Archdeacon. It is very kind of you, but Mrs. Daubeny never touches solids now. Lives entirely on jellies. But she is wonderfully cheerful, wonderfully cheerful. She has nothing to complain of.

[Exit with Lady Hunstanton.]

Mrs. Allonby. [Goes over to Lord Illingworth.] There is a beautiful moon to-night.

Lord Illingworth. Let us go and look at it. To look at anything that is inconstant is charming nowadays.

Mrs. Allonby. You have your looking-glass.

Lord Illingworth. It is unkind. It merely shows me my wrinkles.

Mrs. Allonby. Mine is better behaved. It never tells me the truth.

Lord Illingworth. Then it is in love with you.

[Exeunt Sir John, Lady Stutfield, Mr. Kelvil and Lord Alfred.]

Gerald. [To Lord Illingworth] May I come too?

Lord Illingworth. Do, my dear boy. [Moves towards with Mrs. Allonby and Gerald.]

[Lady Caroline enters, looks rapidly round and goes off in opposite direction to that taken by Sir John and Lady Stutfield.]

Mrs. Arbuthnot. Gerald!

Gerald. What, mother!

[Exit Lord Illingworth with Mrs. Allonby.]

Mrs. Arbuthnot. It is getting late. Let us go home.

Gerald. My dear mother. Do let us wait a little longer. Lord Illingworth is so delightful, and, by the way, mother, I have a great surprise for you. We are starting for India at the end of this month.

Mrs. Arbuthnot. Let us go home.

Gerald. If you really want to, of course, mother, but I must bid good-bye to Lord Illingworth first. I'll be back in five minutes. [Exit.]

Mrs. Arbuthnot. Let him leave me if he chooses, but not with him— not with him! I couldn't bear it. [Walks up and down.]

[Enter Hester.]

249

Hester. What a lovely night it is, Mrs. Arbuthnot.

Mrs. Arbuthnot. Is it?

Hester. Mrs. Arbuthnot, I wish you would let us be friends. You are so different from the other women here. When you came into the Drawing-room this evening, somehow you brought with you a sense of what is good and pure in life. I had been foolish. There are things that are right to say, but that may be said at the wrong time and to the wrong people.

Mrs. Arbuthnot. I heard what you said. I agree with it, Miss Worsley.

Hester. I didn't know you had heard it. But I knew you would agree with me. A woman who has sinned should be punished, shouldn't she?

Mrs. Arbuthnot. Yes.

Hester. She shouldn't be allowed to come into the society of good men and women?

Mrs. Arbuthnot. She should not.

Hester. And the man should be punished in the same way?

Mrs. Arbuthnot. In the same way. And the children, if there are children, in the same way also?

Hester. Yes, it is right that the sins of the parents should be visited on the children. It is a just law. It is God's law.

Mrs. Arbuthnot. It is one of God's terrible laws.

[Moves away to fireplace.]

Hester. You are distressed about your son leaving you, Mrs. Arbuthnot?

Mrs. Arbuthnot. Yes.

Hester. Do you like him going away with Lord Illingworth? Of course there is position, no doubt, and money, but position and money are not everything, are they?

Mrs. Arbuthnot. They are nothing; they bring misery.

250

Hester. Then why do you let your son go with him?

Mrs. Arbuthnot. He wishes it himself.

Hester. But if you asked him he would stay, would he not?

Mrs. Arbuthnot. He has set his heart on going.

Hester. He couldn't refuse you anything. He loves you too much. Ask him to stay. Let me send him in to you. He is on the terrace at this moment with Lord Illingworth. I heard them laughing together as I passed through the Music-room.

Mrs. Arbuthnot. Don't trouble, Miss Worsley, I can wait. It is of no consequence.

Hester. No, I'll tell him you want him. Do—do ask him to stay. [Exit Hester.]

Mrs. Arbuthnot. He won't come—I know he won't come.

[Enter Lady Caroline. She looks round anxiously. Enter Gerald.]

Lady Caroline. Mr. Arbuthnot, may I ask you is Sir John anywhere on the terrace?

Gerald. No, Lady Caroline, he is not on the terrace.

Lady Caroline. It is very curious. It is time for him to retire.

[Exit Lady Caroline.]

Gerald. Dear mother, I am afraid I kept you waiting. I forgot all about it. I am so happy to-night, mother; I have never been so happy.

Mrs. Arbuthnot. At the prospect of going away?

Gerald. Don't put it like that, mother. Of course I am sorry to leave you. Why, you are the best mother in the whole world. But after all, as Lord Illingworth says, it is impossible to live in such a place as Wrockley. You don't mind it. But I'm ambitions; I want something more than that. I want to have a career. I want to do something that will make you proud of me, and

Lord Illingworth is going to help me. He is going to do everything for me.

Mrs. Arbuthnot. Gerald, don't go away with Lord Illingworth. I implore you not to. Gerald, I beg you!

Gerald. Mother, how changeable you are! You don't seem to know your own mind for a single moment. An hour and a half ago in the Drawing-room you agreed to the whole thing; now you turn round and make objections, and try to force me to give up my one chance in life. Yes, my one chance. You don't suppose that men like Lord Illingworth are to be found every day, do you, mother? It is very strange that when I have had such a wonderful piece of good luck, the one person to put difficulties in my way should be my own mother. Besides, you know, mother, I love Hester Worsley. Who could help loving her? I love her more than I have ever told you, far more. And if I had a position, if I had prospects, I could—I could ask her to—Don't you understand now, mother, what it means to me to be Lord Illingworth's secretary? To start like that is to find a career ready for one—before one—waiting for one. If I were Lord Illingworth's secretary I could ask Hester to be my wife. As a wretched bank clerk with a hundred a year it would be an impertinence.

Mrs. Arbuthnot. I fear you need have no hopes of Miss Worsley. I know her views on life. She has just told them to me. [A pause.]

Gerald. Then I have my ambition left, at any rate. That is something—I am glad I have that! You have always tried to crush my ambition, mother—haven't you? You have told me that the world is a wicked place, that success is not worth having, that society is shallow, and all that sort of thing—well, I don't believe it, mother. I think the world must be delightful. I think society must be exquisite. I think success is a thing worth having. You have been wrong in all that you taught me, mother, quite wrong. Lord Illingworth is a successful man. He is a fashionable man. He is a man who lives in the world and for it. Well, I would give anything to be just like Lord Illingworth.

Mrs. Arbuthnot. I would sooner see you dead.

Gerald. Mother, what is your objection to Lord Illingworth? Tell me—

tell me right out. What is it?

Mrs. Arbuthnot. He is a bad man.

Gerald. In what way bad? I don't understand what you mean.

Mrs. Arbuthnot. I will tell you.

Gerald. I suppose you think him bad, because he doesn't believe the same things as you do. Well, men are different from women, mother. It is natural that they should have different views.

Mrs. Arbuthnot. It is not what Lord Illingworth believes, or what he does not believe, that makes him bad. It is what he is.

Gerald. Mother, is it something you know of him? Something you actually know?

Mrs. Arbuthnot. It is something I know.

Gerald. Something you are quite sure of?

Mrs. Arbuthnot. Quite sure of.

Gerald. How long have you known it?

Mrs. Arbuthnot. For twenty years.

Gerald. Is it fair to go back twenty years in any man's career? And what have you or I to do with Lord Illingworth's early life? What business is it of ours?

Mrs. Arbuthnot. What this man has been, he is now, and will be always.

Gerald. Mother, tell me what Lord Illingworth did? If he did anything shameful, I will not go away with him. Surely you know me well enough for that?

Mrs. Arbuthnot. Gerald, come near to me. Quite close to me, as you used to do when you were a little boy, when you were mother's own boy. [Gerald sits down betide his mother. She runs her fingers through his hair, and strokes his hands.] Gerald, there was a girl once, she was very young, she was little over eighteen at the time. George Harford—that was Lord Illingworth's name then—George Harford met her. She knew nothing about life. He—knew everything. He made this girl love him. He made her love him so much that she left her father's house with him one morning. She loved him so much, and he had promised to marry her! He had solemnly promised to marry her, and she had believed him. She was very young, and—and ignorant of what life really is. But he put the marriage off from week to week, and month to month.—She trusted in him all the while. She loved him.— Before her child was born—for she had a child—she implored him for the child's sake to marry her, that the child might have a name, that her sin might not be visited on the child, who was innocent. He refused. After the child was born she left him, taking the child away, and her life was ruined, and her soul ruined, and all that was sweet, and good, and pure in her ruined also. She suffered terribly—she suffers now. She will always suffer. For her there is no joy, no peace, no atonement. She is a woman who drags a chain like a guilty thing. She is a woman who wears a mask, like a thing that is a leper. The fire cannot purify her. The waters cannot quench her anguish. Nothing can heal her! no anodyne can give her sleep! no poppies forgetfulness! She is lost! She is a lost soul!—That is why I call Lord Illingworth a bad man. That is why I don't want my boy to be with him.

Gerald. My dear mother, it all sounds very tragic, of course. But I dare say the girl was just as much to blame as Lord Illingworth was.—After all, would a really nice girl, a girl with any nice feelings at all, go away from her home with a man to whom she was not married, and live with him as his wife? No nice girl would.

Mrs. Arbuthnot. [After a pause.] Gerald, I withdraw all my objections. You are at liberty to go away with Lord Illingworth, when and where you choose.

Gerald. Dear mother, I knew you wouldn't stand in my way. You are the best woman God ever made. And, as for Lord Illingworth, I don't believe he is capable of anything infamous or base. I can't believe it of him—I can't.

Hester. [Outside.] Let me go! Let me go! [Enter Hester in terror, and rushes over to Gerald and flings herself in his arms.]

Hester. Oh! save me—save me from him!

Gerald. From whom?

Hester. He has insulted me! Horribly insulted me! Save me!

Gerald. Who? Who has dared—?

[Lord Illingworth enters at back of stage. Hester breaks from Gerald's arms and points to him.]

Gerald [He is quite beside himself with rage and indignation.] Lord Illingworth, you have insulted the purest thing on God's earth, a thing as pure as my own mother. You have insulted the woman I love most in the world with my own mother. As there is a God in Heaven, I will kill you!

Mrs. Arbuthnot. [Rushing across and catching hold of him] No! no!

Gerald. [Thrusting her back.] Don't hold me, mother. Don't hold me—I'll kill him!

Mrs. Arbuthnot. Gerald!

Gerald. Let me go, I say!

Mrs. Arbuthnot. Stop, Gerald, stop! He is your own father!

[Gerald clutches his mother's hands and looks into her face. She sinks slowly on the ground in shame. Hester steals towards the door. Lord Illingworth frowns and bites his lip. After a time Gerald raises his mother up, puts his am round her, and leads her from the room.]

Act Drop

FOURTH ACT

SCENE

Sitting-room at Mrs. Arbuthnot's. Large open French window at back looking on to garden. Doors R.C. and L.C.

[Gerald Arbuthnot writing at table.]

[Enter Alice R.C. followed by Lady Hunstanton and Mrs. Allonby.]

Alice. Lady Hunstanton and Mrs. Allonby.

[Exit L.C.]

Lady Hunstanton. Good morning, Gerald.

Gerald. [Rising.] Good morning, Lady Hunstanton. Good morning Mrs. Allonby.

Lady Hunstanton. [Sitting down.] We came to inquire for your dear mother, Gerald. I hope she is better?

Gerald. My mother has not come down yet, Lady Hunstanton.

Lady Hunstanton. Ah, I am afraid the heat was too much for her last night. I think there must have been thunder in the air. Or perhaps it was the music. Music makes one feel so romantic—at least it always gets on one's nerves.

Mrs. Allonby. It's the same thing, nowadays.

Lady Hunstanton. I am so glad I don't know what you mean, dear. I am afraid you mean something wrong. Ah, I see you're examining Mrs. Arbuthnot's pretty room. Isn't it nice and old-fashioned?

Mrs. Allonby. [Surveying the room through her lorgnette.] It looks quite the happy English home.

Lady Hunstanton. That's just the word, dear; that just describes it. One feels your mother's good influence in everything she has about her, Gerald.

Mrs. Allonby. Lord Illingworth says that all influence is bad, but that a good influence is the worst in the world.

Lady Hunstanton. When Lord Illingworth knows Mrs. Arbuthnot better he will change his mind. I must certainly bring him here.

Mrs. Allonby. I should like to see Lord Illingworth in a happy English home.

Lady Hunstanton. It would do him a great deal of good, dear. Most women in London, nowadays, seem to furnish their rooms with nothing but orchids, foreigners, and French novels. But here we have the room of a sweet saint. Fresh natural flowers, books that don't shock one, pictures that one can look at without blushing.

Mrs. Allonby. But I like blushing.

Lady Hunstanton. Well, there is a good deal to be said for blushing, if one can do it at the proper moment. Poor dear Hunstanton used to tell me I didn't blush nearly often enough. But then he was so very particular. He wouldn't let me know any of his men friends, except those who were over seventy, like poor Lord Ashton: who afterwards, by the way, was brought into the Divorce Court. A most unfortunate case.

Mrs. Allonby. I delight in men over seventy. They always offer one the devotion of a lifetime. I think seventy an ideal age for a man.

Lady Hunstanton. She is quite incorrigible, Gerald, isn't she? By-the-by, Gerald, I hope your dear mother will come and see me more often now. You and Lord Illingworth start almost immediately, don't you?

Gerald. I have given up my intention of being Lord Illingworth's secretary.

Lady Hunstanton. Surely not, Gerald! It would be most unwise of you. What reason can you have?

Gerald. I don't think I should be suitable for the post.

Mrs. Allonby. I wish Lord Illingworth would ask me to be his secretary. But he says I am not serious enough.

Lady Hunstanton. My dear, you really mustn't talk like that in this house. Mrs. Arbuthnot doesn't know anything about the wicked society in which we all live. She won't go into it. She is far too good. I consider it was a great honour her coming to me last night. It gave quite an atmosphere of respectability to the party.

Mrs. Allonby. Ah, that must have been what you thought was thunder in the air.

Lady Hunstanton. My dear, how can you say that? There is no resemblance between the two things at all. But really, Gerald, what do you mean by not being suitable?

Gerald. Lord Illingworth's views of life and mine are too different.

Lady Hunstanton. But, my dear Gerald, at your age you shouldn't have any views of life. They are quite out of place. You must be guided by others in this matter. Lord Illingworth has made you the most flattering offer, and travelling with him you would see the world—as much of it, at least, as one should look at—under the best auspices possible, and stay with all the right people, which is so important at this solemn moment in your career.

Gerald. I don't want to see the world: I've seen enough of it.

Mrs. Allonby. I hope you don't think you have exhausted life, Mr. Arbuthnot. When a man says that, one knows that life has exhausted him.

Gerald. I don't wish to leave my mother.

Lady Hunstanton. Now, Gerald, that is pure laziness on your part. Not leave your mother! If I were your mother I would insist on your going.

[Enter Alice L.C.]

Alice. Mrs. Arbuthnot's compliments, my lady, but she has a bad headache, and cannot see any one this morning. [Exit R.C.]

Lady Hunstanton. [Rising.] A bad headache! I am so sorry! Perhaps you'll bring her up to Hunstanton this afternoon, if she is better, Gerald.

Gerald. I am afraid not this afternoon, Lady Hunstanton.

Lady Hunstanton. Well, to-morrow, then. Ah, if you had a father, Gerald, he wouldn't let you waste your life here. He would send you off with Lord Illingworth at once. But mothers are so weak. They give up to their sons in everything. We are all heart, all heart. Come, dear, I must call at the rectory and inquire for Mrs. Daubeny, who, I am afraid, is far from well. It is wonderful how the Archdeacon bears up, quite wonderful. He is the most sympathetic of husbands. Quite a model. Good-bye, Gerald, give my fondest love to your mother.

Mrs. Allonby. Good-bye, Mr. Arbuthnot.

Gerald. Good-bye.

[Exit Lady Hunstanton and Mrs. Allonby. Gerald sits down and reads over his letter.]

Gerald. What name can I sign? I, who have no right to any name. [Signs name, puts letter into envelope, addresses it, and is about to seal it, when door L.C. opens and Mrs. Arbuthnot enters. Gerald lays down sealing-wax. Mother and son look at each other.]

Lady Hunstanton. [Through French window at the back.] Good-bye again, Gerald. We are taking the short cut across your pretty garden. Now, remember my advice to you—start at once with Lord Illingworth.

Mrs. Allonby. Au revoir, Mr. Arbuthnot. Mind you bring me back something nice from your travels—not an Indian shawl—on no account an Indian shawl.

[Exeunt.]

Gerald. Mother, I have just written to him.

Mrs. Arbuthnot. To whom?

Gerald. To my father. I have written to tell him to come here at four

259

o'clock this afternoon.

Mrs. Arbuthnot. He shall not come here. He shall not cross the threshold of my house.

Gerald. He must come.

Mrs. Arbuthnot. Gerald, if you are going away with Lord Illingworth, go at once. Go before it kills me: but don't ask me to meet him.

Gerald. Mother, you don't understand. Nothing in the world would induce me to go away with Lord Illingworth, or to leave you. Surely you know me well enough for that. No: I have written to him to say—

Mrs. Arbuthnot. What can you have to say to him?

Gerald. Can't you guess, mother, what I have written in this letter?

Mrs. Arbuthnot. No.

Gerald. Mother, surely you can. Think, think what must be done, now, at once, within the next few days.

Mrs. Arbuthnot. There is nothing to be done.

Gerald. I have written to Lord Illingworth to tell him that he must marry you.

Mrs. Arbuthnot. Marry me?

Gerald. Mother, I will force him to do it. The wrong that has been done you must be repaired. Atonement must be made. Justice may be slow, mother, but it comes in the end. In a few days you shall be Lord Illingworth's lawful wife.

Mrs. Arbuthnot. But, Gerald—

Gerald. I will insist upon his doing it. I will make him do it: he will not dare to refuse.

Mrs. Arbuthnot. But, Gerald, it is I who refuse. I will not marry Lord Illingworth.

260

Gerald. Not marry him? Mother!

Mrs. Arbuthnot. I will not marry him.

Gerald. But you don't understand: it is for your sake I am talking, not for mine. This marriage, this necessary marriage, this marriage which for obvious reasons must inevitably take place, will not help me, will not give me a name that will be really, rightly mine to bear. But surely it will be something for you, that you, my mother, should, however late, become the wife of the man who is my father. Will not that be something?

Mrs. Arbuthnot. I will not marry him.

Gerald. Mother, you must.

Mrs. Arbuthnot. I will not. You talk of atonement for a wrong done. What atonement can be made to me? There is no atonement possible. I am disgraced: he is not. That is all. It is the usual history of a man and a woman as it usually happens, as it always happens. And the ending is the ordinary ending. The woman suffers. The man goes free.

Gerald. I don't know if that is the ordinary ending, mother: I hope it is not. But your life, at any rate, shall not end like that. The man shall make whatever reparation is possible. It is not enough. It does not wipe out the past, I know that. But at least it makes the future better, better for you, mother.

Mrs. Arbuthnot. I refuse to marry Lord Illingworth.

Gerald. If he came to you himself and asked you to be his wife you would give him a different answer. Remember, he is my father.

Mrs. Arbuthnot. If he came himself, which he will not do, my answer would be the same. Remember I am your mother.

Gerald. Mother, you make it terribly difficult for me by talking like that; and I can't understand why you won't look at this matter from the right, from the only proper standpoint. It is to take away the bitterness out of your life, to take away the shadow that lies on your name, that this marriage must take place. There is no alternative: and after the marriage you and I can go away together. But the marriage must take place first. It is a duty that you owe, not merely to yourself, but to all other women—yes: to all the other women in the world, lest he betray more.

Mrs. Arbuthnot. I owe nothing to other women. There is not one of them to help me. There is not one woman in the world to whom I could go for pity, if I would take it, or for sympathy, if I could win it. Women are hard on each other. That girl, last night, good though she is, fled from the room as though I were a tainted thing. She was right. I am a tainted thing. But my wrongs are my own, and I will bear them alone. I must bear them alone. What have women who have not sinned to do with me, or I with them? We do not understand each other.

[Enter Hester behind.]

Gerald. I implore you to do what I ask you.

Mrs. Arbuthnot. What son has ever asked of his mother to make so hideous a sacrifice? None.

Gerald. What mother has ever refused to marry the father of her own child? None.

Mrs. Arbuthnot. Let me be the first, then. I will not do it.

Gerald. Mother, you believe in religion, and you brought me up to believe in it also. Well, surely your religion, the religion that you taught me when I was a boy, mother, must tell you that I am right. You know it, you feel it.

Mrs. Arbuthnot. I do not know it. I do not feel it, nor will I ever stand before God's altar and ask God's blessing on so hideous a mockery as a marriage between me and George Harford. I will not say the words the Church bids us to say. I will not say them. I dare not. How could I swear to love the man I loathe, to honour him who wrought you dishonour, to obey him who, in his mastery, made me to sin? No: marriage is a sacrament for those who love each other. It is not for such as him, or such as me. Gerald,

262

to save you from the world's sneers and taunts I have lied to the world. For twenty years I have lied to the world. I could not tell the world the truth. Who can, ever? But not for my own sake will I lie to God, and in God's presence. No, Gerald, no ceremony, Church-hallowed or State-made, shall ever bind me to George Harford. It may be that I am too bound to him already, who, robbing me, yet left me richer, so that in the mire of my life I found the pearl of price, or what I thought would be so.

Gerald. I don't understand you now.

Mrs. Arbuthnot. Men don't understand what mothers are. I am no different from other women except in the wrong done me and the wrong I did, and my very heavy punishments and great disgrace. And yet, to bear you I had to look on death. To nurture you I had to wrestle with it. Death fought with me for you. All women have to fight with death to keep their children. Death, being childless, wants our children from us. Gerald, when you were naked I clothed you, when you were hungry I gave you food. Night and day all that long winter I tended you. No office is too mean, no care too lowly for the thing we women love—and oh! how I loved you. Not Hannah, Samuel more. And you needed love, for you were weakly, and only love could have kept you alive. Only love can keep any one alive. And boys are careless often and without thinking give pain, and we always fancy that when they come to man's estate and know us better they will repay us. But it is not so. The world draws them from our side, and they make friends with whom they are happier than they are with us, and have amusements from which we are barred, and interests that are not ours: and they are unjust to us often, for when they find life bitter they blame us for it, and when they find it sweet we do not taste its sweetness with them . . . You made many friends and went into their houses and were glad with them, and I, knowing my secret, did not dare to follow, but stayed at home and closed the door, shut out the sun and sat in darkness. What should I have done in honest households? My past was ever with me. . . . And you thought I didn't care for the pleasant things of life. I tell you I longed for them, but did not dare to touch them, feeling I had no right. You thought I was happier working amongst the poor. That was my mission, you imagined. It was not, but where else was I to go? The sick do not ask if the hand that smooths their pillow is pure, nor the dying care if the lips that touch their brow have known the kiss of sin. It was you I thought of all the time; I gave to them the love you did not need: lavished on them a love that was not theirs . . . And you thought I spent too much of my time in going to Church, and in Church duties. But where else could I turn? God's house is the only house where sinners are made welcome, and you were always in my heart, Gerald, too much in my heart. For, though day after day, at morn or evensong, I have knelt in God's house, I have never repented of my sin. How could I repent of my sin when you, my love, were its fruit! Even now that you are bitter to me I cannot repent. I do not. You are more to me than innocence. I would rather be your mother—oh! much rather!—than have been always pure . . . Oh, don't you see? don't you understand? It is my dishonour that has made you so dear to me. It is my disgrace that has bound you so closely to me. It is the price I paid for you—the price of soul and body—that makes me love you as I do. Oh, don't ask me to do this horrible thing. Child of my shame, be still the child of my shame!

Gerald. Mother, I didn't know you loved me so much as that. And I will be a better son to you than I have been. And you and I must never leave each other . . . but, mother . . . I can't help it . . . you must become my father's wife. You must marry him. It is your duty.

Hester. [Running forwards and embracing Mrs. Arbuthnot.] No, no; you shall not. That would be real dishonour, the first you have ever known. That would be real disgrace: the first to touch you. Leave him and come with me. There are other countries than England . . . Oh! other countries over sea, better, wiser, and less unjust lands. The world is very wide and very big.

Mrs. Arbuthnot. No, not for me. For me the world is shrivelled to a palm's breadth, and where I walk there are thorns.

Hester. It shall not be so. We shall somewhere find green valleys and fresh waters, and if we weep, well, we shall weep together. Have we not both loved him?

Gerald. Hester!

Hester. [Waving him back.] Don't, don't! You cannot love me at all,

264

unless you love her also. You cannot honour me, unless she's holier to you. In her all womanhood is martyred. Not she alone, but all of us are stricken in her house.

Gerald. Hester, Hester, what shall I do?

Hester. Do you respect the man who is your father?

Gerald. Respect him? I despise him! He is infamous.

Hester. I thank you for saving me from him last night.

Gerald. Ah, that is nothing. I would die to save you. But you don't tell me what to do now!

Hester. Have I not thanked you for saving me?

Gerald. But what should I do?

Hester. Ask your own heart, not mine. I never had a mother to save, or shame.

Mrs. Arbuthnot. He is hard—he is hard. Let me go away.

Gerald. [Rushes over and kneels down bedside his mother.] Mother, forgive me: I have been to blame.

Mrs. Arbuthnot. Don't kiss my hands: they are cold. My heart is cold: something has broken it.

Hester. Ah, don't say that. Hearts live by being wounded. Pleasure may turn a heart to stone, riches may make it callous, but sorrow—oh, sorrow cannot break it. Besides, what sorrows have you now? Why, at this moment you are more dear to him than ever, dear though you have been, and oh! how dear you have been always. Ah! be kind to him.

Gerald. You are my mother and my father all in one. I need no second parent. It was for you I spoke, for you alone. Oh, say something, mother. Have I but found one love to lose another? Don't tell me that. O mother, you are cruel. [Gets up and flings himself sobbing on a sofa.]

Mrs. Arbuthnot. [To Hester.] But has he found indeed another love?

Hester. You know I have loved him always.

Mrs. Arbuthnot. But we are very poor.

Hester. Who, being loved, is poor? Oh, no one. I hate my riches. They are a burden. Let him share it with me.

Mrs. Arbuthnot. But we are disgraced. We rank among the outcasts Gerald is nameless. The sins of the parents should be visited on the children. It is God's law.

Hester. I was wrong. God's law is only Love.

Mrs. Arbuthnot. [Rises, and taking Hester by the hand, goes slowly over to where Gerald is lying on the sofa with his head buried in his hands. She touches him and he looks up.] Gerald, I cannot give you a father, but I have brought you a wife.

Gerald. Mother, I am not worthy either of her or you.

Mrs. Arbuthnot. So she comes first, you are worthy. And when you are away, Gerald . . . with . . . her—oh, think of me sometimes. Don't forget me. And when you pray, pray for me. We should pray when we are happiest, and you will be happy, Gerald.

Hester. Oh, you don't think of leaving us?

Gerald. Mother, you won't leave us?

Mrs. Arbuthnot. I might bring shame upon you!

Gerald. Mother!

Mrs. Arbuthnot. For a little then: and if you let me, near you always.

Hester. [To Mrs. Arbuthnot.] Come out with us to the garden.

Mrs. Arbuthnot. Later on, later on. [Exeunt Hester and Gerald. Mrs. Arbuthnot goes towards door L.C. Stops at looking-glass over mantelpiece and looks into it. Enter Alice R.C.]

Alice. A gentleman to see you, ma'am.

266

Mrs. Arbuthnot. Say I am not at home. Show me the card. [Takes card from salver and looks at it.] Say I will not see him.

[Lord Illingworth enters. Mrs. Arbuthnot sees him in the glass and starts, but does not turn round. Exit Alice.] What can you have to say to me to-day, George Harford? You can have nothing to say to me. You must leave this house.

Lord Illingworth. Rachel, Gerald knows everything about you and me now, so some arrangement must be come to that will suit us all three. I assure you, he will find in me the most charming and generous of fathers.

Mrs. Arbuthnot. My son may come in at any moment. I saved you last night. I may not be able to save you again. My son feels my dishonour strongly, terribly strongly. I beg you to go.

Lord Illingworth. [Sitting down.] Last night was excessively unfortunate. That silly Puritan girl making a scene merely because I wanted to kiss her. What harm is there in a kiss?

Mrs. Arbuthnot. [Turning round.] A kiss may ruin a human life, George Harford. I know that. I know that too well.

Lord Illingworth. We won't discuss that at present. What is of importance to-day, as yesterday, is still our son. I am extremely fond of him, as you know, and odd though it may seem to you, I admired his conduct last night immensely. He took up the cudgels for that pretty prude with wonderful promptitude. He is just what I should have liked a son of mine to be. Except that no son of mine should ever take the side of the Puritans: that is always an error. Now, what I propose is this.

Mrs. Arbuthnot. Lord Illingworth, no proposition of yours interests me.

Lord Illingworth. According to our ridiculous English laws, I can't legitimise Gerald. But I can leave him my property. Illingworth is entailed, of course, but it is a tedious barrack of a place. He can have Ashby, which is much prettier, Harborough, which has the best shooting in the north of

England, and the house in St. James Square. What more can a gentleman require in this world?

Mrs. Arbuthnot. Nothing more, I am quite sure.

Lord Illingworth. As for a title, a title is really rather a nuisance in these democratic days. As George Harford I had everything I wanted. Now I have merely everything that other people want, which isn't nearly so pleasant. Well, my proposal is this.

Mrs. Arbuthnot. I told you I was not interested, and I beg you to go.

Lord Illingworth. The boy is to be with you for six months in the year, and with me for the other six. That is perfectly fair, is it not? You can have whatever allowance you like, and live where you choose. As for your past, no one knows anything about it except myself and Gerald. There is the Puritan, of course, the Puritan in white muslin, but she doesn't count. She couldn't tell the story without explaining that she objected to being kissed, could she? And all the women would think her a fool and the men think her a bore. And you need not be afraid that Gerald won't be my heir. I needn't tell you I have not the slightest intention of marrying.

Mrs. Arbuthnot. You come too late. My son has no need of you. You are not necessary.

Lord Illingworth. What do you mean, Rachel?

Mrs. Arbuthnot. That you are not necessary to Gerald's career. He does not require you.

Lord Illingworth. I do not understand you.

Mrs. Arbuthnot. Look into the garden. [Lord Illingworth rises and goes towards window.] You had better not let them see you: you bring unpleasant memories. [Lord Illingworth looks out and starts.] She loves him. They love each other. We are safe from you, and we are going away.

Lord Illingworth. Where?

Mrs. Arbuthnot. We will not tell you, and if you find us we will not know you. You seem surprised. What welcome would you get from the girl whose lips you tried to soil, from the boy whose life you have shamed, from the mother whose dishonour comes from you?

Lord Illingworth. You have grown hard, Rachel.

Mrs. Arbuthnot. I was too weak once. It is well for me that I have changed.

Lord Illingworth. I was very young at the time. We men know life too early.

Mrs. Arbuthnot. And we women know life too late. That is the difference between men and women. [A pause.]

Lord Illingworth. Rachel, I want my son. My money may be of no use to him now. I may be of no use to him, but I want my son. Bring us together, Rachel. You can do it if you choose. [Sees letter on table.]

Mrs. Arbuthnot. There is no room in my boy's life for you. He is not interested in you.

Lord Illingworth. Then why does he write to me?

Mrs. Arbuthnot. What do you mean?

Lord Illingworth. What letter is this? [Takes up letter.]

Mrs. Arbuthnot. That—is nothing. Give it to me.

Lord Illingworth. It is addressed to me.

Mrs. Arbuthnot. You are not to open it. I forbid you to open it.

Lord Illingworth. And in Gerald's handwriting.

Mrs. Arbuthnot. It was not to have been sent. It is a letter he wrote to you this morning, before he saw me. But he is sorry now he wrote it, very sorry. You are not to open it. Give it to me.

Lord Illingworth. It belongs to me. [Opens it, sits down and reads it slowly. Mrs. Arbuthnot watches him all the time.] You have read this letter,

269

I suppose, Rachel?

Mrs. Arbuthnot. No.

Lord Illingworth. You know what is in it?

Mrs. Arbuthnot. Yes!

Lord Illingworth. I don't admit for a moment that the boy is right in
what he says. I don't admit that it is any duty of mine to marry you. I deny
it entirely. But to get my son back I am ready—yes, I am ready to marry you,
Rachel—and to treat you always with the deference and respect due to my
wife. I will marry you as soon as you choose. I give you my word of honour.

Mrs. Arbuthnot. You made that promise to me once before and broke
it.

Lord Illingworth. I will keep it now. And that will show you that I love
my son, at least as much as you love him. For when I marry you, Rachel,
there are some ambitions I shall have to surrender. High ambitions, too, if
any ambition is high.

Mrs. Arbuthnot. I decline to marry you, Lord Illingworth.

Lord Illingworth. Are you serious?

Mrs. Arbuthnot. Yes.

Lord Illingworth. Do tell me your reasons. They would interest me
enormously.

Mrs. Arbuthnot. I have already explained them to my son.

Lord Illingworth. I suppose they were intensely sentimental, weren't
they? You women live by your emotions and for them. You have no
philosophy of life.

Mrs. Arbuthnot. You are right. We women live by our emotions and
for them. By our passions, and for them, if you will. I have two passions,
Lord Illingworth: my love of him, my hate of you. You cannot kill those.
They feed each other.

270

Lord Illingworth. What sort of love is that which needs to have hate as its brother?

Mrs. Arbuthnot. It is the sort of love I have for Gerald. Do you think that terrible? Well it is terrible. All love is terrible. All love is a tragedy. I loved you once, Lord Illingworth. Oh, what a tragedy for a woman to have loved you!

Lord Illingworth. So you really refuse to marry me?

Mrs. Arbuthnot. Yes.

Lord Illingworth. Because you hate me?

Mrs. Arbuthnot. Yes.

Lord Illingworth. And does my son hate me as you do?

Mrs. Arbuthnot. No.

Lord Illingworth. I am glad of that, Rachel.

Mrs. Arbuthnot. He merely despises you.

Lord Illingworth. What a pity! What a pity for him, I mean.

Mrs. Arbuthnot. Don't be deceived, George. Children begin by loving their parents. After a time they judge them. Rarely if ever do they forgive them.

Lord Illingworth. [Reads letter over again, very slowly.] May I ask by what arguments you made the boy who wrote this letter, this beautiful, passionate letter, believe that you should not marry his father, the father of your own child?

Mrs. Arbuthnot. It was not I who made him see it. It was another.

Lord Illingworth. What fin-de-siècle person?

Mrs. Arbuthnot. The Puritan, Lord Illingworth. [A pause.]

Lord Illingworth. [Winces, then rises slowly and goes over to table where his hat and gloves are. Mrs. Arbuthnot is standing close to the table. He picks up one of the gloves, and begins pulling it on.] There is not much then for me to do here, Rachel?

Mrs. Arbuthnot. Nothing.

Lord Illingworth. It is good-bye, is it?

Mrs. Arbuthnot. For ever, I hope, this time, Lord Illingworth.

Lord Illingworth. How curious! At this moment you look exactly as you looked the night you left me twenty years ago. You have just the same expression in your mouth. Upon my word, Rachel, no woman ever loved me as you did. Why, you gave yourself to me like a flower, to do anything I liked with. You were the prettiest of playthings, the most fascinating of small romances . . . [Pulls out watch.] Quarter to two! Must be strolling back to Hunstanton. Don't suppose I shall see you there again. I'm sorry, I am, really. It's been an amusing experience to have met amongst people of one's own rank, and treated quite seriously too, one's mistress, and one's—

[Mrs. Arbuthnot snatches up glove and strikes Lord Illingworth across the face with it. Lord Illingworth starts. He is dazed by the insult of his punishment. Then he controls himself, and goes to window and looks out at his son. Sighs and leaves the room.]

Mrs. Arbuthnot. [Falls sobbing on the sofa.] He would have said it. He would have said it.

[Enter Gerald and Hester from the garden.]

Gerald. Well, dear mother. You never came out after all. So we have come in to fetch you. Mother, you have not been crying? [Kneels down beside her.]

Mrs. Arbuthnot. My boy! My boy! My boy! [Running her fingers through his hair.]

Hester. [Coming over.] But you have two children now. You'll let me be your daughter?

Mrs. Arbuthnot. [Looking up.] Would you choose me for a mother?

Hester. You of all women I have ever known.

[They move towards the door leading into garden with their arms round each other's waists. Gerald goes to table L.C. for his hat. On turning round he sees Lord Illingworth's glove lying on the floor, and picks it up.]

Gerald. Hallo, mother, whose glove is this? You have had a visitor. Who was it?

Mrs. Arbuthnot. [Turning round.] Oh! no one. No one in particular. A man of no importance.

CURTAIN

273

AN IDEAL HUSBAND: A PLAY

THE PERSONS OF THE PLAY

THE EARL OF CAVERSHAM, K.G.

VISCOUNT GORING, his Son

SIR ROBERT CHILTERN, Bart., Under-Secretary for Foreign Affairs

VICOMTE DE NANJAC, Attaché at the French Embassy in London

MR. MONTFORD

MASON, Butler to Sir Robert Chiltern

PHIPPS, Lord Goring's Servant

JAMES   }

HAROLD } Footmen

LADY CHILTERN

LADY MARKBY

THE COUNTESS OF BASILDON

MRS. MARCHMONT

MISS MABEL CHILTERN, Sir Robert Chiltern's Sister

MRS. CHEVELEY

THE SCENES OF THE PLAY

ACT I. *The Octagon Room in Sir Robert Chiltern's House in Grosvenor Square.*

ACT II. *Morning-room in Sir Robert Chiltern's House.*

ACT III. *The Library of Lord Goring's House in Curzon Street.*

ACT IV. *Same as Act II.*

TIME: *The Present*

PLACE: *London.*

The action of the play is completed within twenty-four hours.

THEATRE ROYAL, HAYMARKET

Sole Lessee: Mr. Herbert Beerbohm Tree

Managers: Mr. Lewis Waller and Mr. H. H. Morell

January 3rd, 1895

The Earl of Caversham	*Mr. Alfred Bishop.*
Viscount Goring	*Mr. Charles H. Hawtrey.*
Sir Robert Chiltern	*Mr. Lewis Waller.*
Vicomte de Nanjac	*Mr. Cosmo Stuart.*
Mr. Montford	*Mr. Harry Stanford.*
Phipps	*Mr. C. H. Brookfield.*
Mason	*Mr. H. Deane.*
James	*Mr. Charles Meyrick.*
Harold	*Mr. Goodhart.*
Lady Chiltern	*Miss Julia Neilson.*
Lady Markby	*Miss Fanny Brough.*
Countess of Basildon	*Miss Vane Featherston.*
Mrs. Marchmont	*Miss Helen Forsyth.*
Miss Mabel Chiltern	*Miss Maud Millet.*
Mrs. Cheveley	*Miss Florence West.*

FIRST ACT

SCENE

The octagon room at Sir Robert Chiltern's house in Grosvenor Square.

[*The room is brilliantly lighted and full of guests. At the top of the staircase* stands lady chiltern, *a woman of grave Greek beauty, about twenty-seven years of age. She receives the guests as they come up. Over the well of the staircase hangs a great chandelier with wax lights, which illumine a large eighteenth-century French tapestry—representing the Triumph of Love, from a design by Boucher— that is stretched on the staircase wall. On the right is the entrance to the music-room. The sound of a string quartette is faintly heard. The entrance on the left leads to other reception-rooms.* mrs. marchmont *and* lady basildon, *two very pretty women, are seated together on a Louis Seize sofa. They are types of exquisite fragility. Their affectation of manner has a delicate charm. Watteau would have loved to paint them.*]

mrs. marchmont. Going on to the Hartlocks' to-night, Margaret?

lady basildon. I suppose so. Are you?

mrs. marchmont. Yes. Horribly tedious parties they give, don't they?

lady basildon. Horribly tedious! Never know why I go. Never know why I go anywhere.

mrs. marchmont. I come here to be educated.

lady basildon. Ah! I hate being educated!

mrs. marchmont. So do I. It puts one almost on a level with the commercial classes, doesn't it? But dear Gertrude Chiltern is always telling me that I should have some serious purpose in life. So I come here to try to find one.

lady basildon. [Looking round through her lorgnette.] I don't see anybody here to-night whom one could possibly call a serious purpose. The man who took me in to dinner talked to me about his wife the whole time.

mrs. marchmont. How very trivial of him!

lady basildon. Terribly trivial! What did your man talk about?

mrs. marchmont. About myself.

lady basildon. [Languidly.] And were you interested?

mrs. marchmont. [Shaking her head.] Not in the smallest degree.

lady basildon. What martyrs we are, dear Margaret!

mrs. marchmont. [Rising.] And how well it becomes us, Olivia!

[*They rise and go towards the music-room. The* vicomte de nanjac, *a young attaché known for his neckties and his Anglomania, approaches with a low bow, and enters into conversation.*]

mason. [Announcing guests from the top of the staircase.] Mr. and Lady Jane Barford. Lord Caversham.

[Enter lord caversham, an old gentleman of seventy, wearing the riband and star of the Garter. A fine Whig type. Rather like a portrait by Lawrence.]

lord caversham. Good evening, Lady Chiltern! Has my good-for-nothing young son been here?

lady chiltern. [Smiling.] I don't think Lord Goring has arrived yet.

mabel chiltern. [Coming up to lord caversham.] Why do you call Lord Goring good-for-nothing?

[mabel chiltern *is a perfect example of the English type of prettiness, the apple-blossom type. She has all the fragrance and freedom of a flower. There is ripple after ripple of sunlight in her hair, and the little mouth, with its parted lips, is expectant, like the mouth of a child. She has the fascinating tyranny of youth, and the astonishing courage of innocence. To sane people she is not reminiscent of any work of art. But she is really like a Tanagra statuette, and would be rather annoyed if she were told so.*]

282

lord caversham. Because he leads such an idle life.

mabel chiltern. How can you say such a thing? Why, he rides in the Row at ten o'clock in the morning, goes to the Opera three times a week, changes his clothes at least five times a day, and dines out every night of the season. You don't call that leading an idle life, do you?

lord caversham. [Looking at her with a kindly twinkle in his eyes.] You are a very charming young lady!

mabel chiltern. How sweet of you to say that, Lord Caversham! Do come to us more often. You know we are always at home on Wednesdays, and you look so well with your star!

lord caversham. Never go anywhere now. Sick of London Society. Shouldn't mind being introduced to my own tailor; he always votes on the right side. But object strongly to being sent down to dinner with my wife's milliner. Never could stand Lady Caversham's bonnets.

mabel chiltern. Oh, I love London Society! I think it has immensely improved. It is entirely composed now of beautiful idiots and brilliant lunatics. Just what Society should be.

lord caversham. Hum! Which is Goring? Beautiful idiot, or the other thing?

mabel chiltern. [Gravely.] I have been obliged for the present to put Lord Goring into a class quite by himself. But he is developing charmingly!

lord caversham. Into what?

mabel chiltern. [With a little curtsey.] I hope to let you know very soon, Lord Caversham!

mason. [Announcing guests.] Lady Markby. Mrs. Cheveley.

[*Enter* lady markby *and* mrs. cheveley. lady markby *is a pleasant, kindly, popular woman, with gray hair à la marquise and good lace.* mrs. cheveley, *who accompanies her, is tall and rather slight. Lips very thin and highly-coloured, a line of scarlet on a pallid face. Venetian red hair, aquiline nose, and long throat.*

*Rouge accentuates the natural paleness of her complexion. Gray-green eyes that
move restlessly. She is in heliotrope, with diamonds. She looks rather like an
orchid, and makes great demands on one's curiosity. In all her movements she is
extremely graceful. A work of art, on the whole, but showing the influence of too
many schools.*]

lady markby. Good evening, dear Gertrude! So kind of you to let me
bring my friend, Mrs. Cheveley. Two such charming women should know
each other!

lady chiltern. [Advances towards mrs. cheveley with a sweet smile.
Then suddenly stops, and bows rather distantly.] I think Mrs. Cheveley and
I have met before. I did not know she had married a second time.

lady markby. [Genially.] Ah, nowadays people marry as often as they
can, don't they? It is most fashionable. [To duchess of maryborough.] Dear
Duchess, and how is the Duke? Brain still weak, I suppose? Well, that is only
to be expected, is it not? His good father was just the same. There is nothing
like race, is there?

mrs. cheveley. [Playing with her fan.] But have we really met before,
Lady Chiltern? I can't remember where. I have been out of England for so
long.

lady chiltern. We were at school together, Mrs. Cheveley.

mrs. cheveley [Superciliously.] Indeed? I have forgotten all about my
schooldays. I have a vague impression that they were detestable.

lady chiltern. [Coldly.] I am not surprised!

mrs. cheveley. [In her sweetest manner.] Do you know, I am quite
looking forward to meeting your clever husband, Lady Chiltern. Since he has
been at the Foreign Office, he has been so much talked of in Vienna. They
actually succeed in spelling his name right in the newspapers. That in itself
is fame, on the continent.

lady chiltern. I hardly think there will be much in common between
you and my husband, Mrs. Cheveley! [Moves away.]

vicomte de nanjac. Ah! chère Madame, queue surprise! I have not seen you since Berlin!

mrs. cheveley. Not since Berlin, Vicomte. Five years ago!

vicomte de nanjac. And you are younger and more beautiful than ever. How do you manage it?

mrs. cheveley. By making it a rule only to talk to perfectly charming people like yourself.

vicomte de nanjac. Ah! you flatter me. You butter me, as they say here.

mrs. cheveley. Do they say that here? How dreadful of them!

vicomte de nanjac. Yes, they have a wonderful language. It should be more widely known.

[sir robert chiltern *enters. A man of forty, but looking somewhat younger. Clean-shaven, with finely-cut features, dark-haired and dark-eyed. A personality of mark. Not popular—few personalities are. But intensely admired by the few, and deeply respected by the many. The note of his manner is that of perfect distinction, with a slight touch of pride. One feels that he is conscious of the success he has made in life. A nervous temperament, with a tired look. The firmly-chiselled mouth and chin contrast strikingly with the romantic expression in the deep-set eyes. The variance is suggestive of an almost complete separation of passion and intellect, as though thought and emotion were each isolated in its own sphere through some violence of will-power. There is nervousness in the nostrils, and in the pale, thin, pointed hands. It would be inaccurate to call him picturesque. Picturesqueness cannot survive the House of Commons. But Vandyck would have liked to have painted his head.*]

sir robert chiltern. Good evening, Lady Markby! I hope you have brought Sir John with you?

lady markby. Oh! I have brought a much more charming person than Sir John. Sir John's temper since he has taken seriously to politics has become quite unbearable. Really, now that the House of Commons is trying to become useful, it does a great deal of harm.

285

sir robert chiltern. I hope not, Lady Markby. At any rate we do our bes
to waste the public time, don't we? But who is this charming person you have
been kind enough to bring to us?

lady markby. Her name is Mrs. Cheveley! One of the Dorsetshire
Cheveleys, I suppose. But I really don't know. Families are so mixed
nowadays. Indeed, as a rule, everybody turns out to be somebody else.

sir robert chiltern. Mrs. Cheveley? I seem to know the name.

lady markby. She has just arrived from Vienna.

sir robert chiltern. Ah! yes. I think I know whom you mean.

lady markby. Oh! she goes everywhere there, and has such pleasan
scandals about all her friends. I really must go to Vienna next winter. I hope
there is a good chef at the Embassy.

sir robert chiltern. If there is not, the Ambassador will certainly have
to be recalled. Pray point out Mrs. Cheveley to me. I should like to see her

lady markby. Let me introduce you. [To mrs. cheveley.] My dear, Si
Robert Chiltern is dying to know you!

sir robert chiltern. [Bowing.] Every one is dying to know the brillian
Mrs. Cheveley. Our attachés at Vienna write to us about nothing else.

mrs. cheveley. Thank you, Sir Robert. An acquaintance that begin
with a compliment is sure to develop into a real friendship. It starts in the
right manner. And I find that I know Lady Chiltern already.

sir robert chiltern. Really?

mrs. cheveley. Yes. She has just reminded me that we were at schoo
together. I remember it perfectly now. She always got the good conduc
prize. I have a distinct recollection of Lady Chiltern always getting the good
conduct prize!

sir robert chiltern. [Smiling.] And what prizes did you get, Mrs
Cheveley?

286

mrs. cheveley. My prizes came a little later on in life. I don't think any of them were for good conduct. I forget!

sir robert chiltern. I am sure they were for something charming!

mrs. cheveley. I don't know that women are always rewarded for being charming. I think they are usually punished for it! Certainly, more women grow old nowadays through the faithfulness of their admirers than through anything else! At least that is the only way I can account for the terribly haggard look of most of your pretty women in London!

sir robert chiltern. What an appalling philosophy that sounds! To attempt to classify you, Mrs. Cheveley, would be an impertinence. But may I ask, at heart, are you an optimist or a pessimist? Those seem to be the only two fashionable religions left to us nowadays.

mrs. cheveley. Oh, I'm neither. Optimism begins in a broad grin, and Pessimism ends with blue spectacles. Besides, they are both of them merely poses.

sir robert chiltern. You prefer to be natural?

mrs. cheveley. Sometimes. But it is such a very difficult pose to keep up.

sir robert chiltern. What would those modern psychological novelists, of whom we hear so much, say to such a theory as that?

mrs. cheveley. Ah! the strength of women comes from the fact that psychology cannot explain us. Men can be analysed, women . . . merely adored.

sir robert chiltern. You think science cannot grapple with the problem of women?

mrs. cheveley. Science can never grapple with the irrational. That is why it has no future before it, in this world.

sir robert chiltern. And women represent the irrational.

mrs. cheveley. Well-dressed women do.

sir robert chiltern. [With a polite bow.] I fear I could hardly agree with you there. But do sit down. And now tell me, what makes you leave your brilliant Vienna for our gloomy London—or perhaps the question is indiscreet?

mrs. cheveley. Questions are never indiscreet. Answers sometimes are.

sir robert chiltern. Well, at any rate, may I know if it is politics or pleasure?

mrs. cheveley. Politics are my only pleasure. You see nowadays it is not fashionable to flirt till one is forty, or to be romantic till one is forty-five, so we poor women who are under thirty, or say we are, have nothing open to us but politics or philanthropy. And philanthropy seems to me to have become simply the refuge of people who wish to annoy their fellow-creatures. I prefer politics. I think they are more . . . becoming!

sir robert chiltern. A political life is a noble career!

mrs. cheveley. Sometimes. And sometimes it is a clever game, Sir Robert. And sometimes it is a great nuisance.

sir robert chiltern. Which do you find it?

mrs. cheveley. I? A combination of all three. [Drops her fan.]

sir robert chiltern. [Picks up fan.] Allow me!

mrs. cheveley. Thanks.

sir robert chiltern. But you have not told me yet what makes you honour London so suddenly. Our season is almost over.

mrs. cheveley. Oh! I don't care about the London season! It is too matrimonial. People are either hunting for husbands, or hiding from them. I wanted to meet you. It is quite true. You know what a woman's curiosity is. Almost as great as a man's! I wanted immensely to meet you, and . . . to ask you to do something for me.

sir robert chiltern. I hope it is not a little thing, Mrs. Cheveley. I find

288

that little things are so very difficult to do.

mrs. cheveley. [After a moment's reflection.] No, I don't think it is quite a little thing.

sir robert chiltern. I am so glad. Do tell me what it is.

mrs. cheveley. Later on. [Rises.] And now may I walk through your beautiful house? I hear your pictures are charming. Poor Baron Arnheim—you remember the Baron?—used to tell me you had some wonderful Corots.

sir robert chiltern. [With an almost imperceptible start.] Did you know Baron Arnheim well?

mrs. cheveley. [Smiling.] Intimately. Did you?

sir robert chiltern. At one time.

mrs. cheveley. Wonderful man, wasn't he?

sir robert chiltern. [After a pause.] He was very remarkable, in many ways.

mrs. cheveley. I often think it such a pity he never wrote his memoirs. They would have been most interesting.

sir robert chiltern. Yes: he knew men and cities well, like the old Greek.

mrs. cheveley. Without the dreadful disadvantage of having a Penelope waiting at home for him.

mason. Lord Goring.

[*Enter* lord goring. *Thirty-four, but always says he is younger. A well-bred, expressionless face. He is clever, but would not like to be thought so. A flawless dandy, he would be annoyed if he were considered romantic. He plays with life, and is on perfectly good terms with the world. He is fond of being misunderstood. It gives him a post of vantage.*]

sir robert chiltern. Good evening, my dear Arthur! Mrs. Cheveley, allow me to introduce to you Lord Goring, the idlest man in London.

mrs. cheveley. I have met Lord Goring before.

lord goring. [Bowing.] I did not think you would remember me, Mrs. Cheveley.

mrs. cheveley. My memory is under admirable control. And are you still a bachelor?

lord goring. I . . . believe so.

mrs. cheveley. How very romantic!

lord goring. Oh! I am not at all romantic. I am not old enough. I leave romance to my seniors.

sir robert chiltern. Lord Goring is the result of Boodle's Club, Mrs. Cheveley.

mrs. cheveley. He reflects every credit on the institution.

lord goring. May I ask are you staying in London long?

mrs. cheveley. That depends partly on the weather, partly on the cooking, and partly on Sir Robert.

sir robert chiltern. You are not going to plunge us into a European war, I hope?

mrs. cheveley. There is no danger, at present!

[*She nods to* lord goring, *with a look of amusement in her eyes, and goes out with* sir robert chiltern. lord goring *saunters over to* mabel chiltern.]

mabel chiltern. You are very late!

lord goring. Have you missed me?

mabel chiltern. Awfully!

lord goring. Then I am sorry I did not stay away longer. I like being missed.

mabel chiltern. How very selfish of you!

290

lord goring. I am very selfish.

mabel chiltern. You are always telling me of your bad qualities, Lord Goring.

lord goring. I have only told you half of them as yet, Miss Mabel!

mabel chiltern. Are the others very bad?

lord goring. Quite dreadful! When I think of them at night I go to sleep at once.

mabel chiltern. Well, I delight in your bad qualities. I wouldn't have you part with one of them.

lord goring. How very nice of you! But then you are always nice. By the way, I want to ask you a question, Miss Mabel. Who brought Mrs. Cheveley here? That woman in heliotrope, who has just gone out of the room with your brother?

mabel chiltern. Oh, I think Lady Markby brought her. Why do you ask?

lord goring. I haven't seen her for years, that is all.

mabel chiltern. What an absurd reason!

lord goring. All reasons are absurd.

mabel chiltern. What sort of a woman is she?

lord goring. Oh! a genius in the daytime and a beauty at night!

mabel chiltern. I dislike her already.

lord goring. That shows your admirable good taste.

vicomte de nanjac. [Approaching.] Ah, the English young lady is the dragon of good taste, is she not? Quite the dragon of good taste.

lord goring. So the newspapers are always telling us.

vicomte de nanjac. I read all your English newspapers. I find them so amusing.

lord goring. Then, my dear Nanjac, you must certainly read between the lines.

vicomte de nanjac. I should like to, but my professor objects. [To mabel chiltern.] May I have the pleasure of escorting you to the music-room, Mademoiselle?

mabel chiltern. [Looking very disappointed.] Delighted, Vicomte, quite delighted! [Turning to lord goring.] Aren't you coming to the music-room?

lord goring. Not if there is any music going on, Miss Mabel.

mabel chiltern. [Severely.] The music is in German. You would not understand it.

[*Goes out with the v*icomte de nanjac. lord caversham *comes up to his son.*]

lord caversham. Well, sir! what are you doing here? Wasting your life as usual! You should be in bed, sir. You keep too late hours! I heard of you the other night at Lady Rufford's dancing till four o'clock in the morning!

lord goring. Only a quarter to four, father.

lord caversham. Can't make out how you stand London Society. The thing has gone to the dogs, a lot of damned nobodies talking about nothing.

lord goring. I love talking about nothing, father. It is the only thing I know anything about.

lord caversham. You seem to me to be living entirely for pleasure.

lord goring. What else is there to live for, father? Nothing ages like happiness.

lord caversham. You are heartless, sir, very heartless!

lord goring. I hope not, father. Good evening, Lady Basildon!

lady basildon. [Arching two pretty eyebrows.] Are you here? I had no idea you ever came to political parties!

lord goring. I adore political parties. They are the only place left to us where people don't talk politics.

lady basildon. I delight in talking politics. I talk them all day long. But I can't bear listening to them. I don't know how the unfortunate men in the House stand these long debates.

lord goring. By never listening.

lady basildon. Really?

lord goring. [In his most serious manner.] Of course. You see, it is a very dangerous thing to listen. If one listens one may be convinced; and a man who allows himself to be convinced by an argument is a thoroughly unreasonable person.

lady basildon. Ah! that accounts for so much in men that I have never understood, and so much in women that their husbands never appreciate in them!

mrs. marchmont. [With a sigh.] Our husbands never appreciate anything in us. We have to go to others for that!

lady basildon. [Emphatically.] Yes, always to others, have we not?

lord goring. [Smiling.] And those are the views of the two ladies who are known to have the most admirable husbands in London.

mrs. marchmont. That is exactly what we can't stand. My Reginald is quite hopelessly faultless. He is really unendurably so, at times! There is not the smallest element of excitement in knowing him.

lord goring. How terrible! Really, the thing should be more widely known!

lady basildon. Basildon is quite as bad; he is as domestic as if he was a bachelor.

mrs. marchmont. [Pressing lady basildon's hand.] My poor Olivia! We have married perfect husbands, and we are well punished for it.

lord goring. I should have thought it was the husbands who were punished.

mrs. marchmont. [Drawing herself up.] Oh, dear no! They are as happy as possible! And as for trusting us, it is tragic how much they trust us.

lady basildon. Perfectly tragic!

lord goring. Or comic, Lady Basildon?

lady basildon. Certainly not comic, Lord Goring. How unkind of you to suggest such a thing!

mrs. marchmont. I am afraid Lord Goring is in the camp of the enemy, as usual. I saw him talking to that Mrs. Cheveley when he came in.

lord goring. Handsome woman, Mrs. Cheveley!

lady basildon. [Stiffly.] Please don't praise other women in our presence. You might wait for us to do that!

lord goring. I did wait.

mrs. marchmont. Well, we are not going to praise her. I hear she went to the Opera on Monday night, and told Tommy Rufford at supper that, as far as she could see, London Society was entirely made up of dowdies and dandies.

lord goring. She is quite right, too. The men are all dowdies and the women are all dandies, aren't they?

mrs. marchmont. [After a pause.] Oh! do you really think that is what Mrs. Cheveley meant?

lord goring. Of course. And a very sensible remark for Mrs. Cheveley to make, too.

[*Enter* mabel chiltern. *She joins the group.*]

294

mabel chiltern. Why are you talking about Mrs. Cheveley? Everybody is talking about Mrs. Cheveley! Lord Goring says—what did you say, Lord Goring, about Mrs. Cheveley? Oh! I remember, that she was a genius in the daytime and a beauty at night.

lady basildon. What a horrid combination! So very unnatural!

mrs. marchmont. [In her most dreamy manner.] I like looking at geniuses, and listening to beautiful people.

lord goring. Ah! that is morbid of you, Mrs. Marchmont!

mrs. marchmont. [Brightening to a look of real pleasure.] I am so glad to hear you say that. Marchmont and I have been married for seven years, and he has never once told me that I was morbid. Men are so painfully unobservant!

lady basildon. [Turning to her.] I have always said, dear Margaret, that you were the most morbid person in London.

mrs. marchmont. Ah! but you are always sympathetic, Olivia!

mabel chiltern. Is it morbid to have a desire for food? I have a great desire for food. Lord Goring, will you give me some supper?

lord goring. With pleasure, Miss Mabel. [Moves away with her.]

mabel chiltern. How horrid you have been! You have never talked to me the whole evening!

lord goring. How could I? You went away with the child-diplomatist.

mabel chiltern. You might have followed us. Pursuit would have been only polite. I don't think I like you at all this evening!

lord goring. I like you immensely.

mabel chiltern. Well, I wish you'd show it in a more marked way! [They go downstairs.]

mrs. marchmont. Olivia, I have a curious feeling of absolute faintness.

I think I should like some supper very much. I know I should like some supper.

lady basildon. I am positively dying for supper, Margaret!

mrs. marchmont. Men are so horribly selfish, they never think of these things.

lady basildon. Men are grossly material, grossly material!

[*The* vicomte de nanjac *enters from the music-room with some other guests. After having carefully examined all the people present, he approaches* lady basildon.]

vicomte de nanjac. May I have the honour of taking you down to supper, Comtesse?

lady basildon. [Coldly.] I never take supper, thank you, Vicomte. [The vicomte is about to retire. lady basildon, seeing this, rises at once and takes his arm.] But I will come down with you with pleasure.

vicomte de nanjac. I am so fond of eating! I am very English in all my tastes.

lady basildon. You look quite English, Vicomte, quite English.

[*They pass out.* mr. montford, *a perfectly groomed young dandy, approaches* mrs. marchmont.]

mr. montford. Like some supper, Mrs. Marchmont?

mrs. marchmont. [Languidly.] Thank you, Mr. Montford, I never touch supper. [Rises hastily and takes his arm.] But I will sit beside you, and watch you.

mr. montford. I don't know that I like being watched when I am eating!

mrs. marchmont. Then I will watch some one else.

mr. montford. I don't know that I should like that either.

mrs. marchmont. [Severely.] Pray, Mr. Montford, do not make these painful scenes of jealousy in public!

[*They go downstairs with the other guests, passing* sir robert chiltern *and* mrs. cheveley, *who now enter.*]

sir robert chiltern. And are you going to any of our country houses before you leave England, Mrs. Cheveley?

mrs. cheveley. Oh, no! I can't stand your English house-parties. In England people actually try to be brilliant at breakfast. That is so dreadful of them! Only dull people are brilliant at breakfast. And then the family skeleton is always reading family prayers. My stay in England really depends on you, Sir Robert. [Sits down on the sofa.]

sir robert chiltern. [Taking a seat beside her.] Seriously?

mrs. cheveley. Quite seriously. I want to talk to you about a great political and financial scheme, about this Argentine Canal Company, in fact.

sir robert chiltern. What a tedious, practical subject for you to talk about, Mrs. Cheveley!

mrs. cheveley. Oh, I like tedious, practical subjects. What I don't like are tedious, practical people. There is a wide difference. Besides, you are interested, I know, in International Canal schemes. You were Lord Radley's secretary, weren't you, when the Government bought the Suez Canal shares?

sir robert chiltern. Yes. But the Suez Canal was a very great and splendid undertaking. It gave us our direct route to India. It had imperial value. It was necessary that we should have control. This Argentine scheme is a commonplace Stock Exchange swindle.

mrs. cheveley. A speculation, Sir Robert! A brilliant, daring speculation.

sir robert chiltern. Believe me, Mrs. Cheveley, it is a swindle. Let us call things by their proper names. It makes matters simpler. We have all the information about it at the Foreign Office. In fact, I sent out a special Commission to inquire into the matter privately, and they report that the works are hardly begun, and as for the money already subscribed, no one seems to know what has become of it. The whole thing is a second Panama, and with not a quarter of the chance of success that miserable affair ever had. I hope you have not invested in it. I am sure you are far too clever to have done that.

mrs. cheveley. I have invested very largely in it.

sir robert chiltern. Who could have advised you to do such a foolish thing?

mrs. cheveley. Your old friend—and mine.

sir robert chiltern. Who?

mrs. cheveley. Baron Arnheim.

sir robert chiltern. [Frowning.] Ah! yes. I remember hearing, at the time of his death, that he had been mixed up in the whole affair.

mrs. cheveley. It was his last romance. His last but one, to do him justice.

sir robert chiltern. [Rising.] But you have not seen my Corots yet. They are in the music-room. Corots seem to go with music, don't they? May I show them to you?

mrs. cheveley. [Shaking her head.] I am not in a mood to-night for silver twilights, or rose-pink dawns. I want to talk business. [Motions to him with her fan to sit down again beside her.]

sir robert chiltern. I fear I have no advice to give you, Mrs. Cheveley, except to interest yourself in something less dangerous. The success of the Canal depends, of course, on the attitude of England, and I am going to lay the report of the Commissioners before the House to-morrow night.

mrs. cheveley. That you must not do. In your own interests, Sir Robert, to say nothing of mine, you must not do that.

sir robert chiltern. [Looking at her in wonder.] In my own interests? My dear Mrs. Cheveley, what do you mean? [Sits down beside her.]

mrs. cheveley. Sir Robert, I will be quite frank with you. I want you to withdraw the report that you had intended to lay before the House, on the ground that you have reasons to believe that the Commissioners have been prejudiced or misinformed, or something. Then I want you to say a few words to the effect that the Government is going to reconsider the question, and that you have reason to believe that the Canal, if completed, will be of great international value. You know the sort of things ministers say in cases of this kind. A few ordinary platitudes will do. In modern life nothing produces such an effect as a good platitude. It makes the whole world kin. Will you do that for me?

sir robert chiltern. Mrs. Cheveley, you cannot be serious in making me such a proposition!

mrs. cheveley. I am quite serious.

sir robert chiltern. [Coldly.] Pray allow me to believe that you are not.

mrs. cheveley. [Speaking with great deliberation and emphasis.] Ah! but I am. And if you do what I ask you, I . . . will pay you very handsomely!

sir robert chiltern. Pay me!

mrs. cheveley. Yes.

sir robert chiltern. I am afraid I don't quite understand what you mean.

mrs. cheveley. [Leaning back on the sofa and looking at him.] How very disappointing! And I have come all the way from Vienna in order that you should thoroughly understand me.

sir robert chiltern. I fear I don't.

mrs. cheveley. [In her most nonchalant manner.] My dear Sir Robert, you are a man of the world, and you have your price, I suppose. Everybody has nowadays. The drawback is that most people are so dreadfully expensive. I know I am. I hope you will be more reasonable in your terms.

sir robert chiltern. [Rises indignantly.] If you will allow me, I will call your carriage for you. You have lived so long abroad, Mrs. Cheveley, that you

299

seem to be unable to realise that you are talking to an English gentleman.

mrs. cheveley. [Detains him by touching his arm with her fan, and keeping it there while she is talking.] I realise that I am talking to a man who laid the foundation of his fortune by selling to a Stock Exchange speculator a Cabinet secret.

sir robert chiltern. [Biting his lip.] What do you mean?

mrs. cheveley. [Rising and facing him.] I mean that I know the real origin of your wealth and your career, and I have got your letter, too.

sir robert chiltern. What letter?

mrs. cheveley. [Contemptuously.] The letter you wrote to Baron Arnheim, when you were Lord Radley's secretary, telling the Baron to buy Suez Canal shares—a letter written three days before the Government announced its own purchase.

sir robert chiltern. [Hoarsely.] It is not true.

mrs. cheveley. You thought that letter had been destroyed. How foolish of you! It is in my possession.

sir robert chiltern. The affair to which you allude was no more than a speculation. The House of Commons had not yet passed the bill; it might have been rejected.

mrs. cheveley. It was a swindle, Sir Robert. Let us call things by their proper names. It makes everything simpler. And now I am going to sell you that letter, and the price I ask for it is your public support of the Argentine scheme. You made your own fortune out of one canal. You must help me and my friends to make our fortunes out of another!

sir robert chiltern. It is infamous, what you propose—infamous!

mrs. cheveley. Oh, no! This is the game of life as we all have to play it, Sir Robert, sooner or later!

sir robert chiltern. I cannot do what you ask me.

300

mrs. cheveley. You mean you cannot help doing it. You know you are standing on the edge of a precipice. And it is not for you to make terms. It is for you to accept them. Supposing you refuse—

sir robert chiltern. What then?

mrs. cheveley. My dear Sir Robert, what then? You are ruined, that is all! Remember to what a point your Puritanism in England has brought you. In old days nobody pretended to be a bit better than his neighbours. In fact, to be a bit better than one's neighbour was considered excessively vulgar and middle-class. Nowadays, with our modern mania for morality, every one has to pose as a paragon of purity, incorruptibility, and all the other seven deadly virtues—and what is the result? You all go over like ninepins—one after the other. Not a year passes in England without somebody disappearing. Scandals used to lend charm, or at least interest, to a man—now they crush him. And yours is a very nasty scandal. You couldn't survive it. If it were known that as a young man, secretary to a great and important minister, you sold a Cabinet secret for a large sum of money, and that that was the origin of your wealth and career, you would be hounded out of public life, you would disappear completely. And after all, Sir Robert, why should you sacrifice your entire future rather than deal diplomatically with your enemy? For the moment I am your enemy. I admit it! And I am much stronger than you are. The big battalions are on my side. You have a splendid position, but it is your splendid position that makes you so vulnerable. You can't defend it! And I am in attack. Of course I have not talked morality to you. You must admit in fairness that I have spared you that. Years ago you did a clever, unscrupulous thing; it turned out a great success. You owe to it your fortune and position. And now you have got to pay for it. Sooner or later we have all to pay for what we do. You have to pay now. Before I leave you to-night, you have got to promise me to suppress your report, and to speak in the House in favour of this scheme.

sir robert chiltern. What you ask is impossible.

mrs. cheveley. You must make it possible. You are going to make it possible. Sir Robert, you know what your English newspapers are like.

Suppose that when I leave this house I drive down to some newspaper office, and give them this scandal and the proofs of it! Think of their loathsome joy, of the delight they would have in dragging you down, of the mud and mire they would plunge you in. Think of the hypocrite with his greasy smile penning his leading article, and arranging the foulness of the public placard.

sir robert chiltern. Stop! You want me to withdraw the report and to make a short speech stating that I believe there are possibilities in the scheme?

mrs. cheveley. [Sitting down on the sofa.] Those are my terms.

sir robert chiltern. [In a low voice.] I will give you any sum of money you want.

mrs. cheveley. Even you are not rich enough, Sir Robert, to buy back your past. No man is.

sir robert chiltern. I will not do what you ask me. I will not.

mrs. cheveley. You have to. If you don't . . . [Rises from the sofa.]

sir robert chiltern. [Bewildered and unnerved.] Wait a moment! What did you propose? You said that you would give me back my letter, didn't you?

mrs. cheveley. Yes. That is agreed. I will be in the Ladies' Gallery to-morrow night at half-past eleven. If by that time—and you will have had heaps of opportunity—you have made an announcement to the House in the terms I wish, I shall hand you back your letter with the prettiest thanks, and the best, or at any rate the most suitable, compliment I can think of. I intend to play quite fairly with you. One should always play fairly . . . when one has the winning cards. The Baron taught me that . . . amongst other things.

sir robert chiltern. You must let me have time to consider your proposal.

mrs. cheveley. No; you must settle now!

sir robert chiltern. Give me a week—three days!

mrs. cheveley. Impossible! I have got to telegraph to Vienna to-night.

sir robert chiltern. My God! what brought you into my life?

mrs. cheveley. Circumstances. [Moves towards the door.]

sir robert chiltern. Don't go. I consent. The report shall be withdrawn. I will arrange for a question to be put to me on the subject.

mrs. cheveley. Thank you. I knew we should come to an amicable agreement. I understood your nature from the first. I analysed you, though you did not adore me. And now you can get my carriage for me, Sir Robert. I see the people coming up from supper, and Englishmen always get romantic after a meal, and that bores me dreadfully. [Exit sir robert chiltern.]

[*Enter Guests,* lady chiltern, lady markby, lord caversham, lady basildon, mrs. marchmont, vicomte de nanjac, mr. montford.]

lady markby. Well, dear Mrs. Cheveley, I hope you have enjoyed yourself. Sir Robert is very entertaining, is he not?

mrs. cheveley. Most entertaining! I have enjoyed my talk with him immensely.

lady markby. He has had a very interesting and brilliant career. And he has married a most admirable wife. Lady Chiltern is a woman of the very highest principles, I am glad to say. I am a little too old now, myself, to trouble about setting a good example, but I always admire people who do. And Lady Chiltern has a very ennobling effect on life, though her dinner-parties are rather dull sometimes. But one can't have everything, can one? And now I must go, dear. Shall I call for you to-morrow?

mrs. cheveley. Thanks.

lady markby. We might drive in the Park at five. Everything looks so fresh in the Park now!

mrs. cheveley. Except the people!

lady markby. Perhaps the people are a little jaded. I have often observed that the Season as it goes on produces a kind of softening of the brain. However, I think anything is better than high intellectual pressure. That is the most unbecoming thing there is. It makes the noses of the young girls so particularly large. And there is nothing so difficult to marry as a large nose: men don't like them. Good-night, dear! [To lady chiltern.] Good-night, Gertrude! [Goes out on lord caversham's arm.]

mrs. cheveley. What a charming house you have, Lady Chiltern! I have spent a delightful evening. It has been so interesting getting to know your husband.

lady chiltern. Why did you wish to meet my husband, Mrs. Cheveley?

mrs. cheveley. Oh, I will tell you. I wanted to interest him in this Argentine Canal scheme, of which I dare say you have heard. And I found him most susceptible,—susceptible to reason, I mean. A rare thing in a man. I converted him in ten minutes. He is going to make a speech in the House to-morrow night in favour of the idea. We must go to the Ladies' Gallery and hear him! It will be a great occasion!

lady chiltern. There must be some mistake. That scheme could never have my husband's support.

mrs. cheveley. Oh, I assure you it's all settled. I don't regret my tedious journey from Vienna now. It has been a great success. But, of course, for the next twenty-four hours the whole thing is a dead secret.

lady chiltern. [Gently.] A secret? Between whom?

mrs. cheveley. [With a flash of amusement in her eyes.] Between your husband and myself.

sir robert chiltern. [Entering.] Your carriage is here, Mrs. Cheveley!

mrs. cheveley. Thanks! Good evening, Lady Chiltern! Good-night, Lord Goring! I am at Claridge's. Don't you think you might leave a card?

lord goring. If you wish it, Mrs. Cheveley!

mrs. cheveley. Oh, don't be so solemn about it, or I shall be obliged to leave a card on you. In England I suppose that would hardly be considered en règle. Abroad, we are more civilised. Will you see me down, Sir Robert? Now that we have both the same interests at heart we shall be great friends

I hope!

[*Sails out on* sir robert chiltern's *arm.* lady chiltern *goes to the top of the staircase and looks down at them as they descend. Her expression is troubled. After a little time she is joined by some of the guests, and passes with them into another reception-room.*]

mabel chiltern. What a horrid woman!

lord goring. You should go to bed, Miss Mabel.

mabel chiltern. Lord Goring!

lord goring. My father told me to go to bed an hour ago. I don't see why I shouldn't give you the same advice. I always pass on good advice. It is the only thing to do with it. It is never of any use to oneself.

mabel chiltern. Lord Goring, you are always ordering me out of the room. I think it most courageous of you. Especially as I am not going to bed for hours. [Goes over to the sofa.] You can come and sit down if you like, and talk about anything in the world, except the Royal Academy, Mrs. Cheveley, or novels in Scotch dialect. They are not improving subjects. [Catches sight of something that is lying on the sofa half hidden by the cushion.] What is this? Some one has dropped a diamond brooch! Quite beautiful, isn't it? [Shows it to him.] I wish it was mine, but Gertrude won't let me wear anything but pearls, and I am thoroughly sick of pearls. They make one look so plain, so good and so intellectual. I wonder whom the brooch belongs to.

lord goring. I wonder who dropped it.

mabel chiltern. It is a beautiful brooch.

lord goring. It is a handsome bracelet.

mabel chiltern. It isn't a bracelet. It's a brooch.

lord goring. It can be used as a bracelet. [Takes it from her, and, pulling out a green letter-case, puts the ornament carefully in it, and replaces the whole thing in his breast-pocket with the most perfect sang froid.]

mabel chiltern. What are you doing?

lord goring. Miss Mabel, I am going to make a rather strange request to you.

mabel chiltern. [Eagerly.] Oh, pray do! I have been waiting for it all the evening.

lord goring. [Is a little taken aback, but recovers himself.] Don't mention to anybody that I have taken charge of this brooch. Should any one write and claim it, let me know at once.

mabel chiltern. That is a strange request.

lord goring. Well, you see I gave this brooch to somebody once, years ago.

mabel chiltern. You did?

lord goring. Yes.

[lady chiltern enters alone. The other guests have gone.]

mabel chiltern. Then I shall certainly bid you good-night. Good-night, Gertrude! [Exit.]

lady chiltern. Good-night, dear! [To lord goring.] You saw whom Lady Markby brought here to-night?

lord goring. Yes. It was an unpleasant surprise. What did she come here for?

lady chiltern. Apparently to try and lure Robert to uphold some fraudulent scheme in which she is interested. The Argentine Canal, in fact.

lord goring. She has mistaken her man, hasn't she?

lady chiltern. She is incapable of understanding an upright nature like my husband's!

lord goring. Yes. I should fancy she came to grief if she tried to get Robert into her toils. It is extraordinary what astounding mistakes clever women make.

306

lady chiltern. I don't call women of that kind clever. I call them stupid!

lord goring. Same thing often. Good-night, Lady Chiltern!

lady chiltern. Good-night!

[*Enter* sir robert chiltern.]

sir robert chiltern. My dear Arthur, you are not going? Do stop a little!

lord goring. Afraid I can't, thanks. I have promised to look in at the Hartlocks'. I believe they have got a mauve Hungarian band that plays mauve Hungarian music. See you soon. Good-bye!

[*Exit*]

sir robert chiltern. How beautiful you look to-night, Gertrude!

lady chiltern. Robert, it is not true, is it? You are not going to lend your support to this Argentine speculation? You couldn't!

sir robert chiltern. [Starting.] Who told you I intended to do so?

lady chiltern. That woman who has just gone out, Mrs. Cheveley, as she calls herself now. She seemed to taunt me with it. Robert, I know this woman. You don't. We were at school together. She was untruthful, dishonest, an evil influence on every one whose trust or friendship she could win. I hated, I despised her. She stole things, she was a thief. She was sent away for being a thief. Why do you let her influence you?

sir robert chiltern. Gertrude, what you tell me may be true, but it happened many years ago. It is best forgotten! Mrs. Cheveley may have changed since then. No one should be entirely judged by their past.

lady chiltern. [Sadly.] One's past is what one is. It is the only way by which people should be judged.

sir robert chiltern. That is a hard saying, Gertrude!

lady chiltern. It is a true saying, Robert. And what did she mean by boasting that she had got you to lend your support, your name, to a thing I have heard you describe as the most dishonest and fraudulent scheme there has ever been in political life?

sir robert chiltern. [Biting his lip.] I was mistaken in the view I took. We all may make mistakes.

lady chiltern. But you told me yesterday that you had received the report from the Commission, and that it entirely condemned the whole thing.

sir robert chiltern. [Walking up and down.] I have reasons now to believe that the Commission was prejudiced, or, at any rate, misinformed. Besides, Gertrude, public and private life are different things. They have different laws, and move on different lines.

lady chiltern. They should both represent man at his highest. I see no difference between them.

sir robert chiltern. [Stopping.] In the present case, on a matter of practical politics, I have changed my mind. That is all.

lady chiltern. All!

sir robert chiltern. [Sternly.] Yes!

lady chiltern. Robert! Oh! it is horrible that I should have to ask you such a question—Robert, are you telling me the whole truth?

sir robert chiltern. Why do you ask me such a question?

lady chiltern. [After a pause.] Why do you not answer it?

sir robert chiltern. [Sitting down.] Gertrude, truth is a very complex thing, and politics is a very complex business. There are wheels within wheels. One may be under certain obligations to people that one must pay. Sooner or later in political life one has to compromise. Every one does.

lady chiltern. Compromise? Robert, why do you talk so differently to-night from the way I have always heard you talk? Why are you changed?

sir robert chiltern. I am not changed. But circumstances alter things.

lady chiltern. Circumstances should never alter principles!

308

sir robert chiltern. But if I told you—

lady chiltern. What?

sir robert chiltern. That it was necessary, vitally necessary?

lady chiltern. It can never be necessary to do what is not honourable. Or if it be necessary, then what is it that I have loved! But it is not, Robert; tell me it is not. Why should it be? What gain would you get? Money? We have no need of that! And money that comes from a tainted source is a degradation. Power? But power is nothing in itself. It is power to do good that is fine—that, and that only. What is it, then? Robert, tell me why you are going to do this dishonourable thing!

sir robert chiltern. Gertrude, you have no right to use that word. I told you it was a question of rational compromise. It is no more than that.

lady chiltern. Robert, that is all very well for other men, for men who treat life simply as a sordid speculation; but not for you, Robert, not for you. You are different. All your life you have stood apart from others. You have never let the world soil you. To the world, as to myself, you have been an ideal always. Oh! be that ideal still. That great inheritance throw not away— that tower of ivory do not destroy. Robert, men can love what is beneath them—things unworthy, stained, dishonoured. We women worship when we love; and when we lose our worship, we lose everything. Oh! don't kill my love for you, don't kill that!

sir robert chiltern. Gertrude!

lady chiltern. I know that there are men with horrible secrets in their lives—men who have done some shameful thing, and who in some critical moment have to pay for it, by doing some other act of shame—oh! don't tell me you are such as they are! Robert, is there in your life any secret dishonour or disgrace? Tell me, tell me at once, that—

sir robert chiltern. That what?

lady chiltern. [Speaking very slowly.] That our lives may drift apart.

sir robert chiltern. Drift apart?

lady chiltern. That they may be entirely separate. It would be better for us both.

sir robert chiltern. Gertrude, there is nothing in my past life that you might not know.

lady chiltern. I was sure of it, Robert, I was sure of it. But why did you say those dreadful things, things so unlike your real self? Don't let us ever talk about the subject again. You will write, won't you, to Mrs. Cheveley, and tell her that you cannot support this scandalous scheme of hers? If you have given her any promise you must take it back, that is all!

sir robert chiltern. Must I write and tell her that?

lady chiltern. Surely, Robert! What else is there to do?

sir robert chiltern. I might see her personally. It would be better.

lady chiltern. You must never see her again, Robert. She is not a woman you should ever speak to. She is not worthy to talk to a man like you. No you must write to her at once, now, this moment, and let your letter show her that your decision is quite irrevocable!

sir robert chiltern. Write this moment!

lady chiltern. Yes.

sir robert chiltern. But it is so late. It is close on twelve.

lady chiltern. That makes no matter. She must know at once that she has been mistaken in you—and that you are not a man to do anything base or underhand or dishonourable. Write here, Robert. Write that you decline to support this scheme of hers, as you hold it to be a dishonest scheme. Yes—write the word dishonest. She knows what that word means. [sir robert chiltern sits down and writes a letter. His wife takes it up and reads it.] Yes that will do. [Rings bell.] And now the envelope. [He writes the envelope slowly. Enter mason.] Have this letter sent at once to Claridge's Hotel. There is no answer. [Exit mason. lady chiltern kneels down beside her husband and puts her arms around him.] Robert, love gives one an instinct to things

310

I feel to-night that I have saved you from something that might have been a danger to you, from something that might have made men honour you less than they do. I don't think you realise sufficiently, Robert, that you have brought into the political life of our time a nobler atmosphere, a finer attitude towards life, a freer air of purer aims and higher ideals—I know it, and for that I love you, Robert.

sir robert chiltern. Oh, love me always, Gertrude, love me always!

lady chiltern. I will love you always, because you will always be worthy of love. We needs must love the highest when we see it! [Kisses him and rises and goes out.]

[sir robert chiltern *walks up and down for a moment; then sits down and buries his face in his hands. The Servant enters and begins pulling out the lights.* sir robert chiltern *looks up.*]

sir robert chiltern. Put out the lights, Mason, put out the lights!

[*The Servant puts out the lights. The room becomes almost dark. The only light there is comes from the great chandelier that hangs over the staircase and illumines the tapestry of the Triumph of Love.*]

Act Drop

SECOND ACT

SCENE

Morning-room at Sir Robert Chiltern's house.

[lord goring, *dressed in the height of fashion, is lounging in an armchair.* sir robert chiltern *is standing in front of the fireplace. He is evidently in a state of great mental excitement and distress. As the scene progresses he paces nervously up and down the room.*]

lord goring. My dear Robert, it's a very awkward business, very awkward indeed. You should have told your wife the whole thing. Secrets from other people's wives are a necessary luxury in modern life. So, at least, I am always told at the club by people who are bald enough to know better. But no man should have a secret from his own wife. She invariably finds it out. Women have a wonderful instinct about things. They can discover everything except the obvious.

sir robert chiltern. Arthur, I couldn't tell my wife. When could I have told her? Not last night. It would have made a life-long separation between us, and I would have lost the love of the one woman in the world I worship, of the only woman who has ever stirred love within me. Last night it would have been quite impossible. She would have turned from me in horror . . . in horror and in contempt.

lord goring. Is Lady Chiltern as perfect as all that?

sir robert chiltern. Yes; my wife is as perfect as all that.

lord goring. [Taking off his left-hand glove.] What a pity! I beg your pardon, my dear fellow, I didn't quite mean that. But if what you tell me is true, I should like to have a serious talk about life with Lady Chiltern.

sir robert chiltern. It would be quite useless.

lord goring. May I try?

sir robert chiltern. Yes; but nothing could make her alter her views.

lord goring. Well, at the worst it would simply be a psychological experiment.

sir robert chiltern. All such experiments are terribly dangerous.

lord goring. Everything is dangerous, my dear fellow. If it wasn't so, life wouldn't be worth living. . . . Well, I am bound to say that I think you should have told her years ago.

sir robert chiltern. When? When we were engaged? Do you think she would have married me if she had known that the origin of my fortune is such as it is, the basis of my career such as it is, and that I had done a thing that I suppose most men would call shameful and dishonourable?

lord goring. [Slowly.] Yes; most men would call it ugly names. There is no doubt of that.

sir robert chiltern. [Bitterly.] Men who every day do something of the same kind themselves. Men who, each one of them, have worse secrets in their own lives.

lord goring. That is the reason they are so pleased to find out other people's secrets. It distracts public attention from their own.

sir robert chiltern. And, after all, whom did I wrong by what I did? No one.

lord goring. [Looking at him steadily.] Except yourself, Robert.

sir robert chiltern. [After a pause.] Of course I had private information about a certain transaction contemplated by the Government of the day, and I acted on it. Private information is practically the source of every large modern fortune.

lord goring. [Tapping his boot with his cane.] And public scandal invariably the result.

sir robert chiltern. [Pacing up and down the room.] Arthur, do you think that what I did nearly eighteen years ago should be brought up against me now? Do you think it fair that a man's whole career should be ruined for a fault done in one's boyhood almost? I was twenty-two at the time, and I had the double misfortune of being well-born and poor, two unforgiveable things nowadays. Is it fair that the folly, the sin of one's youth, if men choose to call it a sin, should wreck a life like mine, should place me in the pillory, should shatter all that I have worked for, all that I have built up. Is it fair, Arthur?

lord goring. Life is never fair, Robert. And perhaps it is a good thing for most of us that it is not.

sir robert chiltern. Every man of ambition has to fight his century with its own weapons. What this century worships is wealth. The God of this century is wealth. To succeed one must have wealth. At all costs one must have wealth.

lord goring. You underrate yourself, Robert. Believe me, without wealth you could have succeeded just as well.

sir robert chiltern. When I was old, perhaps. When I had lost my passion for power, or could not use it. When I was tired, worn out, disappointed. I wanted my success when I was young. Youth is the time for success. I couldn't wait.

lord goring. Well, you certainly have had your success while you are still young. No one in our day has had such a brilliant success. Under-Secretary for Foreign Affairs at the age of forty—that's good enough for any one, I should think.

sir robert chiltern. And if it is all taken away from me now? If I lose everything over a horrible scandal? If I am hounded from public life?

lord goring. Robert, how could you have sold yourself for money?

sir robert chiltern. [Excitedly.] I did not sell myself for money. I bought success at a great price. That is all.

lord goring. [Gravely.] Yes; you certainly paid a great price for it. But what first made you think of doing such a thing?

sir robert chiltern. Baron Arnheim.

lord goring. Damned scoundrel!

sir robert chiltern. No; he was a man of a most subtle and refined intellect. A man of culture, charm, and distinction. One of the most intellectual men I ever met.

lord goring. Ah! I prefer a gentlemanly fool any day. There is more to be said for stupidity than people imagine. Personally I have a great admiration for stupidity. It is a sort of fellow-feeling, I suppose. But how did he do it? Tell me the whole thing.

sir robert chiltern. [Throws himself into an armchair by the writing-table.] One night after dinner at Lord Radley's the Baron began talking about success in modern life as something that one could reduce to an absolutely definite science. With that wonderfully fascinating quiet voice of his he expounded to us the most terrible of all philosophies, the philosophy of power, preached to us the most marvellous of all gospels, the gospel of gold. I think he saw the effect he had produced on me, for some days afterwards he wrote and asked me to come and see him. He was living then in Park Lane, in the house Lord Woolcomb has now. I remember so well how, with a strange smile on his pale, curved lips, he led me through his wonderful picture gallery, showed me his tapestries, his enamels, his jewels, his carved ivories, made me wonder at the strange loveliness of the luxury in which he lived; and then told me that luxury was nothing but a background, a painted scene in a play, and that power, power over other men, power over the world, was the one thing worth having, the one supreme pleasure worth knowing, the one joy one never tired of, and that in our century only the rich possessed it.

lord goring. [With great deliberation.] A thoroughly shallow creed.

sir robert chiltern. [Rising.] I didn't think so then. I don't think so now. Wealth has given me enormous power. It gave me at the very outset of my life freedom, and freedom is everything. You have never been poor, and never known what ambition is. You cannot understand what a wonderful chance the Baron gave me. Such a chance as few men get.

lord goring. Fortunately for them, if one is to judge by results. But tell me definitely, how did the Baron finally persuade you to—well, to do what you did?

sir robert chiltern. When I was going away he said to me that if I ever could give him any private information of real value he would make me a very rich man. I was dazed at the prospect he held out to me, and my ambition and my desire for power were at that time boundless. Six weeks later certain private documents passed through my hands.

lord goring. [Keeping his eyes steadily fixed on the carpet.] State documents?

sir robert chiltern. Yes. [lord goring sighs, then passes his hand across his forehead and looks up.]

lord goring. I had no idea that you, of all men in the world, could have been so weak, Robert, as to yield to such a temptation as Baron Arnheim held out to you.

sir robert chiltern. Weak? Oh, I am sick of hearing that phrase. Sick of using it about others. Weak? Do you really think, Arthur, that it is weakness that yields to temptation? I tell you that there are terrible temptations that it requires strength, strength and courage, to yield to. To stake all one's life on a single moment, to risk everything on one throw, whether the stake be power or pleasure, I care not—there is no weakness in that. There is a horrible, a terrible courage. I had that courage. I sat down the same afternoon and wrote Baron Arnheim the letter this woman now holds. He made three-quarters of a million over the transaction.

lord goring. And you?

sir robert chiltern. I received from the Baron £110,000.

lord goring. You were worth more, Robert.

sir robert chiltern. No; that money gave me exactly what I wanted, power over others. I went into the House immediately. The Baron advised me in finance from time to time. Before five years I had almost trebled my

316

fortune. Since then everything that I have touched has turned out a success. In all things connected with money I have had a luck so extraordinary that sometimes it has made me almost afraid. I remember having read somewhere, in some strange book, that when the gods wish to punish us they answer our prayers.

lord goring. But tell me, Robert, did you never suffer any regret for what you had done?

sir robert chiltern. No. I felt that I had fought the century with its own weapons, and won.

lord goring. [Sadly.] You thought you had won.

sir robert chiltern. I thought so. [After a long pause.] Arthur, do you despise me for what I have told you?

lord goring. [With deep feeling in his voice.] I am very sorry for you, Robert, very sorry indeed.

sir robert chiltern. I don't say that I suffered any remorse. I didn't. Not remorse in the ordinary, rather silly sense of the word. But I have paid conscience money many times. I had a wild hope that I might disarm destiny. The sum Baron Arnheim gave me I have distributed twice over in public charities since then.

lord goring. [Looking up.] In public charities? Dear me! what a lot of harm you must have done, Robert!

sir robert chiltern. Oh, don't say that, Arthur; don't talk like that!

lord goring. Never mind what I say, Robert! I am always saying what I shouldn't say. In fact, I usually say what I really think. A great mistake nowadays. It makes one so liable to be misunderstood. As regards this dreadful business, I will help you in whatever way I can. Of course you know that.

sir robert chiltern. Thank you, Arthur, thank you. But what is to be done? What can be done?

lord goring. [Leaning back with his hands in his pockets.] Well, the English can't stand a man who is always saying he is in the right, but they are very fond of a man who admits that he has been in the wrong. It is one of the best things in them. However, in your case, Robert, a confession would not do. The money, if you will allow me to say so, is . . . awkward. Besides, if you did make a clean breast of the whole affair, you would never be able to talk morality again. And in England a man who can't talk morality twice a week to a large, popular, immoral audience is quite over as a serious politician. There would be nothing left for him as a profession except Botany or the Church. A confession would be of no use. It would ruin you.

sir robert chiltern. It would ruin me. Arthur, the only thing for me to do now is to fight the thing out.

lord goring. [Rising from his chair.] I was waiting for you to say that, Robert. It is the only thing to do now. And you must begin by telling your wife the whole story.

sir robert chiltern. That I will not do.

lord goring. Robert, believe me, you are wrong.

sir robert chiltern. I couldn't do it. It would kill her love for me. And now about this woman, this Mrs. Cheveley. How can I defend myself against her? You knew her before, Arthur, apparently.

lord goring. Yes.

sir robert chiltern. Did you know her well?

lord goring. [Arranging his necktie.] So little that I got engaged to be married to her once, when I was staying at the Tenbys'. The affair lasted for three days . . . nearly.

sir robert chiltern. Why was it broken off?

lord goring. [Airily.] Oh, I forget. At least, it makes no matter. By the way, have you tried her with money? She used to be confoundedly fond of money.

318

sir robert chiltern. I offered her any sum she wanted. She refused.

lord goring. Then the marvellous gospel of gold breaks down sometimes. The rich can't do everything, after all.

sir robert chiltern. Not everything. I suppose you are right. Arthur, I feel that public disgrace is in store for me. I feel certain of it. I never knew what terror was before. I know it now. It is as if a hand of ice were laid upon one's heart. It is as if one's heart were beating itself to death in some empty hollow.

lord goring. [Striking the table.] Robert, you must fight her. You must fight her.

sir robert chiltern. But how?

lord goring. I can't tell you how at present. I have not the smallest idea. But every one has some weak point. There is some flaw in each one of us. [Strolls to the fireplace and looks at himself in the glass.] My father tells me that even I have faults. Perhaps I have. I don't know.

sir robert chiltern. In defending myself against Mrs. Cheveley, I have a right to use any weapon I can find, have I not?

lord goring. [Still looking in the glass.] In your place I don't think I should have the smallest scruple in doing so. She is thoroughly well able to take care of herself.

sir robert chiltern. [Sits down at the table and takes a pen in his hand.] Well, I shall send a cipher telegram to the Embassy at Vienna, to inquire if there is anything known against her. There may be some secret scandal she might be afraid of.

lord goring. [Settling his buttonhole.] Oh, I should fancy Mrs. Cheveley is one of those very modern women of our time who find a new scandal as becoming as a new bonnet, and air them both in the Park every afternoon at five-thirty. I am sure she adores scandals, and that the sorrow of her life at present is that she can't manage to have enough of them.

sir robert chiltern. [Writing.] Why do you say that?

lord goring. [Turning round.] Well, she wore far too much rouge last night, and not quite enough clothes. That is always a sign of despair in a woman.

sir robert chiltern. [Striking a bell.] But it is worth while my wiring to Vienna, is it not?

lord goring. It is always worth while asking a question, though it is not always worth while answering one.

[*Enter* mason.]

sir robert chiltern. Is Mr. Trafford in his room?

mason. Yes, Sir Robert.

sir robert chiltern. [Puts what he has written into an envelope, which he then carefully closes.] Tell him to have this sent off in cipher at once. There must not be a moment's delay.

mason. Yes, Sir Robert.

sir robert chiltern. Oh! just give that back to me again.

[*Writes something on the envelope.* mason *then goes out with the letter.*]

sir robert chiltern. She must have had some curious hold over Baron Arnheim. I wonder what it was.

lord goring. [Smiling.] I wonder.

sir robert chiltern. I will fight her to the death, as long as my wife knows nothing.

lord goring. [Strongly.] Oh, fight in any case—in any case.

sir robert chiltern. [With a gesture of despair.] If my wife found out, there would be little left to fight for. Well, as soon as I hear from Vienna, I shall let you know the result. It is a chance, just a chance, but I believe in it. And as I fought the age with its own weapons, I will fight her with her weapons. It is only fair, and she looks like a woman with a past, doesn't she?

320

lord goring. Most pretty women do. But there is a fashion in pasts just as there is a fashion in frocks. Perhaps Mrs. Cheveley's past is merely a slightly décolleté one, and they are excessively popular nowadays. Besides, my dear Robert, I should not build too high hopes on frightening Mrs. Cheveley. I should not fancy Mrs. Cheveley is a woman who would be easily frightened. She has survived all her creditors, and she shows wonderful presence of mind.

sir robert chiltern. Oh! I live on hopes now. I clutch at every chance. I feel like a man on a ship that is sinking. The water is round my feet, and the very air is bitter with storm. Hush! I hear my wife's voice.

[*Enter* lady chiltern *in walking dress.*]

lady chiltern. Good afternoon, Lord Goring!

lord goring. Good afternoon, Lady Chiltern! Have you been in the Park?

lady chiltern. No; I have just come from the Woman's Liberal Association, where, by the way, Robert, your name was received with loud applause, and now I have come in to have my tea. [To lord goring.] You will wait and have some tea, won't you?

lord goring. I'll wait for a short time, thanks.

lady chiltern. I will be back in a moment. I am only going to take my hat off.

lord goring. [In his most earnest manner.] Oh! please don't. It is so pretty. One of the prettiest hats I ever saw. I hope the Woman's Liberal Association received it with loud applause.

lady chiltern. [With a smile.] We have much more important work to do than look at each other's bonnets, Lord Goring.

lord goring. Really? What sort of work?

lady chiltern. Oh! dull, useful, delightful things, Factory Acts, Female Inspectors, the Eight Hours' Bill, the Parliamentary Franchise.... Everything, in fact, that you would find thoroughly uninteresting.

lord goring. And never bonnets?

lady chiltern. [With mock indignation.] Never bonnets, never!

[lady chiltern goes out through the door leading to her boudoir.]

sir robert chiltern. [Takes lord goring's hand.] You have been a good friend to me, Arthur, a thoroughly good friend.

lord goring. I don't know that I have been able to do much for you, Robert, as yet. In fact, I have not been able to do anything for you, as far as I can see. I am thoroughly disappointed with myself.

sir robert chiltern. You have enabled me to tell you the truth. That is something. The truth has always stifled me.

lord goring. Ah! the truth is a thing I get rid of as soon as possible! Bad habit, by the way. Makes one very unpopular at the club . . . with the older members. They call it being conceited. Perhaps it is.

sir robert chiltern. I would to God that I had been able to tell the truth . . to live the truth. Ah! that is the great thing in life, to live the truth. [Sighs, and goes towards the door.] I'll see you soon again, Arthur, shan't I?

lord goring. Certainly. Whenever you like. I'm going to look in at the Bachelors' Ball to-night, unless I find something better to do. But I'll come round to-morrow morning. If you should want me to-night by any chance, send round a note to Curzon Street.

sir robert chiltern. Thank you.

[As he reaches the door, lady chiltern enters from her boudoir.]

lady chiltern. You are not going, Robert?

sir robert chiltern. I have some letters to write, dear.

lady chiltern. [Going to him.] You work too hard, Robert. You seem never to think of yourself, and you are looking so tired.

sir robert chiltern. It is nothing, dear, nothing.

[*He kisses her and goes out.*]

lady chiltern. [To lord goring.] Do sit down. I am so glad you have called. I want to talk to you about . . . well, not about bonnets, or the Woman's Liberal Association. You take far too much interest in the first subject, and not nearly enough in the second.

lord goring. You want to talk to me about Mrs. Cheveley?

lady chiltern. Yes. You have guessed it. After you left last night I found out that what she had said was really true. Of course I made Robert write her a letter at once, withdrawing his promise.

lord goring. So he gave me to understand.

lady chiltern. To have kept it would have been the first stain on a career that has been stainless always. Robert must be above reproach. He is not like other men. He cannot afford to do what other men do. [She looks at lord goring, who remains silent.] Don't you agree with me? You are Robert's greatest friend. You are our greatest friend, Lord Goring. No one, except myself, knows Robert better than you do. He has no secrets from me, and I don't think he has any from you.

lord goring. He certainly has no secrets from me. At least I don't think so.

lady chiltern. Then am I not right in my estimate of him? I know I am right. But speak to me frankly.

lord goring. [Looking straight at her.] Quite frankly?

lady chiltern. Surely. You have nothing to conceal, have you?

lord goring. Nothing. But, my dear Lady Chiltern, I think, if you will allow me to say so, that in practical life—

lady chiltern. [Smiling.] Of which you know so little, Lord Goring—

lord goring. Of which I know nothing by experience, though I know something by observation. I think that in practical life there is something about success, actual success, that is a little unscrupulous, something about ambition that is unscrupulous always. Once a man has set his heart and soul on getting to a certain point, if he has to climb the crag, he climbs the crag; if he has to walk in the mire—

lady chiltern. Well?

lord goring. He walks in the mire. Of course I am only talking generally about life.

lady chiltern. [Gravely.] I hope so. Why do you look at me so strangely, Lord Goring?

lord goring. Lady Chiltern, I have sometimes thought that . . . perhaps you are a little hard in some of your views on life. I think that . . . often you don't make sufficient allowances. In every nature there are elements of weakness, or worse than weakness. Supposing, for instance, that—that any public man, my father, or Lord Merton, or Robert, say, had, years ago, written some foolish letter to some one . . .

lady chiltern. What do you mean by a foolish letter?

lord goring. A letter gravely compromising one's position. I am only putting an imaginary case.

lady chiltern. Robert is as incapable of doing a foolish thing as he is of doing a wrong thing.

lord goring. [After a long pause.] Nobody is incapable of doing a foolish thing. Nobody is incapable of doing a wrong thing.

lady chiltern. Are you a Pessimist? What will the other dandies say? They will all have to go into mourning.

lord goring. [Rising.] No, Lady Chiltern, I am not a Pessimist. Indeed I am not sure that I quite know what Pessimism really means. All I do know is that life cannot be understood without much charity, cannot be lived without much charity. It is love, and not German philosophy, that is the true explanation of this world, whatever may be the explanation of the next. And

324

if you are ever in trouble, Lady Chiltern, trust me absolutely, and I will help you in every way I can. If you ever want me, come to me for my assistance, and you shall have it. Come at once to me.

lady chiltern. [Looking at him in surprise.] Lord Goring, you are talking quite seriously. I don't think I ever heard you talk seriously before.

lord goring. [Laughing.] You must excuse me, Lady Chiltern. It won't occur again, if I can help it.

lady chiltern. But I like you to be serious.

[*Enter* mabel chiltern, *in the most ravishing frock.*]

mabel chiltern. Dear Gertrude, don't say such a dreadful thing to Lord Goring. Seriousness would be very unbecoming to him. Good afternoon Lord Goring! Pray be as trivial as you can.

lord goring. I should like to, Miss Mabel, but I am afraid I am . . . a little out of practice this morning; and besides, I have to be going now.

mabel chiltern. Just when I have come in! What dreadful manners you have! I am sure you were very badly brought up.

lord goring. I was.

mabel chiltern. I wish I had brought you up!

lord goring. I am so sorry you didn't.

mabel chiltern. It is too late now, I suppose?

lord goring. [Smiling.] I am not so sure.

mabel chiltern. Will you ride to-morrow morning?

lord goring. Yes, at ten.

mabel chiltern. Don't forget.

lord goring. Of course I shan't. By the way, Lady Chiltern, there is no list of your guests in The Morning Post of to-day. It has apparently been crowded out by the County Council, or the Lambeth Conference, or something equally boring. Could you let me have a list? I have a particular reason for asking you.

lady chiltern. I am sure Mr. Trafford will be able to give you one.

lord goring. Thanks, so much.

mabel chiltern. Tommy is the most useful person in London.

lord goring [Turning to her.] And who is the most ornamental?

mabel chiltern [Triumphantly.] I am.

lord goring. How clever of you to guess it! [Takes up his hat and cane.] Good-bye, Lady Chiltern! You will remember what I said to you, won't you?

lady chiltern. Yes; but I don't know why you said it to me.

lord goring. I hardly know myself. Good-bye, Miss Mabel!

mabel chiltern [With a little moue of disappointment.] I wish you were not going. I have had four wonderful adventures this morning; four and a half, in fact. You might stop and listen to some of them.

lord goring. How very selfish of you to have four and a half! There won't be any left for me.

mabel chiltern. I don't want you to have any. They would not be good for you.

lord goring. That is the first unkind thing you have ever said to me. How charmingly you said it! Ten to-morrow.

mabel chiltern. Sharp.

lord goring. Quite sharp. But don't bring Mr. Trafford.

mabel chiltern. [With a little toss of the head.] Of course I shan't bring Tommy Trafford. Tommy Trafford is in great disgrace.

lord goring. I am delighted to hear it. [Bows and goes out.]

mabel chiltern. Gertrude, I wish you would speak to Tommy Trafford.

lady chiltern. What has poor Mr. Trafford done this time? Robert says he is the best secretary he has ever had.

mabel chiltern. Well, Tommy has proposed to me again. Tommy really does nothing but propose to me. He proposed to me last night in the music-room, when I was quite unprotected, as there was an elaborate trio going on. I didn't dare to make the smallest repartee, I need hardly tell you. If I had, it would have stopped the music at once. Musical people are so absurdly unreasonable. They always want one to be perfectly dumb at the very moment when one is longing to be absolutely deaf. Then he proposed to me in broad daylight this morning, in front of that dreadful statue of Achilles. Really, the things that go on in front of that work of art are quite appalling. The police should interfere. At luncheon I saw by the glare in his eye that he was going to propose again, and I just managed to check him in time by assuring him that I was a bimetallist. Fortunately I don't know what bimetallism means. And I don't believe anybody else does either. But the observation crushed Tommy for ten minutes. He looked quite shocked. And then Tommy is so annoying in the way he proposes. If he proposed at the top of his voice, I should not mind so much. That might produce some effect on the public. But he does it in a horrid confidential way. When Tommy wants to be romantic he talks to one just like a doctor. I am very fond of Tommy, but his methods of proposing are quite out of date. I wish, Gertrude, you would speak to him, and tell him that once a week is quite often enough to propose to any one, and that it should always be done in a manner that attracts some attention.

lady chiltern. Dear Mabel, don't talk like that. Besides, Robert thinks very highly of Mr. Trafford. He believes he has a brilliant future before him.

mabel chiltern. Oh! I wouldn't marry a man with a future before him for anything under the sun.

lady chiltern. Mabel!

mabel chiltern. I know, dear. You married a man with a future, didn't you? But then Robert was a genius, and you have a noble, self-sacrificing character. You can stand geniuses. I have no character at all, and Robert is the only genius I could ever bear. As a rule, I think they are quite impossible. Geniuses talk so much, don't they? Such a bad habit! And they are always thinking about themselves, when I want them to be thinking about me. must go round now and rehearse at Lady Basildon's. You remember, we are having tableaux, don't you? The Triumph of something, I don't know what! I hope it will be triumph of me. Only triumph I am really interested in at present. [Kisses lady chiltern and goes out; then comes running back. Oh, Gertrude, do you know who is coming to see you? That dreadful Mrs Cheveley, in a most lovely gown. Did you ask her?

lady chiltern. [Rising.] Mrs. Cheveley! Coming to see me? Impossible

mabel chiltern. I assure you she is coming upstairs, as large as life and not nearly so natural.

lady chiltern. You need not wait, Mabel. Remember, Lady Basildon is expecting you.

mabel chiltern. Oh! I must shake hands with Lady Markby. She is delightful. I love being scolded by her.

[*Enter* mason.]

mason. Lady Markby. Mrs. Cheveley.

[*Enter* lady markby *and* mrs. cheveley.]

lady chiltern. [Advancing to meet them.] Dear Lady Markby, how nice of you to come and see me! [Shakes hands with her, and bows somewhat distantly to mrs. cheveley.] Won't you sit down, Mrs. Cheveley?

mrs. cheveley. Thanks. Isn't that Miss Chiltern? I should like so much to know her.

lady chiltern. Mabel, Mrs. Cheveley wishes to know you.

[mabel chiltern *gives a little nod.*]

mrs. cheveley [Sitting down.] I thought your frock so charming last

328

night, Miss Chiltern. So simple and . . . suitable.

mabel chiltern. Really? I must tell my dressmaker. It will be such a surprise to her. Good-bye, Lady Markby!

lady markby. Going already?

mabel chiltern. I am so sorry but I am obliged to. I am just off to rehearsal. I have got to stand on my head in some tableaux.

lady markby. On your head, child? Oh! I hope not. I believe it is most unhealthy. [Takes a seat on the sofa next lady chiltern.]

mabel chiltern. But it is for an excellent charity: in aid of the Undeserving, the only people I am really interested in. I am the secretary, and Tommy Trafford is treasurer.

mrs. cheveley. And what is Lord Goring?

mabel chiltern. Oh! Lord Goring is president.

mrs. cheveley. The post should suit him admirably, unless he has deteriorated since I knew him first.

lady markby. [Reflecting.] You are remarkably modern, Mabel. A little too modern, perhaps. Nothing is so dangerous as being too modern. One is apt to grow old-fashioned quite suddenly. I have known many instances of it.

mabel chiltern. What a dreadful prospect!

lady markby. Ah! my dear, you need not be nervous. You will always be as pretty as possible. That is the best fashion there is, and the only fashion that England succeeds in setting.

mabel chiltern. [With a curtsey.] Thank you so much, Lady Markby, for England . . . and myself. [Goes out.]

lady markby. [Turning to lady chiltern.] Dear Gertrude, we just called to know if Mrs. Cheveley's diamond brooch has been found.

lady chiltern. Here?

mrs. cheveley. Yes. I missed it when I got back to Claridge's, and I thought I might possibly have dropped it here.

lady chiltern. I have heard nothing about it. But I will send for the butler and ask. [Touches the bell.]

mrs. cheveley. Oh, pray don't trouble, Lady Chiltern. I dare say I lost it at the Opera, before we came on here.

lady markby. Ah yes, I suppose it must have been at the Opera. The fact is, we all scramble and jostle so much nowadays that I wonder we have anything at all left on us at the end of an evening. I know myself that, when I am coming back from the Drawing Room, I always feel as if I hadn't a shred on me, except a small shred of decent reputation, just enough to prevent the lower classes making painful observations through the windows of the carriage. The fact is that our Society is terribly over-populated. Really, some one should arrange a proper scheme of assisted emigration. It would do a great deal of good.

mrs. cheveley. I quite agree with you, Lady Markby. It is nearly six years since I have been in London for the Season, and I must say Society has become dreadfully mixed. One sees the oddest people everywhere.

lady markby. That is quite true, dear. But one needn't know them. I'm sure I don't know half the people who come to my house. Indeed, from all I hear, I shouldn't like to.

[*Enter* mason.]

lady chiltern. What sort of a brooch was it that you lost, Mrs. Cheveley?

mrs. cheveley. A diamond snake-brooch with a ruby, a rather large ruby.

lady markby. I thought you said there was a sapphire on the head, dear?

mrs. cheveley [Smiling.] No, lady Markby—a ruby.

lady markby. [Nodding her head.] And very becoming, I am quite sure.

lady chiltern. Has a ruby and diamond brooch been found in any of the

330

rooms this morning, Mason?

mason. No, my lady.

mrs. cheveley. It really is of no consequence, Lady Chiltern. I am so sorry to have put you to any inconvenience.

lady chiltern. [Coldly.] Oh, it has been no inconvenience. That will do, Mason. You can bring tea.

[*Exit* mason.]

lady markby. Well, I must say it is most annoying to lose anything. I remember once at Bath, years ago, losing in the Pump Room an exceedingly handsome cameo bracelet that Sir John had given me. I don't think he has ever given me anything since, I am sorry to say. He has sadly degenerated. Really, this horrid House of Commons quite ruins our husbands for us. I think the Lower House by far the greatest blow to a happy married life that there has been since that terrible thing called the Higher Education of Women was invented.

lady chiltern. Ah! it is heresy to say that in this house, Lady Markby. Robert is a great champion of the Higher Education of Women, and so, I am afraid, am I.

mrs. cheveley. The higher education of men is what I should like to see. Men need it so sadly.

lady markby. They do, dear. But I am afraid such a scheme would be quite unpractical. I don't think man has much capacity for development. He has got as far as he can, and that is not far, is it? With regard to women, well, dear Gertrude, you belong to the younger generation, and I am sure it is all right if you approve of it. In my time, of course, we were taught not to understand anything. That was the old system, and wonderfully interesting it was. I assure you that the amount of things I and my poor dear sister were taught not to understand was quite extraordinary. But modern women understand everything, I am told.

mrs. cheveley. Except their husbands. That is the one thing the modern woman never understands.

lady markby. And a very good thing too, dear, I dare say. It might break up many a happy home if they did. Not yours, I need hardly say, Gertrude. You have married a pattern husband. I wish I could say as much for myself. But since Sir John has taken to attending the debates regularly, which he never used to do in the good old days, his language has become quite impossible. He always seems to think that he is addressing the House, and consequently whenever he discusses the state of the agricultural labourer, or the Welsh Church, or something quite improper of that kind, I am obliged to send all the servants out of the room. It is not pleasant to see one's own butler, who has been with one for twenty-three years, actually blushing at the side-board, and the footmen making contortions in corners like persons in circuses. I assure you my life will be quite ruined unless they send John at once to the Upper House. He won't take any interest in politics then, will he? The House of Lords is so sensible. An assembly of gentlemen. But in his present state, Sir John is really a great trial. Why, this morning before breakfast was half over, he stood up on the hearthrug, put his hands in his pockets, and appealed to the country at the top of his voice. I left the table as soon as I had my second cup of tea, I need hardly say. But his violent language could be heard all over the house! I trust, Gertrude, that Sir Robert is not like that?

lady chiltern. But I am very much interested in politics, Lady Markby. I love to hear Robert talk about them.

lady markby. Well, I hope he is not as devoted to Blue Books as Sir John is. I don't think they can be quite improving reading for any one.

mrs. cheveley [Languidly.] I have never read a Blue Book. I prefer books . . . in yellow covers.

lady markby. [Genially unconscious.] Yellow is a gayer colour, is it not? I used to wear yellow a good deal in my early days, and would do so now if Sir John was not so painfully personal in his observations, and a man on the question of dress is always ridiculous, is he not?

mrs. cheveley. Oh, no! I think men are the only authorities on dress.

332

lady markby. Really? One wouldn't say so from the sort of hats they wear? would one?

[*The butler enters, followed by the footman. Tea is set on a small table close to l*ady chiltern.]

lady chiltern. May I give you some tea, Mrs. Cheveley?

mrs. cheveley. Thanks. [The butler hands mrs. cheveley a cup of tea on a salver.]

lady chiltern. Some tea, Lady Markby?

lady markby. No thanks, dear. [The servants go out.] The fact is, I have promised to go round for ten minutes to see poor Lady Brancaster, who is in very great trouble. Her daughter, quite a well-brought-up girl, too, has actually become engaged to be married to a curate in Shropshire. It is very sad, very sad indeed. I can't understand this modern mania for curates. In my time we girls saw them, of course, running about the place like rabbits. But we never took any notice of them, I need hardly say. But I am told that nowadays country society is quite honeycombed with them. I think it most irreligious. And then the eldest son has quarrelled with his father, and it is said that when they meet at the club Lord Brancaster always hides himself behind the money article in The Times. However, I believe that is quite a common occurrence nowadays and that they have to take in extra copies of The Times at all the clubs in St. James's Street; there are so many sons who won't have anything to do with their fathers, and so many fathers who won't speak to their sons. I think myself, it is very much to be regretted.

mrs. cheveley. So do I. Fathers have so much to learn from their sons nowadays.

lady markby. Really, dear? What?

mrs. cheveley. The art of living. The only really Fine Art we have produced in modern times.

lady markby. [Shaking her head.] Ah! I am afraid Lord Brancaster knew a good deal about that. More than his poor wife ever did. [Turning to lady chiltern.] You know Lady Brancaster, don't you, dear?

lady chiltern. Just slightly. She was staying at Langton last autumn when we were there.

lady markby. Well, like all stout women, she looks the very picture of happiness, as no doubt you noticed. But there are many tragedies in her family, besides this affair of the curate. Her own sister, Mrs. Jekyll, had a most unhappy life; through no fault of her own, I am sorry to say. She ultimately was so broken-hearted that she went into a convent, or on to the operatic stage, I forget which. No; I think it was decorative art-needlework she took up. I know she had lost all sense of pleasure in life. [Rising.] And now, Gertrude, if you will allow me, I shall leave Mrs. Cheveley in your charge and call back for her in a quarter of an hour. Or perhaps, dear Mrs. Cheveley, you wouldn't mind waiting in the carriage while I am with Lady Brancaster. As I intend it to be a visit of condolence, I shan't stay long.

mrs. cheveley [Rising.] I don't mind waiting in the carriage at all, provided there is somebody to look at one.

lady markby. Well, I hear the curate is always prowling about the house.

mrs. cheveley. I am afraid I am not fond of girl friends.

lady chiltern [Rising.] Oh, I hope Mrs. Cheveley will stay here a little. I should like to have a few minutes' conversation with her.

mrs. cheveley. How very kind of you, Lady Chiltern! Believe me, nothing would give me greater pleasure.

lady markby. Ah! no doubt you both have many pleasant reminiscences of your schooldays to talk over together. Good-bye, dear Gertrude! Shall I see you at Lady Bonar's to-night? She has discovered a wonderful new genius. He does . . . nothing at all, I believe. That is a great comfort, is it not?

lady chiltern. Robert and I are dining at home by ourselves to-night, and I don't think I shall go anywhere afterwards. Robert, of course, will have to be in the House. But there is nothing interesting on.

lady markby. Dining at home by yourselves? Is that quite prudent?

334

Ah, I forgot, your husband is an exception. Mine is the general rule, and nothing ages a woman so rapidly as having married the general rule. [Exit lady markby.]

mrs. cheveley. Wonderful woman, Lady Markby, isn't she? Talks more and says less than anybody I ever met. She is made to be a public speaker. Much more so than her husband, though he is a typical Englishman, always dull and usually violent.

lady chiltern. [Makes no answer, but remains standing. There is a pause. Then the eyes of the two women meet. lady chiltern looks stern and pale. mrs. cheveley seem rather amused.] Mrs. Cheveley, I think it is right to tell you quite frankly that, had I known who you really were, I should not have invited you to my house last night.

mrs. cheveley [With an impertinent smile.] Really?

lady chiltern. I could not have done so.

mrs. cheveley. I see that after all these years you have not changed a bit, Gertrude.

lady chiltern. I never change.

mrs. cheveley [Elevating her eyebrows.] Then life has taught you nothing?

lady chiltern. It has taught me that a person who has once been guilty of a dishonest and dishonourable action may be guilty of it a second time, and should be shunned.

mrs. cheveley. Would you apply that rule to every one?

lady chiltern. Yes, to every one, without exception.

mrs. cheveley. Then I am sorry for you, Gertrude, very sorry for you.

lady chiltern. You see now, I was sure, that for many reasons any further acquaintance between us during your stay in London is quite impossible?

mrs. cheveley [Leaning back in her chair.] Do you know, Gertrude, I don't mind your talking morality a bit. Morality is simply the attitude we adopt towards people whom we personally dislike. You dislike me. I am quite aware of that. And I have always detested you. And yet I have come here to do you a service.

lady chiltern. [Contemptuously.] Like the service you wished to render my husband last night, I suppose. Thank heaven, I saved him from that.

mrs. cheveley. [Starting to her feet.] It was you who made him write that insolent letter to me? It was you who made him break his promise?

lady chiltern. Yes.

mrs. cheveley. Then you must make him keep it. I give you till to-morrow morning—no more. If by that time your husband does not solemnly bind himself to help me in this great scheme in which I am interested—

lady chiltern. This fraudulent speculation—

mrs. cheveley. Call it what you choose. I hold your husband in the hollow of my hand, and if you are wise you will make him do what I tell him.

lady chiltern. [Rising and going towards her.] You are impertinent. What has my husband to do with you? With a woman like you?

mrs. cheveley [With a bitter laugh.] In this world like meets with like. It is because your husband is himself fraudulent and dishonest that we pair so well together. Between you and him there are chasms. He and I are closer than friends. We are enemies linked together. The same sin binds us.

lady chiltern. How dare you class my husband with yourself? How dare you threaten him or me? Leave my house. You are unfit to enter it.

[sir robert chiltern enters from behind. He hears his wife's last words, and sees to whom they are addressed. He grows deadly pale.]

mrs. cheveley. Your house! A house bought with the price of dishonour. A house, everything in which has been paid for by fraud. [Turns round and sees sir robert chiltern.] Ask him what the origin of his fortune is! Get him to tell you how he sold to a stockbroker a Cabinet secret. Learn from him to what you owe your position.

lady chiltern. It is not true! Robert! It is not true!

mrs. cheveley. [Pointing at him with outstretched finger.] Look at him! Can he deny it? Does he dare to?

sir robert chiltern. Go! Go at once. You have done your worst now.

mrs. cheveley. My worst? I have not yet finished with you, with either of you. I give you both till to-morrow at noon. If by then you don't do what I bid you to do, the whole world shall know the origin of Robert Chiltern.

[sir robert chiltern strikes the bell. Enter mason.]

sir robert chiltern. Show Mrs. Cheveley out.

[mrs. cheveley *starts; then bows with somewhat exaggerated politeness to* lady chiltern, *who makes no sign of response. As she passes by* sir robert chiltern, *who is standing close to the door, she pauses for a moment and looks him straight in the face. She then goes out, followed by the servant, who closes the door after him. The husband and wife are left alone.* lady chiltern *stands like some one in a dreadful dream. Then she turns round and looks at her husband. She looks at him with strange eyes, as though she were seeing him for the first time.*]

lady chiltern. You sold a Cabinet secret for money! You began your life with fraud! You built up your career on dishonour! Oh, tell me it is not true! Lie to me! Lie to me! Tell me it is not true!

sir robert chiltern. What this woman said is quite true. But, Gertrude, listen to me. You don't realise how I was tempted. Let me tell you the whole thing. [Goes towards her.]

lady chiltern. Don't come near me. Don't touch me. I feel as if you had soiled me for ever. Oh! what a mask you have been wearing all these years! A horrible painted mask! You sold yourself for money. Oh! a common thief were better. You put yourself up to sale to the highest bidder! You were bought in the market. You lied to the whole world. And yet you will not lie to me.

sir robert chiltern. [Rushing towards her.] Gertrude! Gertrude!

lady chiltern. [Thrusting him back with outstretched hands.] No, don't speak! Say nothing! Your voice wakes terrible memories—memories of things that made me love you—memories of words that made me love you—memories that now are horrible to me. And how I worshipped you! You were to me something apart from common life, a thing pure, noble, honest, without stain. The world seemed to me finer because you were in it, and goodness more real because you lived. And now—oh, when I think that I made of a man like you my ideal! the ideal of my life!

sir robert chiltern. There was your mistake. There was your error. The error all women commit. Why can't you women love us, faults and all? Why do you place us on monstrous pedestals? We have all feet of clay, women as well as men; but when we men love women, we love them knowing their weaknesses, their follies, their imperfections, love them all the more, it may be, for that reason. It is not the perfect, but the imperfect, who have need of love. It is when we are wounded by our own hands, or by the hands of others, that love should come to cure us—else what use is love at all? All sins, except a sin against itself, Love should forgive. All lives, save loveless lives, true Love should pardon. A man's love is like that. It is wider, larger, more human than a woman's. Women think that they are making ideals of men. What they are making of us are false idols merely. You made your false idol of me, and I had not the courage to come down, show you my wounds, tell you my weaknesses. I was afraid that I might lose your love, as I have lost it now. And so, last night you ruined my life for me—yes, ruined it! What this woman asked of me was nothing compared to what she offered to me. She offered security, peace, stability. The sin of my youth, that I had thought was buried, rose up in front of me, hideous, horrible, with its hands at my throat. I could have killed it for ever, sent it back into its tomb, destroyed its record, burned the one witness against me. You prevented me. No one but you, you know it. And now what is there before me but public disgrace, ruin, terrible shame, the mockery of the world, a lonely dishonoured life, a lonely dishonoured death, it may be, some day? Let women make no more ideals of men! let them not put them on alters and bow before them, or they may ruin

338

other lives as completely as you—you whom I have so wildly loved—have ruined mine!

[*He passes from the room.* lady chiltern *rushes towards him, but the door is closed when she reaches it. Pale with anguish, bewildered, helpless, she sways like a plant in the water. Her hands, outstretched, seem to tremble in the air like blossoms in the mind. Then she flings herself down beside a sofa and buries her face. Her sobs are like the sobs of a child.*]

ACT DROP

THIRD ACT

SCENE

The Library in Lord Goring's house. An Adam room. On the right is the door leading into the hall. On the left, the door of the smoking-room. A pair of folding doors at the back open into the drawing-room. The fire is lit. Phipps, the butler, is arranging some newspapers on the writing-table. The distinction of Phipps is his impassivity. He has been termed by enthusiasts the Ideal Butler. The Sphinx is not so incommunicable. He is a mask with a manner. Of his intellectual or emotional life, history knows nothing. He represents the dominance of form.

[Enter lord goring *in evening dress with a buttonhole. He is wearing a silk hat and Inverness cape. White-gloved, he carries a Louis Seize cane. His are all the delicate fopperies of Fashion. One sees that he stands in immediate relation to modern life, makes it indeed, and so masters it. He is the first well-dressed philosopher in the history of thought.]*

lord goring. Got my second buttonhole for me, Phipps?

phipps. Yes, my lord. [Takes his hat, cane, and cape, and presents new buttonhole on salver.]

lord goring. Rather distinguished thing, Phipps. I am the only person of the smallest importance in London at present who wears a buttonhole.

phipps. Yes, my lord. I have observed that,

lord goring. [Taking out old buttonhole.] You see, Phipps, Fashion is what one wears oneself. What is unfashionable is what other people wear.

phipps. Yes, my lord.

lord goring. Just as vulgarity is simply the conduct of other people.

phipps. Yes, my lord.

lord goring. [Putting in a new buttonhole.] And falsehoods the truths of other people.

phipps. Yes, my lord.

lord goring. Other people are quite dreadful. The only possible society is oneself.

phipps. Yes, my lord.

lord goring. To love oneself is the beginning of a lifelong romance, Phipps.

phipps. Yes, my lord.

lord goring. [Looking at himself in the glass.] Don't think I quite like this buttonhole, Phipps. Makes me look a little too old. Makes me almost in the prime of life, eh, Phipps?

phipps. I don't observe any alteration in your lordship's appearance.

lord goring. You don't, Phipps?

phipps. No, my lord.

lord goring. I am not quite sure. For the future a more trivial buttonhole, Phipps, on Thursday evenings.

phipps. I will speak to the florist, my lord. She has had a loss in her family lately, which perhaps accounts for the lack of triviality your lordship complains of in the buttonhole.

lord goring. Extraordinary thing about the lower classes in England— they are always losing their relations.

phipps. Yes, my lord! They are extremely fortunate in that respect.

lord goring. [Turns round and looks at him. phipps remains impassive.] Hum! Any letters, Phipps?

phipps. Three, my lord. [Hands letters on a salver.]

lord goring. [Takes letters.] Want my cab round in twenty minutes.

phipps. Yes, my lord. [Goes towards door.]

lord goring. [Holds up letter in pink envelope.] Ahem! Phipps, when did this letter arrive?

phipps. It was brought by hand just after your lordship went to the club.

lord goring. That will do. [Exit phipps.] Lady Chiltern's handwriting on Lady Chiltern's pink notepaper. That is rather curious. I thought Robert was to write. Wonder what Lady Chiltern has got to say to me? [Sits at bureau and opens letter, and reads it.] 'I want you. I trust you. I am coming to you. Gertrude.' [Puts down the letter with a puzzled look. Then takes it up, and reads it again slowly.] 'I want you. I trust you. I am coming to you.' So she has found out everything! Poor woman! Poor woman! [Pulls out watch and looks at it.] But what an hour to call! Ten o'clock! I shall have to give up going to the Berkshires. However, it is always nice to be expected, and not to arrive. I am not expected at the Bachelors', so I shall certainly go there. Well, I will make her stand by her husband. That is the only thing for her to do. That is the only thing for any woman to do. It is the growth of the moral sense in women that makes marriage such a hopeless, one-sided institution. Ten o'clock. She should be here soon. I must tell Phipps I am not in to any one else. [Goes towards bell]

[*Enter* phipps.]

phipps. Lord Caversham.

lord goring. Oh, why will parents always appear at the wrong time? Some extraordinary mistake in nature, I suppose. [Enter lord caversham.] Delighted to see you, my dear father. [Goes to meet him.]

lord caversham. Take my cloak off.

lord goring. Is it worth while, father?

lord caversham. Of course it is worth while, sir. Which is the most comfortable chair?

lord goring. This one, father. It is the chair I use myself, when I have

342

visitors.

lord caversham. Thank ye. No draught, I hope, in this room?

lord goring. No, father.

lord caversham. [Sitting down.] Glad to hear it. Can't stand draughts. No draughts at home.

lord goring. Good many breezes, father.

lord caversham. Eh? Eh? Don't understand what you mean. Want to have a serious conversation with you, sir.

lord goring. My dear father! At this hour?

lord caversham. Well, sir, it is only ten o'clock. What is your objection to the hour? I think the hour is an admirable hour!

lord goring. Well, the fact is, father, this is not my day for talking seriously. I am very sorry, but it is not my day.

lord caversham. What do you mean, sir?

lord goring. During the Season, father, I only talk seriously on the first Tuesday in every month, from four to seven.

lord caversham. Well, make it Tuesday, sir, make it Tuesday.

lord goring. But it is after seven, father, and my doctor says I must not have any serious conversation after seven. It makes me talk in my sleep.

lord caversham. Talk in your sleep, sir? What does that matter? You are not married.

lord goring. No, father, I am not married.

lord caversham. Hum! That is what I have come to talk to you about, sir. You have got to get married, and at once. Why, when I was your age, sir, I had been an inconsolable widower for three months, and was already paying my addresses to your admirable mother. Damme, sir, it is your duty to get married. You can't be always living for pleasure. Every man of position is married nowadays. Bachelors are not fashionable any more. They are a damaged lot. Too much is known about them. You must get a wife, sir. Look where your friend Robert Chiltern has got to by probity, hard work, and a sensible marriage with a good woman. Why don't you imitate him, sir? Why don't you take him for your model?

lord goring. I think I shall, father.

lord caversham. I wish you would, sir. Then I should be happy. At present I make your mother's life miserable on your account. You are heartless, sir, quite heartless.

lord goring. I hope not, father.

lord caversham. And it is high time for you to get married. You are thirty-four years of age, sir.

lord goring. Yes, father, but I only admit to thirty-two—thirty-one and a half when I have a really good buttonhole. This buttonhole is not . . . trivial enough.

lord caversham. I tell you you are thirty-four, sir. And there is a draught in your room, besides, which makes your conduct worse. Why did you tell me there was no draught, sir? I feel a draught, sir, I feel it distinctly.

lord goring. So do I, father. It is a dreadful draught. I will come and see you to-morrow, father. We can talk over anything you like. Let me help you on with your cloak, father.

lord caversham. No, sir; I have called this evening for a definite purpose, and I am going to see it through at all costs to my health or yours. Put down my cloak, sir.

lord goring. Certainly, father. But let us go into another room. [Rings bell.] There is a dreadful draught here. [Enter phipps.] Phipps, is there a good fire in the smoking-room?

phipps. Yes, my lord.

lord goring. Come in there, father. Your sneezes are quite heartrending.

344

lord caversham. Well, sir, I suppose I have a right to sneeze when I choose?

lord goring. [Apologetically.] Quite so, father. I was merely expressing sympathy.

lord caversham. Oh, damn sympathy. There is a great deal too much of that sort of thing going on nowadays.

lord goring. I quite agree with you, father. If there was less sympathy in the world there would be less trouble in the world.

lord caversham. [Going towards the smoking-room.] That is a paradox, sir. I hate paradoxes.

lord goring. So do I, father. Everybody one meets is a paradox nowadays. It is a great bore. It makes society so obvious.

lord caversham. [Turning round, and looking at his son beneath his bushy eyebrows.] Do you always really understand what you say, sir?

lord goring. [After some hesitation.] Yes, father, if I listen attentively.

lord caversham. [Indignantly.] If you listen attentively! . . . Conceited young puppy!

[*Goes off grumbling into the smoking-room.* phipps *enters.*]

lord goring. Phipps, there is a lady coming to see me this evening on particular business. Show her into the drawing-room when she arrives. You understand?

phipps. Yes, my lord.

lord goring. It is a matter of the gravest importance, Phipps.

phipps. I understand, my lord.

lord goring. No one else is to be admitted, under any circumstances.

phipps. I understand, my lord. [Bell rings.]

lord goring. Ah! that is probably the lady. I shall see her myself.

345

[*Just as he is going towards the door* lord caversham *enters from the smoking-room.*]

lord caversham. Well, sir? am I to wait attendance on you?

lord goring. [Considerably perplexed.] In a moment, father. Do excuse me. [lord caversham goes back.] Well, remember my instructions, Phipps—into that room.

phipps. Yes, my lord.

[lord goring *goes into the smoking-room.* harold, *the footman shows* mrs. cheveley *in. Lamia-like, she is in green and silver. She has a cloak of black satin, lined with dead rose-leaf silk.*]

harold. What name, madam?

mrs. cheveley. [To phipps, who advances towards her.] Is Lord Goring not here? I was told he was at home?

phipps. His lordship is engaged at present with Lord Caversham, madam.

[*Turns a cold, glassy eye on* harold, *who at once retires.*]

mrs. cheveley. [To herself.] How very filial!

phipps. His lordship told me to ask you, madam, to be kind enough to wait in the drawing-room for him. His lordship will come to you there.

mrs. cheveley. [With a look of surprise.] Lord Goring expects me?

phipps. Yes, madam.

mrs. cheveley. Are you quite sure?

phipps. His lordship told me that if a lady called I was to ask her to wait in the drawing-room. [Goes to the door of the drawing-room and opens it.] His lordship's directions on the subject were very precise.

mrs. cheveley. [To herself] How thoughtful of him! To expect the unexpected shows a thoroughly modern intellect. [Goes towards the drawing-room and looks in.] Ugh! How dreary a bachelor's drawing-room always looks. I shall have to alter all this. [phipps brings the lamp from the writing-table.] No, I don't care for that lamp. It is far too glaring. Light some candles.

phipps. [Replaces lamp.] Certainly, madam.

mrs. cheveley. I hope the candles have very becoming shades.

phipps. We have had no complaints about them, madam, as yet.

[*Passes into the drawing-room and begins to light the candles.*]

mrs. cheveley. [To herself.] I wonder what woman he is waiting for to-night. It will be delightful to catch him. Men always look so silly when they are caught. And they are always being caught. [Looks about room and approaches the writing-table.] What a very interesting room! What a very interesting picture! Wonder what his correspondence is like. [Takes up letters.] Oh, what a very uninteresting correspondence! Bills and cards, debts and dowagers! Who on earth writes to him on pink paper? How silly to write on pink paper! It looks like the beginning of a middle-class romance. Romance should never begin with sentiment. It should begin with science and end with a settlement. [Puts letter down, then takes it up again.] I know that handwriting. That is Gertrude Chiltern's. I remember it perfectly. The ten commandments in every stroke of the pen, and the moral law all over the page. Wonder what Gertrude is writing to him about? Something horrid about me, I suppose. How I detest that woman! [Reads it.] 'I trust you. I want you. I am coming to you. Gertrude.' 'I trust you. I want you. I am coming to you.'

[*A look of triumph comes over her face. She is just about to steal the letter, when* phipps *comes in.*]

phipps. The candles in the drawing-room are lit, madam, as you directed.

mrs. cheveley. Thank you. [Rises hastily and slips the letter under a large silver-cased blotting-book that is lying on the table.]

phipps. I trust the shades will be to your liking, madam. They are the most becoming we have. They are the same as his lordship uses himself when he is dressing for dinner.

mrs. cheveley. [With a smile.] Then I am sure they will be perfectly right.

phipps. [Gravely.] Thank you, madam.

[mrs. cheveley *goes into the drawing-room.* phipps *closes the door and retires. The door is then slowly opened, and* mrs. cheveley *comes out and creeps stealthily towards the writing-table. Suddenly voices are heard from the smoking-room.* mrs. cheveley *grows pale, and stops. The voices grow louder, and she goes back into the drawing-room, biting her lip.*]

[*Enter* lord goring *and* lord caversham.]

lord goring. [Expostulating.] My dear father, if I am to get married, surely you will allow me to choose the time, place, and person? Particularly the person.

lord caversham. [Testily.] That is a matter for me, sir. You would probably make a very poor choice. It is I who should be consulted, not you. There is property at stake. It is not a matter for affection. Affection comes later on in married life.

lord goring. Yes. In married life affection comes when people thoroughly dislike each other, father, doesn't it? [Puts on lord caversham's cloak for him.]

lord caversham. Certainly, sir. I mean certainly not, sir. You are talking very foolishly to-night. What I say is that marriage is a matter for common sense.

lord goring. But women who have common sense are so curiously plain, father, aren't they? Of course I only speak from hearsay.

lord caversham. No woman, plain or pretty, has any common sense at all, sir. Common sense is the privilege of our sex.

lord goring. Quite so. And we men are so self-sacrificing that we never use it, do we, father?

lord caversham. I use it, sir. I use nothing else.

lord goring. So my mother tells me.

lord caversham. It is the secret of your mother's happiness. You are very heartless, sir, very heartless.

lord goring. I hope not, father.

[*Goes out for a moment. Then returns, looking rather put out, with* sir robert chiltern.]

sir robert chiltern. My dear Arthur, what a piece of good luck meeting you on the doorstep! Your servant had just told me you were not at home. How extraordinary!

lord goring. The fact is, I am horribly busy to-night, Robert, and I gave orders I was not at home to any one. Even my father had a comparatively cold reception. He complained of a draught the whole time.

sir robert chiltern. Ah! you must be at home to me, Arthur. You are my best friend. Perhaps by to-morrow you will be my only friend. My wife has discovered everything.

lord goring. Ah! I guessed as much!

sir robert chiltern. [Looking at him.] Really! How?

lord goring. [After some hesitation.] Oh, merely by something in the expression of your face as you came in. Who told her?

sir robert chiltern. Mrs. Cheveley herself. And the woman I love knows that I began my career with an act of low dishonesty, that I built up my life upon sands of shame—that I sold, like a common huckster, the secret that had been intrusted to me as a man of honour. I thank heaven poor Lord Radley died without knowing that I betrayed him. I would to God I had died before I had been so horribly tempted, or had fallen so low. [Burying his face in his hands.]

lord goring. [After a pause.] You have heard nothing from Vienna yet, in answer to your wire?

sir robert chiltern. [Looking up.] Yes; I got a telegram from the first secretary at eight o'clock to-night.

lord goring. Well?

sir robert chiltern. Nothing is absolutely known against her. On the contrary, she occupies a rather high position in society. It is a sort of open secret that Baron Arnheim left her the greater portion of his immense fortune. Beyond that I can learn nothing.

lord goring. She doesn't turn out to be a spy, then?

sir robert chiltern. Oh! spies are of no use nowadays. Their profession is over. The newspapers do their work instead.

lord goring. And thunderingly well they do it.

sir robert chiltern. Arthur, I am parched with thirst. May I ring for something? Some hock and seltzer?

lord goring. Certainly. Let me. [Rings the bell.]

sir robert chiltern. Thanks! I don't know what to do, Arthur, I don't know what to do, and you are my only friend. But what a friend you are— the one friend I can trust. I can trust you absolutely, can't I?

[*Enter* phipps.]

lord goring. My dear Robert, of course. Oh! [To phipps.] Bring some hock and seltzer.

phipps. Yes, my lord.

lord goring. And Phipps!

phipps. Yes, my lord.

lord goring. Will you excuse me for a moment, Robert? I want to give some directions to my servant.

350

SIR ROBERT CHILTERN. Certainly.

LORD GORING. When that lady calls, tell her that I am not expected home this evening. Tell her that I have been suddenly called out of town. You understand?

PHIPPS. The lady is in that room, my lord. You told me to show her into that room, my lord.

LORD GORING. You did perfectly right. [Exit PHIPPS.] What a mess I am in. No; I think I shall get through it. I'll give her a lecture through the door. Awkward thing to manage, though.

SIR ROBERT CHILTERN. Arthur, tell me what I should do. My life seems to have crumbled about me. I am a ship without a rudder in a night without a star.

LORD GORING. Robert, you love your wife, don't you?

SIR ROBERT CHILTERN. I love her more than anything in the world. I used to think ambition the great thing. It is not. Love is the great thing in the world. There is nothing but love, and I love her. But I am defamed in her eyes. I am ignoble in her eyes. There is a wide gulf between us now. She has found me out, Arthur, she has found me out.

LORD GORING. Has she never in her life done some folly—some indiscretion—that she should not forgive your sin?

SIR ROBERT CHILTERN. My wife! Never! She does not know what weakness or temptation is. I am of clay like other men. She stands apart as good women do—pitiless in her perfection—cold and stern and without mercy. But I love her, Arthur. We are childless, and I have no one else to love, no one else to love me. Perhaps if God had sent us children she might have been kinder to me. But God has given us a lonely house. And she has cut my heart in two. Don't let us talk of it. I was brutal to her this evening. But I suppose when sinners talk to saints they are brutal always. I said to her things that were hideously true, on my side, from my stand-point, from the standpoint of men. But don't let us talk of that.

lord goring. Your wife will forgive you. Perhaps at this moment she is forgiving you. She loves you, Robert. Why should she not forgive?

sir robert chiltern. God grant it! God grant it! [Buries his face in his hands.] But there is something more I have to tell you, Arthur.

[*Enter* phipps *with drinks.*]

phipps. [Hands hock and seltzer to sir robert chiltern.] Hock and seltzer, sir.

sir robert chiltern. Thank you.

lord goring. Is your carriage here, Robert?

sir robert chiltern. No; I walked from the club.

lord goring. Sir Robert will take my cab, Phipps.

phipps. Yes, my lord. [Exit.]

lord goring. Robert, you don't mind my sending you away?

sir robert chiltern. Arthur, you must let me stay for five minutes. I have made up my mind what I am going to do to-night in the House. The debate on the Argentine Canal is to begin at eleven. [A chair falls in the drawing-room.] What is that?

lord goring. Nothing.

sir robert chiltern. I heard a chair fall in the next room. Some one has been listening.

lord goring. No, no; there is no one there.

sir robert chiltern. There is some one. There are lights in the room, and the door is ajar. Some one has been listening to every secret of my life. Arthur, what does this mean?

lord goring. Robert, you are excited, unnerved. I tell you there is no one in that room. Sit down, Robert.

sir robert chiltern. Do you give me your word that there is no one there?

lord goring. Yes.

sir robert chiltern. Your word of honour? [Sits down.]

lord goring. Yes.

sir robert chiltern. [Rises.] Arthur, let me see for myself.

lord goring. No, no.

sir robert chiltern. If there is no one there why should I not look in that room? Arthur, you must let me go into that room and satisfy myself. Let me know that no eavesdropper has heard my life's secret. Arthur, you don't realise what I am going through.

lord goring. Robert, this must stop. I have told you that there is no one in that room—that is enough.

sir robert chiltern. [Rushes to the door of the room.] It is not enough. I insist on going into this room. You have told me there is no one there, so what reason can you have for refusing me?

lord goring. For God's sake, don't! There is some one there. Some one whom you must not see.

sir robert chiltern. Ah, I thought so!

lord goring. I forbid you to enter that room.

sir robert chiltern. Stand back. My life is at stake. And I don't care who is there. I will know who it is to whom I have told my secret and my shame. [Enters room.]

lord goring. Great heavens! his own wife!

[sir robert chiltern *comes back, with a look of scorn and anger on his face.*]

sir robert chiltern. What explanation have you to give me for the presence of that woman here?

lord goring. Robert, I swear to you on my honour that that lady is stainless and guiltless of all offence towards you.

353

sir robert chiltern. She is a vile, an infamous thing!

lord goring. Don't say that, Robert! It was for your sake she came here. It was to try and save you she came here. She loves you and no one else.

sir robert chiltern. You are mad. What have I to do with her intrigues with you? Let her remain your mistress! You are well suited to each other. She, corrupt and shameful—you, false as a friend, treacherous as an enemy even—

lord goring. It is not true, Robert. Before heaven, it is not true. In her presence and in yours I will explain all.

sir robert chiltern. Let me pass, sir. You have lied enough upon your word of honour.

[sir robert chiltern *goes out.* lord goring *rushes to the door of the drawing-room, when* mrs. cheveley *comes out, looking radiant and much amused.*]

mrs. cheveley. [With a mock curtsey] Good evening, Lord Goring!

lord goring. Mrs. Cheveley! Great heavens! . . . May I ask what you were doing in my drawing-room?

mrs. cheveley. Merely listening. I have a perfect passion for listening through keyholes. One always hears such wonderful things through them.

lord goring. Doesn't that sound rather like tempting Providence?

mrs. cheveley. Oh! surely Providence can resist temptation by this time. [Makes a sign to him to take her cloak off, which he does.]

lord goring. I am glad you have called. I am going to give you some good advice.

mrs. cheveley. Oh! pray don't. One should never give a woman anything that she can't wear in the evening.

lord goring. I see you are quite as wilful as you used to be.

mrs. cheveley. Far more! I have greatly improved. I have had more

354

experience.

lord goring. Too much experience is a dangerous thing. Pray have a cigarette. Half the pretty women in London smoke cigarettes. Personally I prefer the other half.

mrs. cheveley. Thanks. I never smoke. My dressmaker wouldn't like it, and a woman's first duty in life is to her dressmaker, isn't it? What the second duty is, no one has as yet discovered.

lord goring. You have come here to sell me Robert Chiltern's letter, haven't you?

mrs. cheveley. To offer it to you on conditions. How did you guess that?

lord goring. Because you haven't mentioned the subject. Have you got it with you?

mrs. cheveley. [Sitting down.] Oh, no! A well-made dress has no pockets.

lord goring. What is your price for it?

mrs. cheveley. How absurdly English you are! The English think that a cheque-book can solve every problem in life. Why, my dear Arthur, I have very much more money than you have, and quite as much as Robert Chiltern has got hold of. Money is not what I want.

lord goring. What do you want then, Mrs. Cheveley?

mrs. cheveley. Why don't you call me Laura?

lord goring. I don't like the name.

mrs. cheveley. You used to adore it.

lord goring. Yes: that's why. [mrs. cheveley motions to him to sit down beside her. He smiles, and does so.]

mrs. cheveley. Arthur, you loved me once.

lord goring. Yes.

mrs. cheveley. And you asked me to be your wife.

lord goring. That was the natural result of my loving you.

mrs. cheveley. And you threw me over because you saw, or said you saw, poor old Lord Mortlake trying to have a violent flirtation with me in the conservatory at Tenby.

lord goring. I am under the impression that my lawyer settled that matter with you on certain terms . . . dictated by yourself.

mrs. cheveley. At that time I was poor; you were rich.

lord goring. Quite so. That is why you pretended to love me.

mrs. cheveley. [Shrugging her shoulders.] Poor old Lord Mortlake, who had only two topics of conversation, his gout and his wife! I never could quite make out which of the two he was talking about. He used the most horrible language about them both. Well, you were silly, Arthur. Why, Lord Mortlake was never anything more to me than an amusement. One of those utterly tedious amusements one only finds at an English country house on an English country Sunday. I don't think any one at all morally responsible for what he or she does at an English country house.

lord goring. Yes. I know lots of people think that.

mrs. cheveley. I loved you, Arthur.

lord goring. My dear Mrs. Cheveley, you have always been far too clever to know anything about love.

mrs. cheveley. I did love you. And you loved me. You know you loved me; and love is a very wonderful thing. I suppose that when a man has once loved a woman, he will do anything for her, except continue to love her? [Puts her hand on his.]

lord goring. [Taking his hand away quietly.] Yes: except that.

mrs. cheveley. [After a pause.] I am tired of living abroad. I want to

356

come back to London. I want to have a charming house here. I want to have a salon. If one could only teach the English how to talk, and the Irish how to listen, society here would be quite civilised. Besides, I have arrived at the romantic stage. When I saw you last night at the Chilterns', I knew you were the only person I had ever cared for, if I ever have cared for anybody, Arthur. And so, on the morning of the day you marry me, I will give you Robert Chiltern's letter. That is my offer. I will give it to you now, if you promise to marry me.

lord goring. Now?

mrs. cheveley. [Smiling.] To-morrow.

lord goring. Are you really serious?

mrs. cheveley. Yes, quite serious.

lord goring. I should make you a very bad husband.

mrs. cheveley. I don't mind bad husbands. I have had two. They amused me immensely.

lord goring. You mean that you amused yourself immensely, don't you?

mrs. cheveley. What do you know about my married life?

lord goring. Nothing: but I can read it like a book.

mrs. cheveley. What book?

lord goring. [Rising.] The Book of Numbers.

mrs. cheveley. Do you think it is quite charming of you to be so rude to a woman in your own house?

lord goring. In the case of very fascinating women, sex is a challenge, not a defence.

mrs. cheveley. I suppose that is meant for a compliment. My dear Arthur, women are never disarmed by compliments. Men always are. That is the difference between the two sexes.

lord goring. Women are never disarmed by anything, as far as I know them.

mrs. cheveley. [After a pause.] Then you are going to allow your greatest friend, Robert Chiltern, to be ruined, rather than marry some one who really has considerable attractions left. I thought you would have risen to some great height of self-sacrifice, Arthur. I think you should. And the rest of your life you could spend in contemplating your own perfections.

lord goring. Oh! I do that as it is. And self-sacrifice is a thing that should be put down by law. It is so demoralising to the people for whom one sacrifices oneself. They always go to the bad.

mrs. cheveley. As if anything could demoralise Robert Chiltern! You seem to forget that I know his real character.

lord goring. What you know about him is not his real character. It was an act of folly done in his youth, dishonourable, I admit, shameful, I admit, unworthy of him, I admit, and therefore . . . not his true character.

mrs. cheveley. How you men stand up for each other!

lord goring. How you women war against each other!

mrs. cheveley. [Bitterly.] I only war against one woman, against Gertrude Chiltern. I hate her. I hate her now more than ever.

lord goring. Because you have brought a real tragedy into her life, I suppose.

mrs. cheveley. [With a sneer.] Oh, there is only one real tragedy in a woman's life. The fact that her past is always her lover, and her future invariably her husband.

lord goring. Lady Chiltern knows nothing of the kind of life to which you are alluding.

mrs. cheveley. A woman whose size in gloves is seven and three-quarters never knows much about anything. You know Gertrude has always worn seven and three-quarters? That is one of the reasons why there was never any moral sympathy between us. . . . Well, Arthur, I suppose this romantic interview may be regarded as at an end. You admit it was romantic, don't you? For the privilege of being your wife I was ready to surrender a great prize, the climax of my diplomatic career. You decline. Very well. If Sir Robert doesn't uphold my Argentine scheme, I expose him. Voilà tout.

lord goring. You mustn't do that. It would be vile, horrible, infamous.

mrs. cheveley. [Shrugging her shoulders.] Oh! don't use big words. They mean so little. It is a commercial transaction. That is all. There is no good mixing up sentimentality in it. I offered to sell Robert Chiltern a certain thing. If he won't pay me my price, he will have to pay the world a greater price. There is no more to be said. I must go. Good-bye. Won't you shake hands?

lord goring. With you? No. Your transaction with Robert Chiltern may pass as a loathsome commercial transaction of a loathsome commercial age; but you seem to have forgotten that you came here to-night to talk of love, you whose lips desecrated the word love, you to whom the thing is a book closely sealed, went this afternoon to the house of one of the most noble and gentle women in the world to degrade her husband in her eyes, to try and kill her love for him, to put poison in her heart, and bitterness in her life, to break her idol, and, it may be, spoil her soul. That I cannot forgive you. That was horrible. For that there can be no forgiveness.

mrs. cheveley. Arthur, you are unjust to me. Believe me, you are quite unjust to me. I didn't go to taunt Gertrude at all. I had no idea of doing anything of the kind when I entered. I called with Lady Markby simply to ask whether an ornament, a jewel, that I lost somewhere last night, had been found at the Chilterns'. If you don't believe me, you can ask Lady Markby. She will tell you it is true. The scene that occurred happened after Lady Markby had left, and was really forced on me by Gertrude's rudeness and sneers. I called, oh!—a little out of malice if you like—but really to ask if a diamond brooch of mine had been found. That was the origin of the whole thing.

lord goring. A diamond snake-brooch with a ruby?

mrs. cheveley. Yes. How do you know?

lord goring. Because it is found. In point of fact, I found it myself, and stupidly forgot to tell the butler anything about it as I was leaving. [Goes over to the writing-table and pulls out the drawers.] It is in this drawer. No, that one. This is the brooch, isn't it? [Holds up the brooch.]

mrs. cheveley. Yes. I am so glad to get it back. It was . . a present.

lord goring. Won't you wear it?

mrs. cheveley. Certainly, if you pin it in. [lord goring suddenly clasps it on her arm.] Why do you put it on as a bracelet? I never knew it could he worn as a bracelet.

lord goring. Really?

mrs. cheveley. [Holding out her handsome arm.] No; but it looks very well on me as a bracelet, doesn't it?

lord goring. Yes; much better than when I saw it last.

mrs. cheveley. When did you see it last?

lord goring. [Calmly.] Oh, ten years ago, on Lady Berkshire, from whom you stole it.

mrs. cheveley. [Starting.] What do you mean?

lord goring. I mean that you stole that ornament from my cousin, Mary Berkshire, to whom I gave it when she was married. Suspicion fell on a wretched servant, who was sent away in disgrace. I recognised it last night. I determined to say nothing about it till I had found the thief. I have found the thief now, and I have heard her own confession.

mrs. cheveley. [Tossing her head.] It is not true.

lord goring. You know it is true. Why, thief is written across your face at this moment.

mrs. cheveley. I will deny the whole affair from beginning to end. I will say that I have never seen this wretched thing, that it was never in my possession.

[mrs. cheveley *tries to get the bracelet off her arm, but fails.* lord goring *looks on amused. Her thin fingers tear at the jewel to no purpose. A curse breaks from her.*]

lord goring. The drawback of stealing a thing, Mrs. Cheveley, is that one never knows how wonderful the thing that one steals is. You can't get that bracelet off, unless you know where the spring is. And I see you don't know where the spring is. It is rather difficult to find.

mrs. cheveley. You brute! You coward! [She tries again to unclasp the bracelet, but fails.]

lord goring. Oh! don't use big words. They mean so little.

mrs. cheveley. [Again tears at the bracelet in a paroxysm of rage, with inarticulate sounds. Then stops, and looks at lord goring.] What are you going to do?

lord goring. I am going to ring for my servant. He is an admirable servant. Always comes in the moment one rings for him. When he comes I will tell him to fetch the police.

mrs. cheveley. [Trembling.] The police? What for?

lord goring. To-morrow the Berkshires will prosecute you. That is what the police are for.

mrs. cheveley. [Is now in an agony of physical terror. Her face is distorted. Her mouth awry. A mask has fallen from her. She it, for the moment, dreadful to look at.] Don't do that. I will do anything you want. Anything in the world you want.

lord goring. Give me Robert Chiltern's letter.

mrs. cheveley. Stop! Stop! Let me have time to think.

lord goring. Give me Robert Chiltern's letter.

mrs. cheveley. I have not got it with me. I will give it to you to-morrow.

lord goring. You know you are lying. Give it to me at once. [mrs. cheveley pulls the letter out, and hands it to him. She is horribly pale.] This is it?

mrs. cheveley. [In a hoarse voice.] Yes.

lord goring. [Takes the letter, examines it, sighs, and burns it with the lamp.] For so well-dressed a woman, Mrs. Cheveley, you have moments of admirable common sense. I congratulate you.

mrs. cheveley. [Catches sight of lady chiltern's letter, the cover of which is just showing from under the blotting-book.] Please get me a glass of water.

lord goring. Certainly. [Goes to the corner of the room and pours out a glass of water. While his back is turned mrs. cheveley steals lady chiltern's letter. When lord goring returns the glass she refuses it with a gesture.]

mrs. cheveley. Thank you. Will you help me on with my cloak?

lord goring. With pleasure. [Puts her cloak on.]

mrs. cheveley. Thanks. I am never going to try to harm Robert Chiltern again.

lord goring. Fortunately you have not the chance, Mrs. Cheveley.

mrs. cheveley. Well, if even I had the chance, I wouldn't. On the contrary, I am going to render him a great service.

lord goring. I am charmed to hear it. It is a reformation.

mrs. cheveley. Yes. I can't bear so upright a gentleman, so honourable an English gentleman, being so shamefully deceived, and so—

lord goring. Well?

mrs. cheveley. I find that somehow Gertrude Chiltern's dying speech and confession has strayed into my pocket.

lord goring. What do you mean?

362

mrs. cheveley. [With a bitter note of triumph in her voice.] I mean that I am going to send Robert Chiltern the love-letter his wife wrote to you to-night.

lord goring. Love-letter?

mrs. cheveley. [Laughing.] 'I want you. I trust you. I am coming to you. Gertrude.'

[lord goring rushes to the bureau and takes up the envelope, finds is empty, and turns round.]

lord goring. You wretched woman, must you always be thieving? Give me back that letter. I'll take it from you by force. You shall not leave my room till I have got it.

[He *rushes towards her, but* mrs. cheveley *at once puts her hand on the electric bell that is on the table. The bell sounds with shrill reverberations, and* phipps *enters.*]

mrs. cheveley. [After a pause.] Lord Goring merely rang that you should show me out. Good-night, Lord Goring!

[*Goes out followed by* phipps. *Her face is illumined with evil triumph. There is joy in her eyes. Youth seems to have come back to her. Her last glance is like a swift arrow.* lord goring *bites his lip, and lights his a cigarette.*]

ACT DROPS

FOURTH ACT

SCENE

Same as Act II.

[lord goring *is standing by the fireplace with his hands in his pockets. He is looking rather bored.*]

lord goring. [Pulls out his watch, inspects it, and rings the bell.] It is a great nuisance. I can't find any one in this house to talk to. And I am full of interesting information. I feel like the latest edition of something or other.

[*Enter servant.*]

james. Sir Robert is still at the Foreign Office, my lord.

lord goring. Lady Chiltern not down yet?

james. Her ladyship has not yet left her room. Miss Chiltern has just come in from riding.

lord goring. [To himself.] Ah! that is something.

james. Lord Caversham has been waiting some time in the library for Sir Robert. I told him your lordship was here.

lord goring. Thank you! Would you kindly tell him I've gone?

james. [Bowing.] I shall do so, my lord.

[*Exit* servant.]

lord goring. Really, I don't want to meet my father three days running. It is a great deal too much excitement for any son. I hope to goodness he won't come up. Fathers should be neither seen nor heard. That is the only proper basis for family life. Mothers are different. Mothers are darlings. [Throws himself down into a chair, picks up a paper and begins to read it.]

[*Enter* lord caversham.]

lord caversham. Well, sir, what are you doing here? Wasting your time as usual, I suppose?

lord goring. [Throws down paper and rises.] My dear father, when one pays a visit it is for the purpose of wasting other people's time, not one's own.

lord caversham. Have you been thinking over what I spoke to you about last night?

lord goring. I have been thinking about nothing else.

lord caversham. Engaged to be married yet?

lord goring. [Genially.] Not yet: but I hope to be before lunch-time.

lord caversham. [Caustically.] You can have till dinner-time if it would be of any convenience to you.

lord goring. Thanks awfully, but I think I'd sooner be engaged before lunch.

lord caversham. Humph! Never know when you are serious or not.

lord goring. Neither do I, father.

[*A pause.*]

lord caversham. I suppose you have read The Times this morning?

lord goring. [Airily.] The Times? Certainly not. I only read The Morning Post. All that one should know about modern life is where the Duchesses are; anything else is quite demoralising.

lord caversham. Do you mean to say you have not read The Times leading article on Robert Chiltern's career?

lord goring. Good heavens! No. What does it say?

lord caversham. What should it say, sir? Everything complimentary, of course. Chiltern's speech last night on this Argentine Canal scheme was one of the finest pieces of oratory ever delivered in the House since Canning.

lord goring. Ah! Never heard of Canning. Never wanted to. And did

. . . did Chiltern uphold the scheme?

lord caversham. Uphold it, sir? How little you know him! Why, he denounced it roundly, and the whole system of modern political finance. This speech is the turning-point in his career, as The Times points out. You should read this article, sir. [Opens The Times.] 'Sir Robert Chiltern . . . most rising of our young statesmen . . . Brilliant orator . . . Unblemished career . . . Well-known integrity of character . . . Represents what is best in English public life . . . Noble contrast to the lax morality so common among foreign politicians.' They will never say that of you, sir.

lord goring. I sincerely hope not, father. However, I am delighted at what you tell me about Robert, thoroughly delighted. It shows he has got pluck.

lord caversham. He has got more than pluck, sir, he has got genius.

lord goring. Ah! I prefer pluck. It is not so common, nowadays, as genius is.

lord caversham. I wish you would go into Parliament.

lord goring. My dear father, only people who look dull ever get into the House of Commons, and only people who are dull ever succeed there.

lord caversham. Why don't you try to do something useful in life?

lord goring. I am far too young.

lord caversham. [Testily.] I hate this affectation of youth, sir. It is a great deal too prevalent nowadays.

lord goring. Youth isn't an affectation. Youth is an art.

lord caversham. Why don't you propose to that pretty Miss Chiltern?

lord goring. I am of a very nervous disposition, especially in the morning.

lord caversham. I don't suppose there is the smallest chance of her accepting you.

lord goring. I don't know how the betting stands to-day.

lord caversham. If she did accept you she would be the prettiest fool in England.

lord goring. That is just what I should like to marry. A thoroughly sensible wife would reduce me to a condition of absolute idiocy in less than six months.

lord caversham. You don't deserve her, sir.

lord goring. My dear father, if we men married the women we deserved, we should have a very bad time of it.

[*Enter* mabel chiltern.]

mabel chiltern. Oh! . . . How do you do, Lord Caversham? I hope Lady Caversham is quite well?

lord caversham. Lady Caversham is as usual, as usual.

lord goring. Good morning, Miss Mabel!

mabel chiltern. [Taking no notice at all of lord goring, and addressing herself exclusively to lord caversham.] And Lady Caversham's bonnets . . . are they at all better?

lord caversham. They have had a serious relapse, I am sorry to say.

lord goring. Good morning, Miss Mabel!

mabel chiltern. [To lord caversham.] I hope an operation will not be necessary.

lord caversham. [Smiling at her pertness.] If it is, we shall have to give Lady Caversham a narcotic. Otherwise she would never consent to have a feather touched.

lord goring. [With increased emphasis.] Good morning, Miss Mabel!

mabel chiltern. [Turning round with feigned surprise.] Oh, are you here? Of course you understand that after your breaking your appointment I am never going to speak to you again.

lord goring. Oh, please don't say such a thing. You are the one person in London I really like to have to listen to me.

mabel chiltern. Lord Goring, I never believe a single word that either you or I say to each other.

lord caversham. You are quite right, my dear, quite right . . . as far as he is concerned, I mean.

mabel chiltern. Do you think you could possibly make your son behave a little better occasionally? Just as a change.

lord caversham. I regret to say, Miss Chiltern, that I have no influence at all over my son. I wish I had. If I had, I know what I would make him do.

mabel chiltern. I am afraid that he has one of those terribly weak natures that are not susceptible to influence.

lord caversham. He is very heartless, very heartless.

lord goring. It seems to me that I am a little in the way here.

mabel chiltern. It is very good for you to be in the way, and to know what people say of you behind your back.

lord goring. I don't at all like knowing what people say of me behind my back. It makes me far too conceited.

lord caversham. After that, my dear, I really must bid you good morning.

mabel chiltern. Oh! I hope you are not going to leave me all alone with Lord Goring? Especially at such an early hour in the day.

lord caversham. I am afraid I can't take him with me to Downing Street. It is not the Prime Minster's day for seeing the unemployed.

[*Shakes hands with* mabel chiltern, *takes up his hat and stick, and goes out, with a parting glare of indignation at* lord goring.]

mabel chiltern. [Takes up roses and begins to arrange them in a bowl on

368

the table.] People who don't keep their appointments in the Park are horrid.

lord goring. Detestable.

mabel chiltern. I am glad you admit it. But I wish you wouldn't look so pleased about it.

lord goring. I can't help it. I always look pleased when I am with you.

mabel chiltern. [Sadly.] Then I suppose it is my duty to remain with you?

lord goring. Of course it is.

mabel chiltern. Well, my duty is a thing I never do, on principle. It always depresses me. So I am afraid I must leave you.

lord goring. Please don't, Miss Mabel. I have something very particular to say to you.

mabel chiltern. [Rapturously.] Oh! is it a proposal?

lord goring. [Somewhat taken aback.] Well, yes, it is—I am bound to say it is.

mabel chiltern. [With a sigh of pleasure.] I am so glad. That makes the second to-day.

lord goring. [Indignantly.] The second to-day? What conceited ass has been impertinent enough to dare to propose to you before I had proposed to you?

mabel chiltern. Tommy Trafford, of course. It is one of Tommy's days for proposing. He always proposes on Tuesdays and Thursdays, during the Season.

lord goring. You didn't accept him, I hope?

mabel chiltern. I make it a rule never to accept Tommy. That is why he goes on proposing. Of course, as you didn't turn up this morning, I very nearly said yes. It would have been an excellent lesson both for him and for you if I had. It would have taught you both better manners.

lord goring. Oh! bother Tommy Trafford. Tommy is a silly little ass.
love you.

mabel chiltern. I know. And I think you might have mentioned i
before. I am sure I have given you heaps of opportunities.

lord goring. Mabel, do be serious. Please be serious.

mabel chiltern. Ah! that is the sort of thing a man always says to a gir
before he has been married to her. He never says it afterwards.

lord goring. [Taking hold of her hand.] Mabel, I have told you that
love you. Can't you love me a little in return?

mabel chiltern. You silly Arthur! If you knew anything about . .
anything, which you don't, you would know that I adore you. Every one ir
London knows it except you. It is a public scandal the way I adore you.
have been going about for the last six months telling the whole of society tha
I adore you. I wonder you consent to have anything to say to me. I have n
character left at all. At least, I feel so happy that I am quite sure I have n
character left at all.

lord goring. [Catches her in his arms and kisses her. Then there is ¡
pause of bliss.] Dear! Do you know I was awfully afraid of being refused!

mabel chiltern. [Looking up at him.] But you never have been refuse
yet by anybody, have you, Arthur? I can't imagine any one refusing you.

lord goring. [After kissing her again.] Of course I'm not nearly goo
enough for you, Mabel.

mabel chiltern. [Nestling close to him.] I am so glad, darling. I wa
afraid you were.

lord goring. [After some hesitation.] And I'm . . . I'm a little over thirty

mabel chiltern. Dear, you look weeks younger than that.

lord goring. [Enthusiastically.] How sweet of you to say so! . . . And i

370

is only fair to tell you frankly that I am fearfully extravagant.

mabel chiltern. But so am I, Arthur. So we're sure to agree. And now I must go and see Gertrude.

lord goring. Must you really? [Kisses her.]

mabel chiltern. Yes.

lord goring. Then do tell her I want to talk to her particularly. I have been waiting here all the morning to see either her or Robert.

mabel chiltern. Do you mean to say you didn't come here expressly to propose to me?

lord goring. [Triumphantly.] No; that was a flash of genius.

mabel chiltern. Your first.

lord goring. [With determination.] My last.

mabel chiltern. I am delighted to hear it. Now don't stir. I'll be back in five minutes. And don't fall into any temptations while I am away.

lord goring. Dear Mabel, while you are away, there are none. It makes me horribly dependent on you.

[*Enter* lady chiltern.]

lady chiltern. Good morning, dear! How pretty you are looking!

mabel chiltern. How pale you are looking, Gertrude! It is most becoming!

lady chiltern. Good morning, Lord Goring!

lord goring. [Bowing.] Good morning, Lady Chiltern!

mabel chiltern. [Aside to lord goring.] I shall be in the conservatory under the second palm tree on the left.

lord goring. Second on the left?

mabel chiltern. [With a look of mock surprise.] Yes; the usual palm tree.

[*Blows a kiss to him, unobserved by* lady chiltern, *and goes out.*]

lord goring. Lady Chiltern, I have a certain amount of very good news to tell you. Mrs. Cheveley gave me up Robert's letter last night, and I burned it. Robert is safe.

lady chiltern. [Sinking on the sofa.] Safe! Oh! I am so glad of that. What a good friend you are to him—to us!

lord goring. There is only one person now that could be said to be in any danger.

lady chiltern. Who is that?

lord goring. [Sitting down beside her.] Yourself.

lady chiltern. I? In danger? What do you mean?

lord goring. Danger is too great a word. It is a word I should not have used. But I admit I have something to tell you that may distress you, that terribly distresses me. Yesterday evening you wrote me a very beautiful, womanly letter, asking me for my help. You wrote to me as one of your oldest friends, one of your husband's oldest friends. Mrs. Cheveley stole that letter from my rooms.

lady chiltern. Well, what use is it to her? Why should she not have it?

lord goring. [Rising.] Lady Chiltern, I will be quite frank with you. Mrs. Cheveley puts a certain construction on that letter and proposes to send it to your husband.

lady chiltern. But what construction could she put on it? . . . Oh! not that! not that! If I in—in trouble, and wanting your help, trusting you, propose to come to you . . . that you may advise me . . . assist me . . . Oh! are there women so horrible as that . . .? And she proposes to send it to my husband? Tell me what happened. Tell me all that happened.

lord goring. Mrs. Cheveley was concealed in a room adjoining my

372

library, without my knowledge. I thought that the person who was waiting in that room to see me was yourself. Robert came in unexpectedly. A chair or something fell in the room. He forced his way in, and he discovered her. We had a terrible scene. I still thought it was you. He left me in anger. At the end of everything Mrs. Cheveley got possession of your letter—she stole it, when or how, I don't know.

lady chiltern. At what hour did this happen?

lord goring. At half-past ten. And now I propose that we tell Robert the whole thing at once.

lady chiltern. [Looking at him with amazement that is almost terror.] You want me to tell Robert that the woman you expected was not Mrs. Cheveley, but myself? That it was I whom you thought was concealed in a room in your house, at half-past ten o'clock at night? You want me to tell him that?

lord goring. I think it is better that he should know the exact truth.

lady chiltern. [Rising.] Oh, I couldn't, I couldn't!

lord goring. May I do it?

lady chiltern. No.

lord goring. [Gravely.] You are wrong, Lady Chiltern.

lady chiltern. No. The letter must be intercepted. That is all. But how can I do it? Letters arrive for him every moment of the day. His secretaries open them and hand them to him. I dare not ask the servants to bring me his letters. It would be impossible. Oh! why don't you tell me what to do?

lord goring. Pray be calm, Lady Chiltern, and answer the questions I am going to put to you. You said his secretaries open his letters.

lady chiltern. Yes.

lord goring. Who is with him to-day? Mr. Trafford, isn't it?

lady chiltern. No. Mr. Montford, I think.

lord goring. You can trust him?

lady chiltern. [With a gesture of despair.] Oh! how do I know?

lord goring. He would do what you asked him, wouldn't he?

lady chiltern. I think so.

lord goring. Your letter was on pink paper. He could recognise it without reading it, couldn't he? By the colour?

lady chiltern. I suppose so.

lord goring. Is he in the house now?

lady chiltern. Yes.

lord goring. Then I will go and see him myself, and tell him that a certain letter, written on pink paper, is to be forwarded to Robert to-day, and that at all costs it must not reach him. [Goes to the door, and opens it.] Oh! Robert is coming upstairs with the letter in his hand. It has reached him already.

lady chiltern. [With a cry of pain.] Oh! you have saved his life; what have you done with mine?

[*Enter* sir robert chiltern. *He has the letter in his hand, and is reading it. He comes towards his wife, not noticing lord goring's presence.*]

sir robert chiltern. 'I want you. I trust you. I am coming to you. Gertrude.' Oh, my love! Is this true? Do you indeed trust me, and want me? If so, it was for me to come to you, not for you to write of coming to me. This letter of yours, Gertrude, makes me feel that nothing that the world may do can hurt me now. You want me, Gertrude?

[lord goring, *unseen by* sir robert chiltern, *makes an imploring sign to* lady chiltern *to accept the situation and* sir robert's *error.*]

lady chiltern. Yes.

sir robert chiltern. You trust me, Gertrude?

374

lady chiltern. Yes.

sir robert chiltern. Ah! why did you not add you loved me?

lady chiltern. [Taking his hand.] Because I loved you.

[lord goring *passes into the conservatory.*]

sir robert chiltern. [Kisses her.] Gertrude, you don't know what I feel. When Montford passed me your letter across the table—he had opened it by mistake, I suppose, without looking at the handwriting on the envelope—and I read it—oh! I did not care what disgrace or punishment was in store for me, I only thought you loved me still.

lady chiltern. There is no disgrace in store for you, nor any public shame. Mrs. Cheveley has handed over to Lord Goring the document that was in her possession, and he has destroyed it.

sir robert chiltern. Are you sure of this, Gertrude?

lady chiltern. Yes; Lord Goring has just told me.

sir robert chiltern. Then I am safe! Oh! what a wonderful thing to be safe! For two days I have been in terror. I am safe now. How did Arthur destroy my letter? Tell me.

lady chiltern. He burned it.

sir robert chiltern. I wish I had seen that one sin of my youth burning to ashes. How many men there are in modern life who would like to see their past burning to white ashes before them! Is Arthur still here?

lady chiltern. Yes; he is in the conservatory.

sir robert chiltern. I am so glad now I made that speech last night in the House, so glad. I made it thinking that public disgrace might be the result. But it has not been so.

lady chiltern. Public honour has been the result.

sir robert chiltern. I think so. I fear so, almost. For although I am safe from detection, although every proof against me is destroyed, I suppose, Gertrude . . . I suppose I should retire from public life? [He looks anxiously at his wife.]

lady chiltern. [Eagerly.] Oh yes, Robert, you should do that. It is your duty to do that.

sir robert chiltern. It is much to surrender.

lady chiltern. No; it will be much to gain.

[sir robert chiltern *walks up and down the room with a troubled expression. Then comes over to his wife, and puts his hand on her shoulder.*]

sir robert chiltern. And you would be happy living somewhere alone with me, abroad perhaps, or in the country away from London, away from public life? You would have no regrets?

lady chiltern. Oh! none, Robert.

sir robert chiltern. [Sadly.] And your ambition for me? You used to be ambitious for me.

lady chiltern. Oh, my ambition! I have none now, but that we two may love each other. It was your ambition that led you astray. Let us not talk about ambition.

[lord goring *returns from the conservatory, looking very pleased with himself, and with an entirely new buttonhole that some one has made for him.*]

sir robert chiltern. [Going towards him.] Arthur, I have to thank you for what you have done for me. I don't know how I can repay you. [Shakes hands with him.]

lord goring. My dear fellow, I'll tell you at once. At the present moment, under the usual palm tree . . . I mean in the conservatory . . .

[*Enter* mason.]

mason. Lord Caversham.

lord goring. That admirable father of mine really makes a habit of turning up at the wrong moment. It is very heartless of him, very heartless indeed.

[*Enter* lord caversham. mason *goes out.*]

lord caversham. Good morning, Lady Chiltern! Warmest congratulations to you, Chiltern, on your brilliant speech last night. I have just left the Prime Minister, and you are to have the vacant seat in the Cabinet.

sir robert chiltern. [With a look of joy and triumph.] A seat in the Cabinet?

lord caversham. Yes; here is the Prime Minister's letter. [Hands letter.]

sir robert chiltern. [Takes letter and reads it.] A seat in the Cabinet!

lord caversham. Certainly, and you well deserve it too. You have got what we want so much in political life nowadays—high character, high moral tone, high principles. [To lord goring.] Everything that you have not got, sir, and never will have.

lord goring. I don't like principles, father. I prefer prejudices.

[sir robert chiltern *is on the brink of accepting the Prime Minister's offer, when he sees wife looking at him with her clear, candid eyes. He then realises that it is impossible.*]

sir robert chiltern. I cannot accept this offer, Lord Caversham. I have made up my mind to decline it.

lord caversham. Decline it, sir!

sir robert chiltern. My intention is to retire at once from public life.

lord caversham. [Angrily.] Decline a seat in the Cabinet, and retire from public life? Never heard such damned nonsense in the whole course of my existence. I beg your pardon, Lady Chiltern. Chiltern, I beg your pardon. [To lord goring.] Don't grin like that, sir.

lord goring. No, father.

lord caversham. Lady Chiltern, you are a sensible woman, the most sensible woman in London, the most sensible woman I know. Will you kindly prevent your husband from making such a . . . from taking such . . . Will you kindly do that, Lady Chiltern?

lady chiltern. I think my husband in right in his determination, Lord Caversham. I approve of it.

lord caversham. You approve of it? Good heavens!

lady chiltern. [Taking her husband's hand.] I admire him for it. I admire him immensely for it. I have never admired him so much before. He is finer than even I thought him. [To sir robert chiltern.] You will go and write your letter to the Prime Minister now, won't you? Don't hesitate about it, Robert.

sir robert chiltern. [With a touch of bitterness.] I suppose I had better write it at once. Such offers are not repeated. I will ask you to excuse me for a moment, Lord Caversham.

lady chiltern. I may come with you, Robert, may I not?

sir robert chiltern. Yes, Gertrude.

[lady chiltern *goes out with him.*]

lord caversham. What is the matter with this family? Something wrong here, eh? [Tapping his forehead.] Idiocy? Hereditary, I suppose. Both of them, too. Wife as well as husband. Very sad. Very sad indeed! And they are not an old family. Can't understand it.

lord goring. It is not idiocy, father, I assure you.

lord caversham. What is it then, sir?

lord goring. [After some hesitation.] Well, it is what is called nowadays a high moral tone, father. That is all.

lord caversham. Hate these new-fangled names. Same thing as we used to call idiocy fifty years ago. Shan't stay in this house any longer.

lord goring. [Taking his arm.] Oh! just go in here for a moment, father.

Third palm tree to the left, the usual palm tree.

lord caversham. What, sir?

lord goring. I beg your pardon, father, I forgot. The conservatory, father, the conservatory—there is some one there I want you to talk to.

lord caversham. What about, sir?

lord goring. About me, father,

lord caversham. [Grimly.] Not a subject on which much eloquence is possible.

lord goring. No, father; but the lady is like me. She doesn't care much for eloquence in others. She thinks it a little loud.

[lord caversham goes out into the conservatory. lady chiltern enters.]

lord goring. Lady Chiltern, why are you playing Mrs. Cheveley's cards?

lady chiltern. [Startled.] I don't understand you.

lord goring. Mrs. Cheveley made an attempt to ruin your husband. Either to drive him from public life, or to make him adopt a dishonourable position. From the latter tragedy you saved him. The former you are now thrusting on him. Why should you do him the wrong Mrs. Cheveley tried to do and failed?

lady chiltern. Lord Goring?

lord goring. [Pulling himself together for a great effort, and showing the philosopher that underlies the dandy.] Lady Chiltern, allow me. You wrote me a letter last night in which you said you trusted me and wanted my help. Now is the moment when you really want my help, now is the time when you have got to trust me, to trust in my counsel and judgment. You love Robert. Do you want to kill his love for you? What sort of existence will he have if you rob him of the fruits of his ambition, if you take him from the splendour of a great political career, if you close the doors of public life against him, if you condemn him to sterile failure, he who was made for

379

triumph and success? Women are not meant to judge us, but to forgive us when we need forgiveness. Pardon, not punishment, is their mission. Why should you scourge him with rods for a sin done in his youth, before he knew you, before he knew himself? A man's life is of more value than a woman's. It has larger issues, wider scope, greater ambitions. A woman's life revolves in curves of emotions. It is upon lines of intellect that a man's life progresses. Don't make any terrible mistake, Lady Chiltern. A woman who can keep a man's love, and love him in return, has done all the world wants of women, or should want of them.

lady chiltern. [Troubled and hesitating.] But it is my husband himself who wishes to retire from public life. He feels it is his duty. It was he who first said so.

lord goring. Rather than lose your love, Robert would do anything, wreck his whole career, as he is on the brink of doing now. He is making for you a terrible sacrifice. Take my advice, Lady Chiltern, and do not accept a sacrifice so great. If you do, you will live to repent it bitterly. We men and women are not made to accept such sacrifices from each other. We are not worthy of them. Besides, Robert has been punished enough.

lady chiltern. We have both been punished. I set him up too high.

lord goring. [With deep feeling in his voice.] Do not for that reason set him down now too low. If he has fallen from his altar, do not thrust him into the mire. Failure to Robert would be the very mire of shame. Power is his passion. He would lose everything, even his power to feel love. Your husband's life is at this moment in your hands, your husband's love is in your hands. Don't mar both for him.

[*Enter* sir robert chiltern.]

sir robert chiltern. Gertrude, here is the draft of my letter. Shall I read it to you?

lady chiltern. Let me see it.

[sir robert *hands her the letter. She reads it, and then, with a gesture of*

380

passion, tears it up.]

sir robert chiltern. What are you doing?

lady chiltern. A man's life is of more value than a woman's. It has larger issues, wider scope, greater ambitions. Our lives revolve in curves of emotions. It is upon lines of intellect that a man's life progresses. I have just learnt this, and much else with it, from Lord Goring. And I will not spoil your life for you, nor see you spoil it as a sacrifice to me, a useless sacrifice!

sir robert chiltern. Gertrude! Gertrude!

lady chiltern. You can forget. Men easily forget. And I forgive. That is how women help the world. I see that now.

sir robert chiltern. [Deeply overcome by emotion, embraces her.] My wife! my wife! [To lord goring.] Arthur, it seems that I am always to be in your debt.

lord goring. Oh dear no, Robert. Your debt is to Lady Chiltern, not to me!

sir robert chiltern. I owe you much. And now tell me what you were going to ask me just now as Lord Caversham came in.

lord goring. Robert, you are your sister's guardian, and I want your consent to my marriage with her. That is all.

lady chiltern. Oh, I am so glad! I am so glad! [Shakes hands with lord goring.]

lord goring. Thank you, Lady Chiltern.

sir robert chiltern. [With a troubled look.] My sister to be your wife?

lord goring. Yes.

sir robert chiltern. [Speaking with great firmness.] Arthur, I am very sorry, but the thing is quite out of the question. I have to think of Mabel's future happiness. And I don't think her happiness would be safe in your hands. And I cannot have her sacrificed!

lord goring. Sacrificed!

sir robert chiltern. Yes, utterly sacrificed. Loveless marriages are horrible. But there is one thing worse than an absolutely loveless marriage. A marriage in which there is love, but on one side only; faith, but on one side only; devotion, but on one side only, and in which of the two hearts one is sure to be broken.

lord goring. But I love Mabel. No other woman has any place in my life.

lady chiltern. Robert, if they love each other, why should they not be married?

sir robert chiltern. Arthur cannot bring Mabel the love that she deserves.

lord goring. What reason have you for saying that?

sir robert chiltern. [After a pause.] Do you really require me to tell you?

lord goring. Certainly I do.

sir robert chiltern. As you choose. When I called on you yesterday evening I found Mrs. Cheveley concealed in your rooms. It was between ten and eleven o'clock at night. I do not wish to say anything more. Your relations with Mrs. Cheveley have, as I said to you last night, nothing whatsoever to do with me. I know you were engaged to be married to her once. The fascination she exercised over you then seems to have returned. You spoke to me last night of her as of a woman pure and stainless, a woman whom you respected and honoured. That may be so. But I cannot give my sister's life into your hands. It would be wrong of me. It would be unjust, infamously unjust to her.

lord goring. I have nothing more to say.

lady chiltern. Robert, it was not Mrs. Cheveley whom Lord Goring expected last night.

sir robert chiltern. Not Mrs. Cheveley! Who was it then?

lord goring. Lady Chiltern!

lady chiltern. It was your own wife. Robert, yesterday afternoon Lord Goring told me that if ever I was in trouble I could come to him for help, as he was our oldest and best friend. Later on, after that terrible scene in this room, I wrote to him telling him that I trusted him, that I had need of him, that I was coming to him for help and advice. [sir robert chiltern takes the letter out of his pocket.] Yes, that letter. I didn't go to Lord Goring's, after all. I felt that it is from ourselves alone that help can come. Pride made me think that. Mrs. Cheveley went. She stole my letter and sent it anonymously to you this morning, that you should think . . . Oh! Robert, I cannot tell you what she wished you to think. . . .

sir robert chiltern. What! Had I fallen so low in your eyes that you thought that even for a moment I could have doubted your goodness? Gertrude, Gertrude, you are to me the white image of all good things, and sin can never touch you. Arthur, you can go to Mabel, and you have my best wishes! Oh! stop a moment. There is no name at the beginning of this letter. The brilliant Mrs. Cheveley does not seem to have noticed that. There should be a name.

lady chiltern. Let me write yours. It is you I trust and need. You and none else.

lord goring. Well, really, Lady Chiltern, I think I should have back my own letter.

lady chiltern. [Smiling.] No; you shall have Mabel. [Takes the letter and writes her husband's name on it.]

lord goring. Well, I hope she hasn't changed her mind. It's nearly twenty minutes since I saw her last.

[Enter mabel chiltern and lord caversham.]

mabel chiltern. Lord Goring, I think your father's conversation much more improving than yours. I am only going to talk to Lord Caversham in the future, and always under the usual palm tree.

lord goring. Darling! [Kisses her.]

lord caversham. [Considerably taken aback.] What does this mean, sir? You don't mean to say that this charming, clever young lady has been so foolish as to accept you?

lord goring. Certainly, father! And Chiltern's been wise enough to accept the seat in the Cabinet.

lord caversham. I am very glad to hear that, Chiltern . . . I congratulate you, sir. If the country doesn't go to the dogs or the Radicals, we shall have you Prime Minister, some day.

[*Enter* mason.]

mason. Luncheon is on the table, my Lady!

[mason *goes out.*]

mabel chiltern. You'll stop to luncheon, Lord Caversham, won't you?

lord caversham. With pleasure, and I'll drive you down to Downing Street afterwards, Chiltern. You have a great future before you, a great future. Wish I could say the same for you, sir. [To lord goring.] But your career will have to be entirely domestic.

lord goring. Yes, father, I prefer it domestic.

lord caversham. And if you don't make this young lady an ideal husband, I'll cut you off with a shilling.

mabel chiltern. An ideal husband! Oh, I don't think I should like that. It sounds like something in the next world.

lord caversham. What do you want him to be then, dear?

mabel chiltern. He can be what he chooses. All I want is to be . . . to be . . . oh! a real wife to him.

lord caversham. Upon my word, there is a good deal of common sense in that, Lady Chiltern.

[*They all go out except* sir robert chiltern. *He sinks in a chair, wrapt in*

384

thought. After a little time lady chiltern *returns to look for him.*]

lady chiltern. [Leaning over the back of the chair.] Aren't you coming in, Robert?

sir robert chiltern. [Taking her hand.] Gertrude, is it love you feel for me, or is it pity merely?

lady chiltern. [Kisses him.] It is love, Robert. Love, and only love. For both of us a new life is beginning.

CURTAIN

About Author

Oscar Fingal O'Flahertie Wills Wilde (16 October 1854 – 30 November 1900) was an Irish poet and playwright. After writing in different forms throughout the 1880s, the early 1890s saw him become one of the most popular playwrights in London. He is best remembered for his epigrams and plays, his novel The Picture of Dorian Gray, and the circumstances of his criminal conviction for "gross indecency", imprisonment, and early death at age 46.

Wilde's parents were successful Anglo-Irish intellectuals in Dublin. A young Wilde learned to speak fluent French and German. At university, Wilde read Greats; he demonstrated himself to be an exceptional classicist, first at Trinity College Dublin, then at Oxford. He became associated with the emerging philosophy of aestheticism, led by two of his tutors, Walter Pater and John Ruskin. After university, Wilde moved to London into fashionable cultural and social circles.

As a spokesman for aestheticism, he tried his hand at various literary activities: he published a book of poems, lectured in the United States and Canada on the new "English Renaissance in Art" and interior decoration, and then returned to London where he worked prolifically as a journalist. Known for his biting wit, flamboyant dress and glittering conversational skill, Wilde became one of the best-known personalities of his day. At the turn of the 1890s, he refined his ideas about the supremacy of art in a series of dialogues and essays, and incorporated themes of decadence, duplicity, and beauty into what would be his only novel, The Picture of Dorian Gray (1890). The opportunity to construct aesthetic details precisely, and combine them with larger social themes, drew Wilde to write drama. He wrote Salome (1891) in French while in Paris but it was refused a licence for England due to an absolute prohibition on the portrayal of Biblical subjects on the English stage. Unperturbed, Wilde produced four society comedies in the early 1890s, which made him one of the most successful playwrights of late-Victorian London.

At the height of his fame and success, while The Importance of Being Earnest (1895) was still being performed in London, Wilde had the Marquess of Queensberry prosecuted for criminal libel. The Marquess was the father of Wilde's lover, Lord Alfred Douglas. The libel trial unearthed evidence that caused Wilde to drop his charges and led to his own arrest and trial for gross indecency with men. After two more trials he was convicted and sentenced to two years' hard labour, the maximum penalty, and was jailed from 1895 to 1897. During his last year in prison, he wrote De Profundis (published posthumously in 1905), a long letter which discusses his spiritual journey through his trials, forming a dark counterpoint to his earlier philosophy of pleasure. On his release, he left immediately for France, never to return to Ireland or Britain. There he wrote his last work, The Ballad of Reading Gaol (1898), a long poem commemorating the harsh rhythms of prison life.

Early life

Oscar Wilde was born at 21 Westland Row, Dublin (now home of the Oscar Wilde Centre, Trinity College), the second of three children born to Anglo-Irish Sir William Wilde and Jane Wilde, two years behind his brother William ("Willie"). Wilde's mother had distant Italian ancestry,and under the pseudonym "Speranza" (the Italian word for 'hope'), wrote poetry for the revolutionary Young Irelanders in 1848; she was a lifelong Irish nationalist She read the Young Irelanders' poetry to Oscar and Willie, inculcating a love of these poets in her sons. Lady Wilde's interest in the neo-classical revival showed in the paintings and busts of ancient Greece and Rome in her home

William Wilde was Ireland's leading oto-ophthalmologic (ear and eye) surgeon and was knighted in 1864 for his services as medical adviser and assistant commissioner to the censuses of Ireland. He also wrote books about Irish archaeology and peasant folklore. A renowned philanthropist his dispensary for the care of the city's poor at the rear of Trinity College Dublin, was the forerunner of the Dublin Eye and Ear Hospital, now located at Adelaide Road. On his father's side Wilde was descended from a Dutchman, Colonel de Wilde, who went to Ireland with King William of Orange's invading army in 1690, and numerous Anglo-Irish ancestors On his mother's side, Wilde's ancestors included a bricklayer from County Durham, who emigrated to Ireland sometime in the 1770s.

Wilde was baptised as an infant in St. Mark's Church, Dublin, the local Church of Ireland (Anglican) church. When the church was closed, the records were moved to the nearby St. Ann's Church, Dawson Street. Davis Coakley mentions a second baptism by a Catholic priest, Father Prideaux Fox, who befriended Oscar's mother circa 1859. According to Fox's testimony in Donahoe's Magazine in 1905, Jane Wilde would visit his chapel in Glencree, County Wicklow, for Mass and would take her sons with her. She asked Father Fox in this period to baptise her sons.

Fox described it in this way:

"I am not sure if she ever became a Catholic herself but it was not long before she asked me to instruct two of her children, one of them being the future erratic genius, Oscar Wilde. After a few weeks I baptized these two children, Lady Wilde herself being present on the occasion.

In addition to his children with his wife, Sir William Wilde was the father of three children born out of wedlock before his marriage: Henry Wilson, born in 1838 to one woman, and Emily and Mary Wilde, born in 1847 and 1849, respectively, to a second woman. Sir William acknowledged paternity of his illegitimate or "natural" children and provided for their education, arranging for them to be reared by his relatives rather than with his legitimate children in his family household with his wife.

In 1855, the family moved to No. 1 Merrion Square, where Wilde's sister, Isola, was born in 1857. The Wildes' new home was larger. With both his parents' success and delight in social life, the house soon became the site of a "unique medical and cultural milieu". Guests at their salon included Sheridan Le Fanu, Charles Lever, George Petrie, Isaac Butt, William Rowan Hamilton and Samuel Ferguson.

Until he was nine, Oscar Wilde was educated at home, where a French nursemaid and a German governess taught him their languages. He attended Portora Royal School in Enniskillen, County Fermanagh, from 1864 to 1871. Until his early twenties, Wilde summered at the villa, Moytura House, which his father had built in Cong, County Mayo. There the young Wilde and his brother Willie played with George Moore.

Isola died at age nine of meningitis. Wilde's poem "Requiescat" is written to her memory.

> "Tread lightly, she is near
>
> Under the snow
>
> Speak gently, she can hear
>
> the daisies grow"

University education: 1870s

Trinity College, Dublin

Wilde left Portora with a royal scholarship to read classics at Trinity College, Dublin, from 1871 to 1874, sharing rooms with his older brother Willie Wilde. Trinity, one of the leading classical schools, placed him with scholars such as R. Y. Tyrell, Arthur Palmer, Edward Dowden and his tutor, Professor J. P. Mahaffy, who inspired his interest in Greek literature. As a student Wilde worked with Mahaffy on the latter's book Social Life in Greece. Wilde, despite later reservations, called Mahaffy "my first and best teacher" and "the scholar who showed me how to love Greek things".For his part, Mahaffy boasted of having created Wilde; later, he said Wilde was "the only blot on my tutorship".

The University Philosophical Society also provided an education, as members discussed intellectual and artistic subjects such as Dante Gabriel Rossetti and Algernon Charles Swinburne weekly. Wilde quickly became an established member – the members' suggestion book for 1874 contains two pages of banter (sportingly) mocking Wilde's emergent aestheticism. He presented a paper titled "Aesthetic Morality". At Trinity, Wilde established himself as an outstanding student: he came first in his class in his first year, won a scholarship by competitive examination in his second and, in his finals, won the Berkeley Gold Medal in Greek, the University's highest academic award. He was encouraged to compete for a demyship to Magdalen College, Oxford – which he won easily, having already studied Greek for over nine years.

Magdalen College, Oxford

At Magdalen, he read Greats from 1874 to 1878, and from there he applied to join the Oxford Union, but failed to be elected.

Attracted by its dress, secrecy, and ritual, Wilde petitioned the Apollo Masonic Lodge at Oxford, and was soon raised to the "Sublime Degree of Master Mason".During a resurgent interest in Freemasonry in his third year, he commented he "would be awfully sorry to give it up if I secede from the Protestant Heresy". Wilde's active involvement in Freemasonry lasted only for the time he spent at Oxford; he allowed his membership of the Apollo University Lodge to lapse after failing to pay subscriptions.

Catholicism deeply appealed to him, especially its rich liturgy, and he discussed converting to it with clergy several times. In 1877, Wilde was left speechless after an audience with Pope Pius IX in Rome.He eagerly read the books of Cardinal Newman, a noted Anglican priest who had converted to Catholicism and risen in the church hierarchy. He became more serious in 1878, when he met the Reverend Sebastian Bowden, a priest in the Brompton Oratory who had received some high-profile converts. Neither his father, who threatened to cut off his funds, nor Mahaffy thought much of the plan; but mostly Wilde, the supreme individualist, balked at the last minute from pledging himself to any formal creed. On the appointed day of his baptism, Wilde sent Father Bowden a bunch of altar lilies instead. Wilde did retain a lifelong interest in Catholic theology and liturgy.

While at Magdalen College, Wilde became particularly well known for his role in the aesthetic and decadent movements. He wore his hair long, openly scorned "manly" sports though he occasionally boxed, and he decorated his rooms with peacock feathers, lilies, sunflowers, blue china and other objets d'art. He once remarked to friends, whom he entertained lavishly, "I find it harder and harder every day to live up to my blue china." The line quickly became famous, accepted as a slogan by aesthetes but used against them by critics who sensed in it a terrible vacuousness. Some elements disdained the aesthetes, but their languishing attitudes and showy costumes became a recognised pose. Wilde was once physically attacked by a group of four fellow students, and dealt with them single-handedly, surprising critics. By his third year Wilde had truly begun to develop himself and his myth, and considered his learning to be more expansive than what was within the prescribed texts. This attitude resulted in his being rusticated for one term, after he had returned late to a college term from a trip to Greece with Mahaffy.

Wilde did not meet Walter Pater until his third year, but had been enthralled by his Studies in the History of the Renaissance, published during Wilde's final year in Trinity. Pater argued that man's sensibility to beauty should be refined above all else, and that each moment should be felt to its fullest extent. Years later, in De Profundis, Wilde described Pater's Studies... as "that book that has had such a strange influence over my life".He learned tracts of the book by heart, and carried it with him on travels in later years. Pater gave Wilde his sense of almost flippant devotion to art, though he gained a purpose for it through the lectures and writings of critic John Ruskin. Ruskin despaired at the self-validating aestheticism of Pater, arguing that the importance of art lies in its potential for the betterment of society. Ruskin admired beauty, but believed it must be allied with, and applied to, moral good. When Wilde eagerly attended Ruskin's lecture series The Aesthetic and Mathematic Schools of Art in Florence, he learned about aesthetics as the non-mathematical elements of painting. Despite being given to neither early rising nor manual labour, Wilde volunteered for Ruskin's project to convert a swampy country lane into a smart road neatly edged with flowers.

Wilde won the 1878 Newdigate Prize for his poem "Ravenna", which reflected on his visit there the year before, and he duly read it at Encaenia. In November 1878, he graduated with a double first in his B.A. of Classical Moderations and Literae Humaniores (Greats). Wilde wrote to a friend, "The dons are 'astonied' beyond words – the Bad Boy doing so well in the end!"

Apprenticeship of an aesthete: 1880s

Debut in society

After graduation from Oxford, Wilde returned to Dublin, where he met again Florence Balcombe, a childhood sweetheart. She became engaged to Bram Stoker and they married in 1878. Wilde was disappointed but stoic:

392

he wrote to her, remembering "the two sweet years – the sweetest years of all my youth" during which they had been close. He also stated his intention to "return to England, probably for good." This he did in 1878, only briefly visiting Ireland twice after that.

Unsure of his next step, Wilde wrote to various acquaintances enquiring about Classics positions at Oxford or Cambridge. The Rise of Historical Criticism was his submission for the Chancellor's Essay prize of 1879, which, though no longer a student, he was still eligible to enter. Its subject, "Historical Criticism among the Ancients" seemed ready-made for Wilde – with both his skill in composition and ancient learning – but he struggled to find his voice with the long, flat, scholarly style. Unusually, no prize was awarded that year.

With the last of his inheritance from the sale of his father's houses, he set himself up as a bachelor in London. The 1881 British Census listed Wilde as a boarder at 1 (now 44) Tite Street, Chelsea, where Frank Miles, a society painter, was the head of the household. Wilde spent the next six years in London and Paris, and in the United States, where he travelled to deliver lectures.

He had been publishing lyrics and poems in magazines since entering Trinity College, especially in Kottabos and the Dublin University Magazine. In mid-1881, at 27 years old, he published Poems, which collected, revised and expanded his poems.

The book was generally well received, and sold out its first print run of 750 copies. Punch was less enthusiastic, saying "The poet is Wilde, but his poetry's tame". By a tight vote, the Oxford Union condemned the book for alleged plagiarism. The librarian, who had requested the book for the library, returned the presentation copy to Wilde with a note of apology. Biographer Richard Ellmann argues that Wilde's poem "Hélas!" was a sincere, though flamboyant, attempt to explain the dichotomies the poet saw in himself; one line reads: "To drift with every passion till my soul

Is a stringed lute on which all winds can play".

The book had further printings in 1882. It was bound in a rich, enamel parchment cover (embossed with gilt blossom) and printed on hand-made Dutch paper; over the next few years, Wilde presented many copies to the dignitaries and writers who received him during his lecture tours.

America: 1882

Aestheticism was sufficiently in vogue to be caricatured by Gilbert and Sullivan in Patience (1881). Richard D'Oyly Carte, an English impresario invited Wilde to make a lecture tour of North America, simultaneously priming the pump for the US tour of Patience and selling this most charming aesthete to the American public. Wilde journeyed on the SS Arizona, arriving 2 January 1882, and disembarking the following day. Originally planned to last four months, it continued for almost a year due to the commercial success. Wilde sought to transpose the beauty he saw in art into daily life. This was a practical as well as philosophical project: in Oxford he had surrounded himself with blue china and lilies, and now one of his lectures was on interior design.

When asked to explain reports that he had paraded down Piccadilly in London carrying a lily, long hair flowing, Wilde replied, "It's not whether I did it or not that's important, but whether people believed I did it". Wilde believed that the artist should hold forth higher ideals, and that pleasure and beauty would replace utilitarian ethics.

Wilde and aestheticism were both mercilessly caricatured and criticised in the press; the Springfield Republican, for instance, commented on Wilde's behaviour during his visit to Boston to lecture on aestheticism, suggesting that Wilde's conduct was more a bid for notoriety rather than devotion to beauty and the aesthetic. T. W. Higginson, a cleric and abolitionist, wrote in "Unmanly Manhood" of his general concern that Wilde, "whose only distinction is that he has written a thin volume of very mediocre verse" would improperly influence the behaviour of men and women.

According to biographer Michèle Mendelssohn, Wilde was the subject of anti-Irish caricature and was portrayed as a monkey, a blackface performer and a Christy's Minstrel throughout his career. "Harper's Weekly put a sunflower worshipping monkey dressed as Wilde on the front of the January 1882 issue. The magazine didn't let its reputation for quality impede its expression of what are now considered odious ethnic and racial ideologies. The drawing stimulated other American maligners and, in England, had a full-page reprint in the Lady's Pictorial. ... When the National Republican discussed Wilde, it was to explain 'a few items as to the animal's pedigree.' And on 22 January 1882 the Washington Post illustrated the Wild Man of Borneo alongside Oscar Wilde of England and asked 'How far is it from this to this?' "Though his press reception was hostile, Wilde was well received in diverse settings across America; he drank whiskey with miners in Leadville, Colorado, and was fêted at the most fashionable salons in many cities he visited.

London life and marriage

His earnings, plus expected income from The Duchess of Padua, allowed him to move to Paris between February and mid-May 1883. While there he met Robert Sherard, whom he entertained constantly. "We are dining on the Duchess tonight", Wilde would declare before taking him to an expensive restaurant. In August he briefly returned to New York for the production of Vera, his first play, after it was turned down in London. He reportedly entertained the other passengers with "Ave Imperatrix!, A Poem on England", about the rise and fall of empires. E. C. Stedman, in Victorian Poets, describes this "lyric to England" as "manly verse – a poetic and eloquent invocation". The play was initially well received by the audience, but when the critics wrote lukewarm reviews, attendance fell sharply and the play closed a week after it had opened.

Wilde had to return to England, where he continued to lecture on topics including Personal Impressions of America, The Value of Art in Modern Life, and Dress.

In London, he had been introduced in 1881 to Constance Lloyd, daughter of Horace Lloyd, a wealthy Queen's Counsel, and his wife. She happened to be visiting Dublin in 1884, when Wilde was lecturing at the Gaiety Theatre. He proposed to her, and they married on 29 May 1884 at the Anglican St James's Church, Paddington, in London. Although Constance had an annual allowance of £250, which was generous for a young woman (equivalent to about £25,600 in current value), the Wildes had relatively luxurious tastes. They had preached to others for so long on the subject of design that people expected their home to set new standards. No. 16, Tite Street was duly renovated in seven months at considerable expense. The couple had two sons together, Cyril (1885) and Vyvyan (1886). Wilde became the sole literary signatory of George Bernard Shaw's petition for a pardon of the anarchists arrested (and later executed) after the Haymarket massacre in Chicago in 1886.

Robert Ross had read Wilde's poems before they met at Oxford in 1886. He seemed unrestrained by the Victorian prohibition against homosexuality, and became estranged from his family. By Richard Ellmann's account, he was a precocious seventeen-year-old who "so young and yet so knowing, was determined to seduce Wilde". According to Daniel Mendelsohn, Wilde, who had long alluded to Greek love, was "initiated into homosexual sex" by Ross, while his "marriage had begun to unravel after his wife's second pregnancy, which left him physically repelled".

Prose writing: 1886–91

Journalism and editorship: 1886–89

Criticism over artistic matters in The Pall Mall Gazette provoked a letter in self-defence, and soon Wilde was a contributor to that and other journals during 1885–87. He enjoyed reviewing and journalism; the form suited his style. He could organise and share his views on art, literature and life, yet in a format less tedious than lecturing. Buoyed up, his reviews were largely chatty and positive.Wilde, like his parents before him, also supported the cause of Irish nationalism. When Charles Stewart Parnell was falsely accused of inciting murder, Wilde wrote a series of astute columns defending him in the Daily Chronicle.

His flair, having previously been put mainly into socialising, suited journalism and rapidly attracted notice. With his youth nearly over, and a family to support, in mid-1887 Wilde became the editor of The Lady's World magazine, his name prominently appearing on the cover.He promptly renamed it as The Woman's World and raised its tone, adding serious articles on parenting, culture, and politics, while keeping discussions of fashion and arts. Two pieces of fiction were usually included, one to be read to children, the other for the ladies themselves. Wilde worked hard to solicit good contributions from his wide artistic acquaintance, including those of Lady Wilde and his wife Constance, while his own "Literary and Other Notes" were themselves popular and amusing.

The initial vigour and excitement which he brought to the job began to fade as administration, commuting and office life became tedious. At the same time as Wilde's interest flagged, the publishers became concerned anew about circulation: sales, at the relatively high price of one shilling, remained low. Increasingly sending instructions to the magazine by letter, Wilde began a new period of creative work and his own column appeared less regularly.In October 1889, Wilde had finally found his voice in prose and, at the end of the second volume, Wilde left The Woman's World. The magazine outlasted him by one issue.

If Wilde's period at the helm of the magazine was a mixed success from an organizational point of view, it played a pivotal role in his development as a writer and facilitated his ascent to fame. Whilst Wilde the journalist supplied articles under the guidance of his editors, Wilde the editor was forced to learn to manipulate the literary marketplace on his own terms.

During the late 1880s, Wilde was a close friend of the artist James NcNeill Whistler and they dined together on many occasions. At one of these dinners, Whistler said a bon mot that Wilde found particularly witty, Wilde exclaimed that he wished that he had said it, and Whistler retorted "You will, Oscar, you will".Herbert Vivian—a mutual friend of Wilde and Whistler— attended the dinner and recorded it in his article The Reminiscences of a Short Life which appeared in The Sun in 1889. The article alleged that Wilde had a habit of passing off other people's witticisms as his own—especially Whistler's. Wilde considered Vivian's article to be a scurrilous betrayal, and it directly caused the broken friendship between Wilde and Whistler. The Reminiscences also caused great acrimony between Wilde and Vivian, Wilde accusing Vivian of "the inaccuracy of an eavesdropper with the method of a blackmailer" and banishing Vivian from his circle.

Shorter fiction

Wilde published The Happy Prince and Other Tales in 1888, and had been regularly writing fairy stories for magazines. In 1891 he published two more collections, Lord Arthur Savile's Crime and Other Stories, and in September A House of Pomegranates was dedicated "To Constance Mary Wilde". "The Portrait of Mr. W. H.", which Wilde had begun in 1887, was first published in Blackwood's Edinburgh Magazine in July 1889.It is a short story, which reports a conversation, in which the theory that Shakespeare's sonnets were written out of the poet's love of the boy actor "Willie Hughes", is advanced, retracted, and then propounded again. The only evidence for this is two supposed puns within the sonnets themselves.

The anonymous narrator is at first sceptical, then believing, finally flirtatious with the reader: he concludes that "there is really a great deal to be said of the Willie Hughes theory of Shakespeare's sonnets." By the end fact and fiction have melded together.Arthur Ransome wrote that Wilde "read something of himself into Shakespeare's sonnets" and became fascinated with the "Willie Hughes theory" despite the lack of biographical evidence for the historical William Hughes' existence. Instead of writing a short but serious essay on the question, Wilde tossed the theory amongst the three characters of the story, allowing it to unfold as background to the plot. The story thus is an early masterpiece of Wilde's combining many elements that interested him: conversation, literature and the idea that to shed oneself of an idea one must first convince another of its truth.Ransome concludes that Wilde succeeds precisely because the literary criticism is unveiled with such a deft touch.

Though containing nothing but "special pleading", it would not, he says "be possible to build an airier castle in Spain than this of the imaginary William Hughes" we continue listening nonetheless to be charmed by the telling. "You must believe in Willie Hughes," Wilde told an acquaintance, "I almost do, myself."

Essays and dialogues

Wilde, having tired of journalism, had been busy setting out his aesthetic ideas more fully in a series of longer prose pieces which were published in the major literary-intellectual journals of the day. In January 1889, The Decay of Lying: A Dialogue appeared in The Nineteenth Century, and Pen, Pencil and Poison, a satirical biography of Thomas Griffiths Wainewright, in The Fortnightly Review, edited by Wilde's friend Frank Harris. Two of Wilde's four writings on aesthetics are dialogues: though Wilde had evolved professionally from lecturer to writer, he retained an oral tradition of sorts. Having always excelled as a wit and raconteur, he often composed by assembling phrases, bons mots and witticisms into a longer, cohesive work.

Wilde was concerned about the effect of moralising on art; he believed in art's redemptive, developmental powers: "Art is individualism, and individualism is a disturbing and disintegrating force. There lies its immense value. For what it seeks is to disturb monotony of type, slavery of custom, tyranny of habit, and the reduction of man to the level of a machine." In his only political text, The Soul of Man Under Socialism, he argued political conditions should establish this primacy – private property should be abolished, and cooperation should be substituted for competition. At the same time, he stressed that the government most amenable to artists was no government at all. Wilde envisioned a society where mechanisation has freed human effort from the burden of necessity, effort which can instead be expended on artistic creation. George Orwell summarised, "In effect, the world will be populated by artists, each striving after perfection in the way that seems best to him."

This point of view did not align him with the Fabians, intellectual socialists who advocated using state apparatus to change social conditions, nor did it endear him to the monied classes whom he had previously entertained. Hesketh Pearson, introducing a collection of Wilde's essays in 1950, remarked how The Soul of Man Under Socialism had been an inspirational text for revolutionaries in Tsarist Russia but laments that in the Stalinist era "it is doubtful whether there are any uninspected places in which it could now be hidden".

Wilde considered including this pamphlet and The Portrait of Mr. W.H., his essay-story on Shakespeare's sonnets, in a new anthology in 1891, but eventually decided to limit it to purely aesthetic subjects. Intentions packaged revisions of four essays: The Decay of Lying, Pen, Pencil and Poison, The Truth of Masks (first published 1885), and The Critic as Artist in two parts. For Pearson the biographer, the essays and dialogues exhibit every aspect of Wilde's genius and character: wit, romancer, talker, lecturer, humanist and scholar and concludes that "no other productions of his have as varied an appeal". 1891 turned out to be Wilde's annus mirabilis; apart from his three collections he also produced his only novel.

The Picture of Dorian Gray

The first version of The Picture of Dorian Gray was published as the lead story in the July 1890 edition of Lippincott's Monthly Magazine, along with five others. The story begins with a man painting a picture of Gray. When Gray, who has a "face like ivory and rose leaves", sees his finished portrait, he breaks down. Distraught that his beauty will fade while the portrait stays beautiful, he inadvertently makes a Faustian bargain in which only the painted image grows old while he stays beautiful and young. For Wilde, the purpose of art would be to guide life as if beauty alone were its object. As Gray's portrait allows him to escape the corporeal ravages of his hedonism, Wilde sought to juxtapose the beauty he saw in art with daily life.

Reviewers immediately criticised the novel's decadence and homosexual allusions; The Daily Chronicle for example, called it "unclean", "poisonous", and "heavy with the mephitic odours of moral and spiritual putrefaction". Which he clarified his stance on ethics and aesthetics in art – "If a work of art is rich and vital and complete, those who have artistic instincts will see its beauty and those to whom ethics appeal more strongly will see its moral lesson." He nevertheless revised it extensively for book publication in 1891: six new chapters were added, some overtly decadent passages and homo-eroticism excised, and a preface was included consisting of twenty two epigrams, such as "Books are well written, or badly written. That is all."

Contemporary reviewers and modern critics have postulated numerous possible sources of the story, a search Jershua McCormack argues is futile because Wilde "has tapped a root of Western folklore so deep and ubiquitous that the story has escaped its origins and returned to the oral tradition." Wilde claimed the plot was "an idea that is as old as the history of literature but to which I have given a new form".Modern critic Robin McKie considered the novel to be technically mediocre, saying that the conceit of the plot had guaranteed its fame, but the device is never pushed to its full.On the other hand, Robert McCrum of The Guardian deemed it the 27th best novel ever written in English, calling it "an arresting, and slightly camp, exercise in late-Victorian gothic."

Theatrical career: 1892–95

Salomé

The 1891 census records the Wildes' residence at 16 Tite Street, where he lived with his wife Constance and two sons. Wilde though, not content with being better known than ever in London, returned to Paris in October 1891, this time as a respected writer. He was received at the salons littéraires, including the famous mardis of Stéphane Mallarmé, a renowned symbolist poet of the time. Wilde's two plays during the 1880s, Vera; or, The Nihilists and The Duchess of Padua, had not met with much success. He had continued his interest in the theatre and now, after finding his voice in prose, his thoughts turned again to the dramatic form as the biblical iconography of Salome filled his mind. One evening, after discussing depictions of Salome throughout history, he returned to his hotel and noticed a blank copybook lying on the desk, and it occurred to him to write in it what he had been saying. The result was a new play, Salomé, written rapidly and in French.

A tragedy, it tells the story of Salome, the stepdaughter of the tetrarch Herod Antipas, who, to her stepfather's dismay but mother's delight, requests the head of Jokanaan (John the Baptist) on a silver platter as a reward for dancing the Dance of the Seven Veils. When Wilde returned to London just before Christmas the Paris Echo referred to him as "le great event" of the season. Rehearsals of the play, starring Sarah Bernhardt, began but the play was refused a licence by the Lord Chamberlain, since it depicted biblical characters. Salome was published jointly in Paris and London in 1893, but was not performed until 1896 in Paris, during Wilde's later incarceration.

Comedies of society

Wilde, who had first set out to irritate Victorian society with his dress and talking points, then outrage it with Dorian Gray, his novel of vice hidden beneath art, finally found a way to critique society on its own terms. Lady Windermere's Fan was first performed on 20 February 1892 at St James's Theatre, packed with the cream of society. On the surface a witty comedy, there is subtle subversion underneath: "it concludes with collusive concealment rather than collective disclosure". The audience, like Lady Windermere, are forced to soften harsh social codes in favour of a more nuanced view. The play was enormously popular, touring the country for months, but largely trashed by conservative critics. It was followed by A Woman of No Importance in 1893, another Victorian comedy, revolving around the spectre of illegitimate births, mistaken identities and late revelations. Wilde was commissioned to write two more plays and An Ideal Husband, written in 1894, followed in January 1895.

Peter Raby said these essentially English plays were well-pitched, "Wilde, with one eye on the dramatic genius of Ibsen, and the other on the commercial competition in London's West End, targeted his audience with adroit precision".

Queensberry family

In mid-1891 Lionel Johnson introduced Wilde to Lord Alfred Douglas, Johnson's cousin and an undergraduate at Oxford at the time. Known to his family and friends as "Bosie", he was a handsome and spoilt young man. An intimate friendship sprang up between Wilde and Douglas and by 1893 Wilde was infatuated with Douglas and they consorted together regularly in a tempestuous affair. If Wilde was relatively indiscreet, even flamboyant, in the way he acted, Douglas was reckless in public. Wilde, who was earning up to £100 a week from his plays (his salary at The Woman's World had been £6), indulged Douglas's every whim: material, artistic or sexual.

Douglas soon initiated Wilde into the Victorian underground of gay prostitution and Wilde was introduced to a series of young working-class male prostitutes from 1892 onwards by Alfred Taylor. These infrequent rendezvous usually took the same form: Wilde would meet the boy, offer him gifts, dine him privately and then take him to a hotel room. Unlike Wilde's idealised relations with Ross, John Gray, and Douglas, all of whom remained part of his aesthetic circle, these consorts were uneducated and knew nothing of literature. Soon his public and private lives had become sharply divided; in De Profundis he wrote to Douglas that "It was like feasting with panthers; the danger was half the excitement... I did not know that when they were to strike at me it was to be at another's piping and at another's pay."

Douglas and some Oxford friends founded a journal, The Chameleon, to which Wilde "sent a page of paradoxes originally destined for the Saturday Review". "Phrases and Philosophies for the Use of the Young" was to come under attack six months later at Wilde's trial, where he was forced to defend the magazine to which he had sent his work.In any case, it became unique: The Chameleon was not published again.

Lord Alfred's father, the Marquess of Queensberry, was known for his outspoken atheism, brutish manner and creation of the modern rules of boxing. Queensberry, who feuded regularly with his son, confronted Wilde and Lord Alfred about the nature of their relationship several times, but Wilde was able to mollify him. In June 1894, he called on Wilde at 16 Tite Street, without an appointment, and clarified his stance: "I do not say that you are it, but you look it, and pose at it, which is just as bad. And if I catch you and my son again in any public restaurant I will thrash you" to which Wilde responded: "I don't know what the Queensberry rules are, but the Oscar Wilde rule is to shoot on sight".His account in De Profundis was less triumphant: "It was when, in my library at Tite Street, waving his small hands in the air in epileptic fury, your father... stood uttering every foul word his foul mind could think of, and screaming the loathsome threats he afterwards with such cunning carried out". Queensberry only described the scene once, saying Wilde had "shown him the white feather", meaning he had acted in a cowardly way. Though trying to remain calm, Wilde saw that he was becoming ensnared in a brutal family quarrel. He did not wish to bear Queensberry's insults, but he knew to confront him could lead to disaster were his liaisons disclosed publicly.

The Importance of Being Earnest

Wilde's final play again returns to the theme of switched identities: the play's two protagonists engage in "bunburying" (the maintenance of alternative personas in the town and country) which allows them to escape Victorian social mores.Earnest is even lighter in tone than Wilde's earlier comedies. While their characters often rise to serious themes in moments of crisis, Earnest lacks the by-now stock Wildean characters: there is no "woman with a past", the principals are neither villainous nor cunning, simply idle cultivés, and the idealistic young women are not that innocent. Mostly set in drawing rooms and almost completely lacking in action or violence, Earnest lacks the self-conscious decadence found in The Picture of Dorian Gray and Salome.

The play, now considered Wilde's masterpiece, was rapidly written in Wilde's artistic maturity in late 1894. It was first performed on 14 February 1895, at St James's Theatre in London, Wilde's second collaboration with George Alexander, the actor-manager. Both author and producer assiduously revised, prepared and rehearsed every line, scene and setting in the months before the premiere, creating a carefully constructed representation of late-Victorian society, yet simultaneously mocking it. During rehearsal Alexander requested that Wilde shorten the play from four acts to three, which the author did. Premieres at St James's seemed like "brilliant parties", and the opening of The Importance of Being Earnest was no exception. Allan Aynesworth (who played Algernon) recalled to Hesketh Pearson, "In my fifty-three years of acting, I never remember a greater triumph than [that] first night."Earnest's immediate reception as Wilde's best work to date finally crystallised his fame into a solid artistic reputation. The Importance of Being Earnest remains his most popular play.

Wilde's professional success was mirrored by an escalation in his feud with Queensberry. Queensberry had planned to insult Wilde publicly by throwing a bouquet of rotting vegetables onto the stage; Wilde was tipped off and had Queensberry barred from entering the theatre.Fifteen weeks later Wilde was in prison.

Trials

404

Wilde v. Queensberry

On 18 February 1895, the Marquess left his calling card at Wilde's club, the Albemarle, inscribed: "For Oscar Wilde, posing somdomite" Wilde, encouraged by Douglas and against the advice of his friends, initiated a private prosecution against Queensberry for libel, since the note amounted to a public accusation that Wilde had committed the crime of sodomy.

Queensberry was arrested for criminal libel; a charge carrying a possible sentence of up to two years in prison. Under the 1843 Libel Act, Queensberry could avoid conviction for libel only by demonstrating that his accusation was in fact true, and furthermore that there was some "public benefit" to having made the accusation openly. Queensberry's lawyers thus hired private detectives to find evidence of Wilde's homosexual liaisons.

Wilde's friends had advised him against the prosecution at a Saturday Review meeting at the Café Royal on 24 March 1895; Frank Harris warned him that "they are going to prove sodomy against you" and advised him to flee to France. Wilde and Douglas walked out in a huff, Wilde saying "it is at such moments as these that one sees who are one's true friends". The scene was witnessed by George Bernard Shaw who recalled it to Arthur Ransome a day or so before Ransome's trial for libelling Douglas in 1913. To Ransome it confirmed what he had said in his 1912 book on Wilde; that Douglas's rivalry for Wilde with Robbie Ross and his arguments with his father had resulted in Wilde's public disaster; as Wilde wrote in De Profundis. Douglas lost his case. Shaw included an account of the argument between Harris, Douglas and Wilde in the preface to his play The Dark Lady of the Sonnets.

The libel trial became a cause célèbre as salacious details of Wilde's private life with Taylor and Douglas began to appear in the press. A team of private detectives had directed Queensberry's lawyers, led by Edward Carson QC, to the world of the Victorian underground. Wilde's association with blackmailers and male prostitutes, cross-dressers and homosexual brothels was recorded, and various persons involved were interviewed, some being coerced to appear as witnesses since they too were accomplices to the crimes of which Wilde was accused.

The trial opened on 3 April 1895 before Justice Richard Henn Collins amid scenes of near hysteria both in the press and the public galleries. The extent of the evidence massed against Wilde forced him to declare meekly, "I am the prosecutor in this case" Wilde's lawyer, Sir Edward George Clarke, opened the case by pre-emptively asking Wilde about two suggestive letters Wilde had written to Douglas, which the defence had in its possession. He characterised the first as a "prose sonnet" and admitted that the "poetical language" might seem strange to the court but claimed its intent was innocent. Wilde stated that the letters had been obtained by blackmailers who had attempted to extort money from him, but he had refused, suggesting they should take the £60 (equal to £6,800 today) offered, "unusual for a prose piece of that length". He claimed to regard the letters as works of art rather than something of which to be ashamed.

Carson, a fellow Dubliner who had attended Trinity College, Dublin at the same time as Wilde, cross-examined Wilde on how he perceived the moral content of his works. Wilde replied with characteristic wit and flippancy, claiming that works of art are not capable of being moral or immoral but only well or poorly made, and that only "brutes and illiterates", whose views on art "are incalculably stupid", would make such judgements about art. Carson, a leading barrister, diverged from the normal practice of asking closed questions. Carson pressed Wilde on each topic from every angle, squeezing out nuances of meaning from Wilde's answers, removing them from their aesthetic context and portraying Wilde as evasive and decadent. While Wilde won the most laughs from the court, Carson scored the most legal points To undermine Wilde's credibility, and to justify Queensberry's description of Wilde as a "posing somdomite", Carson drew from the witness an admission of his capacity for "posing", by demonstrating that he had lied about his age on oath. Playing on this, he returned to the topic throughout his cross-examination. Carson also tried to justify Queensberry's characterisation by quoting from Wilde's novel, The Picture of Dorian Gray, referring in particular to a scene in the second chapter, in which Lord Henry Wotton explains his decadent philosophy to Dorian, an "innocent young man", in Carson's words.

Carson then moved to the factual evidence and questioned Wilde about his friendships with younger, lower-class men. Wilde admitted being on a first-name basis and lavishing gifts upon them, but insisted that nothing untoward had occurred and that the men were merely good friends of his. Carson repeatedly pointed out the unusual nature of these relationships and insinuated that the men were prostitutes. Wilde replied that he did not believe in social barriers, and simply enjoyed the society of young men. Then Carson asked Wilde directly whether he had ever kissed a certain servant boy, Wilde responded, "Oh, dear no. He was a particularly plain boy – unfortunately ugly – I pitied him for it." Carson pressed him on the answer, repeatedly asking why the boy's ugliness was relevant. Wilde hesitated, then for the first time became flustered: "You sting me and insult me and try to unnerve me; and at times one says things flippantly when one ought to speak more seriously."

In his opening speech for the defence, Carson announced that he had located several male prostitutes who were to testify that they had had sex with Wilde. On the advice of his lawyers, Wilde dropped the prosecution. Queensberry was found not guilty, as the court declared that his accusation that Wilde was "posing as a Somdomite " was justified, "true in substance and in fact".Under the Libel Act 1843, Queensberry's acquittal rendered Wilde legally liable for the considerable expenses Queensberry had incurred in his defence, which left Wilde bankrupt.

Regina v. Wilde

After Wilde left the court, a warrant for his arrest was applied for on charges of sodomy and gross indecency. Robbie Ross found Wilde at the Cadogan Hotel, Pont Street, Knightsbridge, with Reginald Turner; both men advised Wilde to go at once to Dover and try to get a boat to France; his mother advised him to stay and fight. Wilde, lapsing into inaction, could only say, "The train has gone. It's too late."On 6 April 1895, Wilde was arrested for "gross indecency" under Section 11 of the Criminal Law Amendment Act 1885, a term meaning homosexual acts not amounting to buggery (an offence under a separate statute). At Wilde's instruction, Ross and Wilde's butler forced their way into the bedroom and library of 16 Tite Street, packing some personal effects, manuscripts, and letters. Wilde was then imprisoned on remand at Holloway, where he received daily visits from Douglas.

Events moved quickly and his prosecution opened on 26 April 1895, before Mr Justice Charles. Wilde pleaded not guilty. He had already begged Douglas to leave London for Paris, but Douglas complained bitterly, even wanting to give evidence; he was pressed to go and soon fled to the Hotel du Monde. Fearing persecution, Ross and many others also left the United Kingdom during this time. Under cross examination Wilde was at first hesitant, then spoke eloquently:

> **Charles Gill** (prosecuting): What is "the love that dare not speak its name"?
>
> **Wilde:** "The love that dare not speak its name" in this century is such a great affection of an elder for a younger man as there was between David and Jonathan, such as Plato made the very basis of his philosophy, and such as you find in the sonnets of Michelangelo and Shakespeare. It is that deep spiritual affection that is as pure as it is perfect. It dictates and pervades great works of art, like those of Shakespeare and Michelangelo, and those two letters of mine, such as they are. It is in this century misunderstood, so much misunderstood that it may be described as "the love that dare not speak its name", and on that account of it I am placed where I am now. It is beautiful, it is fine, it is the noblest form of affection. There is nothing unnatural about it. It is intellectual, and it repeatedly exists between an older and a younger man, when the older man has intellect, and the younger man has all the joy, hope and glamour of life before him. That it should be so, the world does not understand. The world mocks at it, and sometimes puts one in the pillory for it.

This response was counter-productive in a legal sense as it only served to reinforce the charges of homosexual behaviour.

The trial ended with the jury unable to reach a verdict. Wilde's counsel, Sir Edward Clarke, was finally able to get a magistrate to allow Wilde and his friends to post bail. The Reverend Stewart Headlam put up most of the £5,000 surety required by the court, having disagreed with Wilde's treatment by the press and the courts. Wilde was freed from Holloway and, shunning attention, went into hiding at the house of Ernest and Ada Leverson, two of his firm friends. Edward Carson approached Frank Lockwood QC, the Solicitor General and asked "Can we not let up on the fellow now?" Lockwood answered that he would like to do so, but feared that the case had become too politicised to be dropped.

The final trial was presided over by Mr Justice Wills. On 25 May 1895 Wilde and Alfred Taylor were convicted of gross indecency and sentenced to two years' hard labour. The judge described the sentence, the maximum allowed, as "totally inadequate for a case such as this", and that the case was "the worst case I have ever tried". Wilde's response "And I? May I say nothing, my Lord?" was drowned out in cries of "Shame" in the courtroom.

Imprisonment

When first I was put into prison some people advised me to try and forget who I was. It was ruinous advice. It is only by realising what I am that I have found comfort of any kind. Now I am advised by others to try on my release to forget that I have ever been in a prison at all. I know that would be equally fatal. It would mean that I would always be haunted by an intolerable sense of disgrace, and that those things that are meant for me as much as for anybody else – the beauty of the sun and moon, the pageant of the seasons, the music of daybreak and the silence of great nights, the rain falling through the leaves, or the dew creeping over the grass and making it silver – would all be tainted for me, and lose their healing power, and their power of communicating joy. To regret one's own experiences is to arrest one's own development. To deny one's own experiences is to put a lie into the lips of one's own life. It is no less than a denial of the soul.

De Profundis

Wilde was incarcerated from 25 May 1895 to 18 May 1897.

He first entered Newgate Prison in London for processing, then was moved to Pentonville Prison, where the "hard labour" to which he had been sentenced consisted of many hours of walking a treadmill and picking oakum (separating the fibres in scraps of old navy ropes), and where prisoners were allowed to read only the Bible and The Pilgrim's Progress.

A few months later he was moved to Wandsworth Prison in London. Inmates there also followed the regimen of "hard labour, hard fare and a hard bed", which wore harshly on Wilde's delicate health. In November he collapsed during chapel from illness and hunger. His right ear drum was ruptured in the fall, an injury that later contributed to his death. He spent two months in the infirmary.

Richard B. Haldane, the Liberal MP and reformer, visited Wilde and had him transferred in November to Reading Gaol, 30 miles (48 km) west of London on 23 November 1895. The transfer itself was the lowest point of his incarceration, as a crowd jeered and spat at him on the railway platform. He spent the remainder of his sentence there, addressed and identified only as "C33" – the occupant of the third cell on the third floor of C ward.

About five months after Wilde arrived at Reading Gaol, Charles Thomas Wooldridge, a trooper in the Royal Horse Guards, was brought to Reading to await his trial for murdering his wife on 29 March 1896; on 17 June Wooldridge was sentenced to death and returned to Reading for his execution, which took place on Tuesday, 7 July 1896 – the first hanging at Reading in 18 years. From Wooldridge's hanging, Wilde later wrote The Ballad of Reading Gaol.

Wilde was not, at first, even allowed paper and pen but Haldane eventually succeeded in allowing access to books and writing materials. Wilde requested, among others: the Bible in French; Italian and German grammars; some Ancient Greek texts, Dante's Divine Comedy, Joris-Karl Huysmans's new French novel about Christian redemption En route, and essays by St Augustine, Cardinal Newman and Walter Pater.

Between January and March 1897 Wilde wrote a 50,000-word letter to Douglas. He was not allowed to send it, but was permitted to take it with him when released from prison. In reflective mode, Wilde coldly examines his career to date, how he had been a colourful agent provocateur in Victorian society, his art, like his paradoxes, seeking to subvert as well as sparkle. His own estimation of himself was: one who "stood in symbolic relations to the art and culture of my age". It was from these heights that his life with Douglas began, and Wilde examines that particularly closely, repudiating him for what Wilde finally sees as his arrogance and vanity: he had not forgotten Douglas' remark, when he was ill, "When you are not on your pedestal you are not interesting." Wilde blamed himself, though, for the ethical degradation of character that he allowed Douglas to bring about in him and took responsibility for his own fall, "I am here for having tried to put your father in prison." The first half concludes with Wilde forgiving Douglas, for his own sake as much as Douglas's. The second half of the letter traces Wilde's spiritual journey of redemption and fulfilment through his prison reading. He realised that his ordeal had filled his soul with the fruit of experience, however bitter it tasted at the time.

> ... I wanted to eat of the fruit of all the trees in the garden of the world ... And so, indeed, I went out, and so I lived. My only mistake was that I confined myself so exclusively to the trees of what seemed to me the sun-lit side of the garden, and shunned the other side for its shadow and its gloom.

Wilde was released from prison on 19 May 1897 and sailed that evening for Dieppe, France. He never returned to the UK.

On his release, he gave the manuscript to Ross, who may or may not have carried out Wilde's instructions to send a copy to Douglas (who later denied having received it). The letter was partially published in 1905 as De Profundis; its complete and correct publication first occurred in 1962 in The Letters of Oscar Wilde.

Decline: 1897–1900

Exile

Though Wilde's health had suffered greatly from the harshness and diet of prison, he had a feeling of spiritual renewal. He immediately wrote to the Society of Jesus requesting a six-month Catholic retreat; when the request was denied, Wilde wept."I intend to be received into the Catholic Church before long", Wilde told a journalist who asked about his religious intentions.

411

He spent his last three years impoverished and in exile. He took the name "Sebastian Melmoth", after Saint Sebastian and the titular character of Melmoth the Wanderer (a Gothic novel by Charles Maturin, Wilde's great uncle). Wilde wrote two long letters to the editor of the Daily Chronicle describing the brutal conditions of English prisons and advocating penal reform. His discussion of the dismissal of Warder Martin for giving biscuit to an anaemic child prisoner repeated the themes of the corruption and degeneration of punishment that he had earlier outlined in The Soul of Man under Socialism.

Wilde spent mid-1897 with Robert Ross in the seaside village of Berneval-le-Grand in northern France, where he wrote The Ballad of Reading Gaol, narrating the execution of Charles Thomas Wooldridge, who murdered his wife in a rage at her infidelity. It moves from an objective story-telling to symbolic identification with the prisoners. No attempt is made to assess the justice of the laws which convicted them but rather the poem highlight the brutalisation of the punishment that all convicts share. Wilde juxtapose the executed man and himself with the line "Yet each man kills the thing he loves". He adopted the proletarian ballad form and the author was credited as "C33", Wilde's cell number in Reading Gaol. He suggested that it be published in Reynolds' Magazine, "because it circulates widely among the criminal classes – to which I now belong – for once I will be read by my peer – a new experience for me". It was an immediate roaring commercial success going through seven editions in less than two years, only after which "[Oscar]" was added to the title page, though many in literary circles had known Wilde to be the author. It brought him a small amount of money.

Although Douglas had been the cause of his misfortunes, he and Wilde were reunited in August 1897 at Rouen. This meeting was disapproved of by the friends and families of both men. Constance Wilde was already refusing to meet Wilde or allow him to see their sons, though she sent him money – three pounds a week. During the latter part of 1897, Wilde and Douglas lived together near Naples for a few months until they were separated by their families under the threat of cutting off all funds.

Wilde's final address was at the dingy Hôtel d'Alsace (now known as L'Hôtel), on rue des Beaux-Arts in Saint-Germain-des-Prés, Paris. "This poverty really breaks one's heart: it is so sale , so utterly depressing, so hopeless. Pray do what you can" he wrote to his publisher. He corrected and published An Ideal Husband and The Importance of Being Earnest, the proofs of which, according to Ellmann, show a man "very much in command of himself and of the play" but he refused to write anything else: "I can write, but have lost the joy of writing".

He wandered the boulevards alone and spent what little money he had on alcohol. A series of embarrassing chance encounters with hostile English visitors, or Frenchmen he had known in better days, drowned his spirit. Soon Wilde was sufficiently confined to his hotel to joke, on one of his final trips outside, "My wallpaper and I are fighting a duel to the death. One of us has got to go". On 12 October 1900 he sent a telegram to Ross: "Terribly weak. Please come". His moods fluctuated; Max Beerbohm relates how their mutual friend Reginald 'Reggie' Turner had found Wilde very depressed after a nightmare. "I dreamt that I had died, and was supping with the dead!" "I am sure", Turner replied, "that you must have been the life and soul of the party." Turner was one of the few of the old circle who remained with Wilde to the end and was at his bedside when he died.

Death

By 25 November 1900 Wilde had developed meningitis, then called "cerebral meningitis". Robbie Ross arrived on 29 November, sent for a priest, and Wilde was conditionally baptised into the Catholic Church by Fr Cuthbert Dunne, a Passionist priest from Dublin, Wilde having been baptised in the Church of Ireland and having moreover a recollection of Catholic baptism as a child, a fact later attested to by the minister of the sacrament, Fr Lawrence Fox. Fr Dunne recorded the baptism,

> As the voiture rolled through the dark streets that wintry night, the sad story of Oscar Wilde was in part repeated to me... Robert Ross knelt by the bedside, assisting me as best he could while I administered conditional baptism, and afterwards answering the responses while I

gave Extreme Unction to the prostrate man and recited the prayers for the dying. As the man was in a semi-comatose condition, I did not venture to administer the Holy Viaticum; still I must add that he could be roused and was roused from this state in my presence. When roused, he gave signs of being inwardly conscious... Indeed I was fully satisfied that he understood me when told that I was about to receive him into the Catholic Church and gave him the Last Sacraments... And when I repeated close to his ear the Holy Names, the Acts of Contrition, Faith, Hope and Charity, with acts of humble resignation to the Will of God, he tried all through to say the words after me.

Wilde died of meningitis on 30 November 1900. Different opinions are given as to the cause of the disease: Richard Ellmann claimed it was syphilitic; Merlin Holland, Wilde's grandson, thought this to be a misconception, noting that Wilde's meningitis followed a surgical intervention, perhaps a mastoidectomy; Wilde's physicians, Dr Paul Cleiss and A'Court Tucker, reported that the condition stemmed from an old suppuration of the right ear (from the prison injury, see above) treated for several years (une ancienne suppuration de l'oreille droite d'ailleurs en traitement depuis plusieurs années) and made no allusion to syphilis.

Burial

Wilde was initially buried in the Cimetière de Bagneux outside Paris; in 1909 his remains were disinterred and transferred to Père Lachaise Cemetery, inside the city. His tomb there was designed by Sir Jacob Epstein. It was commissioned by Robert Ross, who asked for a small compartment to be made for his own ashes, which were duly transferred in 1950. The modernist angel depicted as a relief on the tomb was originally complete with male genitalia, which were initially censored by French Authorities with a golden leaf. The genitals have since been vandalised; their current whereabouts are unknown. In 2000, Leon Johnson, a multimedia artist, installed a silver prosthesis to replace them. In 2011, the tomb was cleaned of the many lipstick marks left there by admirers and a glass barrier was installed to prevent further marks or damage.

The epitaph is a verse from The Ballad of Reading Gaol,

And alien tears will fill for him

Pity's long-broken urn,

For his mourners will be outcast men,

And outcasts always mourn.

Posthumous pardon

In 2017, Wilde was among an estimated 50,000 men who were pardoned for homosexual acts that were no longer considered offences under the Policing and Crime Act 2017. The Act is known informally as the Alan Turing law.

Honours

In 2014 Wilde was one of the inaugural honorees in the Rainbow Honor Walk, a walk of fame in San Francisco's Castro neighbourhood noting LGBTQ people who have "made significant contributions in their fields."

Biographies

Wilde's life has been the subject of numerous biographies since his death. The earliest were memoirs by those who knew him: often they are personal or impressionistic accounts which can be good character sketches, but are sometimes factually unreliable. Frank Harris, his friend and editor, wrote a biography, Oscar Wilde: His Life and Confessions (1916); though prone to exaggeration and sometimes factually inaccurate, it offers a good literary portrait of Wilde. Lord Alfred Douglas wrote two books about his relationship with Wilde. Oscar Wilde and Myself (1914), largely ghost-written by T. W. H. Crosland, vindictively reacted to Douglas's discovery that De Profundis was addressed to him and defensively tried to distance him from Wilde's scandalous reputation. Both authors later regretted their work. Later, in Oscar Wilde: A Summing Up (1939) and his Autobiography he was more sympathetic to Wilde. Of Wilde's other close friends, Robert Sherard; Robert Ross, his literary executor; and Charles Ricketts variously published biographies, reminiscences or correspondence. The first more or less objective biography of Wilde came about when Hesketh Pearson wrote Oscar Wilde: His Life and Wit (1946). In 1954 Wilde's son Vyvyan Holland published his memoir Son of Oscar Wilde, which recounts the difficulties Wilde's wife and children faced after his imprisonment. It was revised and updated by Merlin Holland in 1989.

Oscar Wilde, a critical study by Arthur Ransome was published in 1912. The book only briefly mentioned Wilde's life, but subsequently Ransome (and The Times Book Club) were sued for libel by Lord Alfred Douglas. In April 1913 Douglas lost the libel action after a reading of De Profundis refuted his claims.

Richard Ellmann wrote his 1987 biography Oscar Wilde, for which he posthumously won a National (USA) Book Critics Circle Award in 1988and a Pulitzer Prize in 1989. The book was the basis for the 1997 film Wilde, directed by Brian Gilbert and starring Stephen Fry as the title character.

Neil McKenna's 2003 biography, The Secret Life of Oscar Wilde, offers an exploration of Wilde's sexuality. Often speculative in nature, it was widely criticised for its pure conjecture and lack of scholarly rigour. Thomas Wright's Oscar's Books (2008) explores Wilde's reading from his childhood in Dublin to his death in Paris. After tracking down many books that once belonged to Wilde's Tite Street library (dispersed at the time of his trials), Wright was the first to examine Wilde's marginalia.

> Later on, I think everyone will recognise his achievements; his plays and essays will endure. Of course, you may think with others that his personality and conversation were far more wonderful than anything he wrote, so that his written works give only a pale reflection of his power. Perhaps that is so, and of course, it will be impossible to reproduce what is gone forever.

Robert Ross, 23 December 1900

In 2018, Matthew Sturgis' "Oscar: A Life," was published in London. The book incorporates rediscovered letters and other documents and is the most extensively researched biography of Wilde to appear since 1988.

416

Parisian literati, also produced several biographies and monographs on him. André Gide wrote In Memoriam, Oscar Wilde and Wilde also features in his journals. Thomas Louis, who had earlier translated books on Wilde into French, produced his own L'esprit d'Oscar Wilde in 1920. Modern books include Philippe Jullian's Oscar Wilde, and L'affaire Oscar Wilde, ou, Du danger de laisser la justice mettre le nez dans nos draps (The Oscar Wilde Affair, or, On the Danger of Allowing Justice to put its Nose in our Sheets) by Odon Vallet, a French religious historian. (Source: Wikipedia)

NOTABLE WORKS

ESSAYS

"The Decay of Lying" First published in Nineteenth Century (1889) republished in Intentions (1891).

"Pen, Pencil and Poison" First published in the Fortnightly Review (1889), republished in Intentions (1891).

"The Soul of Man under Socialism" First published in the Fortnightly Review (1891), republished in The Soul of Man (1895), privately printed.

Intentions (1891) Wilde revised his dialogues on aesthetic subjects for publication in this volume, which comprises:

- "The Critic as Artist"
- "The Decay of Lying"
- "Pen, Pencil and Poison"
- "The Truth of Masks"

"Phrases and Philosophies for the Use of the Young" first published in the Oxford student magazine The Chameleon, December 1894)

"A Few Maxims For The Instruction Of The Over-Educated" First published, anonymously, in the 1894 November 17 issue of Saturday Review

FICTION

Novel

The Picture of Dorian Gray (1890/1891). The first version of "The Picture of Dorian Gray" was published, in a form highly edited by the magazine, as the lead story in the July 1890 edition of Lippincott's Monthly Magazine. Wilde published the longer and revised version in book form in 1891, with an added preface.

Stories

"The Portrait of Mr. W. H." (1889)

The Happy Prince and Other Tales (1888, a collection of fairy tales) consisting of:

- "The Happy Prince"
- "The Nightingale and the Rose"
- "The Selfish Giant"
- "The Devoted Friend"
- "The Remarkable Rocket"

A House of Pomegranates (1891, fairy tales)

Lord Arthur Savile's Crime and Other Stories (1891) Including "The Canterville Ghost" first published in periodical form in 1887.

Complete Short Fiction. Penguin Classics, 2003. Edited with an Introduction and Notes by Ian Small. Contains all works listed above plus Poems in Prose (1894) and one very short 'Elder-tree' (fragment).

POEMS

Ravenna (1878) Winner of the Newdigate Prize.

Poems (1881) Wilde's collection of poetry and first publication.

The Sphinx (1894)

Poems in Prose (1894)

The Ballad of Reading Gaol (1898)

PLAYS

Vera; or, The Nihilists (1880)

The Duchess of Padua (1883)

Lady Windermere's Fan (1892)

A Woman of No Importance (1893)

Salomé (French version) (1893, first performed in Paris 1896)

Salomé: A Tragedy in One Act: Translated from the French of Oscar Wilde by Lord Alfred Douglas, illustrated by Aubrey Beardsley (1894)

An Ideal Husband (1895) (text)

The Importance of Being Earnest (1895) (text)

La Sainte Courtisane and A Florentine Tragedy Fragmentary. First published 1908 in Methuen's Collected Works

(Dates are dates of first performance, which approximate better to the probable date of composition than dates of publication.)

The Importance of Being Earnest and Other Plays. Penguin Classics, 2000. Edited with an Introduction, Commentaries and Notes by Richard Allen Cave. Contains all from above save the first two. Salome is in English.

As an appendix there is one excised scene from The Importance of Being Earnest.

POSTHUMOUS (PREVIOUSLY UNPUBLISHED)

De Profundis (Written 1895-97, in Reading Gaol). Expurgated edition published 1905; suppressed portions 1913, expanded version in The Letters of Oscar Wilde (1962).

The Rise of Historical Criticism (Written while at college) First published in 1905 (Sherwood Press, Hartford, CT) privately printed. Reprinted in Miscellanies, the last volume of the First Collected Edition (1908).

The First Collected Edition (Methuen & Co., 14 volumes) appeared in 1908 and contained many previously unpublished works.

The Second Collected Edition (Methuen & Co., 12 volumes) appeared in installments between 1909–11 and contained several other unpublished works.

The Letters of Oscar Wilde (Written 1868-1900) Published in 1962. Republished as The Complete Letters of Oscar Wilde (2000), with letters discovered since 1962, and new annotations by Merlin Holland.

The Women of Homer (Written 1876, while at college). First published in Oscar Wilde: The Women of Homer (2008) by The Oscar Wilde Society.

The Philosophy of Dress First published in The New-York Tribune (1885), published for the first time in book form in Oscar Wilde On Dress (2013).

MISATTRIBUTED

Teleny, or The Reverse of the Medal (Paris, 1893) has been attributed to Wilde, but its authorship is unclear. One theory is that it was a combined effort by several of Wilde's friends, which he may have edited.

Constance On September 14, 2011, Wilde's grandson Merlin Holland contested Wilde's claimed authorship of this play entitled Constance, scheduled to open that week in the King's Head Theatre. It was not, in fact, "Oscar Wilde's final play," as its producers were claiming. Holland said Wilde did sketch out the play's scenario in 1894, but "never wrote a word" of it, and that "it is dishonest to foist this on the public." The Artistic Director Adam Spreadbury-Maher of the King's Head Theatre and producer of Constance pointed out that Wilde's son, Vyvyan Holland, wrote in 1954, "a significant amount of the dialogue (of Constance) bears the authentic stamp of my father's hand". There is further proof that the developed scenario that Constance was reconstituted from was written by Wilde between 1897 and his death in 1900, rather than the 1894 George Alexander scenario which Merlin Holland quotes.

CPSIA information can be obtained
at www.ICGtesting.com
Printed in the USA
LVHW042059170820
663425LV00002B/190